I0691898

Also by Cathryn Grant

Cathryn Grant

THE WOMAN IN THE CELLAR

An Alexandra Mallory Novel

D2C Perspectives

1

Sydney, Australia

My mind seems to need something to constantly pick over. A problem to chew on, as if my psyche is ravenously hungry at all times. I can't stop devouring. Are all minds like that? Maybe so. We're all so busy inside our own heads, we forget to notice that all those heads moving around us are also buzzing with thoughts and plans, desires and memories.

I suppose the difference between my mind and many other minds is that my thoughts aren't fed, and made more obsessive, by worry and fear and regret.

In one of my high school English classes, I read a story by John Updike that was one of two or three I never forgot. It was the story of a teenage boy who was consumed with appreciation for a girl's body when she and her friends walked into the A&P where he worked. He asserted that it was doubtful there was a mind inside her skull, but rather a little buzz, the sound of a bee caught in a glass jar. Her thoughts were nothing more than the relentless buzzing of an insect, a language he would never comprehend.

It's not clear to me if this story was one of millions of instances in which some men think of women as sub-standard in their intellect and even, their humanity. It wasn't only that her thoughts were impossible to interpret, he suggested they really were quite meaningless. Or was it truly a sweet coming-of-age story meant to illustrate the confusion of sexual awakening and the alien nature of the opposite sex?

The story was written in the early sixties. Obviously, many boys now are more astute, and women have become quite adept at making sure males know what's on their minds. Still, I can't get that story out of my own head. It's lingered all my life, while nearly every other short story that was required reading has evaporated.

Along with my ravenously hungry psyche, I have an equally voracious desire for food.

I love every single aspect of eating. I succumb like a lover to the aroma of sizzling beef, the smell of garlic sautéing in olive oil. I adore the smells of a traditional Thanksgiving dinner, a meal I was not likely to enjoy in Australia, where November is on the cusp of summer. A turkey with stuffing and mashed potatoes was not the optimal meal in humid, eighty-five-degree weather.

I like beautiful plates and flatware, and tables set as if they're works of art in themselves — elegantly arranged fresh flowers, candles, or a large glass container filled with polished stones. Recently, I saw a photograph of a table set with black dishes, silver utensils, and sleek glassware. Lined up down the center of the table were twelve hand-blown glass vases, each holding a single red rose. Those vases had such seductive lines you felt they had the softness of human flesh, not unlike the lifelike quality of the figure carved out of wood that dominated the corner of Sean's bedroom.

The conversation that surrounds a meal is as enticing as the food, increasing the pleasure of eating, and vice versa.

There aren't many foods I don't love. I love good steak and rich seafood, pork ribs and their cousin, bacon. I love fried chicken, and stir-fried chicken in a spicy sauce. I love every vegetable I can think of, especially with drizzled butter and a dusting of salt, along with bread and pasta, potatoes and rice. I love Italian, Indian, Mexican, Thai, French, and Chinese food, to name a few. I'm not as consumed by longing for sweets, but I enjoy the occasional chocolate chip cookie, and I'll never turn down a moist, chewy brownie.

I'm always thinking about my next meal, stopping to study menus posted on the exterior walls of restaurants.

Maybe that's why I have such a need to run and lift weights, countering my insistent attention to filling my stomach.

I'm hungry. A lot.

All animals eat. All the time. The life of a wildcat or a hawk or a shark is a relentless hunt for food.

One of the problems my mind gnawed on as if it were a plate of baby back ribs, succulent with tangy barbecue sauce, was Carmen Dunn and her Facebook trolling of our fledgling company.

I knew Sean hadn't given me the full story about her. It wasn't as if that was a great intuitive conclusion on my part, he'd flat out told me she was his ex's sister. But first, he'd lied, calling her a friend, and insisting that was *all I needed to know*.

I'd been quite sure it was not all I needed to know. I was still sure.

The other problem my mind chewed on was the telescope that I'd stolen from the man I'd murdered next door. The expensive, powerful telescope sat on my closet floor, concealed in a rolled-up rug, inside my locked bedroom. Taking the telescope was one of those occasionally impulsive things I've done throughout my life. A terrible risk.

At the time, all I could think of was how much I loved looking at Saturn and its rings, Jupiter and her moons. I wanted that for myself.

My mind had leapt ahead to that day when I'll have a magnificent home of my own. After realizing the magic of studying the solar system, a telescope was something I now desired as part of that perfect environment I've been building in my mind all my life. But acquiring a large telescope before I owned the home was premature.

Since the telescope became mine, I'd only used it twice.

Now I had to keep Gavin from ever entering my closet, no matter how casually. And Tess was giving me sideways glances because I was locking my door in a house occupied by people who supposedly trusted one another.

2

It was Friday evening. According to Tess's suggestion that we plan for more time outside of the claustrophobic vault that was Sean's house and the four TruthTeller employees, a schedule had been set for evening meals. Each of us had an assigned night for cooking. No one was required to be there, but if you planned to be out, it was noted on our shared calendar at least two days in advance so the proper amount of food could be purchased for the meal.

It continuously struck me odd, that there were only four people living inside the six-bedroom, six-bathroom, six-thousand square foot house, but it continued to feel like a prison. Or worse, something from a dystopian novel. A place that was often pleasantly calm and quiet and yet you imagined you could hear the constant heartbeats of your housemates. Or at least I did. I think Tess felt that too, otherwise she wouldn't have made an issue out of it. She pushed Sean to be more proactive, as she put it, in making sure we felt plenty of freedom to conduct private lives outside of our endeavor.

Sean was fully convinced that a copious amount of togetherness was essential for fostering creativity, but so far, I'd seen very few creative ideas growing out of our shared meals and movie nights, our conversations over drinks and the occasional joint. I suppose it didn't help that there had been a steady parade of murder and the associated police presence. Maybe that increased the oppressive sense that you had to watch every movement, every word.

Maybe the claustrophobia wasn't the house and our tangled work and social lives at all. Maybe it was Sean himself.

At any rate, the idea was we would share our meals on weeknights. The weekend evenings were now set apart for time on our own, presumably outside of the house. But forced free time can become as claustrophobic as forced companionship.

I didn't have a car and I didn't know anyone in Australia outside of the woman across the street. Well, I had known others, but they were dead, from suicide and murder. Fortunately, the Cronulla police force, even with help from the Sydney police department, had no information to suggest Detective Bender's death had been anything but suicide.

Tess had a car, but also had little to no social life outside of Sean's house. At first, she'd been happy to throw herself into work and forget about the outside world. Now, I saw her desire for escape in every gesture.

So there we were, inside that gorgeous, expensively-decorated house, pressed together, wanting something else, but not quite sure what that might be or how to get it.

Gavin was a bit of a loner, so he was happy to take his free time inside his room, working on his own software projects or interacting with other geeks online.

The solution, Sean announced, was obvious.

He opened four bottles of beer, handed them around, and suggested we all have a seat on the patio while he outlined his next big idea.

We would throw a dinner party.

Although he was funding the company himself and didn't need financial investors, what about word of mouth investors — people who would give their *time* to promote the benefits of the TruthTeller app? Fans who believed in our product? People who were well-connected and would talk it up. He would call the dinner party WOTT — Word of Mouth TruthTeller.

Tess rolled her eyes.

Since my chair was placed slightly behind Sean's, out of his line of sight, it was easy to slip out. I went into the house, my bare feet silent on the tile floor. I placed my nearly untouched beer on the middle shelf of the fridge. Hopefully when one of the guys came in for another, they would take that one. I don't like beer. No matter how much it seems to be an Australian thing, I was tired of drinking it to be polite. Drinking beer was like swallowing a bottle of soapy water.

I mixed a martini, took a sip, and returned to the patio.

"Where did you go?" Sean said.

I raised my glass.

"Right. But you missed my idea."

I smiled.

"I'll start over," he said.

Tess rolled her eyes again. It was unlike her, to mock him behind his back while he spoke, eagerly thrusting his arms out to the sides. Of course, she had turned into such a contradiction, I was no longer sure what I would classify as being *like her*. Maybe that had been the case from the first time I met her, but her cool and confident exterior misled me for a rather long time. In some ways, she was as chameleon-like as I am, which might have been part of the connection between us, even if we weren't entirely aware of it. Or at least I hadn't been aware of it until that moment.

Sean didn't see her expression. His untied hair swept

across his shoulders and around the sides of his face as he continued talking about how eating together fosters a sense of community. I couldn't disagree with that.

His bare feet tapped on the tile each time he took steps in any direction, almost pacing, driven by energy that flowed from his fascination with his own thoughts. It seemed as if our togetherness generated ideas in his head after all. Maybe that's what he was after. Maybe he didn't care about our ideas at all, he just wanted us there to feed his bottomless energy, a man oozing with creativity, sucking thoughts and life out of us as if he were sucking the marrow out of chicken bones.

"Not just one dinner party, was what I said when you snuck out." He turned to look at me, then faced Tess and Gavin again. "We'll have a series of dinners. We'll generate old-world word-of-mouth buzz. Relying solely on the internet, on social media is a bad idea."

"Social media works," Gavin said. "It's been demonstrated."

Gavin didn't used to think that. Was he defending my role as social media manager? Had he done research on my behalf? I took a sip of my drink and glanced at him. He was staring into the opening of his beer bottle.

"Does it?" Sean avoided looking at me as well. "It gets attention, but does it get buyers?"

"We don't have anything to sell yet," Tess said.

"Advance enthusiasm. We need to build word of mouth, create pent-up demand."

"Don't oversell," Gavin said. He stared at the ground now. It wasn't clear whether he was avoiding everyone's eyes, or just being his usual withdrawn, minimalist self.

"We'll gather a group of people I know — not just

technology peeps, but artists, maybe a musician or two. Even people who you wouldn't think of as patrons for a business — possibly some surfers, a bartender or waitress…"

"So basically all your mates and former co-workers," Gavin said.

"Yes. If you want to put it that way. I wasn't thinking in those terms, but of course they have to be people I know. I know there's been concern that we're too ingrown, isolated. This way, we'll have opportunities for expanded interaction, you'll make new friends, and we'll generate leads. Like I said, organic word of mouth." He stopped suddenly. He gave each one of us in turn a long stare, waiting for our enthusiastic agreement, our praise for his revolutionary plan. His desire for affirmation was spread across the smile that consumed his face.

"How many dinner parties?" Tess said.

I took a sip of my martini. "A good question. And I have another. Who is doing all this planning and cooking?"

Sean flopped down in a lounge chair. He pulled his feet up and crossed his legs at his ankles, hiding that beautiful shark tattooed on the top of his foot.

I felt like shark bait at that moment — Sean circling silently, or not so silently. His grin exposing nearly all of his teeth, ready to bite into our freedom once again. I wondered if he realized he had just finished setting up a structure to theoretically offer us time that belonged solely to us, and now he was circling again, ready to consume more of our psychic energy.

"I don't think we want to set limits right now. I'm thinking once a month, but probably three dinners in the next six weeks, to kick things off, build momentum. We'll get people excited and integrate the dinners into their routine. It will be like a salon. A place where people gather to discuss big ideas…"

"We know what a salon is," Tess said.

Gavin stared at Sean, his face inscrutable.

"And as far as the cooking," Sean said, "I'm happy to do it. I don't want this to be a burden on anyone. It should be exciting and generate fresh energy, not a sense of obligation."

"Does that mean we aren't required to attend?" I looked directly at him and sucked an olive off the stir stick.

He glared back at me and said nothing.

3

Despite the fact that it was Friday night and we were *on our own* dinner-wise, after Sean made his dinner salon proposal, the four of us went to a steak house. He spent the evening selling Tess on his idea, refusing to meet my eyes during the entire meal.

The steak was mouth-watering and my martini was top notch, as was the wine we had with dinner.

I relished my meal — filet mignon, au gratin potatoes, green beans, and a side dish of sautéed mushrooms — as well as Gavin's hand on my leg. As I lingered over each bite, my mind was fed by thoughts of going to Gavin's room when we got home. It was also entertaining watching Sean work so hard to stir up Tess's support, to try to get her to feel what he was feeling. It was clear he believed he needed her as enthused as he was in order to bring the rest of us along.

The dinner party idea wasn't a bad one.

I was excited to meet new people. And I knew I wouldn't be asked to cook because I'd made it pretty clear that food preparation wasn't my specialty. When it was my night for organizing dinner, I walked to the shop for meat pies or called for a pizza. Besides, Sean would want to do all the cooking because it would give him total control. He could choose the menu, the timing, the wine…and the guest list.

We needed something to kick things up. Our app was now scheduled to launch at the end of July. It wasn't an ideal time for the rest of the world, with most Europeans on vacation for a month, and half of the US vacationing at any given time between June and August. But in Australia, fall was nearing its end, and the energy that comes with cooler weather was still driving more action. The seasonal cycle affects us on a deeper level than we sometimes recognize. Fall is the time to stop languishing, to get serious.

While we were cooing over the various indulgent ways to eat chocolate that were demonstrated in our desserts, Sean slipped away from the table. When the meal was over, he informed us the bill had been taken care of and we simply left. A gracious gesture, always making sure we didn't have to pay for anything whatsoever. Or, as I was starting to realize now that the pleasure of never spending money was growing more familiar, a way to control our relationship to him.

No matter how much he said we owed him nothing, there was a sense of indebtedness. Aside from that, which wasn't something that bothered me, there was an imbalance of power. And a lot of that imbalance was inside his own head. He assumed as CEO he made the final decisions, but he made all the decisions.

We walked out of the restaurant and climbed into the waiting Uber minivan Sean had ordered. We rode home, our stomachs humming with good food and our heads buzzing with a fair amount of alcohol. Our ears were filled with the rather nice voice of the Uber driver, singing along with an Australian group I'd never heard of, but who Sean and Gavin were both quite familiar with. They demonstrated this by silently mouthing the words of the chorus.

At the house, Sean disappeared upstairs and returned a moment later, wearing his swim trunks. He headed out to the backyard. Tess wandered up the stairs to her room and when we heard the door close, Gavin and I went up and locked ourselves in his room.

Tess knew Gavin and I were having sex, so we didn't work overtime to hide it, but we were still unclear about Sean's awareness, and there was no sense inviting his scrutiny. I didn't want him poking into any area of my life, and Gavin seemed to feel the same way.

With both of us contented after a satisfying end to the evening, we fell asleep, our legs tangled around each other, the sound of Sean splashing in the pool as he swam laps working its way into our dreams.

When I woke at two, my throat and mouth were dry. Gavin was propped up, the pillows stuffed behind his back and neck. He held a half-empty bottle of water. He took a sip and handed it to me, seeming to know I was awake even though I hadn't moved or spoken. The room was dark enough that he couldn't see my eyes. He must have been aware that my breathing had shifted.

"Is he still swimming?" I sat up and took a sip of water.

"Did the sound of him swimming give you nightmares?" I felt his body shift as he enjoyed making me squirm. I'm not sure what it is about men that makes them enjoy watching women squirm. They love to make us laugh, and seem equally delighted to make us shiver in fear or disgust or outrage. Any sort of heightened response gives them a sense of power, I suppose. Maybe it all comes back to sex. They want to see us lose control to our animal nature, to forget about our work hassles and the state of our hair and the style of our shoes, our career goals and financial aspirations.

"Are you hoping it did?" I said.

"You said you wanted me to teach you how to swim. When?"

"Soon."

"What are you waiting for?"

"Spring? Summer?"

"You're avoiding it," he said. "You think you're ready to dive in, but really, you're trying to fool your brain into thinking you've handled it by talking about it instead of doing it."

"Don't analyze me."

"Why not?"

"Because you're wrong."

"Am I?"

I took the bottle out of his hand and drank some more. He was wrong. I couldn't see the fun of immersing half my body, and ultimately my entire body, in water when the air was cold, the sky cloudy, and a breeze slicing my skin with even more cold. The weather was causing me to wait, not some hardly noticeable self-protective device formed in my subconscious.

"Once you're in the water, you don't notice the air temperature."

"I suppose I don't want Sean watching. It would be nice to have another pool."

I could imagine Sean, seeing my weakness, thinking I would never be accomplished enough to stand up to another attempt to toss me into the pool, that I'd never put in enough time to become truly comfortable in the water. Just like learning another language, if learning happens during childhood, the skill and comfort with water is ingrained, built into your body's instincts before your brain is fully formed. It becomes a deeper, seemingly integral part of you.

Instead, knowing the water was primed to take my life was a very deep and possibly permanent piece of me.

"That's understandable," he said. "We could go to a beach."

I thought of waves, rising up, crashing over me, massive arms pulling me down. I'd seen waves toss full-grown men on their heads as if they were bits of broken wood. "I think the surf would complicate things."

"There's an area near Bondi Beach where they've built walls to form a sea-water swimming pool. At low tide, you won't experience waves. And now that I think of it, the salt water will make you more buoyant. Learning to let go and yield to the water will be easier."

I didn't like the idea of letting go at all. Letting go meant giving the water power over me. But until I learned, anyone who was adept in the water had even more power over me. And so did the water itself, for that matter. "That sounds interesting."

"If we go early in the morning it won't be crowded. And that's another benefit of winter."

I considered this. Trading my morning run, which filled me with euphoria, for a battle with instincts that were perfectly natural, was a difficult choice. Water puts forth a constant effort to push its way into every opening in my head, as I fight the sense that my body is solid and heavy, filled with bone and muscle, destined to sink. If salt helped, I was up for that.

4

Melbourne, Australia

Tess was glad to be out of that house. Glad to be visiting Melbourne again, but disappointed she wasn't able to actually spend time in the city. She'd flown down, taken a transport van to animal quarantine, and now she stood in line waiting for Damien. Once she completed the paperwork, they would transfer the cockatoo, still in his travel crate, to the plane she was taking for her return to Sydney.

Thinking of what the poor bird had been through in the past few months made her feel like she might cry. She was horribly selfish for moving him to Australia. How long would she be here? She loved the country, hated her living situation, and was on the fence about her job.

Possibly, if she bought her own place, the job might become interesting again. Possibly.

The difficulty with a start-up as small as TruthTeller was that most people went into start-ups for three reasons. The first was a love for the technology, a love for technology in general, which she did not have. The other was a gamble hoping for phenomenal success that would dramatically change your financial situation. There was a third that embodied her attraction — the pure adrenaline required to create something out of nothing and find a niche for it in the marketplace.

What she'd loved about her previous marketing jobs was the interaction with smart people. She loved the analytical side and the creation of complex programs designed to deliver impact in a crowded field. She enjoyed the challenge of translating technology features into words that described how a product would benefit customers and solve their problems. She loved articulating those details to customers, moving them toward making the decision to choose her company, her products. She loved beating competitors.

TruthTeller didn't have any real competitors, but neither did it have business benefits. She supposed she hadn't made a solid transition to the consumer marketplace.

And now, she was holed up inside a home that, no matter how spacious and filled with pleasing aesthetics, was stifling.

The quarantine release line inched forward. She couldn't believe there were so many people bringing animals into the country on any given day. As she'd passed the vast area filled with individual glass-walled rooms to house each creature, she'd seen a horse doing time while medical professionals ensured it wasn't carrying any diseases that would impact the Australian equine population.

A horse!

She couldn't imagine the animal flying, it was hard enough on a human. The poor thing must have been terrified, no matter how much was done to provide comfort.

Her thoughts returned to the individuals who comprised a company that hardly had enough employees to be worthy of the name *company*. Sean was full of ideas, eager to get their product to market, fanatical about its importance to the world, but not always inclined to listen to input — Alex's or her own, for that matter. Recently, his quirky and controlling side had overwhelmed his cheerful, easy-going nature. At least it had seemed easy-going when she met him, when they discussed partnering over the app. Now she realized it wasn't that at all. Minor instability could be mis-read as easy-going.

And Alex. The woman was like a drug. Being around her unpredictable behavior and utter lack of concern for what anyone thought of her choices was addictive. She was entertaining and alluring. Tess constantly found herself hoping for Alex's approval, which never really came. She hated that about their relationship. Alex was her employee. The power balance between them was completely distorted. And yet, she didn't want to let go. She wanted to form a bona fide friendship with Alex. In one sweeping emotion she wanted to push Alex away and draw her closer.

Gavin was a self-contained geek, happy to be working on software, sitting alone in his room for hours at a time.

They were a disconnected group, each pursuing their own goals.

Sometimes, Tess worried the app was a foolish gimmick that would have a limited customer base. How often could you even use it? How many life-altering decisions did a person make in the few decades from their early twenties to their late fifties? Three? Five?

Maybe some people would value the app to guide them every step of the way, assisting with the most minor choices. Maybe it would have appeal for those who couldn't make up their minds about a vacation destination or whether they should remodel the kitchen.

There were probably more of those than she realized. Otherwise, why the popularity of an endless stream of online self-assessment tools? The interest in comparing yourself to superheroes and Disney characters seemed insatiable.

Finally, there was only one person remaining between her and the clerk who would give her access to her beloved pet. She was stunned by how much she'd missed him. He was a bird! How could she feel so much affection for a creature with wings and a deadly-looking beak? It was almost as if his conversation meant something in her life. She smiled, thinking about the adorable tilt of his head when he was studying her while he ate dinner, or the shriek of his mocking laugh from another room, startling her so that she had to remind herself that it wasn't another human being who'd entered her house and was laughing at her.

The man in front of her, a guy not much taller than herself with a shaved head, moved away and was led into the room where the animals were viewed and signed off for the next leg of their journeys.

She gave the clerk her name, the breed of her pet, and his ID number. After a surprisingly few number of taps on the computer keyboard, the release form began printing. Why had the line moved so slowly if the process was this quick?

She took the form, smiled and thanked the woman, and turned to follow the guy with the shaved head.

Forty minutes later, Damien was safely tagged for the final leg of his journey. She was riding in a transport van back to the main terminal.

5

Her flight wasn't for another ninety minutes. She'd been assured the quarantine release process was quick, but she hadn't wanted to trust an unfamiliar bureaucracy. She wanted to be sure there were no obstacles and that Damien was on that plane with her, arriving in Sydney by dinnertime.

As she walked along the concourse, she passed a few eateries before arriving at a cocktail lounge done up like an Irish pub. A drink sounded good. She wasn't hungry and sitting in a stiff plastic chair for an hour before sitting again on a plane was not appealing.

She sat at one of several small round tables, hung her bag on the back of the chair, and looked around. Early afternoon, in the middle of the week, the place was less than half full. A server approached her.

"A glass of Yarra Valley Chardonnay, please," Tess said. She smiled, hearing Damien's voice in her head, announcing — *Chardonnay time*. She couldn't wait to put him into the human-sized cage she'd purchased.

Sean had been adamant that he didn't want the bird loose in the house, especially with all the wild cockatoos that enjoyed breakfast in his yard. The captive bird would fly at the windows and incite the others to do the same. He'd agreed she could buy a six-by-eight-foot cage that was tall enough for Tess to stand up in. There was plenty of room for it in the massive foyer, nestled behind the curving staircase.

Damien would have a perch and lots of space to move around. She could let him out whenever she liked, but he couldn't have free run of the house.

This was another reason she was seriously considering looking for a place of her own, no matter how it undermined Sean's vision for collaboration. She was done with the work-life-integration experiment. She was going to lose her mind, speaking to the same three people day in and day out. Seeing her bird in a cage would be too much.

The chardonnay arrived. She paid for it and settled back, looking around the room for a second time.

A man at a nearby table raised his glass of red wine toward her. He took a sip and smiled, then looked away before she could return the gesture. Maybe that was for the best. She didn't need to be flirting in an airport bar, no matter how hungry she was to talk to a man who wasn't a colleague.

She took a sip of wine and thought about Sean. He wouldn't take well to a suggestion that she move out of his home, but living there wasn't written into her contract. The whole idea had been a sweeping gesture of utopian enthusiasm and generosity on his part. She'd gone along because…well…she supposed it was because she was infected with the novelty of Australia and Australians.

She didn't want to rent, and it probably wasn't possible with a large bird anyway. Buying a place while still paying the mortgage on her San Francisco condo would be tight, but she had plenty for a solid down payment. And even in Sydney, property wasn't listed at the shocking prices she was used to in the Bay Area. It was doable. In fact, if she lowered her demands, she might be able to buy a small, older house outright.

"Are you waiting for anyone?"

She looked up. The man with the red wine stood a few feet from her. She smiled. "Just my bird."

She thought the rather bizarre response might turn him away, but he laughed. He gestured toward the two empty chairs. "Which seat belongs to your bird?"

"Neither one. Go ahead."

He took the chair to her right. "So, a fellow American." She smiled.

"Where're you headed? Trystan, by the way."

"Tess. And I'm headed home to Sydney."

He took a sip of wine. "An ex pat. What's that like?"

"I don't think about it much, so I guess that means I'm feeling at home."

He asked how long she'd been in Australia. She told him about the start-up, but didn't describe the app, obviously. She explained the situation with Damien.

He peppered her with questions about Sydney, about the Australians, about the beaches. He was here on business, flying to Sydney for the last three days of meetings then back home to New York. "I don't mean to overstep, but with your bird coming to stay, does that mean you're making this permanent?"

"What's permanent?"

He smiled and leaned back in his chair. "True enough. Do you own a place here?"

"The start-up team is sharing a home." That was enough. She wasn't telling him any more. And it was a little personal, although he made it sound as if he had similar thoughts for himself, so maybe he was just looking for general information.

"Can't let go of that old college roomie feeling?" He laughed.

"No. It's not that. We…start-ups require long hours. So living together made sense. It keeps the creativity flowing without artificial limits to the work day."

He smiled but said nothing.

She took a long sip of wine and sat forward slightly, ready to get up. She only had a few minutes left.

"Sorry if I offended," he said.

"You didn't. I know it sounds strange, and juvenile. But it works. So far. It's an enormous house, we all have en suite bedrooms."

"You don't have to explain."

"I'm not." But she was, and as she took her last swallow of wine, she knew she was moving out of Sean's house. It was crushing her. There would be no debate about it. She'd given it her all, and after two months, it was time to mix things up. She needed space, and not just square footage. "I'm boarding in a few minutes."

He pulled a card out of his shirt pocket. "Here's my card. Do you mind if I ask for yours?"

"Nope." She reached into her bag and took out her card holder. She handed a card to him. "Good to meet you."

"Likewise," he said.

She walked quickly out of the bar and turned in the direction of her gate. As she went to drop it into her bag, she looked down at his card. She read the slender black print. Her lips parted slightly and she slowed as she tucked it into an inside pocket.

6

Listening to my brain gnawing on the Carmen situation, I was becoming more obsessed with her place in Sean's life. Obsessed with knowing what she was after. Obsessed with trying to find out what he was hiding. And I had no doubt he was hiding something. I wondered what her next move might be, and I wondered how long Sean would pretend her interest in him was nothing important.

I couldn't imagine what he'd done that had made a woman so angry she was stalking his company profile, coming close to harassing him in front of his potential customers.

The comments she'd posted were nothing in the world of online bullying, but still, she was provoking him. She was mocking his failure to demonstrate complete honesty because he'd delegated interaction on our Facebook page to me, yet called his app TruthTeller. I shouldn't even use the word bully. She wasn't bullying anyone, she was asking questions. And she was challenging hypocrisy.

Still, it was one of those things that can spiral out of control in the often socially alienated world of social media.

Sean was a difficult man to deal with. His desire to control and his arrogance were concealed by his sexy good looks, but it was right below the surface, and emerged easily when you spent every day of the week with him. His moods shifted more often than Tess's. You never knew which Sean you were going to get — *nature-loving, laid-back Aussie* guy, or *entitled-rich* guy, or *I'm-in-charge* guy, or secretive and stubborn *I-don't-know-what* guy. But I couldn't imagine him doing something so awful that a woman would stalk him. And she was definitely headed in that direction.

He'd lied to the police about the woman's body found in his swimming pool, and lied about his relationship with her. But the lies weren't to cover up anything he'd done wrong. He simply withheld information that wouldn't have mattered anyway. She killed herself. His lies didn't hurt anyone.

I couldn't see him doing something that incited stalking, and lying about it. But I had to know what was going on.

It was time to do a little harassing of my own.

Of course a company's social media manager shouldn't be harassing potential customers. She should watch every word posted online. But I know what you have to do to get attention on social media. And being polite and watching your words usually isn't it. I'd noticed our page engagement dropping precipitously since Carmen stopped sparring with me. The two women who liked and loved and laughed at every word she posted had disappeared into the shadows. They hadn't liked a single thing I'd posted in the past five or six days.

I went into the office, loving the quiet of having it to myself while Tess was in Melbourne picking up Damien. I opened the window halfway to allow lots of fresh air into the room. I sat at the desk and clicked to the Facebook page for TruthTeller.

I scrolled back and re-read the last exchange between

Carmen and me, with my phony last name.

Carmen Dunn: *"Lucky" belongs to those who are born lucky.*

Alex Teller: *Fair enough.*

Carmen Dunn: *Why are you posting all the updates on this page, if it's Sean's company?*

Alex Teller: *I'm in charge of social media.*

Carmen Dunn: *So even that's a misrepresentation — you only talk to us because you're paid to.*

Alex Teller: *Lots of people do social media as a job.*

As we'd typed our messages at each other, Jane and Lara had weighed in on every line Carmen posted, adding thumbs and hearts and faces with open mouths — her own personal Greek chorus.

Carmen Dunn: *If this app is so special, he should be here talking about it.*

Alex Teller: *He will.*

Carmen Dunn: *When?*

Alex Teller: *When the timing is right.*

Carmen Dunn: *Dodging the truth again?*

Alex Teller: *Seriously. He's busy with the product right now. It's revolutionary. That sort of innovation doesn't happen without a lot of hard work.*

Carmen Dunn: *I'm sure.*

Carmen Dunn: *"TruthTeller". Makes me want to laugh and puke at the same time.*

Jane and Lara had added yellow faces with open mouths.

Alex Teller: *That's harsh.*

Carmen Dunn: *Truth is important to me — it's not a sales pitch.*

Alex Teller: *We all tell the truth when it's convenient, and avoid it when it's not.*

My next post had been a winking face in its own comment box. Then…

Alex Teller: *That's why we need an app like TruthTeller, don't we, Carmen?*

It wasn't clear why she'd never responded to my final comment. I didn't have the sense from what had gone on before that she was planning to back down. And I didn't think she *had* backed down. Perhaps she was regrouping for her next assault.

I put the cursor in a box and typed a note to Carmen.

Alex Teller: *Are you still interested in buying the statue?*

I leaned back and looked out the window. Five cockatoos were busy in the large tree near the edge of the front lawn. They were eating and chatting, like several friends having lunch together. There's something strangely human about those birds, and I don't think it's just their ability to speak. Tess said they were intelligent. She'd informed me they can solve puzzles on par with the ability of four-year-old humans. That intelligence must come out in their eyes, the movement of their bodies, making them seem human. They don't behave like any other kind of bird I've seen, even other large birds, like crows, which I understand are also smart.

Cockatoos give the impression they're smiling at you, waiting politely for you to speak. Maybe it's the yellow crown. Yellow is a friendly color. The playful curl of those yellow feathers adds to the friendliness.

Ten minutes had passed. There was no activity on the Facebook page.

That was okay, I can be patient when I have a plan.

I went into the kitchen, poured sparkling water into a glass, and cut a wedge out of a lime sitting in a bowl with several others. I dropped it in the water, enjoyed the brief fizz, took a sip, and walked back to the office. The office beside it, shared by Gavin and Sean, was empty. The lights were out and the shutters were closed tightly.

From the doorway of my office, I could see the Facebook page had changed. A new message from Carmen.

I went in, sat down, took another sip, and put down the glass.

Carmen Dunn: *I never said that.*

Alex Teller: *You didn't? I was sure you asked about the price.*

Carmen Dunn: *I wanted to know what Sean paid for it.*

Alex Teller: *Oh. My mistake.*

I added a shocked-looking emoji.

I waited. Nothing. I drank some sparkling water. The lime tapped my upper lip. Still nothing.

Alex Teller: *If you want to know more about the statue, should we start a private chat? I know you think we should be open, since our reason for existing is to promote truth telling. And we absolutely do, but the statue is a prized possession of Sean's, so it seems fair to discuss it privately.*

Carmen Dunn: *Then why was the photograph posted at all?*

Alex Teller: *Because it's so beautiful, I just had to share it.*

Carmen Dunn: *Thank you for being honest.*

Alex Teller: *You're welcome.*

I wasn't at all honest. It's funny how telling people something that makes you look bad can make them think you're telling the truth. Who would lie to make herself look bad? The whole purpose of lying is to improve or protect your reputation. At least that's how most people see it.

I lie for other reasons.

7

In Sean's opinion, the cage for Tess's cockatoo robbed the entryway of its dramatic appearance. The open feeling was blemished. Once the bird was there, the area would take on the appearance of a zoo. On the other hand, he was glad she'd moved the bird to Australia. It meant she was all-in with him and TruthTeller. After that night when she'd stood in his room, naked, and he'd sent her away, he'd wondered whether they were on shaky ground. Even though he'd explained why he couldn't be with any woman for a while, he'd worried the rejection would change things.

Tess insisted it didn't matter, that it was a simple request for sex. There was no emotional attachment, no desire for a relationship behind it.

He didn't believe her. No woman, no human being, took rejection, no matter how valid, with such equanimity.

The bird was moving in, and it meant all was good between them. The TruthTeller venture would continue without any upsets or change in the dynamic among the four of them. He turned away from the cage. He smiled, seeing the cage in a new light. It was symbolic of permanence.

Restricting his sex life appeared absurd on the surface, but it was the right thing to do. He couldn't escape the burden of what he'd done — inadvertently creating a child and setting in motion the events that lead to its death. Besides, celibacy felt good, better than he would have imagined. He was content with the knowledge that he was suffering after he'd caused so much of it himself. Of course, Terri hadn't suffered for a long period of time. There would have been terror as she fell, but then it was over. The same was true of her child…his child. But they were both dead, and that was unbearable — two lives cut impossibly short, even if they weren't conscious of it.

Thinking of their deaths made the smile slide off his face.

He turned again and studied the cage. His original instinct had been right. He didn't like it. Empty, it made him look like a pervert. It looked like the setup for some kind of torture-freak or serial killer that kept victims prisoner in his foyer before killing them. He shuddered. He should move on to more pleasant things, like planning the first dinner party. But the cage was bothering him. Maybe once the bird was inside…

Tess would be back any minute from her trip to Melbourne.

He felt sorry for her bird. If it caught sight of the wild cockatoos, it would go out of its mind. He hoped he didn't wind up with a large, mentally unbalanced bird living in his foyer. It wasn't at all the mood he wanted to set with the guests that would be coming into his home. He closed his eyes for a moment.

That's where he needed to keep his thoughts — on the dinner. It was a fantastic idea, something outside normal expectations. He couldn't wait to get started.

The front door opened and Tess stepped inside. She pushed the door wider and moved out of the way. An Uber driver pushing a hand dolly wheeled a large crate into the foyer. He eased the dolly from beneath the crate. Tess handed him some cash. He thanked her and left.

"Finally. Poor Damien," she said. "Get some pliers and a claw-heeled hammer so we can get him out."

The sound of the bird murmuring came from inside the crate.

"Shouldn't we move that into the cage, first? Before we release him?"

"He's not going to take off. Don't worry."

He was worried, but he smiled. A large bird confined for months, sedated for its flight, was not going to be a pleasant creature.

"I thought you loved wildlife," she said.

"I do."

"Then why do you look like Tippi Hedren?"

"Tippi who?"

"The actress in that Hitchcock film, *The Birds*. You look like you're terrified that Damien is going to open the back doors at night and every cockatoo in Sydney is going to swoop through your house, looking for eyes to gouge out."

He shivered. "They're gentle birds. I'm just not sure about keeping them captive. I'm not sure I like it."

"That's all he's ever known."

"So?" He turned and went to the garage. He came back carrying a hammer and pliers.

Dismantling the crate was relatively easy, a simple matter of prying loose the boards. They didn't need the pliers at all. As the slats fell away, the pristine white bird was revealed. It tipped its head and stared at Sean, keeping its crown low. Sean was pleased the bird didn't view him as a threat. At the same time, the bird looked a bit loopy.

"He was sedated again?"

"Yes. I hate that he's had to go through all of that."

"Maybe he would have been better off staying in your old home."

"Well I want him with me, and it looks like I'm going to be here for the foreseeable future."

His mood lifted, pleased to hear that, although he wasn't sure about *foreseeable*. She managed to say it in such a way that *foreseeable* might mean the next five hours. Of course she couldn't mean that, but there was something forced about her voice.

"And he talks?" Sean said.

"Yes. What time is it, Damien?"

The cockatoo turned his head at the sound of Tess's voice, but said nothing. He closed his eyes in a long, slow blink. Opening them but continuing to fight the heavy, sluggish movement of his eyelids.

"I guess he's still coming out of it," Tess said.

"Clearly."

She knelt and placed her forearm in front of Damien's feet. She placed the other hand on the side of his wing and nudged him toward her wrist.

The bird lifted one foot, then lowered it back to the mat where he stood. Scattered around his feet were bits of apple and a few drops of shit.

Sean did love wildlife. It was one of the things that made the world a magnificent place. Understanding the other inhabitants of the planet was a lifelong pursuit. He'd spent countless hours, possibly entire weeks of his life underwater, observing fish and sea mammals, coral and starfish and anemones. He could never get enough. He loved living in

Australia where creatures that didn't exist anywhere else on the planet had chosen to make their home.

But wildlife should be just that — wild. He did not approve of keeping a magnificent creature like a cockatoo contained inside a cage, or even inside a house. They belonged outdoors. If that meant a shorter lifespan, that was the way it was supposed to be. They were not there for human entertainment.

Human beings had a way of possessing everything, wanting to close it off and charge admission, taint it. Private beaches, exotic animals, and even the very air that rightfully belonged to everyone. Surfing and diving didn't interfere with the natural cycles of the earth. But jet skis and beachside amusement parks and wild animals kept inside cages horrified him.

Tess picked up the bird and carried him into the cage. She placed him on a black mat. She picked up the water dish and went to the kitchen, returning a moment later with a bowl of fresh water. "I need to get him something to eat, but I'll wait until he's more alert. I think he'll ask for it when he's ready."

"I'm not sure how I feel about him being here."

"You said…"

He waved his hand at her. "I know. It's just the reality of seeing him inside that cage. It breaks my heart, if you really want to know."

"He's perfectly happy. I've had him for nearly a year now. Look how beautiful his feathers are. He's healthy, and once he gets his energy back, you'll see how he is. He loves to talk, loves human interaction."

"And what about flying? What about avian interaction?

You think he's happy just sitting on a perch and chatting up your guests?"

She looked at him but didn't respond. Her expression was calm and uncaring. Clearly, she didn't give a shit what he thought about the situation.

8

The foyer was silent for a moment. Then, a scratching sound marred the quiet as Damien made a tentative step toward exploring his new environment.

"I appreciate you letting him stay here for now," Tess said.

Sean crossed his arms, gripping his biceps. "Of course. It's no problem. He's your pet and he belongs here. I'm just not comfortable with captivity, you know?"

She wanted to laugh. Hadn't she and Alex been virtual captives since the day they moved in? They were held captive by luxury and ease and inertia, by an unpredictable schedule and Sean's enthusiasm — expected to splash around in the pool, get drunk, smoke dope, watch movies, talking and thinking incessantly about their work. And the funny thing was, they rarely discussed their work. She could recall fewer than ten conversations that took place over a meal or during a game of pool. She'd only used the billiards table once…the four of them shooting a few games, and during that game not a single word was said about marketing the app, or how to enhance its features.

Despite spending all her time in Sean's house, she was certain she'd given less focused attention to her work than she would have if she'd clocked in thirty or forty hours a week at an office downtown.

"He won't have to endure the cage for long," she said.

"What?"

"I know it was a lot, getting the cage in here, but it's temporary."

He shrugged. "Don't misinterpret. I didn't mean he can't stay here. He's an amazing bird, and I'm sure he'll demonstrate that in a few hours. He's perfectly welcome. I know it's important to you, having him here."

"I've made a decision," she said.

"That sounds threatening."

"How on earth can my making a decision be considered a threat? Or do you like to keep all the decision-making in your hands?"

He laughed. "Come on, Tess. Don't be pissy."

"I'm not being pissy. I'm trying to tell you about a decision and you're ridiculing me."

"I'm not. Truly. Let's go get a beer."

She stared at him.

"Or wine. Would you like a glass of wine?"

She sighed. He wasn't going to make it easy. She had a feeling he knew what was coming. He was trying to divert her with comments about her behavior. He probably regretted criticizing her for having a captive cockatoo, but it wasn't that at all. Would he rather see a dead cockatoo lying in his backyard, the victim of an inadequate food supply or a predator? There was nothing wrong with keeping Damien safe. She wasn't sure whether cockatoos had predators, but all animals did, so surely there was at least one. Even if it was something unlikely to be found in suburban Sydney — a crocodile or something like that. "Sure. A glass of wine would be nice. But I want to keep an eye on Damien."

"No worries." He gestured toward the bench beside the

staircase. "Have a seat. I'll be back. White or red?"

"White, please. Chardonnay, if you have it."

Damien shrieked behind her. *Chardonnay time!* She laughed. She felt better already. It was a fantastical thought, but she felt Damien was urging her on, giving her courage to shatter a portion of Sean's vision.

"Impressive," Sean said.

"They talk a lot, so I suppose not really, but it does make me smile. Every time."

He nodded and headed toward the kitchen.

A moment later he was back with a beer for himself and a wineglass half filled with silky yellow liquid. He handed the glass to her and raised his bottle.

"Cheers," she said.

He sat beside her and took a long swallow. "I wanted to talk to you about the menu for the dinner party."

"I didn't join this company to work part time as your de facto hostess."

"That's not it at all. I want to run my ideas past you. I value your input."

"And *I* wanted to tell you about a decision I've made. Don't try to hijack the conversation."

"We weren't having a conversation." He laughed. "When I was pouring your wine, I thought about the dinner party. That's all. I'd been meaning to ask…"

"I'm not planning a dinner party. It's an interesting idea, but it's not my area of expertise. I'm here to make sure this app is a success in the marketplace. I…"

"Hold on. Don't dismiss it too fast. I see this gathering as a marketing opportunity."

"That's great. And if you want to do it, I'm definitely

going to be here, and I'll engage with the participants."

"Guests," he said.

"But I've been doing some thinking. I need a change in my environment."

Even though he sat several inches away from her, she felt his body stiffen, heard his breathing become more shallow.

Damien scuffled across the mat. She heard the tap of his beak against the ceramic bowl. Good, he was drinking water. The day before, she'd purchased two mangos. As soon as he started chattering, she would cut one up for him.

"I'm not asking you to do any work for it. I just want to bounce ideas off you. We're a team. And you know your role isn't limited to marketing. We discussed it. I see you as a contributor to the strategic direction of the company."

She took a sip of wine and stood. "Please stop interrupting."

"I thought we were having a conversation?"

Now she wasn't sure if he was trying to fuck with her head or just grabbing every random thought to try to delay the inevitable. He surely knew. Her complaints over the past few weeks regarding their lack of freedom, her suggestions that they needed to institute enforced time apart…he had to know. "Living here is not working for me."

"You brought the bird all this way and now you're taking him back to the states? That's almost abuse, Tess."

He *was* trying to fuck with her head. "I don't mean living in Australia. I meant living in your house. The work-life-play thing is a great vision, and something worth pursuing, if the others are interested. But I need my own place."

"Is this because I wouldn't…because of my vow, and…"

"Of course not. I resent you suggesting that."

"It won't work if only part of the team lives here."

"Our objective is to find a market for the app. To make money on sales of the app. To enhance our customers' lives, if you want to consider the larger mission, not just our business goals. Living in this house contributes nothing to making any of that happen. In fact, I'm concerned it hinders that objective."

"Not true."

"For me, it is absolutely true. I signed on for the challenge of introducing people to a unique product."

"And we need creative energy for that."

"People get creative energy in different ways. I get creative energy by doing things that take my mind off work, not by seeing my co-workers across the breakfast table." She laughed and took a sip of wine. She imagined eating breakfast and reading the news without interruption. She imagined coming and going without others observing and commenting on her habits. She imagined inviting a man over for dinner, or overnight. She imagined pouring her heart out to Damien while he listened and chortled and helped her avoid taking herself too seriously. She imagined meeting new people, and not just the ones Sean chose for her, a contrived evening at a dinner party.

"It will have a terrible effect on the others," he said.

"I don't think so. But again, it's not my purpose here to consider how others work best. If you're concerned about that, hire an HR consulting firm. The objective is to sell the app. I don't see that we've had any creative synergy with this set-up."

"You haven't given it a chance."

"I've given it as much chance as I'm going to. I'll be

looking for a place and hope to be out by the end of July."

"So you're just telling me? We aren't going to discuss it? You're making an executive decision without me?"

She took another long swallow of wine and glanced at Damien. He looked back at her. "It's not an executive decision. It has nothing to do with TruthTeller. It's a personal decision. And there's nothing to discuss."

Damien bobbed his head and she had to force herself not to smile. It was unbelievable how much she'd missed him.

For whatever reason, maybe to stretch her neck, she looked up at the landing. Alex stood leaning on the rail, looking down.

9

Portland, Oregon

Long before my brother Jake and I started running together, when I was a little kid, I thought he was the most interesting of my three brothers. Eric was the smart, social one, the leader of the pack. Tom was the athletic and charming, and even smarter one. But Jake had a quiet way of running circles around both. A different kind of intelligence. One that wasn't about impressing teachers and our parents by earning good grades.

At least once a week he came home with a backpack full of books he'd taken out of the school library. Unless they were doing homework, the other two weren't all that interested in reading. Of course they read the Bible, as we were all required to do. They read biographies of so-called great people of faith, another requirement. That always struck me as funny because people of faith are supposed to be humble and reject the spotlight. But then, they didn't know they would be tagged as great after they died, so I suppose it wasn't really their fault.

Jake didn't bring home paperback detective stories. He didn't bring home adventure stories written for boys, as a lot of books were, and still are — girl books and boy books. Of course there are books that aren't segregated by gender — Harry Potter is the one everyone thinks of. But the Mallory kids weren't allowed to read those kinds of books. It featured magic, which was *the work of Satan*. I read the series in college.

The books we read while we were under our parents' watchful eyes, written for grade school kids and teenagers, were channeled toward one gender or the other, starting with the picture on the front cover. A girl saves her horse. A boy builds a fort and keeps the bullies out.

Jake devoured books about the planet. He poured over information about volcanos and natural disasters. He read about climate change and dinosaurs. Most of all, he loved to read about the ocean. In that area, he did branch out, or should I say deeper. He read *Twenty Thousand Leagues Under the Sea*. This lead him to the story of Atlantis and an interest in sharks. My father was thrilled with his interest in *Twenty Thousand Leagues Under the Sea*. He slapped Jake on the back — *Good choice, Jake, not the vapid stuff being printed now. A story for men.*

All those stories taking place so far below the surface of the ocean must have flooded his brain. He finally stumbled upon a book called *The Book of Sharks*. It was filled with information about their habits and diet, details about rare species, photographs and drawings, and accounts of shark and human interaction.

My mother was nervous about the effect the book would have on him. She worried about nightmares. She worried he might be showing a little too much fascination with gore and the bizarre. My father, for once, thought a little latitude was a good thing. They should encourage his intellectual curiosity. And there was nothing wrong with knowing the realities of something deadly — it developed respect, a healthy fear.

This knowledge was *not* appropriate for a young girl.

The pictures were terrifying and would produce nightmares, my mother said, having spent rather a long time viewing them herself. The stories were harrowing. There was nothing in *The Book of Sharks* that I needed to know. I would never in my life encounter a shark outside of an aquarium, so I didn't need to read about the things they might do to the human body. I should focus my attention on reading uplifting stories, on learning about gardening or cooking, not brutal creatures determined to maul human beings.

It was okay for Jake, barely, to know these things.

The Book of Sharks was kept in a prominent spot on his nightstand.

One afternoon, while Jake was still at school, I slipped into his room, grabbed the book, and walked quietly in my stocking feet, back to my room. I slid the book under my bed and went downstairs.

My mother was pleased to know I wanted a healthy snack — just apple slices. She was happy to cut them up and arrange them on a plate for me. I was doing my spelling homework, I told her. I wanted to surprise her after dinner when she would realize that on a Wednesday, I had already learned all the words for the test on Friday.

I quietly closed my bedroom door. She preferred our doors open, so she could glance at what we were doing when she walked by. Closing them wasn't absolutely forbidden, but it definitely invited more interest.

Still, closing it was the safer choice. She would most likely stay downstairs because she knew I wanted to surprise her with my spelling excellence. She knew what I was doing in my room, no need to check. On the off chance that she did come up, it was better to get a reprimand for unnecessarily closing my door than it was to be caught looking at *The Book of Sharks.* I would have time, when I heard the top stair creak, to slide the book under the bed and lean over my list of spelling words.

I placed my clock on the floor in front of me. I had thirty minutes, maybe more, to enjoy the book before Jake arrived home. I'd allowed myself five minutes to open my door, check for my mother, and get in and out of Jake's room.

The stories were indeed fantastic. I understood why he was so taken with the book, why he'd been studying it for several weeks now. He'd renewed it twice already, and since no other kid in the school had asked about the book, they allowed him to keep checking it out.

I read about a shark that followed a sailboat for ten miles, swimming right beside it, keeping the occupants from enjoying their trip as all eyes were on the shark, watching for that threatening fin cutting through the water. There was another story of a shark body-slamming a kayak while the guy tried to paddle fast enough to escape. Eventually, he did, landing exhausted on a deserted beach, miles from where he'd set out.

I read about a man who had parts of both arms torn off and his leg damaged with bites, but managed to live.

I was starting the story of a shark that swam into the mouth of a river when I saw the minute hand tick past the five. I wrote down the page number and closed the book.

When I came out of Jake's room. He was just reaching the top of the stairs.

"What are you doing in my room?"

"I wasn't."

"Don't lie."

I stared at him.

"I know you were in there. Why else would you be in that part of the hallway?"

I started toward my room.

He leaped up the last step and took several long strides, reaching my door before I did. He folded his arms and looked down at me. "Why were you in my room? And don't lie."

"No reason."

"There was a reason, or you wouldn't have lied."

I tried to slip around him but he stuck out his leg and blocked me. As I lifted one foot to step over, he grabbed my shoulder. "Tell me now. Or I'll tell mom you were in there."

"She won't care."

"Want to bet?"

I whispered.

"What did you say?"

"Lean down," I said. "So she won't hear."

He bent slightly.

"I wanted to see the shark book."

"I thought you hated water? Why would you want to look at pictures of the ocean?"

"I'm not *in* the water. I'm interested in the sharks."

"Well she doesn't want you to see that stuff. You're too young."

"It's because I'm a girl. Not because of my age."

"Maybe."

"Shh."

"Okay." He began whispering again. "I'll let you borrow it, but stay out of my stuff."

I nodded. "Can I have it now?"

"No. Later." He moved away from my doorway and down the hall. In a loud whisper, he called back, "And don't think you can lie to me. Ever."

10

I saw Tess look up at me, I saw her realize that I'd listened to her conversation with Sean.

So…she was moving out. I hadn't anticipated it, but it wasn't surprising. It was clear the minute I saw that cage that it wasn't going to be a long-term solution for housing Damien.

To Tess, Damien was part of her family. He was her entire family. She wouldn't want him locked up like a prisoner. She wanted him to feel he had free run of the house, even if he didn't choose to take advantage of it.

She hadn't seemed very happy. All the drive and confidence that had drawn me to her when we first met had faded inside of Sean's house, making her personality as stark and empty as the house next door — room after room of white tile floors and white walls and white carpet. A recipe for snow blindness.

All of us had been cranky while the police were showing up to question us every other day. Maybe the investigation into Karen's death had gutted Sean's vision. Maybe his dinner parties would revive us. Who knew. Either way, Tess would be gone.

I walked toward my room, trying to imagine what it would be like without her. Would she come to the office inside of his house every day? She hadn't said a word about how her new living situation would play out in practical terms. Would he allow her a key, or would she ring the front bell every morning while we were eating breakfast?

From my perspective on the second floor, their faces hidden from view, it had sounded as if she was more committed to TruthTeller than ever. It sounded as if she thought living here was keeping her from doing her best work. That seemed to be lost on Sean. He seemed to care more about keeping us in his sphere of influence than he did about actually launching the damn product into the world.

I could see Tess's point. Everything was a distraction.

I stopped at my door and took the key out of my pocket.

"You heard?" Tess said.

I turned. She was coming toward me. Her dark hair, silky and grown past her shoulders now, brushed across her arms as she walked. Her long legs moved gracefully, her shoes sank into the carpet, making it appear as if she were striding across the front lawn.

She stopped a few feet away. "Everything?"

I nodded. "Yup." I stuck the key in the lock.

"What do you think?"

"Whatever works."

"I'm not abandoning you."

I laughed and pushed open my door just wide enough to slip into my room. "I don't feel abandoned. I'll be fine."

"I just can't…"

"I heard your explanation."

"I guess so. Can I come in for a minute?"

I thought about the telescope. She hadn't been in my room since I'd taken it. She hadn't been in my room to see that the area rug I bought wasn't spiffing up the beige carpet as I'd said, but was wrapped around the telescope. She wouldn't be able to see into my closet from the main part of my room. And I could usher her out to the balcony, insist I needed a smoke.

"If you don't want me to come in, just say so."

"No, it's fine."

She laughed. "Such a friendly invitation."

"I was going to have a smoke. Do you mind?"

"Of course not."

She followed me into the room. I got a glass and filled it with an inch of water. I picked up my cigarettes and lighter off my desk. With Tess following, I went onto the balcony, closing the door behind us.

"Can I have one?" she said.

"Really? I didn't know you smoked. You never…"

"Lots of people have, at one point or another. Right?"

"It's a nasty habit, but hard to let go of," I said.

She nodded. "And sometimes, nothing else suffices."

She was right about that. I held out the pack and she removed a cigarette. I lit both of them and put the glass on the balcony floor between us. We smoked in silence for several minutes. Nothing about her movements or her release of the smoke into a thin, graceful stream, made it seem as if smoking was a long-abandoned habit. She gave the impression it was her second or third smoke of the day.

I tapped my ash into the glass. "How do you think he took it?"

"You heard."

"I don't think he's going to let go that easily," I said.

"Maybe not. But nothing will change when I'm not living here."

"Do you really believe that?"

"Nothing important. All of this…" she waved her arm around toward the room behind us, "…is bullshit. It feels like we're in college."

"A little." It was far nicer than anything I'd experienced in college, than anything I'd experienced in my life, actually, except for the month or two I house-sat and bird-sat in her Russian Hill condo. But she was right about the dynamic between the four of us. I suppose the petty fights over someone eating another person's food that occupied college life weren't part of our lives now, but petty, prurient curiosity over who was having sex and who wasn't remained the same. I liked our set-up. And despite knowing things would shift, possibly dramatically, without Tess, I wasn't ready to give up all the freebies.

Living in a luxury home and saving nearly my entire paycheck was something I couldn't have imagined falling into my hands. But now that it had, I was thrilled. I liked knowing I was making huge leaps toward my goal of buying my own property.

"Are you pissed?" she said.

"Of course not. You do what you have to do."

"You're okay staying here with the two of them?"

"Of course." I noticed it didn't seem to be anywhere in her thoughts that she might invite me to escape with her. Not that I wanted to live with her, I preferred being close to Gavin. And I preferred the house over whatever smaller place Tess might choose. I doubted she could afford anything remotely like it on her own. Her deal for TruthTeller was lucrative, but she still had a mortgage in San Francisco.

"Why are you so quiet?" she said.

"No reason."

"It's just so stifling living here."

"It might be the same when you leave."

"Why?"

"Maybe it's Sean, not the house, not the roommates. Maybe it's being in business with him at all."

She put the cigarette to her lips and drew smoke into her mouth and lungs. She let it out quickly, but said nothing.

"Have you looked for a place?" I said.

"I love browsing real estate websites. I'm always looking at what's out there."

"Have you found anything that works for you?"

"Not yet. But I have a good idea where to start."

"How are you going to manage buying a place and moving out by July? It takes more than a month, doesn't it?"

She shrugged. "Yes. But I wanted him to face the reality. I didn't want him thinking I was hanging around for another six or eight months and that he could figure out some way to deflate my motivation." She took another drag on her cigarette.

I nodded.

I suppose when all of our creature comforts are met, not making a change is easy. There's nothing pushing you. Maybe that's why parents send their kids away to college. The lure of parentally-funded freedom drives us to spend four more years in school, and after that, the school sees to it that you're out. No cocoon protecting you.

"Why did he think you were leaving?" I said.

"What do you mean?"

"He said something about a vow?"

She shrugged one shoulder. She dropped her cigarette into the glass and stood. "Thanks for the smoke."

"What was he talking about?"

"I'm not sure."

"He seemed to think there was a reason."

"There is. I need my own space. I need my own life."

She put her hand on the handle of the balcony door. "I keep forgetting to ask. Why did you start locking your bedroom door?"

"It feels more private."

"You're the one who goes prowling through other rooms. Do you really think Sean will come into yours without an invitation?"

"I just feel more comfortable."

"Is Gavin's paranoia rubbing off on you?"

"He's not paranoid."

"Okay, his extreme caution, then."

"Maybe it is."

"How can you live here, if you don't trust the people sharing the house?"

I really don't trust anyone, but Tess wouldn't understand that. Leaving my door unlocked before I was trying to hide a large telescope hadn't been an indication of trust.

The door was locked so no one would stumble across the telescope. Taking it had been a mistake and I needed to be rid of it. Soon. Her curiosity over the locked door proved it.

I dropped my cigarette in the glass of water and stood. "Like you said, it's a little too cozy. It's nice to have some sense that at least one space belongs only to you."

"Did I say it was too cozy?"

I smiled. "I think you did."
She looked uncertain, but she didn't argue.

11

Bondi Beach would be crowded on a Sunday, even in the winter. If I wanted my first swim lesson, which I'd lied and said I was looking forward to, we needed to be there before sunrise.

At six a.m. I was standing on the front patio while Gavin backed his little blue Triumph Spitfire out of the garage. It was a car that looked in danger from even a mid-sized SUV, in danger of being crushed by a single wheel climbing over the hood of the car, but we didn't have to take a freeway to get to Bondi, so I figured it would be okay.

Riding with the top down, cool, dark air blowing across my skin felt good, and I saw the appeal of the tiny car. Besides, you can die in a Volvo, given the right circumstances, despite their claims of superior safety. So why not enjoy the ride in a very cute and compact car? The trunk was large enough for a single suitcase and a duffel bag. Now, it held nothing but a canvas bag with two large towels.

Swimming was a sport that required nothing but a small piece of spandex. No goggles, no flippers, no rubber tubes, according to Gavin. Just me and the water. I wasn't sure if he'd said that to make me confront reality, or if he wasn't thinking about what that sounded like to someone who does not want to face off against a large body of water without any supporting equipment.

We parked and walked toward the empty beach, the sky

growing pale gray around us. At the far end, two men in tiny bathing suits with tight caps on their heads were striding into the waves. At the same moment, they dove into the surf. They seemed to be gone for a very long time, but eventually their latex-covered heads bounced up like billiard balls. They began swimming parallel to the beach, looking as if they belonged in the water, that propelling their bodies through swelling, curling waves, their feet unable to touch the sand below, was as easy as strolling along a sidewalk.

Gavin turned to the right. The swimmers disappeared from my sight as I followed him toward the rocks on the opposite side of the famous beach.

Bondi Beach is the epitome of the Australian lifestyle. First off, it's a beautiful beach with pristine white sand and sparkling blue water, great for surfing. Oddly enough, there's a shark net stretched across part of the bay, allowing swimmers and surfers to play without fear of attack. I imagined sharks, lined up on the opposite side of the net, smelling the small drops of blood leaking from stubbed toes and shaving cuts, frustrated in their quest.

The nearby buildings were constructed in the early part of the last century. The area offers some of the best bars, restaurants, and cafes in Sydney. Tourists from all over Australia and the world consider it a must-see destination. It appeared to be one of those *see-and-be-seen* beaches, like Malibu or the French Riviera.

To our right was a hotel and rows of huge homes looking out over the water. In front of the hotel pool was another rectangular pool built to allow the ocean to wash into it. As Gavin had promised, during low tide, it looked like any other swimming pool, the water still and flat.

He dropped our bag on a concrete bench beside the pool. He pulled off his sweatshirt and kicked off his flip-flops. "Ready when you are." He walked into the water until it reached his hips.

I took off my sweatshirt and slid my skirt down over my hips. I'd purchased a new one-piece swimsuit for the occasion. I figured it would make me feel more like an otter, or a dolphin, maybe even a shark...more acclimated to water. Bikinis are made for splashing around and looking cute, but not for turning myself into a creature that's at one with the water.

Not that I had such high expectations, but I figured dressing the part couldn't hurt. I'd worked my hair into a single fishtail braid to further my effort to be a creature that moved through water unimpeded, like those guys in the waves. I resisted the urge to check on their progress, keeping my eyes on Gavin's face.

The water was cool but comfortable. I walked toward Gavin, trying not to shiver from thoughts of what the water might do to me despite the pleasing temperature.

"You look great," he said.

I smiled. I was pretty sure that looking good wasn't helpful, and I didn't want to be thinking about how I looked. I wanted to think about how I would manage to put my face into water and feel it pushing into my nostrils, lapping around my ears, trying to pry open my lips. I shivered despite my best effort.

"Okay. So I'm going to take this as if you were a child. Don't be put off. It really does work, taking a playful approach. Okay? Swimming is fun. Don't think about anything but the fun of each thing you're doing."

I nodded.

He moved deeper into the water until it reached his chest. "Come with me."

I followed slowly.

"I want you to put your face in the water and blow air out of your mouth. Try to make the largest bubbles you can imagine."

I laughed. "Seriously?"

"Absolutely." He put his face in the water and demonstrated.

I took a deep breath.

"Don't do that. Just put your face in and blow."

"How can I blow if I don't have enough air inside?"

"You have more than you think."

He waited.

This was it. Either I was going to do this or I wasn't. Besides, I could pull my head out at any moment. My father was ten thousand miles away. Gavin would never in a hundred years put his hand on the back of my head and push. Yet, I felt something there. Possibly the hand of god shoving me under the water.

I shook my head, dislodging the imagined downward press of fingers. I stuck my nose, brow, and lips into the water, leaving my ears well above the surface. I blew, hearing the bubbles, then lifted my head. I tasted salt. My eyes blurred as I opened them and water filmed across the surface.

"Well done," he said.

"Thank you. Do I get a gold star?"

"Possibly." He touched my nose, wiping away a drop of water. "Do it again."

He had me do it fifteen or twenty more times, and by the

last time, it didn't seem like such a big deal. I felt ridiculously impressed with myself. Of course, my feet were firmly planted on the bottom of the pool. The water couldn't sweep me away in this position. At least I didn't think it could.

After that, we moved on to a lesson in floating. It was much more pleasant than pushing my nose and mouth into the water, but also defied logic even more than blowing air into something somewhat solid and listening to the rumble like my breath was a storm of its own.

He held me in his arms, which was nice. He moved his hands so one was beneath my upper thighs and the other under my shoulders, bringing up the reminder of less supportive hands on my skull. He insisted the water would hold me. All I had to do was relax. "Pretend you're having sex. Just let your body forget itself."

For several minutes he stood holding my body while I tried to keep my head back and unwind the tension in my shoulders. The conscious directing of my muscles to unclench was like yoga, and nothing like sex, which pretty much takes care of itself.

And then, I was floating. My lower legs drifted below the surface, but the rest of me remained above the water. I felt it holding me and heard Gavin's muffled voice with that lovely accent, talking about weightlessness. I wondered if I might fall asleep, but of course, that could never happen.

That was it for the first lesson.

We dried off, kissed for a while, and then walked across the street to get coffee and scones.

We sat at an outdoor table and gobbled scones as if we'd swum ten miles, instead of lying in a pool, trying to convince all the hidden parts of my brain that the water would not attempt to smother me.

He mentioned Tess moving out and Sean's worry that everything might fall apart in the aftermath.

"Is that what he said?" I took a sip of my latte, enjoying the flood of warmth.

"Yes."

"Is he going to try to talk her out of it?"

"I'm not sure. Sometimes, I have no idea what he's up to. Right now, he's mostly thinking about his dinner party. Maybe he thinks it will be so outstanding, she'll change her mind."

I smiled and picked up my second scone. Blueberry. "I'm sure it will work out. We'll still launch the app on the same timeline." I took a bite of my scone.

He was quiet for a moment. "I wonder what he really wants. It almost seems as if he doesn't care all that much about the app any more. He talks about it a lot, but he constantly delays. He keeps asking me to make changes, minor tweaks, things that could be done after it's out there in the wild."

"I guess he wants it to be perfect," I said.

"Nothing is perfect."

"As close as he can get."

"Do you ever wonder if it's just a game?" Gavin said.

"What do you mean?"

"That he just wants to keep us all in this house, living like some sort of artificial family. That he doesn't care much about the app. It's a smokescreen."

I laughed. "That's crazy."

"It's like the dinner party. Another reason to delay getting the app out while we spend an evening asking random people to talk it up for us. Like that's going to happen."

I shrugged. "You know him better than I do."

"I've known him longer, that's all. I don't actually know him at all. At least that's how it feels most of the time."

I finished my scone and looked out at the water. I wondered whether I would ever dive into the surf and go swimming out there with no end in sight.

12

The afternoon following my first swim lesson, Tess went out looking at real estate. True to his word that Sean had a constant flow of updates to the app, Gavin retreated to his room to make some more adjustments to the code. Sean was in his room, where he'd been since just after we returned from my swim lesson.

I took Damien out of his cage. I put him on my shoulder and carried him and his perch into the office, settling him beside me. There were no cockatoos on the front lawn in the afternoon, so I figured he would stay calm during his first opportunity to get a better look outdoors. Of course, he wasn't used to the outdoors after living in a high rise, so maybe I was attributing human desire to him.

I sat down and opened Facebook.

There was nothing new, but I had an idea to spark more activity — I would do some recording during the dinner party. Weeks ago, I'd promised the page fans who were intrigued by our living and working together, that I'd post some clips from our lives. Now that our unconventional work environment was fracturing, I wondered if talking about Sean's vision had been the best approach. Still, for now it was my only idea, and surely I'd find something interesting at a dinner party. If nothing else, there would be plenty of alcohol and you can usually count on that to provide entertaining behavior.

Keeping my back to Damien, I spoke, trusting he'd know I was speaking to him since he was the only other living being in the room. "For now, I'm going to find out what this Carmen is up to."

Dangerous woman.

I smiled. "Me or Carmen?"

He didn't respond, but it didn't matter.

I opened a message window and typed a note to her.

Alex: *So you aren't interested in purchasing the statue?*

While I waited for a reply, I surfed the web. It was nearly twenty minutes before a tiny *one* inside a red disk appeared to let me know I had a single message. I slowly released my breath, not aware I'd been holding it. For now, it looked like she was willing to chat privately, letting go of her crusade for public truth telling.

Carmen: *Is he selling it?*

Alex: *I could ask.*

Carmen: *You're offering to sell it and you don't have his permission?*

Alex: *To be honest, no. But I could still ask. I'm just curious about why you're so interested in it.*

Carmen: *Why don't you ask him.*

Alex: *I did.*

Carmen: *What did he say?*

Alex: *Not much.*

Her response was an emoji with its mouth in a straight line.

I had no idea how to interpret that. It seemed as if she was playing my own game back at me — mislead by using emojis, appear to be communicating while saying nothing at all. Clearly she was well aware of that.

Behind me, Damien was murmuring. *Dangerous woman. Delicious mango. Pleased to meet you.*

I smiled and leaned back in the chair. If Sean caught me at this, he would be pissed. But at the same time, I couldn't carry on with our Facebook updates, knowing Carmen was out there, ready to strike at any time, undermining my effort to draw our fans slowly toward the app. I had to know what she was really after. Then, maybe I could get her to abandon her assault. That last part was a long shot, but it was worth trying. It's always worth trying.

You never know what's going to happen in this world. People go along assuming one day will be like another, and most of the time, I suppose they are. And I suppose those of us in developed countries could do a better job of valuing that stability and sameness. There are a large number of people on this planet, the majority, who have no clue what's going to happen from one day to the next, from one moment to the next. They have no idea where they'll find their next bit of food or their next glass of water or a place to sleep.

All that aside, lots of strange and amazing things happen out of nowhere. And for me, when I get bored, I like to make things happen. Admittedly, I like to see how people respond to the unexpected.

Sean was making a terrible mistake, thinking he could just ignore Carmen, that she would go away and leave his company alone, his brand intact, what little there was of it. She was angry with something, angry at him, and she was not going away unless someone dealt with her rage. Obviously that someone was me.

Although maybe Gavin was right. Maybe Sean didn't care about making our company successful. I laughed to myself.

Did Gavin really believe that or was he just frustrated because he had to keep making minor updates, feeling like his job was never finished, deprived of the creative energy of doing something new and different? Gavin had struck me as a man who wanted things to be right, but maybe there was a limit to his desire for quality. Maybe he thought additional quality at this point wouldn't be noticed by customers. If he was tired of what seemed like unnecessary changes, it made sense that he would think Sean was treating all of this like some elaborate, senseless game. To me, his suspicion seemed absurd.

For now, I would focus on Carmen. Once we had a dinner party or two, and Tess moved out, then we would see how things re-shaped themselves.

Alex: *Is there anything I can do to help resolve the situation?*

After fifteen minutes, there was no response. I tried again.

Alex: *Is this about his statue, or something else?*

The bubbles began floating across the space below my comment. She was heated, typing fast, bubbles bouncing furiously, or so it seemed. I probably imagined it.

Carmen: *It's not his statue!*

Alex: *???*

There were no bubbles to suggest she had anything more to say. My mind drifted to the bubbles I'd blown into the salt water, rumbling in my ears, air rushing out of me, the only way to keep water from rushing into me. It was a clever trick, but what happened once you ran out of air?

I waited for several more minutes. She wasn't going to respond.

There had to be a way to get her talking to me. I turned

and looked at Damien. He studied me, keeping his eyes focused on mine, looking as if he were waiting for me to speak. I was waiting for Carmen and he was waiting for me.

"What do you think, Damien?"

Dangerous woman.

"That's all?"

He laughed.

13

The speed with which Sean had managed to pull his dinner party list together surprised and impressed me. The invitees must have been people eager to see him again, or simply acquaintances who thought highly of him and valued an invite to dinner at his place over other social possibilities, or…people craving a peek at his magnificent home.

It was scheduled for the Saturday after he first suggested the idea — July 1.

Gavin was doing all the cooking. He wanted to — *no pressure, no obligation.* He assured me. He assured Tess. He didn't see it as an infringement on his role with the company at all. He loved to cook.

The dining room table was set with white plates on silver placemats. A spray of silver-painted dried branches stood in a large thick glass vase in the center of the table. The chandelier was on, the lights dim until after sunset. There would be four men and two women, and the four of us. We were serving champagne and three varieties of wine. A decadent tiramisu sat in the refrigerator, and beside it, a platter of cheese, the hard cheeses already sliced. The soft cheeses were still wrapped in plastic. Red grapes and candied nuts were ready in covered bowls beside packages of flatbread and crackers that would accompany the post-dessert cheese course.

I was standing beside Gavin, holding a knife that was so

sharp, it left a little slice in my skin when I pressed the blade against my fingertip. I wore jeans and a T-shirt and a black apron with a kangaroo on the front. My clothes were easily washed, but Gavin insisted on the apron. He thought it looked cute. And he thought it would make me take my role more seriously. My makeup was already on, and my hair brushed out into a long, soft curtain. After I finished helping, all I had to do was slip into my dress and shoes.

After appetizers of stuffed mushrooms and bacon-wrapped shrimp that Sean would pass while all of us stood around drinking champagne and getting to know one another, we would enter the dining room for the meal.

The first item on the menu was endive salad, plum tomatoes, and finely chopped hard-boiled egg with a light, creamy mustard dressing. This was followed by grilled swordfish and vegetables, the vegetables drizzled with olive oil and seasoned with nothing but salt and pepper — sliced peppers, squash, eggplant, and red onions. I was in charge of making risotto. I held the knife, ready to slice mushrooms into paper-thin semi-circles, cutting the slices in half again so mushrooms didn't overwhelm each bite of risotto.

On the counter in front of me was the recipe for the risotto, which Gavin was walking me through. He acted as if it were the periodic table of elements, so complex he had to describe each facet. I listened patiently, giving him a delicate smile every time he glanced at me.

"Put down the knife and wash and dry the mushrooms," he said.

I did as I was told, scrubbing each one until it was a buffed white orb. I dried them and placed them on the cutting board. I popped out the stems, dropping them into the compost container. I picked up that magnificent knife. I ran the blade through the first mushroom, making a precise cut that left a perfect sliver. It fell on the cutting board like a slightly large, utterly unique snowflake.

"You cut those like you're performing surgery," Gavin said.

"That's good to know. Something to add to my résumé."

He laughed. He turned to the swordfish and began spreading a thin layer of soft butter on each piece then dusting them with salt, pepper, and rosemary. He went to work on the rest of his vegetables, quickly outpacing me as I drew the blade through each mushroom multiple times, letting it sink slowly, carefully into the flesh.

He poured us both a glass of Chardonnay and I went outside with him while he began grilling the vegetables. They would be kept warm in a drawer beneath the grill. The swordfish wouldn't be cooked until the guests were well into their appetizers.

Once the risotto was cooking, we left the food and went to our rooms to dress.

As I slipped off my jeans and glimpsed my black lace underpants in the mirror, cut high on my thighs, rather small in the back, I thought about Gavin. I was overcome with a desire to abandon our dinner party obligations, slip into his room, and pull him onto the bed. It was inconvenient to be feeling desire for his body at the same time I was looking forward to all that delicious food, and trying to work out how I was going to shoot a film without being observed. I like my mind settled in one place at a time, not split and running in opposite directions.

I pushed the thought away and pulled off my T-shirt. I

eased the short, fitted black dress off the hanger, raised my arms, and let the dress slide down my body. I zipped the side, put on a silver arrow pendant, and stepped into my highest black heels. It was the first time I'd gotten fully dressed up in Australia, except for my side trip to stage Detective Bender's suicide. And that outfit had been so not me that I hadn't felt particularly dressed up.

Although I was prepared to film parts of the dinner, hoping to find something entertaining, or better, intriguing and provocative, I was still on the fence about the best path forward. Sean was worried about the things I'd exposed on Facebook. Was he still poking around on the page when I wasn't aware of it?

Just because he'd confronted me before about my interaction with Carmen, didn't mean he wasn't still watching the conversation lurch forward and stop, predicting better than I could when she was going to strike.

It's easy to forget that eyeballs you aren't even aware of are paying attention to the words that flow from your fingertips on social media. Curious strangers are scrutinizing every photograph, nefarious strangers are looking at a photograph's metadata for clues about your location. If people really stopped and thought about that, they might be more hesitant to blast out every upset that passes through their minds, every emotion that flutters across their lives.

If I spent more time on Twitter, if I looked for ways to be flamboyant in that arena, Sean wouldn't be on to me. Yet. I could perform my job and get some interest for TruthTeller.

When I delivered a report to him, he'd be so pleased with the numbers, he might not investigate. Besides, it's not exactly easy to travel back in time on Twitter. Launch enough tweets and earlier comments get so buried, only the truly diligent will find them.

That is, if he wanted genuine market attention for TruthTeller at all. Gavin's assessment of Sean's motivation hovered at the edge of my thoughts. Was it even believable that Sean was playing some game with us, using the app in some bizarre scheme to acquire roommates? I couldn't imagine spending so much to pay people excellent salaries if you weren't serious about making money with your app. I couldn't be sure whether Gavin was just irritated and over-reacting to the re-dos, or if he knew something more that he wasn't saying.

Maybe this was why Gavin hadn't wanted stock in the company.

14

The entire focus of the dinner party had shifted. Sean wished he could go back and push the re-start button, wherever that was. This was supposed to be an intellectual gathering of like-minded yet wildly divergent people. The people who comprised TruthTeller had sparked the idea. Gavin, Tess, and Alexandra were impossibly different from one another and in that variation, he found endless stimulation.

Expanding that through frequent meals shared with other people who had moved in and out of his life at various times would be mind-blowing. Before the party began, he couldn't wait to sit back in his chair at the head of the table, listening to them talk, watching food move into their mouths, jaws working, tongues poking out to lick lips, throats contracting as they swallowed. He saw their hands, reaching for glasses filled with silken wine. He almost felt the wine as it slipped across their tongues, and without anyone observing its path, seeped into their bloodstreams.

With the satiation of good food, the warm glow of dopamine, their thoughts would open like flowers. The wine would make them more willing to expose those thoughts to the others.

It was what everyone truly wanted — another person to listen. When people spoke without censoring every word, it made conversation much more interesting. A rich meal eased the self-conscious desire to fit in, to say what was acceptable so one might imagine she or he was welcomed. The truth came out.

Truth telling.

He smiled.

But now. Tess had spoiled everything. Or had she? Maybe he'd spoiled it.

There was no doubt in his mind, no matter how she denied it, that she was moving out because he'd rejected her. Seeing her standing naked at the foot of his bed had shaken him deeply. No matter how many times she tried to frame it as an act of confidence, as something that had no emotion tied to it, she hadn't persuaded him.

No woman, no human being, likes to know their naked body isn't of interest. The object of their desire is supposed to be aroused at the mere sight of skin. He had been, but he'd made a vow, and he'd carried it on for this long. He wasn't taking a hammer to it this late in the game.

Sometimes he wondered who he was doing it for. No one would ever know whether or not he'd failed. But he felt there was some cosmic justice, there had to be, the world made no sense without it. And this overarching justice, even though it failed every moment of every day, had to prevail at some point in time. After life was over, or possibly not until the world blew itself up or burned itself out, but at some point, there would be justice. And then, he would be glad for keeping his promise. Because then, someone or some...*thing*, or possibly all of humanity, would notice he'd paid his debt.

And now, she was moving out. Because she didn't understand. He'd tried to give her an explanation, but she acted as if it wasn't important. She'd lied to his face that all was okay between them, and then made plans to move out.

With Tess gone, the balance of the house would be destroyed. With Tess gone, he felt even more alone. Gavin was a good guy, and they got along, shared some similar ideas, liked to take life easy, more or less. But Alex. Without Tess, he was afraid Alex wouldn't be held in check. And she definitely needed someone holding her in check.

He'd been right from the moment he first took her hand in his, shaking it, looking into her eyes. She was a predator.

After Lisa bled to death in her front yard, he'd been ashamed of that reaction, briefly. After he learned the nature of Lisa's husband, he'd thought *predator* was too vicious a way to describe Alexandra Mallory. But now, he was sure of it.

He'd known it was the truth when she entered his room and sat in his chair as if it belonged to her. He knew it when she photographed his statue and posted it on the internet. He knew it when she went into Gavin's room late at night, thinking no one knew they were having sex. He knew it when she engaged in a chat with Carmen, egging her on. Alex didn't give a shit about the reputation of the company, she wanted to poke Carmen and see how far she'd go. Alex wanted an entry point into his life, she wanted power over him.

Tess kept all that under control, even though she didn't realize it.

Besides, he liked Tess. There would be no marketing of the app without Tess, no future for TruthTeller without her. She was smart, interesting. And, she was excellent to look at. Vow or no vow, he loved looking at her. She was confident and quietly in possession of herself. They all needed her.

Now, the dinner party had transformed from a gathering of like-spirited people into a performance, something he hoped would open Tess's eyes, force her to recognize what she was losing. A dinner that would make her see that people craved a solid, tightly-knit community. Living by herself would make her miserable. She just didn't see that yet.

His guests were standing around the pool drinking champagne. He walked among them with a plate of stuffed mushrooms. His guests were like robots in the way they plucked each plump mushroom cap filled with minced garlic and ground pork off the plate, popping them into their mouths, chewing and nodding as they listened to someone talk Rugby League, about the latest film releases, about government screw-ups, about business. Always business.

There was Chris, the only other American in the group, a husky guy with a blonde buzz cut who had worked as a product manager at the company that acquired Sean's first startup. Chris was talking a mile a minute to Sylvie, an art gallery owner in Sydney, and Mimi, an actress who made and sold leather bracelets to supplement her income. Both women were small and slim, wearing black dresses, as were Tess and Alex. That's the only dress color most women seemed to possess. It was the safe choice, he supposed. Especially for a dinner party. You didn't call attention to yourself but looked classy and sexy, without being slutty, all at the same time.

Gavin stood beside the grill carrying on an animated conversation with Oscar, a sports promoter, and Henry, a veterinarian. The vet was a scuba diving friend. At first, Sean had dismissed the thought of inviting him. But then it occurred to him that a vet saw people every day who faced huge and potentially shattering decisions about their pets. He was a perfect sounding board for the TruthTeller app.

It was impossible to guess what Gavin and those two had

in common — certainly not diving or the health problems of animals. Most likely sports, but he couldn't be sure. Gavin was doing most of the talking, an anomaly on its own. Sean hadn't heard Gavin talk for such a lengthy amount of time since he'd moved into the house. It was as if sharing living space had forced him to retreat, a turtle returning to its shell when there was too much stimulation. Funny how Gavin thought there was too much stimulation and Tess, not enough.

He went into the kitchen and put down the nearly empty plate. He refilled his champagne glass. Beer would have been preferable, but he wanted to set a certain mood, wanted especially to catch Tess's attention, so champagne it was. To him, it was like drinking perfumed air. He took another sip and popped a mushroom into his mouth. It was cold. He went to the warming drawer and took out another tray of mushrooms.

From the corner of his eye, he saw a flicker of movement. He turned. Gavin was signaling that the swordfish was ready.

Midway through dinner, he began to relax. The food was excellent. It had been served at the perfect temperature despite the inevitable chaos of people putting down partially full champagne glasses, looking for a place to dump wadded up cocktail napkins, making last minute trips to use the toilet, and crisscrossing each other as they found their chairs, indicated by a tiny silver card lying on each plate.

Now, with a solid Cab to chase the dizzying effects of champagne and a meal that surpassed his expectations, the hum of conversation and quiet laughter that assured him everyone was having a good time, he felt satisfied. There wasn't anyone sitting a few inches too far from the edge of the table, silent and disengaged. He was the only one mentally stepping outside of the party to observe the overall flow of the evening.

Watching Tess made him particularly happy. Her long, dark hair was tucked behind both ears, exposing thick gold earrings. He'd never seen her with her hair pushed so casually out of the way, as if she'd forgotten herself and was simply caught up in the moment. She was seated beside Ian, a guy who worked in finance. Sean knew him from the sale of his company. Even after years of shared lunches and dinners and a day at a cricket match, he still wasn't entirely sure what the guy actually did, but whatever it was, he raked in money. On the other side was Mimi. That arrangement had been a risk because the two women had nothing in common. But Mimi was funny and talkative, and he figured it might work just because it was hard not to like Mimi. She was a true entertainer. Tess looked entertained.

This was the key. He'd been brilliant, planning this party. Tess didn't need her own space, she didn't need distance between her and the rest of the team. She needed the opposite. More people. She was stifled and uninspired. She needed lively interaction and conversation. She needed variety and the challenge of new ideas.

He'd spent two days trying to decide who should be at the foot of the table. It couldn't be Tess, she would feel pressured into assuming the role of a hostess which would make her imagine she was being pressed into taking more ownership of the house and the party than she wanted. Putting Gavin there seemed weird, and the same for a guest, who might wonder why they were chosen for a somewhat honorary position.

So of course, it was Alex. Seeing her across from him — a pseudo husband and wife — was uncomfortable, but for the most part, he'd kept his attention on Tess.

Now, he glanced in Alex's direction. He'd been wrong about everyone being engaged. Alex had moved her chair a few inches back from the table. Her dinner plate glistened as if she'd licked it clean. She wasn't talking. She was looking directly at him, a tiny smile on her face.

There was no doubt, that woman was a predator, and he still didn't know what she wanted.

15

More than anything, I wanted a second piece of swordfish. And several more slices of grilled eggplant. Another scoop of creamy risotto. But everything was gone. The platters and bowls were scraped clean. The others appeared satisfied, drinking wine, the thought of dessert and that luscious cheese plate the furthest thing from their minds.

But I wanted more. Not a lot. Just a few bites. Half a plate, maybe. I wasn't starving. Not even what you'd call hungry, but there was a faint nagging in my stomach. On top of that was the memory of those veggies and the blackened brand marks from the grill that made them so tasty, and the melt-in-your-mouth swordfish, firm and pure in its taste, instead of drowning in a sauce or too much seasoning.

I took a sip of wine. Before dinner, I'd wanted a martini. Champagne is fine, but a martini would have set the stage, and that little extra opening tang from the olives might have avoided the situation I found myself in now.

There was a way to distract myself from my hunger, I just needed to figure out how to do it without attracting attention.

I pushed my chair a few more inches away from the table. A moment earlier, Sean had looked at me, holding my gaze for several long seconds before turning his head slowly as if he were counting his guests, mentally tapping each one on the head like a child that he needed to count off, assuring himself they were all present, well-fed and comfortable and happy.

Now, his scrutiny was back on Tess.

The look he gave her was difficult to interpret. If I didn't know him better, I might think it was love. I might think it was at least lust, that they'd found a satisfactory arrangement similar to mine and Gavin's. But it wasn't love, and I didn't think it was lust. I know the look of lust and I think I would have recognized it.

There was something else going on.

Grief, because she was leaving? Possibly.

Helplessness? Loneliness? Anger that his utopian workplace had cracks in its foundation?

None of those quite fit.

I continued to watch him watch her. I inched my chair out farther. He glanced my way but didn't pause. Immediately his eyes were back on Tess, who was laughing and chatting as if this was the best party she'd attended all year. Maybe it was.

I stood.

Sean looked at me. I smiled and slipped away from my place. I headed toward the bathroom. As I glanced back over my shoulder, I saw he was watching where I was headed. Then, he looked away. He seemed to have made the obvious, but mistaken assumption that I needed to pee.

Once I was out of his range of sight, I turned toward the living room, my heals clicking on the tile. When I reached the carpet, I slipped my shoes off. My phone sat on one of the small tables near the front of the room, beside a narrow vase with a single white rose. I placed my nose close to the petals and inhaled. Delicious. The craving in my stomach dissipated. I picked up my phone.

Creeping toward the edge of the living room, I had an

angled view of the dining room. Sean hadn't moved. I hurried out and around the back of the glass enclosed atrium where the turtles hid in the greenery and swam around their small pond. Damien murmured, but fortunately he looked like he was falling asleep. I opened my camera app and changed the setting to video.

I inched around the glass enclosure, getting a better angle into the dining room. Closing in on Sean's face to capture his expression cut out the other guests. At the same time, if I wanted to show the object of his attention, I needed a wider shot that would include Tess and her constantly moving head, her lips expelling words, her eyes laughing. I wished I had a more sophisticated camera.

There had to be a way to make it work. I re-positioned my phone and looked at the scene. I pressed record and let it run for about twenty seconds, taking in Tess on the left side of the screen, Sean at the right. I tapped pause. Of course... the solution was simple. I would film him watching her, then I would zoom in on her excited, happy, slightly tipsy face for half a minute. Then I'd stop and focus on his face for a few seconds longer, the intensity of his gaze, that unreadable expression. The two threads would come together during editing.

The beauty of his expression was that every person who viewed the film would interpret it differently — lust, love, envy, hatred, sadness. The list could be even longer, since we do tend to project biases onto everything we observe.

At the end, I had about five minutes recorded. With some editing, it would be a perfect ninety-second clip, the maximum length of most on-line attention spans. Although that might be an exaggeration, I'd found myself clicking away from videos after twenty seconds. Hopefully this was compelling enough to keep people engaged for several minutes. I'd edit it with an upbeat song, maybe a song that suggested some of those possible interpretations, or maybe some classical music.

If I posted it on Facebook, Sean would be furious. But only if I made a comment suggesting what I thought was going on, not that I'd figured that out yet. But if I ignored the subliminal communication and made a comment about his salon idea and how much admiration he had for his executive vice president of marketing, it wouldn't look malevolent.

I would explain, if he even saw it, that people were curious about what it was like — living and working together. I could talk about the intellectual stimulation of our arrangement. I giggled to myself. Stimulation, yes. Intellectual, absolutely not.

Viewers could draw their own conclusions. If they made comments about what might be going on between the two of them, it wasn't my fault.

When I first explained Sean's vision on our Facebook page, there had been comments about sexual tension. The video would enflame those people, confirming their beliefs about the inevitable results of living with co-workers. It would draw others into the discussion as well. But still, it was worth the risk. I'd told him repeatedly — if you want to get attention online, you have to be flamboyant. Over the top.

People want blood, they want conflict. They want to know that living in a luxury house and working with the same people was not as utopian as it might appear.

The video might suggest danger — Sean ready to rip Tess's lucrative job out of her hands. People love the threat of danger. Look at those images that get so much attention, showing that glass-floored footbridge crossing a deep gorge in China, or even the impossibly narrow trails winding down into the Grand Canyon. Consider the views and excitement and trending that results from people who face a gunman or a raging tiger. Along with the threat of physical danger, they love hearing about the downfall of the privileged. People want excitement, an adrenaline rush, and in the world of social media, they want even more of it — we're an easily bored species.

16

Tess had gone out shopping, taking the whole day off, she'd said. I wondered whether she was shopping for houses, not clothes, despite her comment about needing a new pair of boots. But she isn't the type to lie, so maybe the boots were a truthful destination. I didn't recall seeing her wearing boots since I'd arrived and possibly she really did need a new pair. I have a bit of a boot fetish myself, so I could understand that. But the entire day?

I went into the office and spent nearly an hour editing the video of Sean and Tess. To make it interesting, I ended up having to cut it to forty-five seconds. It opened on a close-up of Sean's face, as he stared at something beyond the frame with a craving look, a look that made it seem like he saw something no one else was able to see, something outside of reality. Maybe he was insane.

I laughed. Of course he wasn't, but there was something in that expression…

Next, the video drew back and captured most of the guests seated around the table, the wine like drops of blood in the slightly blurred image of all that white and silver. The camera had focused on the rose, giving a two- or three-second image that was sharp and clear. Even though Sean's face, now in the background, wasn't as well-defined, that look on his face was still evident. A look that I think he was unaware of, as if he wasn't having any focused thoughts, but something far back in his mind, his subconscious taking control of his eyes and mouth and jaw.

The image faded for half a second before it drew close to Tess. She was smiling and laughing. She looked like someone else entirely, relaxed, shedding her VP persona. She almost looked like a little girl. There was nothing about the set of her face or mouth suggesting she felt smothered in the house. She appeared to be in love with life, and captivated by her new acquaintances.

The camera moved slowly back to Sean, his face unchanged.

After listening to fifteen or twenty selections, I decided against a pop song. It would distract as people got caught up in the lyrics, and their own love or hatred of the artist. Their reaction to the music would color what they saw on the screen. I tried a section of a piano concerto by Rachmaninoff. It worked perfectly.

As I watched the finished video, playing it seven or eight times, I couldn't make a final decision about whether or not to post it. I was lying to myself if I thought Sean wouldn't be pissed. Tess too.

Tess was so intent on developing our social media presence and yet, like Sean, she didn't get it. You can't hide yourself and be successful. Of course, I had every intention of continuing to hide my own self. I know how dangerous that environment is, how it will cut your life open and hand pieces of you out to the world. I would continue with my semi-fake names, directing attention to the people and things around me.

My deliberately low profile could be considered hypocritical, but then, I hadn't known what the job was when

I made the move to Australia and I figured I was making the best of what I'd been given. I wasn't the one who wanted to use social media. I was just doing my job, using the tools, following the methods that had a chance of working.

A red circle with a *one* inside appeared on the message icon at the top of the page. I minimized the video and clicked my notifications — one new message from Carmen Dunn.

My skin turned pleasantly cool. She was back, and I hadn't had to do a single thing to lure her. She couldn't wait to tell me what was on her mind. When she'd refused to answer my string of question marks, a non-question, really, I'd thought that might be the end of it.

I should have known. She was a woman upset about something, very upset, and she'd found an avenue to vent or get revenge or whatever it was she wanted, and she couldn't stop herself from continuing down that path. It consumed her. Now, I was in charge. When someone is consumed, it's easy to step in and take control without them even noticing.

I clicked.

Carmen: *What did Sean tell you about me?*

Alex: *Not much.*

Carmen: *Don't be a bitch!!!*

Alex: *I'm telling the truth.*

Carmen: *Ha. Ha.*

I could string her along a bit more, piss her off more than she was. Or I could yield. But she hadn't answered my question yet. She owed me.

Alex: *Who does the statue belong to? You never answered.*

Carmen: *You first.*

Alex: *I asked you a question days ago.*

Carmen: *What did he say about me?*

Alex: *He said you're his ex's sister.*

Carmen: *What else did he say?*

There was nothing to tell her. There was obviously a lot more behind what Sean had said, and all the things he hadn't said. He'd made that clear in the intensity with which he ordered me, and I had no doubt, it was an order, to get rid of her. He'd told me she needed to fuck off and it was my job to figure out how to make that happen. Surely he hadn't meant for me to say that to her on our TruthTeller page, for the entire world to see.

Alex: *He was vague. He told me how he knew you and said I should turn the conversation to other topics.*

Carmen: *Ha. I bet he did.*

She knew him well.

Alex: *And the statue?*

Carmen: *What about it?*

Alex: *You said it didn't belong to him.*

There was no response. I waited. I wished I had an espresso or at least a glass of water. Staring at the screen made time pass slowly. I stood and walked to the window. The front yard was empty — no birds digging for their morning snacks. Usually early mornings were filled with the chatter of magpies and kookaburras, like the background chatter of colleagues in an office building.

I returned to the desk. Still no response from Carmen.

Alex: *Still waiting.*

I added a winking emoji.

Carmen: *I think we should meet face-to-face.*

Alex: *Why?*

Carmen: *Because that's what I prefer.*

Alex: *Okay. Sure. Where and when?*

Carmen: *Do you like scotch?*

She was making this too much work. Of course I'd rather have a martini, but what the hell.

Alex: *Never tried it.*

Carmen: *There's an underground whiskey bar on Clarence. The Baxter Inn.*

Alex: *Ok.*

Carmen: *Does Thursday, July 19 work?*

July nineteenth? It was the third. I had to wait over two weeks? This had better be interesting, not some BS about disputed ownership between Sean and his ex.

Alex: *That's weeks away.*

Carmen: *I live in Cooktown, in Queensland. That's the soonest I can get down there.*

Alex: *Ok.*

Carmen: *Sean is not the "truth teller" you seem to think he is.*

I smiled. Who is?

I didn't comment on her rather inflammatory comment. We said good-bye and she said she'd confirm a few days before.

Two weeks. I stood and went into the kitchen. Instead of espresso, I began mixing a martini.

I was eaten alive with curiosity. I had to find out more, not just to satisfy my relentless interest in other people, but also to find out whether there was anything that might impact me. I couldn't see why, but without knowing the history between Carmen and Sean, anything could happen.

Even if my lucrative deal with TruthTeller ended the next day, it would have been worth it. But if the end was closer than I realized, I preferred to know as soon as I could.

17

Standing in the water beside Gavin, ready for my second swim lesson, I was startled to realize that I was resisting it more now than I had during all those weeks before I actually got into the water.

Blowing bubbles was easy, but even a child recognized that swimming involved putting your face in the water for more than five seconds at a time. It meant lifting your feet off the bottom of the pool. Floating on my back hadn't been terrible. Once I connected it to yoga, once I realized that a lifetime spent observing a sponge bobbing in a dishpan of soapy water proved that not everything sank, floating seemed within the realm of possibility. Although connecting the buoyancy of that sponge to the human body was more difficult.

A sponge doesn't contain muscle, or bones. Still, I'd seen boats float. I'd taken physics in high school and knew the basics of density related to size. And of course I'd seen other people swim. I'd watched the Olympics, I'd seen all kinds of movies where people dove and swam and ventured into deep water.

Floating on my back had been a somewhat simple step.

But that wasn't swimming. If I wanted to conquer water and reverse the position of power, I couldn't just learn to swim on my back. If you're on a boat and it goes down, or if your CEO tosses you into a swimming pool, you need to swim up from the depths. You can't just cruise along kicking your feet, sweeping your arms overhead, gazing at the sky.

Face in the water. That was what I didn't want and that was what I needed to face, so to speak.

Gavin explained very patiently, and without a condescending tone whatsoever, that floating on my stomach was exactly the same as floating on my back.

"Not at all," I said. "It's definitely not *exactly* the same."

"It is. You relax, let the water hold you, think of yourself as weightless."

"And stop breathing?"

"You release your breath slowly, blowing bubbles."

"And then what?"

"Why don't we try it? Things work better, they're easier to grasp, if you do them instead of hearing them explained."

He was right, but I wasn't ready.

"Are you ready?" he said.

"No."

"Let me know when you are."

I put my arm around his neck and turned my face close to his — "Never."

"Well, then."

"I'll never be ready. But I suppose...Okay. Show me what to do."

Like the time before, he positioned himself to support my body, one arm poised to cradle my upper legs and the other ready to place just below my collarbone.

"Sink into my arms."

"That sounds nice."

He smiled. "See?"

"For how long?"

"What feels comfortable?" he said.

"Three seconds."

"Hardly enough time to relax. How about if you hold your breath and count to twenty."

I remained with my feet firmly on the sand.

"Take a breath and let it out slowly right now, and count. To see what it feels like. That way you'll know it's possible and you won't panic."

"I'm not going to panic. I…"

"Try it," he said.

I took in a small breath and held onto it for a moment before slowly blowing it out while he counted out loud, more slowly than I would have liked. But it worked. He eased past eight and I knew I could keep going for another half second, maybe two.

"Okay. Now floating," he said.

I lowered my shoulders close to the water and let myself rest on his arms. I put my chin into the water. I lowered my face and let my shoulders and torso relax as best I could. Then I realized I wasn't counting. I jerked my head out of the water, gasping for air as if I'd been beneath the surface for twenty minutes.

"What happened," he said.

"I forgot to count."

He laughed. "Try again."

I couldn't. I didn't want to. But neither would I admit that to him. I took a long, deep breath, and sealed my lips against each other.

"That's going to make it worse. You'll feel like you're holding it, your body wants to expel it all at once."

I nodded and released the air.

I tried again and the same thing happened, my mind went blank, I felt the water intruding into my nose. I thought about the bubbles I was supposed to be blowing, but I couldn't. I wanted to breathe. I wanted air coming in, not just seeping out, leaving me lifeless. I thrashed away from him and tried to stand. My feet couldn't seem to find the bottom. He grabbed my arm and kept me from slipping under.

"What are you so afraid of?"

I had no plans to tell him about my baptism, ever. Or rather, my aborted baptism. Watching the memory circle inside my mind made it appear simultaneously horrific, unimportant, and massively overblown, almost sad. Maybe it was the forced repentance I'd choked on, not the water at all.

"I'll try again," I said.

We continued on for another fifteen minutes or so. He held me, I put my chin in the water, lowered my face, tried to relax. But my body refused to consider the slow release of air and the relaxing of my muscles with my face submerged. Two of the three, but not all at once.

Finally, I moved out of his arms. "I'm done."

"I don't think it's a good idea to quit until you try it successfully at least once."

"I believe I've tried it more than once. Several times more than once."

"You aren't going to sink."

"I'm not going to breathe either."

"You kept your face in the water. And you floated on your back. It's a simple matter of putting the two together."

I moved my hand across the surface of the water, my palm flat. I realized that just standing in the water, enjoying it stroking my skin like this was a step forward. He didn't see that. He was pushing too hard. And yet, usually going all in is better. Forge ahead and deal with the consequences when they arise, don't imagine them ahead of time, since you really don't ever know what is going to happen. Especially don't imagine things going wrong. It's a waste of time.

How else would I have killed the people I had? It wasn't by assuming I couldn't get the upper hand with them. It wasn't by assuming I'd be caught in the act. Gavin was right. Still, I just couldn't.

"You must have had a very traumatic experience with water," he said.

I shrugged.

"Do you remember it?"

I shrugged again.

"I assume that means yes."

"Don't assume anything."

"You would have said no, if you didn't. Something is making you fight the water."

He had that right. All my life, the water had been a worthy opponent, a superior opponent. I'd managed to avoid a confrontation and it didn't seem necessary to invite a struggle that I'd inevitably lose.

"I'm right here. Even if it were possible to sink, I wouldn't let you go far."

"I'm not giving up entirely, but that's enough for today."

I could feel him yield to me, even though he said nothing.

As we moved toward the steps leading out of the pool, he put his arm around my waist.

"It must have been terrible, whatever it was."

I remained silent.

There was no point in talking about it. Giving him the

details wouldn't do anything to assist my swim lessons.

"It doesn't seem right," he said.

"What doesn't?"

"We all have these memories of events from when we were little kids, teenagers, the past. Sometimes they aren't even that terrible, in context of the really terrible things in the world. Not even traumas, if you view them on a grand scale, but traumatic to a child. And one, maybe two events end up shaping our entire lives. They try to dictate who we are. It's quite amazing. When you think of the hours and hours and months and years of life, and one twenty-minute or two-hour incident influences everything."

I thought it was a bit of an exaggeration, but I saw his point.

18

The estate agent's name was Cheryl. She was in her late forties, dressed in a skirt and flats, managing to look casual and professional at the same time. She had blonde hair swept into a messy bun at the nape of her neck. Her makeup was light, giving her an honest and open appearance. She seemed to be a listener, which in Tess's experience, was somewhat rare in the real estate profession, even though there was a lot of pretense at listening.

Tess and Cheryl met at the estate agent's office. Home sales were different in Australia. Property usually sold at an auction, with all the bidding on public display. You knew the look of the people you were competing against and you knew what they were offering. You could guess which of your competitors were developers wanting to tear down a house, which were investors, and which were looking for a home.

Australians didn't have to navigate the blind submission of a bid, later discovering they'd been outdone by fifty or a hundred grand. Worse yet, were the situations she'd heard about in which people were exhausted from repeatedly bidding and losing out. At the end of their ropes, they went immediately to their upper limit, offered fifty or even a hundred thousand dollars over the asking price, finding out later they could have saved thirty, forty, fifty thousand dollars. It was painful even thinking about it.

After Cheryl asked about Tess's desired areas, the type of

home she wanted, and a few other get-acquainted questions, they went out to do some looking. Cheryl showed her several townhouses, called villas for a reason Tess couldn't figure out. When she asked, Cheryl stared at her as if she were asking why water was called water.

All of the places they viewed were nice. She and Cheryl chatted about views and floor plans, storage space and carpet versus hardwood floors. Each time they entered the front door of a property, Tess's heart raced. The feeling brought home how desperately she wanted to escape the other three employees of TruthTeller, the house that wasn't her home.

Sean's idea was insane, now that she'd experienced it. Living with colleagues was both juvenile and extremely invasive. People needed their privacy, their own lives. Maybe blending work and your private life had worked hundreds of years ago, or still did in farming communities, but even at that, people didn't live in the same house. They merged work and play and social activity, but they didn't sleep thirty feet from each other. They didn't eat every single meal together. They didn't face each other over coffee in the morning and drinks at night.

It was exhausting. If she'd wanted all that, she would have a family. And even a family spent time away from each other. They didn't go to work at the same fucking office, once again sitting fifteen or twenty feet away from each other for ten hours a day.

What she still hadn't figured out was why the three of them had stayed so long in Sean's state of limbo. They'd always been free to go out, but none of them did. Sure, their roommates were all reasonably interesting people. And it hadn't stopped Alex and Gavin from hooking up. But hooking up wasn't even what she wanted, despite that ill-considered visit to Sean's bedroom, a blatant and awkward invitation for sex. She was glad now that he'd said no.

He was so certain she was moving out because she was insulted or hurt or ashamed over that incident. But it was none of those things. She was moving out to get a life. The past few months had demonstrated to her how easily the human spirit could be cowed. Offer enough comforts, enough security, passable social interaction, an environment where little effort was required for quite a nice life, and everyone stayed put.

The recurring nightmare hadn't been specific, but she'd woken multiple times feeling as if she couldn't breathe. Although she hadn't recalled a dream, not even the flash of a scene, when she woke, her mind rambled. She saw herself three or four years from now, the app doing well, updates and ideas for expansion keeping them relatively busy, time flying past. Suddenly, she would be nearly forty years old.

She would have no friends, no real stimulation in her career, no man. Of course she wouldn't wait that long. That could never happen, but it could. It wasn't outside the realm of possibility. Time had a way of racing past without you really noticing. You thought about things you wanted to do or should do, and then the days continued their steady unfolding and those things remained at the back of your mind, never urgent enough that you took action.

No, although it seemed far-fetched, in many ways, it wasn't.

For her entire life, her career had come first. It wasn't shameful to say she wanted a relationship, that she might even want a child. She remembered her brief conversation about parenthood when she and Alex first met. She hadn't even known her own thoughts, and she'd wondered if the desire for a child was just the normal human inclination to desire what you didn't have. Like wanting a horse, or a yacht…but did you really want those things?

She laughed to herself, glad she was in the master bedroom alone, not giggling uncontrollably in front of Cheryl or the listing agent or the other couple viewing the townhouse…villa…where she stood now.

She wasn't comparing a horse and a child, just the idea of thinking you're missing out on something. Wanting a child was not just biology and not just the desire to fit in with society. She would enjoy raising a human being. And it didn't have to be her child, she would be happy to adopt. That's what made her recognize the desire as genuine and not self-serving, not the result of a restless desire for change.

They looked at two more homes that Cheryl said were *must-sees*, but likely candidates for a heated auction that would drive the price beyond what Tess wanted to pay.

"There is one more…" She took a step back and deliberately moved her eyes from the crown of Tess's head to her feet. "I don't know if it's you."

"What does that mean?"

"You're very sophisticated. There's an air about you."

Tess laughed. "Is there?"

"Oh yes. Classy. And so I think I tend to see you in a modern home, and you said that's what you like. But still…"

"What?"

They walked slowly along the sidewalk toward Cheryl's car. It was parked under a eucalyptus tree, which gave it filtered shade. The air was cool enough, they didn't really need to park in the shade. Cheryl had joked about the spot, telling Tess that eucalyptus branches often came crashing down without warning. The trees were called widow-makers for their tendency to take out people without the preliminary sound of splintering wood, crushing them to death. Tess had lived among eucalyptus trees all her years in Northern California, but had never heard of their danger, or their morbid nickname. Nevertheless, Cheryl had parked under the tree, which struck Tess as odd. It seemed riskier than necessary.

"The property is an old whaling cottage. But it's been updated nicely. It's small, but unique."

"Sure, why not," Tess said.

The house captivated her the moment Cheryl pulled the car to the curb. It was surrounded by trees and a lawn that wasn't manicured into an outdoor carpet. There were huge plants hugging the front porch, spilling flowers against the posts and along the railing.

There was no imported tile walkway like Sean's house, no massive walls of glass and stucco. The exterior was pale blue with black trim. Inside, it was light and extraordinarily quiet. Sean's house was quiet, but it was the quiet of excess space and top-of-the-line insulation and an exclusive neighborhood. This was the quiet of a park.

It had two bedrooms and a single bathroom. There were five steps leading up to the master bedroom which featured a small balcony. The highlight was a narrow sunroom with bifold doors on two sides. The small dining room also had bifold doors opening to the terra-cotta tiled patio.

Standing on the back porch, the doors to the eating area completely open behind her, looking out at more grass and trees and flowers, she turned toward Cheryl. "When is the auction?"

Cheryl smiled. "See, you do have class. But it's not fake classiness. You're the real deal. Genuine."

"Thank you," Tess said.

"The auction is Saturday."

Tess's phone vibrated against her hip bone. She pulled it out of the front pocket of her jeans and looked at the display. A text message. It wasn't anyone on her contact list, but it was a US number. She tapped open the message.

This is Trystan Vogel. If you recall, we met in the Melbourne airport. I'm back in Sydney again — second week of July. Would like to grab a drink and quick chat if you're game. Business.

She dropped her phone into her purse. Business didn't exactly fit with what he had printed on his *business* card.

19

The morning after my failed floating lesson, I went for a run before the sun came up. It was a cold, wintery day with thick clouds pushing a chilly wind along the sidewalks and across the vacant front yards. It was July! I felt like all the hot, lazy July days of my life existed only in my imagination. July felt like a word, an idea that the Southern Hemisphere had stripped of its essence.

Running felt good, despite the disorienting weather. Especially after being cowed by water twice in the past week. On the pavement, I was in control. I gulped in air as much and as often as I wanted. I moved freely without having to ration the thing that keeps us alive — oxygen moving in an out as it pleases. I felt I could run for hours. I felt my body taking charge. I wasn't required to relax and yield and trust some other force to take care of me, a force waiting to suffocate me.

I'd mapped out a six-mile route, longer than what I'd been doing lately. I needed to work harder, to forget the water, to remember how strong and fit I was.

Now that Carmen had moved to the back of my mind, a problem I wouldn't be able to deal with for two weeks, my thoughts began nibbling again at the telescope on my closet floor.

Wind pushed against my face, keeping my skin cool. My legs moved with long strides and my feet hit the pavement with such a solid thud I felt that the earth was doing her part to keep me stable. Maybe this swimming thing was a bad idea. I'd managed to avoid water nearly all my life. Sean knew better than to ever toss me in the pool again, and how many situations like that would I face in the future? Possibly none.

And yet, I was still conscious of the oceans and lakes and swimming pools and rivers lurking out there, knowing they had power over me.

I turned the corner and headed toward a large park with winding pathways that made for a tranquil run.

The telescope. I needed to think about the telescope.

It had been hard enough getting it into the house while my roommates slept. How on earth would I get it back out? Carrying it to my room from next door had been very risky, but in a sleeping suburban neighborhood, dead after midnight, not completely insane. Trying to get an Uber to show up and then maneuvering the telescope out of the house and into the trunk would increase the odds of being seen.

At the time, all I could think of was how much I wanted a telescope in my future home, how I might have a room dedicated to stargazing, and how the scope I'd stolen would look in this imagined room — sleek and classy.

The space would be circular, with narrow windows, all of which would open without screens so the telescope could be directed out any one of the windows and into the darkness. The interior wall would feature a long, curved wood bench, fixed to the wall, and made comfortable with cushions. If I wanted to host a stargazing party, there would be plenty of seats. Scattered in front of this long, curving bench would be small tables to hold drinks and snacks. The room would have unobtrusive wireless speakers near the ceiling. Stargazing is better in silence, based on my brief experience, but options are nice. If it was a stargazing party, music would entertain those waiting their turn to gaze.

As I ran, going faster and faster, almost as if I were making a futile effort to outrun a tsunami, I thought about the reality of possessing a telescope that had belonged to such a despicable man. What had I been thinking? I didn't want his telescope at all. Selecting a new one would be so much more fun, and by the time this magnificent home of mine came into being, the cost of a telescope would be insignificant. If nothing else, by the time my future home materialized, technology would have moved forward and I'd find a telescope that was even more sophisticated.

I entered the park, slowing a bit as the pathway was narrower than the sidewalk. It was cooler, with densely planted trees and shrubs, making me feel secluded and refreshed as sweat evaporated off my back and scalp.

Why had I thought I wanted a telescope that had been used to invade women's lives, staring at them as they undressed and slept and had sex?

I suppose the reality that I'd been rid of John, that I'd put a stop to his stalking, leering behavior made the telescope seem like a prize. Now, it was nothing of the sort. I had to get rid of it. I didn't feel even the slightest prick of temptation suggesting I might want one last glimpse of Jupiter or Saturn up close. No. The sooner I could unload it, the better. But how? There was no one I could ask to help me without exposing what I'd done.

I wasn't inclined to put it on an internet bazaar like eBay. I couldn't very well walk into a shop and try to get at least some of its value. That, too, would be a slender thread connecting me to John's death.

It seemed as if my only choice would be to take it out in the middle of the night and abandon it in a park or on a street corner. But that would involve an Uber driver.

When I'd taken it, I was high on the victory of removing a perverted man from the earth. I had wanted to take the object he cared about the most and have it as my own. Even though he was dead, it felt good to deprive of him of the object he'd used to invade women's private worlds.

At the same time, I was still enraptured by my close-up view of the billions of stars out there, silently watching us every night. I wanted to look up closely and touch each one. I wanted to stroke the soft curve of Jupiter with its muted colors. I wanted that every night.

Suddenly, I was sweating a lot more. Sweating as if I were running during the afternoon, as if someone were following me, possibly that tsunami. An enormous wave was pursuing me, rising up twenty or thirty feet above my head, making the graceful curl that waves do, revealing the underbelly of smooth, glistening water, before its weight forces it to bend and it crashes with a roar, sweeping away everything in its path.

20

Portland

Jake had decided I couldn't take *The Book of Sharks* to my room, I had to come into his room and look at it with him sitting beside me. The book belonged to the school library and he didn't need me mauling pages for which he'd get in trouble.

He'd become obsessed with sharks after reading *Twenty Thousand Leagues Under the Sea* because the account of Captain Nemo saving a pearl diver from a shark attack had gripped him more than any other part of the novel. It was clear from the look on his face that he wanted to battle a shark with his bare hands. I suppose he believed that learning what *The Book of Sharks* had to tell him would give him an advantage.

He fantasized about taking on a fifteen-hundred-pound white shark armed with a mouthful of teeth that look like knife blades, growing in multiple rows for a steady supply of replacements. He would open the book to a photograph of a shark, its jaw open wide, and study the teeth. Speculating what those teeth felt like kept him going for half an hour.

Ripping through human flesh, slicing you right down to the bone… "That's what they do," he said. "They've rescued shark bite victims with their bones exposed. I'm not kidding."

I tried to picture this. There were no photographs of uncovered bone in the book.

"Can you imagine the blood? And when there's blood, more sharks come."

"I don't like thinking about blood," I said.

"Then why are you so interested in sharks? That's what they do. They're vicious, bloody killers. Nemo was incredible, attacking that beast with just a hunting knife. Can you imagine?"

I couldn't, and I didn't want to. I wished the shark had escaped.

"He could've been torn into chum," Jake said.

I nodded.

"The shark was seven or eight times Nemo's weight. The deep sea is their home turf. Nemo was at a disadvantage in so many ways."

"He had a diving suit, so he could breathe," I said.

Jake turned the page. "Look at this one."

A shark was shown from the side, it's long body spreading across the page, a diver in the background to provide context for the size.

"I can hardly imagine what it's like for a man to go up against something like that," Jake said.

"It's a story," I said.

"Yes, but it happens in real life. Divers get attacked by sharks. They have their legs or arms chewed off. Sometimes they get away and sometimes they don't."

I knew this. I was sitting right beside him, reading the book, but I said nothing.

He turned more pages, half of them filled with text, the rest dominated by photographs. He didn't want to read the text while I was a captive audience. He seemed to enjoy watching me shiver when he mentioned blood. "I wonder why they like blood so much?" he said.

"I don't know."

"There's no other creature like it. No other creature hunts blood like sharks do."

I nodded.

"They're pure muscle. Well, not muscle exactly, but solid. I wonder what it would feel like to have one bash into you." He continued turning pages, talking about what it would feel like to fight a shark, talking about wanting to go under water and discover that world for himself. "It's like a whole other universe," he said. "All you can hear is your own breathing."

I nodded.

"And it's dangerous. You can be deprived of oxygen, you can get sick coming to the surface too fast. You can get attacked by sharks."

"Do other fish eat people?"

He shrugged.

"I think I'm gonna learn to scuba dive when I get older," he said. "I need to know what it's like down there."

I didn't say anything. I wasn't sure anyone in my family truly understood how I felt about water. They'd seen me thrashing and choking that day I was supposed to be baptized. And later, they knew I refused to learn how to swim. Jake and the others knew I didn't like it. But I'm not sure any of them thought much about what it all meant. My mother, maybe.

I had no desire ever to be in the ocean, with all that water above me, swallowed by water, and nothing but a little tube helping me breathe.

"What if a shark bites the breathing tube?" I said.

"That wouldn't happen."

"It could."

"The tubes are plastic. They want meat."

"The sharks are just defending themselves. They probably don't think human beings belong under water. And they don't. Otherwise, they'd have gills."

"Man can go anywhere. We rule the animal kingdom. We're at the top of the food chain. We can fly and go down to the bottom of the ocean. We can go into space, to other planets."

"It doesn't seem right to invade their territory."

He laughed. "We're supposed to subdue the earth because we're smarter. We can think, they can't."

"How do you know?"

"Because they don't communicate, dummy."

"How do you know?"

"You're nuts." He closed the book. "It seems like you're on the shark's side instead of the human beings they want to tear into pieces."

"I just wonder why Nemo had to kill the shark. She was just doing what was natural," I said. "Maybe she was hungry."

"She?"

"Well there must be girl sharks, not just boy sharks."

"Yeah."

He didn't seem as excited about hand-to-hand combat with a girl shark. I picked up the book and opened it.

"Be careful."

I turned to the image we'd been looking at a minute earlier. "It doesn't say if it's a girl or a boy."

"It looks like a guy. Very fierce," he said.

"Well it's not like the girls are smiling and have long eye lashes."

He laughed. "You're weird."

"It just doesn't seem right for humans to go into the water where the sharks live, and then kill them because they don't want to get eaten."

"Why do you have to turn everything into a headache?"

"I don't."

"People kill animals. That's how it is."

"I know."

"Where do you think hamburgers come from?"

"I know." I handed the book to him. "But this is different. The shark was minding its own business. And the pearl diver was trying to take something out of an oyster. So it wasn't like he was all innocent."

"That's what mankind does. We conquer nature."

I stretched out on the floor, flat on my back. I closed my eyes and tried to picture the shark swimming around, not realizing it would be attacked by a human with a large knife, only watching out for its usual predators. "What kind of fish kill sharks?"

"I don't think any. That's why mankind needs to do it. I said, we're at the top of the food chain."

"But we don't eat shark meat."

"Some people do. Shark fin soup. It's a delicacy in China."

I shivered and sat up.

"I need to do my homework," he said.

"Can I take the book?"

"You better not wreck it."

"I won't."

He handed it to me. "If you do, and I get a fine, you have to pay it."

"I won't wreck it." I went to my bedroom and closed the door. I sat on the floor near the window where the late afternoon sun was coming through, forming a rectangle on the carpet. I looked at every page of the book and wondered if I'd ever see a shark outside of an aquarium. Probably not.

21

Tess knocked on Alex's bedroom door. She was met with silence from within. She touched the handle. She pressed gently, careful to keep if from suddenly depressing and making a sound, or worse, opening the door before she was invited in. The handle moved only a fraction of an inch. Still locked.

She was pretty sure Alex was inside, so locking it wasn't quite as odd as it was watching her whip out the key every time she approached her room. Why the sudden locking? What did she know about Sean, or Gavin for that matter, that she was hiding from Tess? Or what was she up to inside that room? But Tess had been in there just a few days earlier. Everything had looked perfectly normal.

She knocked again.

"Yes?" Alex's voice was faint.

"It's me. I wanted to run something by you, if you have a minute."

The door opened a few inches. "Let's go sit in the living room."

"Your room is fine, it's quick. It's nothing about work."

"I'd still rather go downstairs. A glass of wine, maybe?"

Tess stepped back. "Alright."

When they were seated on one of the living room sofas,

wine glasses in hand, Tess tapped her glass against Alex's.

Damien laughed from his cage in the hallway, then shouted — *Chardonnay time!*

"He has excellent hearing," Alex said.

"He does." Tess took a sip of wine. "So I…"

"Did you get new boots the other day? I never saw them."

"I did. I'll show you later. I wanted to ask you about this guy I met."

Alex settled back. She crossed her legs and held her wineglass out from her body slightly, as if she enjoyed holding it, but didn't have much interest in drinking the wine.

"When I picked up Damien in Melbourne, I stopped in a bar in the terminal…to pass the time while I waited for my flight."

Alex nodded.

"I met this guy."

Alex smiled. "Sounds interesting."

Tess glared at her. There'd been nothing in her mention of meeting a guy to suggest she'd encountered him in a flirty way. Why did Alex have to turn it into that? "We weren't flirting."

"I didn't think you were."

Tess took a sip of wine, followed by a deep breath. Maybe the insinuation was in her own mind. Trystan was good looking, easy to talk to. Was that shaping her thoughts? But she hadn't felt a spark. And this wasn't about that, even if she had. "We talked for a few minutes, nothing else. He's American. From New York."

"Okay."

"There wasn't much to it, just an info exchange, really.

And we traded business cards."

Alex nodded, still holding the glass away from her body. "So that's what you wanted to run by me? You're not just moving out, you're looking for a new job."

Tess put her glass on the coffee table.

"Not at all. We just started talking. I've never met him before. It wasn't planned."

Finally, Alex took a sip of wine. She re-crossed her legs.

"His card was weird, though. He didn't have a company name. Just a title, if you can call it that…email, and phone."

"Between jobs?"

"It wasn't even a job title. It said *Provocateur.*"

Alex laughed. "Are you serious?"

"Yes. So I'm not sure what that means."

"It means someone who…"

"I know what the word means. I don't know what it means in the context of a business card."

"You didn't ask? I would have."

"We exchanged cards as I was leaving. I didn't look at it until I was on my way to the gate."

"I wonder what it means."

"He texted me. He'll be back in Sydney next week and he wants to meet. He said it's business."

"There's your chance. To find out about a career we've never heard of. Provoking people until they react. How do you get paid for that, I wonder?"

"I have no idea. Do you think I should meet with him?"

"Absolutely." Alex took a long swallow of wine. "You should tell him you're inviting me."

"I don't think so."

"Is he self-employed? Is that a real job? Does he get

paid? How did he get into that, whatever *that* is? So many questions."

Tess picked up her glass. Actually, the title fit Alex. She smiled.

"What's so funny?"

"Nothing. I didn't realize you'd be so fascinated."

Alex sipped her wine. She put the glass on the table and stood. She crossed the room and looked out at the backyard, gazing toward the swimming pool. The focus of her eyes seemed far away. It was clear she was trying to figure out how to get herself included in the meeting with Trystan. But there was no way Tess was inviting her.

Meeting with him was outside the norm of how she usually did things. Usually she would ask for a discussion topic. And *business* was not a topic. Yet since she'd receive his message, she couldn't stop thinking about it. He hadn't sent a follow-up text. Was he giving her room to decide? Or had he assumed she wasn't interested? In that case, you would think he would provide more information, trying to get her to change her mind. But if his job was to provoke, of course he wanted to provoke her curiosity.

Alex turned to face her. "You're sure you aren't looking for another job?"

"I'm sure. I'm not going to walk out right when the app is poised to launch. Wanting a home of my own has nothing to do with the company. I'm not the one who's behaving oddly here." She waved her hand to the side to indicate the room, the entire house, their entwined lives.

"If you're not looking for a job, what do you think the provocateur wants? Did he give any hint when you met him?"

"None. I was surprised when I got the text."

"You'll tell me all about it, after you meet him?"

Tess smiled. "You won't be able to stop me."

"You don't think he's hitting on you? That he just said business so you'll agree to meet him?"

"I don't think so. Even when I was talking to him. He was very...there wasn't any sub-text."

Alex returned to the coffee table. She picked up her wine glass and took a sip. "It seems obvious to me. You're curious, you meet. There's nothing to lose. Why did you want my opinion?"

"Good question. I guess because of the job title." She laughed. "It's clearly not a normal meeting."

"What are you afraid might happen?"

"Again, good question. I suppose I just needed to hear it out loud."

"Text him right now."

Tess pulled her phone out of her pocket. She opened the message and replied that she'd be glad to meet. Trystan's response was immediate — *Good. There's a nice bar at Cafe Sydney.*

They arranged a date and time. She put her phone on the table.

"All set?" Alex said.

"Cafe Sydney. Thursday."

"Nice."

"I know. Seems kind of a high-end place for a quick meeting."

"I guess you might as well have a view and all the amenities, even if it's only half an hour."

Tess finished her wine. She was probably making too much of it. The job title was what did it. Who called themselves that? He wanted to unsettle people. Why else print it on a business card?

22

Weekends were supposed to be our own, under the new *arrangement.* No planned group meals. Everyone doing their own thing. The only problem was, none of us seemed to have our own thing to do, except maybe Tess. And even she had a slim selection.

It seemed as if we were connected to each other in a way we couldn't break away from.

So here we were again. Sean was barbecuing burgers and at some point, had mentioned it casually to each of us.

Now, there was a feast large enough for a block party spread out on the patio table. He had the heat lamps and the gas fire pit turned on, all of which did a good job of keeping the cool evening air outside the cover of the patio.

There were bowls of potato chips and pretzels, a platter with pickles and beetroot, sliced onions and tomatoes. He'd made an enormous bowl of pasta salad and another was filled with greens and chopped marinated artichoke hearts and Kalamata olives. He'd made a plate of fried halloumi cheese for snacking while we waited for the burgers.

We piled vegetables onto our burgers and sat around the table. Sean and Gavin, as always, had a bottle of beer beside their plates. Tess had a glass of white wine and I had a glass of Zin. I couldn't imagine white wine with a hamburger, but she seemed to relish it.

As we gobbled down the perfectly cooked food, Sean

talked about the next dinner party. The first one had been even more successful than he'd hoped. The sports promoter and the gallery owner both wanted to try out the app. They were excited to tell people about it, which was exactly what he'd envisioned.

"I guess we'll be ready to launch in September, right Gav?"

"Sure," Gavin said. He took a good-sized bite of his burger. Beet juice stained his lips. His eyes had a glazed look. He was probably thinking about the constant delays, the minor flaws he was constantly fixing.

I'd thought the date had been moved to August, but I said nothing.

Sean asked Tess about the marketing plan, but seemed strangely uninterested in the social media aspect. When she mentioned Facebook, he talked over her and quickly circled back to the next dinner party — two weeks away, was what he thought best. He'd already reached out to a few of the previous guests. The actress was filming that weekend and couldn't make it, so he'd invited another woman he knew.

"You guys can also invite people. We don't want it to get too large, but one or two more interesting people in the mix would be good."

No one spoke.

After a few minutes of silent eating, Tess pushed her plate to the side. She put a potato chip in her mouth and crunched down, chewing slowly. She swallowed and took a tiny, almost ceremonial sip of wine. "I have some news."

It felt as if all of our body heat and the heat from the lamps and the fire were sucked into the night air. No one breathed. We all knew what was coming. Sean looked ill, his face suddenly blanched and his eyelids jittering slightly as if he was afraid to blink and miss something. Or, he was trying to think of a way to forestall the inevitable.

"I attended an auction yesterday," Tess said. "It looks like I now own a home in Sydney."

"Congratulations," Gavin said. He sounded genuine.

"Can't wait to see it," I said.

"I think you'll be surprised," she said. "It's nothing at all like my condo."

Sean seemed to glower at this mention of her former life. As if he felt left out, somehow. As if she hadn't existed outside of him and his largesse, and he loathed this reminder, that indeed she had. He continued eating his burger, plowing through it as if he hadn't eaten all day. Maybe he hadn't.

We watched him eat. After a minute or so, it began to look as if I'd misinterpreted his response. Now, he behaved as if he hadn't heard what she'd said. He didn't look in her direction, didn't show any further reaction on his face. All he did was open his mouth, take a bite, chew, swallow, open his mouth again...

It was so childish. She had a right to move into her own place. The whole thing had been an experiment and it was never a condition of employment. He was sulking. Upset that Tess, and possibly none of us, shared his fantasies.

Finally, the burger was gone.

"Nothing I can do to persuade you to stay?" he said. He swallowed some beer. He still wasn't looking at her. His gaze was focused in the direction of the swimming pool, although he couldn't actually see it from where he was sitting. And it was dark. The firelight didn't cast a long enough glow to sweep over the surface of the water.

"I won the auction. It's my house," she said.

"No reason you can't rent it out."

"Come on Sean."

He took another swallow of beer. "I had a very specific vision. I thought we all shared it."

No one spoke.

"Maybe this is an American thing. You're all so independent, you love your isolation, your self-reliance. It's in your blood. Maybe that's the problem. I should have thought of the cultural differences before asking you to join the company."

Tess laughed. "You really think that? Besides, Alex isn't going anywhere, and she's American."

"It's only a matter of time. And the whole point was that all of us work together, and *play* together."

"We are working together," Tess said.

"What happens when we're eating breakfast and we come up with some thoughts for advertising and you're not here?"

She laughed again. "You'll tell me when I arrive for work. Thirty minutes later."

"We're supposed to connect. We're a unit. The shared energy is what makes it unique."

"You don't have to live together to share energy," Tess said.

"We're a family."

"In my experience, businesses that think they're families go off the rails. You can go too far, mixing business and personal. Trust me."

"Then why did you agree at all?"

"Because I believe in the product, Sean. It seemed like something worth experimenting with. But I don't need to sleep in the same house to believe the product is a good idea and that there's a market for it."

Sean pushed his chair away from the table. He picked up his bottle and poured the rest of the contents down his throat. He lowered the bottle, gripping it with such a tight fist, I thought it might shatter. Or that he might hurl it across the yard. He looked both eerily calm and furious at the same time, a disturbing combination. In a low voice, he said, "You just don't get it."

"What don't I get?"

He slammed the bottle on the table.

"Chill out," Gavin said.

"I have a vision."

"And you're confusing some weird communal living view of the world with a business. Not gonna work," Gavin said.

I stared at him, surprised. I'd never heard him contradict Sean so directly.

Sean ignored him.

Like children rushing for their pacifiers, we all grabbed the drink in front of us and took a few reassuring sips. The alcohol didn't do much to disarm the tension that bound us together. Rather ironic, since Sean wanted shared creativity to draw us close, forming life-long friendships. I'd never heard him use the word family before. It was jarring, and for me, was not the most pleasing illustration. I suppose that considering my siblings brought up pleasant memories, but not my parents.

My father. The man who tried to drown me.

That's melodramatic, I know. He didn't set out to drown me, and he would have been horrified if I had been sucked under the water and come up lifeless. But at the time, and in my dreams since that day, and often in my memory, and definitely when I tried to float with my face buried in the water, the sensation of drowning was my experience.

Sean moved away from the table. "The content of this app, and the vision of this company are tightly integrated. Maybe, Tess, you should consider whether your future lives here with us, or not. I'd rather have a pure, high-energy launch of our app into the market than have it dragged down by a lack of unity." He looked at Tess, then Gavin. "I think we'll delay the launch until October. It's probably a better time of year anyway."

He went into the house and disappeared from view, leaving us with dishes to clear away and food to wrap up, and a heavy silence that covered everything.

23

I was seated beside Tess, driving to north Sydney. She was eager to show me the cottage she'd purchased. Neither of us had said a word about Sean's blow-up, melt-down, whatever you want to call it. There was an impression he might be losing his grip, but neither of us had mentioned that either.

When Gavin and I had whispered with our heads beside each other on a single pillow in his bed the night before, all our talk had been a review of his erratic behavior, how upset he was about Tess moving out, how he seemed to be getting more controlling, and how we could not believe he wanted to delay announcing the app until October.

We didn't voice any thoughts that he was mentally unbalanced.

I didn't truly think he was. It was something else. But that something else was difficult to define. A loss of control came the closest, but that was a trite way to describe what was going on.

I was curious to know what Tess was thinking. I was on the verge of asking her, but also wanting to hear what she said first. Would she be angry or pitying? Would she announce she planned to look for another job, as he'd basically told her to do?

How did he think we were going to market this thing without Tess? I was pretty sure he didn't believe I was qualified to do her job. And in a lot of ways, I wasn't. I didn't know how to work with the traditional media or anything like that. I didn't know much about budgeting or setting up global campaigns. Not that I couldn't figure it out, but it was more work than I wanted. It was also a fruitless train of thought because Sean would dismiss the idea without discussion.

The way things stood, I wasn't that good with the job I had. I'd generated some flurries of attention and I was busy digging into the CEO's private life for no relevant purpose. I wasn't sure there was a single person out there who planned to buy the app because of my savvy social media marketing.

What a mess.

I wanted to laugh, but it was doubtful anyone else would find it funny. I was happy with all the money I'd saved, and I'd had some good times in that house, but how much longer would it last?

So far, all Tess wanted to talk about was her new house. It was so unique, so well-put-together, so secluded but located in a friendly neighborhood, so perfect for Damien. She couldn't wait to create her own environment, eat meals when she pleased, cook the food she preferred — and that did not include a steady diet of *burgers* and barbecued anything, except maybe grilled fish.

That was the closest she'd ventured to making a comment about Sean and the scene he'd created the night before.

Burgers.

I love burgers. The aroma of sizzling beef, the juicy, satisfying texture between my teeth, on my tongue, the crunch of pickles and onion, the accompanying sweetness of tomato. I love burgers with cheese. I've had them with Swiss cheese and sautéed mushrooms, a delicious combination.

Thinking about it made me want to try a burger place Gavin had mentioned in a suburb of Sydney, but the timing was all wrong, now that Tess seemed to be on a vendetta against burgers, and animal flesh in general. Except fish. I guess their flesh didn't count.

She turned off the highway. "Did you see Sean this morning?"

"No."

"I wonder if he's calmed down," she said.

"We can only hope."

She gave a single, staccato laugh.

"What do you think is going on?" I said.

"Who knows. Obviously I triggered something with my decision to get my own place. He's sure going out of his way to try to ruin my experience."

"What are you going to do?"

"About what?" She put on her signal and made a left.

I was finally getting used to a car remaining close to the curb when it turned left, and veering out into the middle of an intersection for a right turn. I no longer clutched the dashboard, imagining a collision. It was probably time for me to think about taking a shot at driving. Immediately I thought of my swimming lessons and changed my mental direction… one thing at a time.

"We're almost there," she said. She entered and circled through a roundabout, and then made two more left turns, the last onto a narrow street, bordered by ancient trees, crowding close as if they wanted to see who was passing by. There were no sidewalks, the lawns running right out to the pavement which made it feel tropical and earthy, less suburban. Glimpses of houses were possible through large front lawns filled with shrubs and more trees. But they weren't precisely arranged and landscaped like the expensive yards in Sean's neighborhood.

She pulled to the side of the road in front of a narrow lot with a long path leading to a small dark blue house.

We got out of the car and walked up the path. "Cheryl's meeting us here, since obviously I don't have a key yet." We leaned against the railing of the front porch to wait.

The house was indeed charming, but it did not seem to fit Tess. It looked like something out of another era, while Tess gives an air of being ultra contemporary. Maybe she needed a counterpoint. She'd said it was an old whaling cottage.

"We could walk around to the back, but I really want to show you that last. You'll love how the dining area completely opens up on to the patio."

It didn't sound that remarkable. A lot of dining areas open onto patios. And in my limited experience of Australia, they all seemed to do that. At least that's how it was with the stately homes in Sean's neighborhood.

"So what are you going to do?" I said.

"About what?"

"It seemed like Sean was suggesting you should leave the company."

"Did it?" She looked across the street, squinting slightly.

"That's how it sounded to me."

"We'll see what happens. He's just upset. He clearly has trouble accepting change. And as we already knew, he thinks everyone should have the same enthusiasm for things that he does. In some ways, he's a child."

"What about him moving the product announcement out

again? Are you worried about that?"

"Not if he isn't. Look, he's paying us. If he has a bottomless pit of money and he wants to keep delaying, that's his business."

I was surprised she seemed to view it more like I did. It wasn't what I'd expected.

"If I get bored, then maybe I'll look around."

"You don't seem very concerned."

She shrugged. "I'm focused on the house. On getting Damien out of that cage. I didn't bring him all this way to watch him sit in a prison."

"He hardly left his room at your condo."

"But it was his choice."

I wasn't sure it was his choice, since his wings had to be trimmed to prevent him soaring around the house. It really wasn't fair to a creature born to fly, and I'd tried not to think about it. Tess said it was for his safety, to prevent him landing on the stove or flying into a ceiling fan. She said Damien was chatty and friendly *because* he was restricted to very brief, indoor flights. Still, it was unnatural.

Maybe that's what Sean didn't like. Maybe that's why he'd suddenly become so irritable. He was very fond of his country and its national treasures — The Great Barrier Reef, the utterly unique wildlife, the self-contained continent. Maybe it pained him to see Damien unable to fly, cage or not.

A small, bright yellow car pulled up behind Tess's car. A moment later, a woman with a blonde ponytail, wearing a yellow turtleneck sweater and a black skirt, popped out of the car. Obviously a fan of yellow, maybe to reflect her hair color.

Smiling, she waved eagerly, opened the rear door, and reached into the back seat.

As she walked toward us, it wasn't clear what she'd been rummaging for in the back seat of her car. Her hands were empty and her left hand rested lightly on a small yellow purse that dangled from her shoulder. She hugged Tess, moved as if she planned to hug me while chirping that I *must be Alex*. I held her off with a rapid handshake.

The house really was quite unusual. I wasn't sure I could see Tess inside of it, but I could see myself there. It was perfect for the indoor-outdoor Australian lifestyle with its bifold doors. It was small without seeming confining and I could imagine waking there in the silence, making breakfast for one, and sitting in the garden. I could see myself in that secluded, overgrown yard, smoking a cigarette and drinking a martini, listening to the tropical birds who are both more ominous and more friendly-sounding than most North American birds.

Cheryl chattered about its perfection the entire time, a melodic backdrop to my tour of the rooms. Tess echoed her comments as if they both needed to reassure themselves it was the right home for Tess.

Twenty minutes later when the yellow car and its yellow occupant darted away from the front of Tess's house, my mind raced back to our unfinished conversation. "So you're definitely not looking for another job?" I said.

"Not now. I already told you…"

"I know."

"Are you worried?" she said.

"No. Just trying to decide whether I should consider my options."

"Besides," Tess said, "Our visas identify TruthTeller as our employer. We can't just hop to another job without some government paperwork. And I really don't know what's involved with making that kind of change."

I had conveniently put this out of my head, and I'm not sure why. We were more tethered to Sean than I'd cared to think about.

24

Cafe Sydney was on the top floor of Customs House — the customs building constructed in the nineteenth century that for the past twenty-five years or so had been used for exhibitions and events as well as housing the city library. In the center of the lobby floor, visible through plexiglass panels, was a model of Sydney, built to scale, every building faithfully replicated.

The restaurant overlooked the harbor. The indoor area featured a number of slightly raised booths. In front of those was a row of tables, and with a step down, the dining area spilled onto a large patio. The arrangement gave nearly every diner a panoramic view of the Sydney Harbor.

Trystan was seated at the bar, a counter formed into a square with the bartender and alcohol in the center. This section was elevated enough to provide a glimpse of the water. Behind the bar were small tables formed from simple blocks of wood, positioned in front of a cushioned bench that ran along the back wall.

Trystan wore a long-sleeved button-down white shirt and blue jeans, and as she drew closer, she saw he had on expensive loafers. He didn't look obviously American as some visitors did. Whenever she had that thought, she wondered whether she also had that American look. She tried to figure out what it was — a facial expression, a view of the world that's demonstrated in posture and demeanor, that despite thousands of variations in viewpoints, was similar in a specific way, coming from having grown up in the most privileged country on the planet? She wasn't sure, but she could often pick out Americans before they spoke. Maybe that's why he'd chosen to approach her in the airport bar. After six months of living here, it was possible she still had that look.

She slid onto a stool beside him.

"Thanks for meeting with me. What would you like to drink?"

She felt rushed, shoved past the usual dance of two people meeting for the first time. "A glass of Chardonnay, please."

He ordered two glasses of wine and then turned to take in what he could of the view. "Have you ever eaten here?"

"No. It's on my list." Another thing that would be great about escaping the inertia of Sean's house — more eating out. As the bartender placed the wine in front of her, Tess smiled and touched the base of her glass. "Thank you." The bartender returned the smile before she moved toward three women seated at the opposite corner of the bar.

"It's pricey, but amazing food," he said. "And of course the view. Hence the priciness. Although the food isn't the kind served in a place that knows you'll pay for the view and tolerate lower quality. It really is absolutely incredible."

"I've heard great things about it.

"What should we drink to?" he raised his glass but kept it close, avoiding tapping it against hers.

The first thing that darted through her mind was *provocation*, but she wanted to hold her thoughts to herself, wait to see what this was all about. "To great views," she said.

"Agreed."

She took a small sip of wine.

"I looked you up online, of course," he said. "Which is why I asked to meet."

Why hadn't she done the same? It was what you did. Instead, she'd let the unconventional job title throw her off course, discussing the encounter with Alex rather than doing her most basic research. She could blame it on the distraction of her new house, or her disinterest in whatever he might be selling.

Even though Sean might be losing it a bit and might have screwed up ideas, she still loved the concept behind the app and still believed in the company. She wasn't ready to bail yet and therefore she had no reason to investigate Trystan. "And what did you find?" she said.

"When I saw you in O'Brien's, I knew you had an impressive background."

"How on earth would you know that?"

"I always know. I'm sure you do as well, you just don't want to admit it. All you have to do is observe someone — the way they sit and walk, how they handle themselves, and you can get a good idea whether they've contributed something worthwhile to the world."

Sometimes she could, but it wasn't fail-safe. She sipped her wine.

"I guessed you might be well-connected professionally and indeed you are."

So, he was looking for something from her. Possibly a job of his own. Maybe provocateur wasn't all that well-paying. Maybe it was a declining industry. She smiled into her wine.

"Should I tell you a bit about myself?"

Did he realize she hadn't bothered to research him? Was his work life concealed, no LinkedIn profile, nothing that Google would pop up in terms of interviews in the media or charitable events or even a marriage or children? An alumni association?

She took a sip of wine. "Please do."

"I'm an entrepreneur, which I suppose is obvious. Much of my work involves connecting the right people. I also do a lot of consulting. Nothing structured, more of a mentoring type role. I help executives take a fresh look at their company, their leadership team, their own style, and the reasons for their stagnation. I ask questions that a typical consulting firm would avoid. I look for ways to shake up the status quo and help them break out of the boxes they've built around themselves."

"Sounds interesting."

"In all industries — technology, media, entertainment, politics. I even worked with a preacher who wanted to build one of those mega church enterprises that's an industry of its own."

She nodded.

"I've worked with executives in the auto industry, college professors, and physicians."

"Why would a physician need shaking out of the status quo?"

"It's a very competitive field. And if you want to make a name for yourself…"

She didn't think she would like to have a physician who was intent on making a name for herself, but maybe that wasn't fair. A career was a career, everyone had ambition.

"How did you get into that?" she said.

"Natural talent."

She smiled.

"Yes, I'm honest about my strengths. People spend far too much time putting on poses of false humility. I know what I'm good at, I know where I fail, and I'm not afraid to talk about it."

"Where do you fail?"

"Golf."

"That's an easy answer. A cop-out, I think."

"Nope. I lack the mental discipline to practice, and so I don't do well. It's a game of practice."

"Most sports are."

"Maybe so. You're a bit of a provocateur yourself," he said.

She wasn't, but he seemed to bring something out in her. Maybe that was his skill.

"I need your help because I'm looking for a personal assistant and I thought you might be able to point me toward some suitable candidates. Obviously I have a lot of my own connections, but I need to look outside of my purview."

"Isn't that what recruiters are for?"

"This is different. I think you probably know a lot of people and might be able to make a connection to someone who's professional but also a bit avant-garde. A personal recommendation, not a suggestion based on bullet points. This isn't just an administrative role."

She still thought his confidence in his weakness was a charade. There was nothing shameful about being bad at golf. It didn't counter the boast about his natural talent. Everyone was bad at golf, or at least the majority of people who weren't professionals. Only someone pursuing a professional career had time for all that practice. He was right about that. So claiming he didn't have the discipline was absurd.

A weakness should show a vulnerable area, to tone down the arrogance of proclaiming your *natural talent*.

"This is different because I can't choose someone based on a résumé alone. I need a complete picture, and I need a person who has the potential to get me, to get what I do, someone who *believes* in what I do, and anticipates my thoughts."

"Good luck with that," Tess said.

"I believe that person is out there. I just need to locate him, or her. And I'm doing that by talking to people who give a vibe of having solid instincts, and a savvy approach to their own career."

"And that's me?"

"Absolutely."

"I'll give it some thought." If Alex wasn't critical to their social media marketing...But Alex would never want to be anyone's assistant. She was certainly one of a kind, definitely avant-garde. She would get what the guy did, that was for sure.

"No one springs immediately to mind?" he said. "That's how instinct usually is. Your first thought is the perfect solution."

"No." She picked up her glass and took several sips of wine. It occurred to her that he could utilize the TruthTeller app in his search for candidates. She also wondered if he knew she was lying. She had the feeling he did, as if he could see right into her head, watching Alex's name parade across her frontal lobe.

"I'm asking a lot of people in different arenas."

"Women you meet in airport bars?"

He laughed. "Occasionally."

While he talked more about his role, she studied the other people sitting nearby. The additional talking didn't provide a lot of additional insight. Part of her thought there was something to it, a person whose function was to break you out of your confines, but another part of her thought he was a bullshitter. A con-man of the first order. Another, very tiny voice at the back of her mind whispered that she could use someone who would force her out of the confining spaces of her life.

"Our company is having a dinner party tomorrow night," she said. "If you're free, it would be great to have you join us. It's informal, and an eclectic mix of people. You'd fit right in. We need a provocateur."

"Absolutely. I'd love to."

She'd hardly taken a breath before his answer flowed out, as if he'd been waiting for an invite since she first sat beside him. She had no idea why she'd asked him. Sean said they were free to invite others, but this guy was a complete stranger. And she had a feeling he and Alex might be an explosive combination.

25

It was pouring rain the night of Sean's dinner party.

I was supposed to call it the TruthTeller dinner party. Sean reminded me of this several times a day, but it was his idea, his food, his friends and former co-workers, his house. I couldn't think of a single thing that made it a TruthTeller event, except that all four of us were there.

Anita Goyant, the woman he'd invited to replace the actress, was the first to arrive. I answered the door and I knew she would be a problem the minute she took a step back and eyed me up and down.

"Are you Sean's girlfriend?" she said.

I laughed. "No. I just live here."

"Oh. I'm a little confused. He said this was…" she took another step back. She had curly brown hair that didn't quite reach her shoulders. Her eyes were a rich dark brown, but she was the type who forces them open wider than they should be, in an effort to look charming and, so she probably thought, more attractive. Sexier. She wasn't wearing a lot of eye makeup, or any makeup, except for pink lipstick. The out-of-style shade of it looked oddly good.

She wore a casual long black dress with spaghetti straps, no bra, and black flip-flops. The dress was damp around the hem where it had dragged through puddles of water. The rain and cold breeze hadn't forced her to succumb to a coat of any kind. I had to admire her for that. She was carrying a tiny green purse and a large black umbrella that she held away from her body, revealing rather well-developed biceps.

She shook the umbrella, spraying water across the doormat. "So you are…?"

"I'm Alex." I stepped back. "Come in."

She glowered at me for half a second, turned and leaned the umbrella against one of the patio chairs, and followed me inside.

Damien laughed hysterically. I wanted to join him.

"Oh. A bird," she said.

"Yes."

"Someone should set him free."

"He's perfectly happy." I wasn't sure he was, but I imagined he would be in Tess's new home.

"And I'm Anita," she said. "Thanks for asking."

"Would you like a glass of champagne?" Sean was obsessed with champagne. Maybe it was just as well, not serving cocktails, considering all the wine consumed during dinner and the drinks following dessert at the previous party, but I longed for a martini. Champagne looks gorgeous in the glass, and it's okay with brunch, but it's not my favorite.

She followed me to the billiards room where a long, narrow cherrywood table held champagne flutes, several bottles in chillers, and a tray of chicken satay, made by Gavin. I filled a glass and handed it to her.

"You're sure you aren't Sean's girlfriend?"

"Definitely sure."

She took a long swallow of champagne. "I was worried, the way you opened the door with such a…" she waved her hand beside her head, catching a long, narrow turquoise ring in a strand of hair. She slid her hand away and extracted the hair from the filigree around the turquoise. "…An air of ownership."

I smiled. I poured a glass of champagne for myself and took a sip.

She leaned toward me as if we were close friends and there were other people standing nearby, yearning to hear our secrets. She spoke in a loud whisper. "I didn't think he had a girlfriend any more and when I saw you, I was worried. Always hoping, right?" She grinned, her pink-painted lips stretched wide in a way that was still attractive, but made her look slightly unglued.

I couldn't help myself. "Hoping for what?"

She stepped back. She moved her champagne glass to her right hand and held out her left, wiggling her fingers, lifting her ring finger slightly.

"I'm not sure what you mean."

She rolled her eyes. "You know what I mean."

"I don't."

"He's gorgeous, you idiot. And…" she lifted her head slightly, indicating the room around us.

"Rich?"

"Well that's kind of tacky to say, but he knows how to take care of a girl."

"Do girls need taking care of?"

"Silly." She slapped my wrist with her ringless left hand. "Of course we do."

"Why don't I introduce you to the rest of the team." I started toward the door. "Have you met many of Sean's friends? I don't recall how you know him."

"We belong to the same gym. Or we did. Ages ago. I'm a personal trainer."

"Sounds fun. Do you like it?"

"Love it. I just *love* it." She juggled the glass and formed a heart with her hands. Her fingers were curved like commas, the knuckles of both hands pressed against each other, the glass pinched precariously between her thumb and first finger, leaning so far to the right the champagne was brushing against the lip of the glass. "Love. It." She reasserted her grip on the glass. "You look like you work out."

"I do. Let's go into the other room."

She followed me to the great room and immediately slipped away from me. A moment later, she'd attached herself to Sean's side.

The doorbell rang again and I returned to what looked to be my default duty of greeting newcomers. It was actually a role I preferred over standing in the other room sipping champagne. I liked watching them enter, seeing whether they tried to dominate the encounter or hung back, observing whether they were drawn to the staircase or the bird cage or the atrium of plants and turtles. Usually, people were drawn to that staircase, even if they'd seen it before. But Damien's enormous cage went a long way toward pulling their attention to that first, it was so unusual and just a little bit weird because it was large enough to hold a human being, or two.

Still, they marveled at the staircase. As it was meant to, the elegant curve captivated their eyes, leading them up to the second floor where there was really nothing to see. But they had to look.

A few commented on Damien, a few walked up close to his cage and spoke to him. He laughed but refused to speak, being the little control freak that he is. There would be no showing off his abilities unless he was in the mood.

26

The last to arrive was Trystan, the provocateur.

Tess had told me he was coming and filled me in on the job description for a self-titled provocateur. It sounded intriguing, as if there might be more to it than what he'd said. I had a general idea of why he was paid for what he did, but still wondered how in demand those services would be. Her comments were vague, as if she'd lost interest, which made it surprising that she'd invited him to dinner. She'd sounded bored with the whole thing.

Most people, no matter what they say, don't really want to be shaken out of the status quo. And if they do want to go to the next level and change course and all those things that are said to be important in reaching the pinnacles of life, they don't want someone else pointing out what aspects of their personality and behavior are preventing them from doing so.

No one truly wants to hear what their flaws are. They want to self-analyze. They want to be in charge. They'd rather take a written personality test or career self-assessment or attend seminars or listen to generic motivational talks than have someone observe them in daily life and comment on their deficiencies.

At least that's how I'd feel. Maybe I'm different. I suppose I don't know many who have reached the so-called pinnacle, however that's defined. Unless you count Sean. Did creating a company that someone else wanted to purchase put you at the pinnacle? Did having a lot of money put you there? Or were there other requirements? Power? Fame? Admiration? Talent? Charm?

Trystan was a good-looking man in a rather typical way. He met all the check boxes — taller than average, thick brown hair, intense brown eyes, an appealing smile. But there was something plastic about him. Something manufactured. It's possible my frame of reference had changed, spending all my time with down-to-earth Australians.

For all his idiosyncrasies, and worse, Sean wasn't obviously conscious of his good looks. He was comfortable in his skin and didn't seem to think much about his appearance, although I suppose a tattoo across the bones of your foot says something about trying to get attention for your appearance. As does long hair on a man.

Gavin wasn't traditionally gorgeous, but again, he was comfortable in his skin and that is much hotter than a perfectly-regulated tan and expensive clothes, and teeth that have been nicely arranged by a few years in a torture device.

He extended his hand. "Trystan."

I took his hand. "Alex."

"Nice to meet you. You're part of the start-up?"

"Yes."

I moved away from the doorway and he walked inside. He ignored the staircase entirely and went to the birdcage. "Hello there, fella."

I followed. "How do you now it's a fella?" I said.

He laughed. "What's its name?"

"Damien."

"So I'll go with fella." He leaned closer to the cage. "Do you talk?"

Damien adjusted his position on his perch. *Nice to meet you. Chardonnay time.*

Trystan turned toward me, grinning. "It never gets old, listening to them talk, does it?"

"No, it doesn't." I was impressed. For some reason, Damien had let go of his aloofness. His crown was lowered and he seemed to accept Trystan on the spot. Was that the same deal as it's supposed to be with dogs? If the dog mistrusts a stranger, you should put up a barrier, but if the dog greets someone with exuberance, that person is deemed safe and acceptable? I wasn't even sure I bought it with dogs, much less a bird.

We went to the billiards room where I poured him a glass of champagne. He picked up a stick of chicken satay. I took one for myself and we wandered to the great room where most of the others were gathered, a few moving cautiously out to the center of the patio where they were protected from the pounding rain.

Sean hadn't roped Gavin into cooking this time. He'd done it all himself, except for the chicken satay.

The kitchen was filled with the aroma of roasting game hens, wild rice, and carrots with a sweet glaze. There was a salad made of arugula, raspberries, and almond slices, and another with romaine lettuce, cherry tomatoes, and thinly sliced red onion. He'd bought fresh rolls. Scoops of softened butter were sitting in tiny dishes beside each dinner plate.

Dessert would be bowls of gelato with shortbread biscuits, the preferred Australian word for cookies.

After all the burgers and ribs he'd made for us, I was surprised and impressed by his cooking skills.

The food was as delicious as it smelled. The conversation

was as lively as the last time. Once again, I was seated at the foot of the table, and once again, Sean's attention was consumed by Tess.

Anita sat one chair away from Sean where she tried tirelessly throughout the meal to capture his interest. She delivered a steady flow of anecdotes in a raised voice, her head turned toward him, ignoring those who were actually listening to her stories, which weren't half bad. Maybe they just interested me because they were all about her weight-training clients. Some of them were funny.

She laughed too loudly, and sometimes stopped herself mid-sentence to listen to the few words Sean had to say, offering a comment no matter how unnecessary. When Sean requested the plate of rolls, she asked him whether he needed any other dishes passed. When he stood to refill wine glasses, she complimented his skill in providing dripless pours.

It would have been fantastic to shoot a video of Anita melting over him, but unless I could ensure shots that didn't show her face, that would be my riskiest post yet. Unless… maybe I could pitch it to her as something flattering. Her fifteen minutes of fame. But she'd have to be insanely stupid to believe that, because if I got the images I wanted, they would not present her in a good light. I tossed out the idea. She was a lot of things, but she wasn't stupid.

I turned my attention to Trystan. He was drinking in the atmosphere. I hadn't seen any evidence of the provocateur, but possibly he was keeping that at bay until dessert, or maybe he liked to stay in the shadows entirely until he could hand out a few of those business cards and start everyone guessing. Perhaps he liked to make a mysterious exit, leaving the cards behind.

We chatted about the US and he told me about his favorite places to eat in New York. He was shocked I'd never been there and insisted it was the greatest city in the world. There are millions of people in Paris and London, LA and Chicago, Singapore, Tokyo, Dubai, and Cairo, not to mention Sydney and Melbourne and a host of other places who would violently disagree with him, but I didn't point that out. He seemed completely oblivious to this possibility.

In the end, it was all quite pleasant. The only one who seemed to have a less than fantastic time was Sean — eyeing Tess, glaring at her as if he could make her stay — roping her in and tying her down with the intensity of his gaze.

As I was seeing everyone out the front door, Anita grabbed my arm. She leaned close, touching my ear with her lips. I tried to pull away, but she had an iron grasp of my upper arm.

"I'll be back tomorrow to clean up. Don't tell him."

"That's not necessary."

"It is. Such a terrific party, and doing all that work, all by himself! I think he'll appreciate the help."

"It will be taken care of tonight."

She gave me a knowing smile. "I don't think that's likely. It's one o'clock in the morning."

"I said it will be taken care of."

She released my arm. "Don't tell him."

"Please don't show up here."

She smiled and glided out the door, picked up her umbrella, and walked into the night. The clouds had pulled away, revealing glittering stars overhead.

27

As she'd promised, and as I'd hoped she would talk herself out of, realizing how bat-shit crazy and pathetic it was, Anita showed up at the front door the next morning at seven o'clock.

I knew this because I was returning from my run, planning to spend the next forty-five minutes in the weight room. I'd lift weights and do twenty minutes of yoga, relishing the quiet as my housemates slept off champagne and gelato and wine.

No matter how much I overindulge, I rarely let it stop me from running the next day. In fact, it's better to get out of bed and run or lift weights so those toxins can ooze out with my sweat. There's no point in spending half of the following day lying around like a slug, hoping it slowly makes its way out of your body while you try to chase it with orange juice. Why not be done with it as soon as possible?

The start of my run had been difficult — my breath tight, fighting the rest of my body, and my muscles screaming that a firm bed, warm sheets, and a soft blanket would be so much better. I paid no attention. By the time I hit the one-mile mark, my blood was moving more freely and my lungs were washed with clean air. The early morning air does feel clean, even when your mind knows it's not as pristine as it could be. Before dawn and just after sunrise, it smells and tastes pure and healthy. And maybe, at that point in the day, it *is* cleaner, the night air having pushed the smog and pollutants to the side so the earth can get a breathing break of her own.

When I returned, Anita was standing on the front patio, pressing the doorbell.

I paused outside the front gate and watched to see who would answer Sean's door, and what Anita would do.

She had to raise her hand, the one with the turquoise ring, three times, pressing her finger on the button before the door opened.

I couldn't immediately see who it was. I opened the gate quietly and moved closer. Gavin stood there in his boxer shorts. Seeing his half naked body, now that I was warmed and refreshed, I wanted to skip the weights and yoga and crawl into his bed, feeling his warm, sleepy skin on mine.

Anita began talking and gesturing. Gavin looked at her as if he had no idea who she was. The more she talked, the more he looked like he also had no idea what she was saying. She moved close enough that he was forced to take a few steps back.

She wore jeans, Converse shoes without socks, and a black tank top. The sleeves of a pink sweatshirt were tied around her shoulders. When she turned, possibly sensing my presence, I saw that the intense pink lipstick had been left in its tube.

She turned back and put her hand on Gavin's chest. He took another step away from the door, but she moved with him. A moment later, she was inside the house.

Why had he let her inside? I'd washed the dishes and cleaned up the kitchen the night before. I don't like getting up to a messy kitchen, decaying food smeared on plates and flatware, rank alcohol sitting in half-empty glasses, and counters with sticky puddles, and bits of spilled food, petrified and clinging to the granite.

Besides, she'd been so insistent with her plan to show up, I needed to be sure that if she was that bold, if she talked her way into the house, there would be nothing for her to do.

It wasn't as if I was overly territorial, trying to protect Sean or stake some sort of claim for my position in a house that wasn't mine, for which I didn't even pay rent. Clearly she was going to insert herself into Sean's life, and there was nothing I could do about that. But the thought of having her around all the time made my skin crawl. She would upset the dynamic of our house far more than Tess's move.

I strolled up the walkway and went inside. I closed the door softly behind me.

Gavin and Anita had already moved to the kitchen. I heard their voices, hers loud and grating, asking who had cleaned up.

"I don't know," Gavin said. "I crashed the minute the last person was out the door."

"Was it her?"

"Who?"

"That girl who lives here. The one that had the super high heels and the short dress."

"Alex?"

"She's not the type to wash dishes."

I walked toward the kitchen. My running shoes squeaked on the tile. When I entered the room, they were both facing the doorway, waiting for me. Gavin stood with his legs spread and his arms crossed over his bare chest. He seemed to have angled his arms to cover the maximum area possible.

Anita was beside him, one hand in the front pocket of her jeans, the other fiddling with the elastic strap around her ponytail. "You cleaned up?"

"I don't like a mess in the morning." What was wrong with her? She acted like she was ready to move in, like she had some authority from Sean to take care of his dinner party clean-up. In all the time I'd lived there, I'd never seen her at the house or heard Sean mention her name.

She narrowed her eyes. "You? I'm not sure I believe...I told you I was coming."

"And I said it would be taken care of."

"You just wanted to make sure I couldn't help him."

"He doesn't need your help."

She raised her voice. "You're not his wife."

I laughed.

Gavin looked surprised, but was also laughing silently.

"I wanted to help. He needs a girl who knows how to work hard. Not eye candy. I wanted to do one small thing, and you took it away from me, just for spite."

"It had nothing to do with you, or with spite."

"Why? Tell me why you had to do that."

"I live here. I told you, I don't like waking up to a dirty kitchen." It was beyond ridiculous. "You should go now. Call him or text him and work it out with him later."

"Where is he?"

"Asleep," Gavin said.

"Tell him I'm here."

"I'm going back to bed." Gavin walked around her and left the room rather quickly, I thought, anxious to escape whatever was going to happen.

It wouldn't have surprised me if she suddenly darted past

me and ran up the stairs, hunting for Sean.

"Please tell him I'm here."

"You need to leave. I don't know why you want to be his housekeeper, or whatever it is you want, but he invited you to fill a slot at his dinner party. That's all. It's not your job to clean the kitchen, and it's a little weird to just show up here so early when everyone's still sleeping."

"You're not."

"Text him later," I said.

"I wanted to do something to help him, to share the work."

"So you mentioned."

"Why are you being so mean?"

"Why are you acting like a teenager? You're an adult woman. Have some self-respect."

"What do you know?" She nearly spit as she said it.

I took her wrist and tugged her toward me. She yielded, tripping behind me as I went to the foyer and opened the front door. "Please don't show up again unless Sean invites you."

"Fuck you," she said. "Just because you live here and work for him doesn't give you ownership rights."

"I have no interest in *ownership rights*. And I'm pretty sure they aren't up for grabs. For anyone." I pushed her gently out the front door and closed it behind her.

I returned to the kitchen and started making espresso. Possibly, there was something off about her that was more deeply rooted than I'd realized. Maybe the invite to the dinner party made her think there was more to it than just a social gathering for people who might become enamored with Sean's app.

28

On the drive to Bondi Beach for my swim lesson that afternoon, Gavin and I talked about Anita.

Mostly Gavin talked.

"I've never met her before, and I'm not sure what made him think to invite her. Listening to her this morning, I thought she might be certifiably wacko. Showing up like that...I think she has stalker potential. I told Sean and he blew it off. She used to be his trainer and they slept together once or twice, but it wasn't anything, and that was how she wanted it, so it's all cool. He invited her because she's friendly and he thought she'd be fun. He was a little worried she talked too much, that she didn't shut up long enough for people to move into a deeper conversation."

"Is there some sort of conversation he wants to have?"

"Who knows."

"Don't parties usually take on a life of their own? People talk about whatever's happening in their lives or the world at the time, or whatever they're thinking on a particular day."

"Yep."

"They tell their stories and feed on each other. It's not something you control." I laughed. "If he wants to decide what we'll talk about like he's planning a conversation menu, he should give us lists of questions for each other."

Gavin laughed with me. "I don't know what he's expecting. I just hope she doesn't show up again. She rang the bell ten or twelve times. She held it down until I felt like it was inside my head. Not a cool way to wake up after a night of too much wine." He rubbed the side of his head as if the hangover might still be crouching in the corner of his skull. "It gives a different kind of hangover than beer."

"It does."

"What do you think she wants? How weird is it to have someone want to come wash up for you? I've never heard anything like it."

"She wants to hook up with him," I said.

He nodded. "And washing plates is the way to do that?"

"Not in my experience."

Keeping his gaze on the road, he smiled slightly. "Do you think she's dangerous?"

I considered this. Despite Sean's dinner invitation, there was a sense that Anita had appeared out of nowhere. If three is considered a pattern, there were now three women who had thrown themselves at Sean. Karen coming naked into his backyard. Anita showing up to wash his dishes. And Carmen. They were captivated by his appearance, his you-can't-stop-staring good looks. But also, at least in Anita's case, his money. Did this sort of thing happen a lot with him? Was that what I'd find out from Carmen?

Was Anita dangerous? It was hard to say. She had no filters, and she was clearly hoping Sean would fall for her. But cleaning up the kitchen? There was nothing threatening about that. It was more pathetic than dangerous. Showing up at seven in the morning was concerning. At least she hadn't returned before dawn, or tried to get into the house, or wandered into the backyard and startled one of us coming downstairs for a glass of water at three a.m. to wash away the effects of wine and champagne.

"Do you?" Gavin said. He turned into the parking lot.

"No. Probably not."

Across from us the beach spread out with smooth, soothing fine-grained sand, comforting and warm. And beyond that, the silky blue water and the canopy of blue overhead. The rain had washed away every single cloud and there was nothing but blue as far as I could see. It was California-blue, unusual for Sydney where there are almost always a few clouds hovering somewhere, at least as long as I'd been there. The waves were gentle, white-foamed edges collapsing softly on the sand before they ran up the beach in gentle strokes, their long fingers reaching to take over more space.

I didn't really want to talk about Anita, but seeing the ocean and watching those waves made me think it was a better alternative to walking into that pool and putting my face in the water.

I hated that it was controlling me still. I wanted it to be easy. I wanted all the thoughts I'd had as a child, and they *were* childish thoughts, wiped away. I wanted to face it like a blank slate without believing it was trying to kill me. Everyone else seemed able to do that. It couldn't be that hard. But all those people had learned to love the water when they were children, ignorant of its danger. They had parents who showed them water was playful and fun.

Gavin turned off the engine. "There's something not right about her and I hope she doesn't come back. I felt very uncomfortable around her."

That made me smile, although I kept it to myself. I wondered what he picked up in Anita that he didn't see inside of me. He was completely oblivious that I might be far more dangerous than Anita.

Unless, I wasn't.

29

With the question of Anita unresolved, Gavin opened his door and I did the same. We walked in silence to the pool.

Gavin peeled off his T-shirt as he kicked off his flip-flops. Despite all that blue sky, the air was cold. It was winter after all. Not as chilly as a San Francisco Bay Area winter, but still winter. Gavin didn't shiver or look to have any goosebumps on his skin. He sauntered along the edge for a few yards and then dove in, gliding just below the surface. The water was probably warmer than the air, but still, going into a large pool of water was even less appealing than usual. I'd agreed to the lesson. I refused to admit defeat, refused to make excuses, even though an excuse was…excusable.

I took off my dress and kicked my flip-flops on top of Gavin's. The thin soles and narrow straps made them look delicate beside the thick rubber of his. His flip-flops looked like they were designed for a mountain trek. As I took a step away from the pile of discarded clothes, the edge of my foot brushed against his shirt. The warmth of his skin still lived in the cotton, whispering that there were so many things more pleasant than walking into a pool of water.

Waves of apprehension flowed through me as I approached the water. I had to conquer this today. Taking it slowly, waiting for something to change that would make putting my face in the water more pleasant, was not working. This required a force of will. I wasn't expecting a full-out experience of swimming, but I had to get my face in the water and float despite thoughts of death sloshing around inside my brain.

As I moved through the water toward him, it lapped higher on my body with each step. He stretched his arms overhead and bent his head back, looking up at the sky. When I was closer, he lowered his arms. "I was thinking. Maybe we rushed this."

I waited, shivering slightly at the cold air washing across the damp skin of my arms.

"You need to really absorb the idea that your body floats. I think we should spend all of today with you floating on your back. It's a gorgeous sky, you can just look up and relax and let the water hold you."

I could have kissed him.

I put my arms around his waist and pulled him closer. He bent slightly and we kissed for a very long time. It occurred to me, while his tongue was deep inside my mouth, and my body was melting beneath me, no longer trembling from cold, that people loved swimming pools and water vacations because all that water could be quite seductive in more ways than one.

After a while, he turned my head gently away so I was facing toward the open ocean. He put his lips close to my ear. "We should continue this right here. Or get back to the house. Or get started floating."

I laughed. "Aren't we already floating?" I looked toward the edge of the surf. It was filling with swimmers. A man was pushing an umbrella into the sand close to the water line while his toddlers ran up and down with the ebb and flow of the waves.

I moved away from Gavin. "Finish floating, then we'll

finish what else we started."

He put his arms behind my shoulders and thighs as he had before. I rested there for several minutes, letting the water hold me. The cool air continuing to brush across my wet skin didn't invite thoughts of relaxing, of easing myself into a state approaching sleep, as he'd suggested. Sleep sounded dangerous, so it was just as well it was the furthest thought from my mind.

Finally, I managed to exert authority over my muscles, thinking of each group, willing them not to contract. It sounds counter-intuitive, but it was successful because I managed to remain afloat. Unless it was the water doing all the work. Maybe it liked me a bit after all, maybe it wanted me to float on its surface, trusting it more than I trusted any other force of nature and certainly more than I trusted most human beings.

It's difficult to have confidence in another human being when it's impossible to know what runs around inside their skull. I always know what's inside my own head. With another person, it's a total mystery, made riskier by the fact they might deliberately mislead you. And I know this of course, because I'm often misleading.

I might be enclosed in Gavin's arms, thinking about the lovely muscles of his chest and shoulders. Most people might assume the man or woman holding them is having similar thoughts, thinking about kissing or stroking the other's leg. But you don't know that at all. The other person might be thinking about the burrito they had for lunch or the bit of code they need to write that afternoon. The person holding you might be thinking about his sister's dead finger that he'd felt the compulsion to preserve under his bed for going on fifteen years. He might be thinking about ending your relationship or eating dinner or another woman or a TV show or nothing at all. The other person might very well be thinking of killing you.

I definitely had no idea what was inside of Sean's head. He'd hired me to do social media, or at least agreed with Tess that was my responsibility, and an important one. Yet he'd done nothing but undermine it. I didn't understand what was going on with Carmen and it was completely unclear how his past was bleeding into my job and how it might swell or suddenly erupt all over me.

On the other hand, he knew exactly what was going on. He had information that affected my job but he was determined to keep it to himself, and suggested I was intruding where I didn't belong if I dared to ask.

Now, there was this oddity of a woman who was supposed to be part of a cast of whatever show he was running at these dinner parties. Like an unruly cast member from a stage performance, she'd leaped past the fourth wall and landed in our midst.

Water was possibly *more* trustworthy than human beings. You knew what to expect from any body of water. There were rules for encountering it, and if you followed those rules — respecting it when it was fierce, learning to control your breath, understanding the dynamics of floating, then it all worked out.

Of course those who have faced tsunamis know differently, but for the most part, it was possible water was manageable and I'd mistakenly viewed it as a threat with a will of its own. It might have a will that could be bent to mine.

These were the things rolling through my mind like

gentle waves themselves, as I let the water hold me, and realized it might not be so terrible, as long as I kept my face toward the sky.

30

When we arrived back at Sean's house, our skin was dry and warm from running the heater in the car. The garage was empty, meaning — no Sean, no Tess. It would make for a pleasant rest of the morning in Gavin's bed and then a breakfast of bacon and hash browns and eggs with cheese and tomatoes and onions. Sour cream on the eggs sounded good also.

The way the list of ingredients was unfolding in my mind made me think I wanted food more than sex. I suppose all the adrenaline that it took for me to simply lie on my back and trust the salt water had stirred my appetite.

We entered through the side door and hung the towels in the laundry room. Gavin headed toward the foyer and was three steps up the staircase before I started after him. At the top, he looped his arm around my neck and we walked side-by-side down the hallway. When we reached my door, he stopped while I continued walking, which had the effect of half strangling me. I ducked out of the circle of his arm.

"Where are you going?" he said.

"Trying to avoid being decapitated."

"If you didn't keep walking, that wouldn't be an issue," he said.

"Aren't we going to your room?"

"We're always in my room. Besides, if we stay in your room, I won't see the computer staring at me reminding me of Sean's feature update list."

"I prefer your room."

"What difference does it make?"

"Exactly."

"What's the problem? Do you have a dead body in there?" He laughed. He tried to press down on the door handle. "You do have a dead body."

"Which is a good reason to use your room," I said.

He stared at me, unnerved, I suppose, by my easy agreement. He held out his hand. "Give me the key."

"If this is foreplay, it's not working," I said.

"It would be different, for a change. And to avoid the computer. Don't you care whether I'm distracted?"

"You can close your eyes."

"How would I look at your gorgeous body with my eyes closed?"

"I think you have a solid memory of it by now. And like they said in Grease…"

"What?"

"You never saw that 70s movie, Grease? In one of the songs, Olivia Newton John tells John Travolta that he could feel his way to her. I thought you'd be familiar with the music, since she's Aussie."

"Be careful with our authenticity, Ms. Alexandra."

"Why?"

"She lives in Australia. She wasn't born here, therefore not Aussie. But we're off topic here."

I grabbed his hand and tugged gently. "Do you want to do this or argue about which bed to use?"

"What's the big deal?" He pressed on the door handle again as if it would somehow magically open.

It wasn't that he might trip over the telescope. But it had been on my mind, a lot. And being on my mind made it feel larger than it was. It made the rug seem like a completely inadequate disguise, and it was. If anyone saw the rolled-up rug, they'd wonder about that in itself.

Knowing it was there, knowing every one of my housemates would recognize it, had transformed it into a huge object in my mind, filling the entire closet floor, obvious by its shape, suspiciously hard if a curious toe was pushed against the rug. I felt like it dominated my room and sat in plain sight for the most casual observer. It wasn't of course, but I couldn't stop thinking about it. A bit like *The Telltale Heart*.

"I'm starting to think there is something in there you don't want me to see. When did you start locking your door?"

"I took a page from your playbook."

"I think it's slightly different," he said.

"Is it?"

"Why don't you want me in your room? I don't get it? You're making a huge deal out of it for no reason."

"You're making a huge deal out of it for no reason."

He took a step away from me.

Now, hunger definitely had superseded sex. My stomach rumbled. I wasn't feeling all that excited anymore. Without the artificial heat of the car, my damp swimsuit clung to my skin, my wet hair was cold against my head and upper back. And most of all, Gavin was annoying me. Why the hell did he care what room we used? It was absurd.

"Are you going to unlock your door?" he said.

"What's the problem? Why is locking your door okay and locking mine isn't?"

"I let you inside whenever you want."

"And I want to go to your room now, yet you're not letting me."

"You're acting like a child."

We stood looking at each other, breathing heavily from irritation, not desire. The longer we stood there, the more I wanted something to eat. My stomach rumbled again. Now, I had no interest in sex whatsoever. The only thing I had to figure out was how to get him away from my room and thinking of something else. That something would have to be more engaging than a plate of eggs and bacon.

"It's dirty, okay? I haven't cleaned up, and…"

"The house cleaners were here last week."

"I don't mean vacuuming. I have clothes everywhere, and the sink has hair in it."

"I don't care about clothes everywhere. What's wrong with you?"

"I'm tired of arguing about this. And I'm hungry."

"So you want brekkie more than me?"

I moved up close and wrapped my arms around his waist. "Never. But all that outdoor air and the exertion of floating…I know it doesn't seem like exertion to you. It almost sounds funny — that floating takes energy. But for me, it did, fighting my thoughts regarding water."

"I can see that. Mental strain can be exhausting."

"So now, I want to eat. I want to cook for you and eat with you. And after…maybe you don't care about dirty clothes and hair in the sink, but I do. And that's what matters. You might be distracted by your computer, I'm distracted by the mess. And it's more than distracting, it makes me feel decidedly not sexy. So…your choice."

He took my earlobe between his thumb and forefinger and rubbed it gently. "Okay, you win."

I almost always do. But I hadn't thought there was a battle between Gavin and me. And so far, there hadn't been a winner or a loser.

31

I cooked *brekkie* and we ate without talking. After my last piece of bacon, I put my fingers in Gavin's mouth and he sucked on them gently. We left the dishes on the bar and headed upstairs. Without any discussion we went straight to his room, un-locking and locking the door, and into his bed.

Peeling off my still-damp bathing suit was like working with plastic cling wrap, but he managed quite well.

We also didn't speak while we explored and satisfied each other's bodies, taking our time, enjoying the warmth of each other's flesh and the comfort of a well-appointed bed. His hair and skin smelled as fresh as the ocean air. After the extreme concentration and effort to relax during my swim lesson, every touch of Gavin's fingers and mouth, every wave of pleasure, felt more intense than usual. I think he felt the same, although he didn't say. Neither did I.

After a bit of sleep, I got out of bed and picked up my swimsuit. There was a damp spot on the carpet which I hoped wouldn't decay into a nasty odor of salt water and dead skin. I slipped into my dress and went to the side of the bed. I put my hand on his shoulder and shook gently. "I'm going to shower. See you later."

He grunted.

After my shower, I dried my hair and put on makeup. Just to be different, because it had been the same shoulder-length medium brown since I re-dyed it after killing Detective

Bender, I parted my hair on the opposite side. I wished I had a jar of instant color, because I would have added a red streak right then. It was time for a trip to a salon. The whole works — hair color and cut, massage, mani, pedi, followed by a martini to complete an entire day of self-care. I decided to book a few appointments before Sean's next dinner party.

I dressed in red leggings and a red tank top covered by a long, loose white sweater. Since the outfit was plenty warm, I put on black gladiator sandals. It was a bright outfit, but it helped counter the fact that my hair was less than remarkable.

I went downstairs to clean up the dishes from our breakfast.

Sean was standing near Damien's cage, watching the bird, who was ignoring him.

"Has he talked to you much?" I said.

He turned. "It's not talking, it's mimicking."

"Okay. Whatever." I started toward the kitchen. I stopped and turned. "By the way, what's the deal with Anita?"

"What deal?"

"Did you know she showed up here at seven a.m. this morning?"

"Yes, Gav mentioned it."

"And he told you she wanted to clean up the dishes from last night?"

"Why?"

I shrugged. "You tell me."

"I don't know why she would do that."

"She's very…into you."

He stared at me.

I waited for several seconds.

"She's been texting me all day, but she didn't say she'd been here."

"Did you ever…"

"I invited her to dinner because I stopped by the gym looking for someone else. I ran into her and we talked for a few minutes. She asked why I wasn't working with a trainer any more. We talked about that and then she mentioned she was lonely."

"I thought you wanted vibrant, connected people at your dinner soirées, not people who complain about being lonely."

"She isn't normally like that. She's a good trainer. I thought she'd add something to the group, a different perspective. She went on a bit too much, but it worked out fine, don't you think?"

"I think it's bizarre for someone to show up at your door wanting to wash your dishes."

"Don't read into it."

I laughed. Damien laughed with me. "It's impossible not to read into it. She definitely has plans for you." I smiled. "Thinks you're a good catch. An eligible bachelor."

He rolled his eyes. "Maybe you can get rid of her. Give her a call and tell her I haven't responded to her texts because…"

"That's not my job. Getting rid of your stalker girlfriends."

"I told you she's not…"

"Carmen. Anita. Who else might pop up on the front doorstep?"

He stared at me, his mouth open, his eyes wide, a spasm of potential nausea riding across his lips. "Was Carmen here?"

"No."

"Oh. Good. Good." His face resumed a neutral expression but he still looked slightly ill. "Why can't you just tell Anita something for me. As a friend. I wasn't saying it's your job. But easy enough and saves me…"

"You need to deal with your own issues."

"You seem good at that sort of interaction, though. Putting things out there in plain language. Being clear about how things are going to be. You're a natural. A predator knows how to mark her territory."

I laughed, longer this time. Damien joined again, increasing his sense of hilarity as if I were a stand-up comic giving him a private show. "A *predator*? My *territory*?"

He didn't laugh. His face was solemn, desperately trying to make sure I understood his point. "Yes. You're a predator."

"Why would you say that?" I didn't believe he had the nerve, first of all. It was a slick attempt to change this from his problem with a potential stalker into something I should do for him because it fit my nature, or some such nonsense.

"You know you are. You go after what you want and you aren't sidetracked by convention. Watching you these past few months, it's been quite fascinating."

"Predators have prey," I said.

"Yes." He leaned against Damien's cage. "That's one thing I haven't figured out. Who *is* your prey?" He held up three fingers.

I knew who he would tick off. As he went through the names of my housemates, I smiled and wondered if he had any idea what I was thinking. Of course he didn't. Because he had it wrong.

My prey wasn't a person. My prey was the life I want,

taking tiny steps all the time, always fine-tuning my dreams.

Lately, I think my steps are too tiny. Sure, my bank account had swelled significantly while I was in Australia, but not nearly at the rate it needs to in order for me to have the kind of home and the life I want. Specifically, a life in which I don't have to do stupid jobs like making PowerPoint slides or tweeting in the hopes of saying something so incredibly enticing that millions will follow me, hang on my every word, and spend their money on the product I'm selling, just because I'm the one selling it.

"You're wrong," I said.

"I don't think I am. For sure Gavin is your prey." He winked. "But he's not enough. You always want more."

So, he did know about Gavin and me. I sort of respected him for knowing. I was pretty sure Tess hadn't told him, and so I respected him for not being blind or naïve or oblivious.

Damien spoke in a low voice, almost as if he were trying to whisper. *Dangerous woman.*

This time, Sean laughed, loud and hard. "Smart bird. So come on, please get in touch with Anita for me, and tell her to get lost."

"You always think it's that easy, don't you."

"What?"

"That you can get someone out of your life by saying get lost. When someone thinks you owe them, it's not so easy."

"I guess. Well can't you be a mate? Help me out? Please?" He tipped his head slightly, giving me a coy, pleading expression. It was very unlike him, even joking around.

"No. Text her back and tell her what you need to say. But since she thinks she can show up at your house, I would make sure it's firm."

"It is rather unsettling, that she came over here." He started toward the kitchen and I followed, uncertain whether he thought that since he'd asked, I would still comply, even though I'd said *no*.

"While you're at it," he said. "Why don't you figure out a way to keep Tess from bailing on us."

Without saying anything more, as if by mutual agreement to end the conversation, we started cleaning up the breakfast dishes and pans. While we worked, I studied the shark tattooed on his foot and wondered if it takes one to know one.

32

Whether they evolved slowly into their various selves or were dumped into the world's oceans in a single glut by some sort of intelligently creative explosion, the oceans are filled with sharks. There are over four hundred-seventy species.

Predators.

I'm not sure why that term is associated with sharks more than other sea life. They're all predators.

Even cuddly little sea otters prey on shellfish. Most people don't think of shellfish as sentient beings. They don't elicit warm feelings because they lack fur and faces and appendages. The more we see ourselves in animals, the more we like them. I suppose the human connection to dogs more so than to chimpanzees would be the exception to that.

But most of us aren't emotional about globs of rubbery flesh that live inside hard shells, poking out delicate antennae, peering with bulbous, alien eyes, creeping along the ocean floor like the hunchback of Notre Dame. So if otters want to crack the shells of clams and mussels and gobble them up, we'll photograph and film their adorable little murders all day long.

Sharks have a different reputation. And it might be that blood thing. They smell it and they come. They know where you're weak, they know when you're losing blood. They *know* that blood flowing out into the water means easy prey. So they aren't patrolling for food per se. They're sniffing for blood. Although surely the blood suggests to them food is available, so I'm not really sure why they're slapped with the predator label more than most.

But seeking blood, fixating on blood does make them seem ominous. Other animals stalk their prey by sight or sound or the smell of the creatures' sweat and fur and skin. Sharks smell the blood, so I suppose they're stalking death.

Sharks are beautiful creatures. Their wicked teeth, constantly replenishing, further proving their predatory tendencies, their ability to tear prey into a thousand shreds, make them seem vicious by human standards. The shape of their jaws and their open mouths revealing those rows of teeth don't make for a pleasing expression. It appears leering, mocking, the grin of something that wants to eat you alive. Or dead.

But they swim with such grace. And their speed is impressive. White sharks can swim twenty-five miles an hour, and close to thirty miles an hour in short bursts. And they hardly appear to move a muscle to do it. They glide forward, tails undulating, dorsal fins giving stability. They move with the speed and precision of a machine.

I've watched them at the aquarium for hours, and I've longed to see them in the wild. Given my antagonism toward water and boats, it didn't seem like that would ever happen. But if I learned to swim, which suddenly seemed believable, maybe anything was possible.

Whatever the reasons, sharks are considered more predatory, but there's nothing immoral about their attacks on vulnerable swimmers and surfers. When they kill, they aren't vicious, or perverted for desiring blood. Those are attributes placed on them by the humankind.

The predatory behavior of sharks is accepted as the natural order of the planet. But when it comes to predators in the human race, everyone gets fussy.

Murder is a crime, punishable by being locked up for decades, and often, by death. In the eyes of the law and most of humanity, there's no excuse for deliberate murder.

Except when there is.

War. That's okay, if you're the defender. If your side has the high ground in the dispute. If your side is crusading for what's *right*, it's justified by those in agreement with your beliefs. Being a blatant aggressor, not so much.

And self-defense, that's okay. But only if the loss of your own life is absolutely in the realm of possibility.

If predators exist in the animal kingdom, might they exist in human social structure? Might someone like me have a place in the natural order of things?

This idea had been slow to grow on me. I certainly didn't think about it when I was ten years old, looking at *The Book of Sharks*. I didn't think about it when I was in college and committed my first murder. But as I've moved forward, taking the lives of people who were predators of a different kind, it's come to mind more and more often. Maybe there needs to be a predator for those predators. Although they don't bring physical life to an end, they prey upon women — harass, belittle, marginalize, subjugate, punish, abuse. They effectively end the movement of women through their lives, which is a different kind of death. A death of their life force, their spirit.

Either way, I've grown very fond of sharks. It's not an opinion I share very often because most people think they're terrifying and vicious. Cruel, almost. They view sharks as deadly killers that maul adorable ocean-dwelling mammals, not to mention human beings. Sharks are the enemy. Just look at those teeth and you can see where their heads are at. But sharks didn't make any choice to have mouths that resemble a rack of knives. They are what they are.

I wondered what the shark tattooed on Sean's left foot meant to him. Yes, it was a beautiful piece of artwork. But he'd chosen a shark for a reason. It wasn't to intimidate business contacts because the tattoo was hidden in all circumstances related to business, except for the informal atmosphere of TruthTeller.

People choose tattoos because the image and design have deep symbolism for the bearer. The shark symbolized something to Sean. It reflected a part of how he saw himself. I had to believe that meant he knew very well he was also a predator. Whatever that meant to him.

33

I decided to post the video of Sean eyeing Tess on our Facebook page.

My decision came from pure predatory behavior. If he saw it, I wanted Sean to realize that although he might have control over certain aspects of my employment, he was not going to start pulling me into his personal problems, starting with Tess's decision to leave our little commune. Tess was leaving the house because he was a control freak. That's not the same as a predator, although there are similarities. And that similar streak in my own make-up is not lost on me.

This was the problem with our living situation — blurred lines. It was obvious from the start, but I don't think I realized how much the blurred lines of our relationships would blur the edges of the job I was hired to do. He treated me like a buddy who could help him with girl problems, and at the same time, he wanted me to be a social media star, generating tens of thousands of leads for our app, building excitement and demand.

Maybe that's why he kept delaying the announcement — he was terrified no one really wanted the app. Talking about it repeatedly at dinner parties might reassure him there was interest, but it was also going to thin his guest list. So far, he hadn't done a thing to raise the topic, spending his time focused on Tess. So for now, the guests were eager to return.

As long as he continued paying me a salary to get

attention on social media, I was going to do everything I could think of, short of betraying my own identity, to get that attention. The page needed a boost, a flood of comments and shares and likes and most of all, curiosity that brought people back more often, feeding their need for updates, longing to be part of the inner circle. Maybe that would translate to sales, at some point. It was certainly a better bet than a dinner party with an art gallery owner and a sports promoter, a guy Tess picked up at the airport and a personal-trainer-turned-stalker.

The video was edited and ready to go. All I had to do was write something pithy. I stared out the window, calmed as always by the lush greenery crowding close to the house, trying to think of the best approach.

I could talk about the gorgeous environment of Sean's dining room, describe the menu and hope that inciting envy got people engaged. But that seemed like a long shot. Sure, if someone is already famous, envy will bring out comments and attention. But TruthTeller was the new kid in the fourth-grade class, longing for someone to notice him and offer a seat at the lunch table.

The first step was to make people feel important, necessary. Noticed.

If I asked them to voice an opinion as to what Sean was thinking as he watched Tess, ignoring his other guests, their curiosity would be aroused. It might even spark debate — women, or men, who were captivated by his good looks wanting him to gaze at them in the same way, assuming it was lust or love. Some women might see it as predatory, a man who won't take no for an answer as he stares at a beautiful woman. And men...I wasn't sure how some men might interpret his expression. That unknown might really mix it up.

You never know how many different opinions there are on any topic until you make a statement online. And then, the world lets you know, tearing any opinion into fine shreds.

I decided to keep it simple — *Our CEO: What is he thinking? What does he want?*

I uploaded the video and clicked post.

Within seven minutes, the video had been viewed five times. That was good, although no reactions yet, not even the easy and innocuous thumb.

I went to the kitchen and made an espresso. I poured it over ice and added heavy cream, stirring it vigorously. I took a sip. Cold liquid and the electricity of caffeine shot into my bloodstream. I took another sip and returned to the office. I closed the door and settled on the small couch. I looked at one of the magazines on the coffee table. Tess had subscribed to several, as if she expected all kinds of meetings in her office, which had been the norm at CoastalCreative.

Was she surprised it hadn't happened that way, yet? Was she disappointed? Had she not even noticed? I flipped through glossy pages, pausing to read The Top Ten Tips for Social Media Success and the Five Essential Things you needed to know about Marketing on Twitter. When I got to an article about how Instagram can shoot your social cachet into the stratosphere, I closed the magazine. I took a few more fortifying sips of my icy coffee and returned to the desk.

There was one share, twenty-three thumbs up, five surprised emojis, and two comments.

A woman named Alicia had this to say: *He's proving why living and working together is not sustainable. There are too many layers, the potential for hidden agendas.*

Very clever of her. I didn't remember her name from the flurry of activity we'd had a month or so ago over Sean's vision, but I didn't remember many of those names at all, there had been so many. Presumably she was one who viewed his vision as a threat to couples and families.

The next comment was from Tami: *She's in trouble, and he's contemplating how to reprimand her.*

Then, in parentheses, Tami added — *(Is that you? I can't be sure from your profile picture, although it also looks like it could be the other woman who works there. If it's you, I'm thinking he doesn't like your approach to Facebook.)*

I laughed. Even with the closed door, Damien heard me, echoing my belly laugh with the precise timbre of my voice. I stood and picked up my drink. I wondered whether I could get some video of Damien, especially calling out *Chardonnay time*, before he moved out with Tess.

34

The Baxter Inn entrance was off an alley with a nondescript entrance that looked like nothing more than a door to a storage room. I opened the door and was faced with the tiniest of vestibules and stairs leading down to the cellar. I was wearing a skirt, thick black tights, and a black T-shirt under a short leather jacket with knee-high boots. Because the boots had a hard sole, prone to skidding, and the stairs were concrete coated with glossy paint, I stepped down slowly, curious about why this place was so popular if it was so dingy.

I passed through the door at the foot of the stairs and immediately reversed my opinion.

The room was dark, with the atmosphere of an ancient library. There were wide support posts along the center of the room. They were decorated with iron sconces that held fat candles. The enormous candles looked as if they'd been burning for fifty years, judging by the layers of hardened wax lying in strings on the sides of the candles that dripped the night away.

Two-top oak tables were arranged to the right of the support posts. Booths with plank benches lined the far wall. There was music playing, but at a volume that provided soothing background sound, softer than the lyrical buzz of conversation. The ceiling was low over the tables and higher over the bar area.

The bar ran along the left side of the room. Most of the seats were occupied on a Thursday evening. The shelves behind the bar itself were filled, counter to ceiling, with bottles of scotch, whiskey, and rye. There were easily five or six hundred different kinds. Wheeling ladders that are often used in libraries were placed at intervals in front of the shelves.

As I watched, a woman grabbed one of the ladders, swung her foot onto the second rung and scrambled up three more. She leaned to her left and grabbed a bottle off the shelf, scurrying back down to the floor. She eased out the cork and poured a thin stream of gold into a glass.

I studied the bar for several seconds, wondering if I might find something I liked since there were more than enough choices. Sitting on the bar were leather menus as robust as books. Several people were leafing through the copies placed in front of them.

I turned the other way, thinking of Carmen with her pixie haircut and her pointed chin.

Suddenly, a woman was beside me. She touched my arm with a firm press of her fingers. "Alex?"

I turned. "Yes."

The pixie haircut photograph she used on Facebook was obviously ancient. Her hair reached to the middle of her back, wavy and thick and slightly tangled. Like her sharp chin and the shape of her face in general, her shoulders and hips had sharp angles. She had a few inches on me. She wore flat boots, faded, torn jeans tucked into the boots, and a white low-cut blouse. Her neck was draped with chains, each one holding a tiny charm. Before she caught my eye, I noticed a kangaroo, a tiny gold cat, a pair of gold dice, and a locket.

"I'm Carmen. I have a table. There's too much talking about scotch if you sit at the bar." She smiled, but her eyes didn't follow the lead. She gestured toward a booth in the back corner where a large black purse sat prominently on the table and a pale pink coat was draped across the bench. "First, what do you want to drink?"

"I don't know anything about scotch. Get whatever you think is good." I pulled two tens out of my purse and held them out.

She waved them away. "Do you want a shot or something mixed?"

"A shot is good."

She turned and headed toward the bar.

I went to the table. I unzipped her purse a few inches and tucked the bills inside. I sat down and pushed the purse over against the wall. I glanced at the bar. It was rather trusting of her that she wasn't looking my direction, not at all worried about her purse.

A few minutes later she approached the table and placed two small glasses in the center. "This is Balblair."

I smiled.

"It's smooth, not too much peat. Most newbie scotch drinkers like it." She slid in across from me and picked up one of the glasses. "Cheers."

I touched her glass and took an exploratory sip.

"What do you think?"

"It will take some getting used to."

"It does grow on you." She took another sip.

I expected I would remain a martini drinker, but this was okay. It was soothing. I could see how it would be nice on a cold evening by a fire, maybe even more satisfying than an icy cold martini. But I do like the chill of a cold drink, even when the weather is cold.

I put down my glass. "So tell me about the statue. You said it doesn't belong to Sean."

"We should get to know each other first, don't you think?"

I didn't see why. We weren't there to become friends. "You kept my curiosity stoked for two weeks. So it's at the top of my mind. And I answered *your* question."

"Yes. But there's more to the story than just the statue."

"Like what?"

"Has Sean ever mentioned Terri?"

"I assume that's your sister?"

She nodded.

"That's all he told me."

She looked down. She picked up the drink and put the glass to her lips. She eased a tiny thread of dark gold alcohol into her mouth. "He really didn't say anything about her?"

"No." I put my hand around my glass, trying to decide whether I was ready for another taste of the burning liquid.

"He didn't bother to tell you she's dead?"

I kept my gaze on the scotch. This changed things. It changed my thoughts about Sean, and it changed how I viewed Carmen's behavior. "How did she die?"

"We were climbing. In Nepal. It was supposed to be a spiritual reconnection for both of us — with each other, with life. But things didn't go well from the start."

"Why?"

"The first day out, she told me she was pregnant. Not a great condition for a climb like that."

"Pregnant by Sean?" I picked up the glass and took a

deep sip. The alcohol flamed through my mouth and down my throat, but not with any more intensity than the thought of Sean with a child. A child that never came into being.

"Yes."

"Did he know?"

"Yes. But they weren't together when she told him."

"Oh." It was getting more complicated. It certainly explained something about Sean. The guy had ghosts I wasn't aware of. I suppose we all have ghosts that others aren't aware of. I know I do.

"The fourth day of our trip, she slipped and fell into a gorge. It was awful." Carmen's eyes filled with tears, but they didn't roll down her face, taking her thick mascara and artfully smudged eye liner with them.

"It sounds terrible."

She nodded. "So…Terri and I didn't get to sort things out between us. And that was so hard. So unfair…it's still hard. You have no idea."

"I guess when someone dies unexpectedly…"

"Especially when things were such a mess."

"Because of her pregnancy?"

"Not just…"

I waited. If I'd had a martini, I would have eaten an olive, taken another sip, but with this stuff, I wasn't sure. It didn't seem to be hitting me any harder than a martini. But at the rate this story was going, I could see another shot of scotch in my future.

Carmen got up and walked to the bar. She returned with a bowl of pretzel twists. "You looked like you need something to blunt the edge of the scotch." She smiled, her eyes still watery.

I ate a few pretzels and waited for the rest of the story. It was clear there was another piece coming.

She didn't speak.

Finally my curiosity won out. "Why were things a mess?"

She sighed. "This is why I said I wanted to get to know you. All of a sudden, I'm not sure why I'm telling you this. I don't know you at all. And I'm not sure…some of the things you post. Like that video. What was that about?"

"Just trying to get attention for the app."

"Is he okay with that?" She stared at me for a moment. "He doesn't know, does he?"

"Not yet." I gave her a triumphant smile.

"Why doesn't he use the Facebook page? Isn't this company his new…"

She stumbled and caught her breath over the obvious word she'd wanted to use there. She pushed her hair away from her eyebrow where it was falling, creeping across the edge of her eye like a spider with long, dark legs. She grabbed a handful of pretzels and put them all in her mouth at once. She chewed and swallowed, taking her time with it. "He should be out there himself, not you."

I shrugged. "He can't do everything."

"I need to talk to him."

"I can't help with that. The only reason I'm here is you were going to tell me about the statue." I took a sip of burning liquid. I ate two pretzels to chase it. I realized the flavor of the scotch might be growing on me. It wasn't much stronger than a martini, just different.

"Why can't you get him to post on Facebook so I can talk to him?"

What was this? First, Sean telling me to deal with women

he had dismissed from his life, and now one of them putting me in the same position. I wasn't a go-between. This wasn't a high stakes negotiation, or high school, for that matter.

Right now, it felt more like high school.

"I can't text him. He blocked me." Her voice was suddenly fierce, angry.

"Why do you need to talk to him?"

"I need to talk to him about the statue."

"Did it belong to your sister or something?"

"I have to talk to him."

"So you didn't lure me here to tell me its history, you did it to try to get me to do something for you?"

"I didn't lure you. I need to talk to him."

I took a sip of scotch. "I can't help with that."

"You have to try."

"If you can't get him to talk to you, what on earth makes you think I can? It makes no sense."

"Please."

I shook my head.

"It's..." she started to cry, the tears falling down her cheeks this time, black sludge following.

"Tell me what's going on."

"My sister and I wanted to hike in Nepal because it's supposed to be a spiritual place. We needed to heal our relationship. I was angry with her, and I shouldn't have been."

I stared at her. Had she pushed her sister? That couldn't be. And she wouldn't be telling me about it if she had. Besides, people don't do that. I do, but most people don't. It never even enters their minds.

35

"I don't know what's going on here, and aside from something I can't influence, I'm not sure what you want from me," I said.

"That's the only thing I want. You're the only person I know who can help. It's imperative that I talk to him."

"I work for Sean, I don't want to get sucked into his personal life."

"He used to be my boyfriend."

"You and Sean?"

She nodded. She wiped her finger under her right eye and blinked rapidly. "Before he got with Terri."

"Oh, that's messy."

"I told you it was a mess."

"I'm still not sure why you're telling me."

"I need to get to Sean and I have no one who can help. Except you. Please. You have to help me."

"Even if I wanted to get in the middle of his stuff, he's not going to listen to me. He didn't even want me chatting with you on Facebook."

She nodded. She finished her scotch and pushed the glass to the center of the table.

I took a sip of mine, glad I'd taken it more slowly. When the glass was empty, I was leaving. I felt like I'd been underground for hours, in the cellar of a stately old house, a different world where people disappeared into thick, rich alcohol that was an acquired taste. Most people like their alcohol cut with something sweet, or at least some sort of complementary flavor. And this stuff, a lot of it very expensive, according to the menu I'd looked at while she was ordering, was meant to be swallowed straight, no ice.

Scotch reminded me of sex — warm and seductive, leaving a nice heated glow as it made its way through your body. I wondered if that's what turned people into scotch aficionados.

I swallowed the last of it. "Thanks for the drink. I should get going."

She grabbed my wrist. "Please."

"You're not listening to me. I can't do anything to get him to talk to you."

"It's been so hard. My sister dead. And that sweet little child never had a single breath. I don't think you have any idea of the pain. And he…"

"Maybe not."

"I feel like a huge hole was blown out of my chest. I can hardly breathe. There's this cold wind, like an arctic blizzard, blowing through that hole, freezing the edges. It makes me so cold I don't know what I'm supposed to do."

"It sounds awful."

"I was with him and then he just…he just cut me out of his life. And later, a long time after, when I thought I had him out of my system, he started seeing my sister. Things didn't go very well between her and me, obviously. And then, he did the same to her. Right before he sold his company. Maybe it was the money, he knew he was going to be filthy rich. And I…all I wanted was to take care of my sister and her baby, to make things better. And she fell off the trail and down that canyon and…I don't want her to be dead!" The last words came out in a long, pitiful wail.

Several other drinkers turned to look at us, one of the men holding my gaze as if I were the one who had elicited that painful cry. I glared back at them until they turned their heads in another direction.

"I'll tell you about the statue, if you really have to know, if you can get Sean to talk to me," she said. "Then you'll understand."

"But why do you need to talk to him?"

"It's complicated."

"That's not a reason."

She said nothing.

"He seems very determined not to be in touch with you," I said.

She stared at me as if I'd said something completely irrelevant.

"You said you would tell me about the statue today. And here I am. Yet, no info."

"I know. I wanted you to meet me. To know what he did to us."

Part of me no longer cared what the story was with the statue. I assumed it was related to whatever hurt feelings and three-way drama had transpired between Carmen and Terri, Terri and Sean, Sean and Carmen. "I don't know how many times I can say this — he's not going to listen to me."

"Will you try? You don't have anything to lose."

"I work for him. Do you understand what that means? I can't be nagging him about someone he's made it clear he doesn't want to be in touch with. It would be better if you let it go, put it in the past." I ate a pretzel. "All those platitudes.

Concentrate on positive memories of your sister."

She stood suddenly. "You know what you're forcing me into, don't you?"

I shook my head. I didn't stand, tipping my head slightly to look up at her, towering over me with all that thick, dark hair brushing her cheeks.

"I have to talk to him. Nothing else matters in my life right now except getting his attention."

I waited.

"You're forcing me to use Facebook to get to him."

"Your call."

"I mean the TruthTeller page. If you're so fucking worried about your job, maybe you should worry about that. I could bring down that page."

"You could. But that won't get him talking to you."

"We'll see." Her expression softened slightly, as if she remembered I wasn't the one she hated, or whatever it was roiling inside of her — rage, hate, unrelieved grief, a fair amount of helplessness which is its own kind of wrath. "But I will use that page to provoke him into responding. I know he must look at it once in a while, maybe more than anyone realizes. Even you."

"How can you know that?"

"I know him. He likes to know what's going on."

I shrugged.

"I'll get to him on that page," she said. "It might take time, but like I said, it's pretty much all I'm living for." She walked away, her figure growing dimmer as she passed out of the light of the candles and into the shadows near the base of the stairs. A moment later, she was gone.

36

True to her word, Carmen got busy on our Facebook page before I arrived back at the house.

Luckily for me, Tess wasn't in the office. She wasn't home at all. She rarely was lately, off seeing to the details for her house, although I had no idea what sort of details. It had been nicely and authentically remodeled, she wasn't doing any major work that required choosing tile or bathroom fixtures or even paint colors. I suppose she had to be shopping for furniture.

She was sending daily reports to all three of us, so clearly she was working occasionally, using her laptop in her bedroom, or from a cafe, or wherever she was.

Damien was holding his own. After traveling all this way to be with her, I would have expected him to be put out that he sat alone in that cage all day and night. When I passed by, Tess was never there talking to him. He chattered at me when I was in the vicinity, but he wasn't shrieking or exhibiting any signs of unhappiness. Maybe after being cooped up in quarantine, his new home felt like a palace. Maybe there'd been so many other creatures, he was content with the solitude.

I went into the office, closed the door, and launched the Facebook page.

There were eighteen comments and twenty-four thumbs up for the video.

All but two of the comments were from women, and every single one thought Sean was in love with Tess. They were wrong, I didn't know what I'd captured in that video, but I was certain he was not in love with her. Although, I knew him, and for utter strangers, it might look very much like love, or lust. I acknowledged that. I was just disappointed with their lack of creativity. The best one so far had been Tami's, even though she mistakenly thought it was me in the video, she seemed to put more thought into her response.

The final comment was from Carmen.

He looks like a man hiding the truth.

I let the mouse hover over the bottom edge of her comment. It was my job to make people feel important by acknowledging and responding to what they had to say. But with her, I wasn't sure. First of all, it was a nonsensical comment. How can a man look like he's hiding the truth? If he's hiding it, then it wouldn't be visible on his face. I suppose she meant looking like he was lying. Second of all, or maybe that was first of all, it was clearly self-serving. I suppose that was to be expected. She'd said she wanted to force him to react. Of course she would post things that might spark anger, enough to make him respond to her.

How could I *like* the comment? That's the problem with those damn thumbs. Are they signs of agreement only or are they acknowledgements that you understand what the other is saying even if you don't agree? Or are they just polite conventions, like saying *how are you* when you have no interest in knowing *how* someone is, beyond *fine*. Meaningless words, meaningless thumbs.

I clicked the surprised face. It seemed more fitting, more non-committal.

Then I realized — she was going to use me to get to him after all. My refusal to help her get in touch with him meant nothing. By using Facebook to get through to him, she was forcing me to make this kind of decision for every single thing she posted. And if others responded to her comments, it would get worse.

I ran back up the page, liking all the other comments. Carmen was the only one who received the yellow face.

One person had written that Sean was trying to hide his feelings for Tess because he didn't want to jeopardize the success of his company. She added — *A well-publicized harassment charge could destroy it. And it if wasn't that at all, if his feelings were returned, a love affair could devastate it even more thoroughly.*

Which is more dangerous, harassment or love?

Most would say harassment, but history says love. Unrequited love. But you could say that even mutual love has brought down nations. After Marc Antony's affair with Cleopatra helped contribute to a split in the Roman government and led to the famous lovers' suicide, the Roman Empire prospered as it solidified under a single ruler. But Egypt was never the same. Except for a brief reign by her son, Cleopatra was the last pharaoh and the once-breathtaking kingdom of Egypt became a province of the Roman Empire.

I clicked reply and took my hands off the keyboard for a moment. After I'd composed my thoughts, I began typing, my only desire to get the conversation rolling, to draw in more curious commenters.

It's interesting that you thought of harassment before love.

Instead of hovering over the page, waiting for more, I

clicked over to Twitter. I'd sadly neglected it while I was fiddling with the video. For the next half hour I re-tweeted like a crazed gull, grabbing bites of information and flinging them across the waves. My mind was blank in terms of coming up with something worthwhile to say on behalf of TruthTeller, but skimming the world's thoughts and re-tweeting the most interesting can keep you busy for hours.

People are very witty on Twitter. Maybe because wit is part of its name.

37

I sent a text message to Tess and suggested we go out to dinner. She responded immediately and eagerly, if you can feel such a thing as eagerness through a text message, and I think you can. Even without emojis, you can feel enthusiasm in the words that are chosen, you can feel the level of interest in whether or not more details are added to the plan. She not only suggested a place, Uncle Ming's dumpling bar, she said she'd make a reservation.

We left the house at three, long before it was time for Gavin to begin preparing dinner. Neither of us had spoken to Sean.

The Uber dropped us off right in front of the restaurant. We walked to a door that opened to stairs leading underground. It was looking as if wintertime in downtown Sydney was all going to be spent in cellars. Being below street level naturally increases your sense of being confined. If it were to come to that, the avenues of escape are fewer, and more likely to be blocked. Floods come to mind. So do earthquakes and armed robbery, but Sydney doesn't have earthquakes and they have very few guns, so perhaps the underground threat was much less than I imagined. There was still the thought of a flood, water pouring in and seeking its lowest spot, filling up the space, consuming everyone trapped inside.

At the bottom of the stairs was a square lobby, two walls

lined with cushioned benches. The hostess checked our reservation and grabbed some menus. Strings of red beads were hung like a curtain in the doorway that led into the restaurant itself. We followed her through the opening, the strands plucking at our hair.

Uncle Ming's is an opium den-inspired cocktail and dumpling bar. Uncle Ming reportedly began his career as a policeman in Shanghai, collecting protection money from opium traders. For unknown, but easily guessed reasons, he had to leave China in the late 1920s. He settled in Sydney where he opened a place for locals to meet and have a drink.

It was a charming, atmospheric place. The free-standing tables were small, but the booths were larger, and secluded, with half walls that formed tiny private rooms. The music was thumping and the bar was as crowded as the eating area. Later, I discovered the restrooms had Chinese language lessons piped in. You could learn to ask *where is the train station* while you peed. I was pretty sure I wouldn't remember the phrase, but I wished I could. I was tempted to linger at the sink, soaping my hands a second time so I could learn how to greet people and ask for a taxi as well.

We both ordered an Empire's Sun which featured Tanqueray Ten, lychee liqueur, rose, and lavender. It was refreshing and carried quite a kick.

Instead of displaying the food on small, constantly circling carts like most Dim Sum places, ordering was off the menu. We started with vegetable egg rolls, steamed pork dumplings, and barbecued chicken wings. I could have done without the mess of the wings, but they were tasty, so I suppose it made up for all the sticky sauce on my fingertips.

Tess talked about her new house for nearly twenty

minutes. She had indeed been furniture shopping as well as organizing the schedule for cleaners and a gardener and other minor work that the place needed in order to perfect it for her move-in.

By the time she wound down, we'd consumed all the food and were looking at the menu again. This time, we ordered a different drink — Chang Mai Chillers, also with Tanqueray Ten, mixed with Amaretto and passionfruit.

The thing about Dim Sum is you keep eating it, because you're ordering a few bites at a time. When your tiny plate is filled, there's no doubt you can consume it easily. Even if you're full, it's only a bit more. And then it's replaced with another small portion, still easy to consume, just a few more bites. It's the same with Tapas. Before you know it, your stomach is ready to explode. The poor organ has been filled to overflowing for half an hour and you didn't even notice, the flavors taking over your brain, along with all the feel-good chemicals that rush out when your body's presented with spicy sauce and soft noodles, meat and the crunch of delicately sliced vegetables.

"I meant to ask you…" I kept my tone casual, hoping she wouldn't see the abrupt change of subject as anything more than a randomly surfacing memory. "What do you know about Sean's ex-girlfriend?"

"What does that have to do with anything?" Tess closed her chopsticks around a chicken dumpling.

"I guess she died."

"How do you know?" Her voice sounded off, as if she'd let slip something she wasn't supposed to.

"Did you know?"

She took a sip of her drink and said nothing. The music

filled the room, swelling around us, making the silence seem less awkward than it might under normal circumstances.

"A woman who used to know him was making comments on his Facebook page."

"What woman?"

Carmen felt like such a part of my life, I was sure I'd discussed her and her effort at sabotage with everyone, to one extent or another. But now, I couldn't remember whether I'd mentioned her to Tess at all. Maybe I hadn't.

Tess closed her lips around the straw in her drink, then pulled it out of her mouth without taking a sip. "And why are you in such an intimate conversation with her that she's telling you about Sean's ex?"

"She's the ex's sister."

Tess gave a single nod and held my gaze.

"Did you know his girlfriend died?"

"I don't see why that's anything we need to talk about."

"I just thought it was…she was pregnant. Did you know that?"

She continued to hold my gaze.

"Did you know?"

She sighed. "Yes. I knew. So what?"

"It's just…it explains a lot about him."

"What does it explain?"

"He has secrets."

"I don't think it's such a big secret."

"Well he acted like it was a secret. When I asked him, so I could figure out where Carmen was coming from, he didn't tell me any of that. He told me to get rid of her, to not let her post on our page, as if I can control that."

"And yet, you are allowing it. It sounds like you're

encouraging her."

"No. It was a private chat."

"That's worse."

"Why?"

"You should gently discourage her. You need to focus on customers. Not trolls."

"If I ignore her, she might attack us, dominate the page."

"Well you need to get a handle on it."

I took a long sip of my drink. I swished the other half of my dumpling around in the puddle of chili oil and popped it in my mouth. I chewed carefully and tried to think about what I wanted to say. "I was surprised that he'd been through something so tragic and never said anything."

"Why would he?"

"Well for one thing, this woman is putting stuff on our page and I asked him who she was and he didn't say a word about it."

"Because it has nothing to do with her making comments on Facebook. I'm thinking you don't have this social media thing under control at all."

"Have you tried it? Getting people to be fascinated by your bullshit is harder than you might think."

She laughed.

I was pleased that she'd laughed. She did see some of the stupidity of my job. In so many ways my job was easy — screwing around online. But in the important ways, it was next to impossible. I felt like I was biding my time, creating vapor until Sean and Tess woke up and realized it was completely unnecessary. Maybe the people who did nothing more than post lame ads to keep their brand out there had it right. Maybe we should have done paid advertising on all the sites and not tried to do it for free, thinking we could make something viral, when in reality, nothing can be *made* viral. The very nature of a virus is something that has a will and direction of its own. It comes on unexpectedly, choosing its own path through the public consciousness.

"This woman wants something from him. I'm not really sure what, and it would have been helpful to know the whole story. That's all I'm saying. Her sister died. It puts her activity in a different light."

Tess leaned back in her chair. She moved away from the table and crossed her legs, showing off her new brown leather riding boots. They were exquisite, and I wanted a pair like them. It's silly the way women love riding boots when they haven't been near a horse in ten years, but there's something sleek and casual about them. They're comfortable and they look classy. What more could you want?

"I don't know why he didn't tell you." She pushed her glass to the side. "Let's get another drink. I can't eat any more, but a drink would be nice. I feel like getting a little drunk."

"Celebrating your escape to freedom?"

"Something like that."

We ordered another round of Empire's Sun.

I was feeling a slight buzz. Diving into the third drink intensified the feeling. I had the impression the drinks had gotten stronger with each order. Maybe it was a thank you to people who lingered and enjoyed the atmosphere. I smiled and took another sip. "Is there anything else I should know about his ex, and her sister?"

"As far as I know, that's it."

"She's pretty upset. It sounds like she hasn't gotten over

her sister's death."

"I'm not sure what that has to do with Sean."

"Well there is something else."

"What?"

"He hasn't said anything to you about Carmen?"

She shook her head.

"He used to be with her too. Both sisters."

"I don't imagine that ended well."

"It's hard to see how it could."

"Then you know everything you need to. She obviously has an agenda. Figure out how to manage it."

Tess wasn't much help. I'd thought she would know more. I could tell there was nothing left. "It will be strange without you in the house."

"But more professional, I think."

"Maybe."

"Have you thought about getting your own place?" she said.

"No."

I'd thought the three drinks might ease things between us, which had grown into something I no longer recognized. I still considered her a friend, and I think she saw me the same way, but it wasn't like it had been when we worked at CoastalCreative.

Still, it was possible she saw it differently, because after that, she suggested a fourth drink. Then the conversation shifted significantly — to our thoughts about Australia and Australian lifestyle and Australian men. And it felt like we were friends again.

38

Sean watched headlights scoop the darkness from the front of the house, flashing briefly through the windows beside the front door, as a car turned into the driveway. He took a few steps back from the door and glanced at the bird, who was watching him.

His crown feathers were down, the bird clearly comfortable with Sean's presence in the shadowy foyer at well past midnight. But it was definitely keeping an eye on him. Sean worried about the poor thing. The foyer hadn't been the best choice for the cage location. Most of the day, the bird was alone out here. The isolation had made him louder. He laughed harder and shouted his favorite phrases to make sure he was heard.

He should probably give some thought to suggesting they move the bird to the great room. If Tess stayed, that is. He was still working out how he was going to make sure that happened. He couldn't allow her to leave. Yes, she'd purchased a house, but that could be fixed. He needed her here. He needed her steadying presence, her incredible calm. Most of all, he needed the balance of four.

Groups of three were nothing but conflict and back-stabbing and ever-shifting allegiances. Only in geometry was the triangle considered an unbreakable structure. When it came to human beings, a triangle was weak, prone to fracture and misery.

Look at the situation with Carmen and Terri and him over the years. Of course they hadn't been a threesome in the physical sense. They hadn't even spent a lot of time with all three of them together, but the desires of the third person in the triangle were always present, influencing the other two. Carmen on one side, Terri on the other. The two of them ganging up on him, or one of them whispering to him about the other. Carmen always jealous of her more beautiful and more confident sister, Terri always suspicious that Carmen was trying to worm her way back into Sean's life.

It was exhausting.

He wanted balance. He wanted four. He wanted…it was just…familiar to him.

The house was silent, but he couldn't pick up any sounds of them getting out of the car.

A moment later, a key scraped the inside of the lock, the mechanism turned, and the door opened.

Tess stepped inside first. Alex lingered on the patio behind her.

Sean smiled. "So glad you're going out. That's fantastic. See, this is working."

Tess gave him what could only be described as a pitying smile. "We just had dinner. It's normal. Not something worth waiting up to comment on."

He ignored the smile, and her tone, and her caustic words. "Did you meet anyone interesting?"

"Just Alex." She laughed.

The bird laughed with her. Alex joined the chorus.

"But you didn't meet her. You already…" He was confused.

Alex closed the door. "I need to crash."

Tess tugged Alex toward her in a grandiose hug. They laughed harder.

"Empire's Sun!" Tess said as if she were getting ready to lead a rugby cheer.

"Empire's Sun!" Alex shouted. She wriggled out of Tess's arm and moved toward the stairs.

They were drunk. Not falling down drunk, but definitely feeling it. He'd never seen either one of them like this, for all the evenings they'd spent drinking, or getting high.

He wasn't sure whether he should read something into it. How much had they had? Or were they putting it on, trying to deliver some sort of message about having a great time without him and Gav? Maybe just without him. He felt his face contort into a disapproving grimace. He didn't want it to, but the muscles contracted with a will of their own. He tried to combat it with an extra large smile.

"What's so funny?" Alex said.

"Nothing."

"You're grinning like a mad man."

"Just amused that you're drunk."

"Not drunk," Alex said. "Relaxed." She walked up the stairs, taking great care with the placement of each foot in the way that people aware of how drunk they are tend to do. She disappeared down the hallway.

Tess pressed the switch for the patio light and started up the stairs.

"It's good that you had fun. Had a chance to relax," he said.

Tess continued walking. She didn't even look back down in his direction.

He turned out the foyer light and went into the kitchen.

He took a beer out of the fridge, opened it, swallowed a goodly amount, and went into the billiards room. Now, he wouldn't be able to sleep at all.

He took another swallow of beer and put the bottle on a table. He chalked a cue, racked the balls, and broke them. Balls scattered like mice racing toward hiding spots when a cat creeps into the yard. He picked solids and began knocking them in.

After he'd sunk four, he rested the cue against the table and took a few more swigs of beer. He went to the glass door and looked out at the dark yard.

There had to be a way to keep Tess in the house. A half idea was forming in his head. He'd known since she made her announcement that he wasn't going to let her go easily. She didn't get to act so enthused about the vision for the company and then abandon the others mid-stream. Not even mid-stream. Sure she could still do her job while living elsewhere, but that wasn't the point. There was so much more to their venture than just the app.

He'd messed up. A lot. The murder investigations hadn't helped. Karen drowning in his pool…But he also hadn't implemented enough structure. He hadn't made it clear what was expected.

Why was it so hard to communicate a vision to other people? It was the one small thing, and yet a great thing, that gave him doubts about his leadership ability. He wanted them enthused, driving toward a mutual goal. He wanted the same energy he felt coursing through his own veins flowing through theirs, pushing them forward. He wanted them to experience what burned inside of him, that intense desire to help the world see that life could be entirely different.

Life didn't have to go on the same way, decade after decade, the human race marching to early graves because of epic internal conflicts between loving their work and resenting its drain on their personal lives. And yes, of course it was more difficult when workers had families, but they weren't there yet. This was the embryonic stage, and he couldn't even get three people to fully commit to the experiment.

Maybe it was unrealistic. Maybe…He refused to consider that. Tess had thrown a grenade into the middle of everything and he couldn't let her simply walk out. They hadn't even introduced the product yet. This was the most critical phase.

Watching her stumble in the front door with Alex at her side had poked something at the back of his mind. As she grabbed Alex in that hug, a wild gesture unlike anything he'd ever seen from her, he'd realized there was much more to the relationship between those two women than he'd recognized. He'd known they were friends, known they were close, but…

Relationships between women were tricky. You never knew what was really going on. They could act like the most bitter of enemies, and then you discovered they were as intimate as sisters, even when they were sisters. He shivered.

He'd always known Tess thought highly of Alex, but tonight, he'd seen something else. A need, bordering on love in Tess's eyes. Tess needed Alex, maybe more than she even recognized. Alex filled some vacant spot that Tess felt in her own psyche. She would never let go of Alex, or let anything come between them. She would defend Alex to the death, despite the friction he'd sometimes seen between them. None of that mattered.

Alex was the key to keeping Tess in this house. It was so obvious. Why hadn't he seen it weeks ago? He downed the rest of his beer and left the pool game incomplete.

39

Tess was surprised at what a good time she'd had with Alex. For the first time in quite a while, they'd both forgotten themselves and the boss-employee stumbling block. They drank more than they should have and probably said a few things they shouldn't have, but it was so good to be out of that house. She'd felt like a normal human being, two friends hanging out after work, strangers to everyone around them.

Until they got home. Sean had stood in the entryway like a father waiting for his curfew-busting teenage daughters. He tried too hard to be friendly and approving, when really, he was angry about something. Whether it was his lingering upset that she was leaving his cozy little prison or jealousy over her and Alex, or something else entirely, she didn't care.

She felt she could breathe.

She turned over and tugged the pillow into the curve of her neck. She should get up. It was past ten, but the bed was so warm and comforting.

Part of the reason for not wanting to get up was knowing that all kinds of social land mines awaited her downstairs. For years, she'd enjoyed her first cup of coffee alone. Now, even a simple cup of espresso required a lot of back and forth discussion over who was having some, or what other drink they preferred on any given morning.

In less than four weeks, she would be rising when she pleased, facing nothing but the view of her own back patio and garden. The only voice would be Damien's. The only cup of coffee she would brew would be her own. And it wouldn't be espresso every damn day.

She got up and went to the desk. She flipped open her leather-bound notebook and went to the back page. She counted out the days until the house belonged to her. Every morning, she would mark off one day. It would remind her of how fast the time was moving, no matter how it felt, the sense of interminable waiting.

She took a shower and dressed in jeans and a white turtleneck sweater. A partial blow-dry was enough, ditto for a bit of mascara and lip gloss. The gloss wasn't even necessary since she'd be eating breakfast.

Her stomach growled and rumbled with its desire for food, for something to soak up the alcohol, along with the inevitable insulin rush from all those noodles. But they were so good. She hadn't eaten that much in ages, and she'd felt she couldn't stop.

In the kitchen, the oven was on and the smell of baking eggs and cheese filled the room. "I made a quiche," Sean said.

His voice startled her. She hadn't noticed him, sitting on the couch facing the empty TV screen, his back to the kitchen. The rest of the space appeared dark in contrast to the sunlight spilling into the kitchen area. She walked toward the opening between the two rooms. "I didn't see you there."

He spoke without turning to look at her. "The quiche will be done in ten minutes. And it'll be great with buttered toast, don't you think?"

"Sounds good," she said.

She returned to the kitchen counter and began measuring out espresso beans to make herself a cup. She didn't offer one to Sean. When he heard the grinder chewing beans, he didn't ask.

A few minutes later, he entered the kitchen. He grabbed two oven mitts, opened the oven door, and pulled out the baking dish. He set the quiche on a sandstone trivet. "Give it a minute to cool and settle," he said.

"Sure." She walked toward the windows and looked outside. The air in the room felt heavy. Maybe it was the heat from the oven, the thick smell of cheese. She heard bread drop into the toaster and the sounds of him removing butter and jam from the fridge, pouring orange juice.

"Ready?" he said.

She turned from the window and went to the bar. "Where are the others?"

"I don't know. Sleeping, I assume."

"I doubt Alex is sleeping. I'm sure she went for a run."

"After the way you two sounded last night, I can't imagine she's running."

"Drinking never stops her."

He cut a wedge of quiche and put it on a plate. He handed her the plate with several slices of already buttered toast.

She picked up a piece of toast and took a bite, followed by a sip of espresso.

"I wanted to talk to you about something," he said. "First. Can I apologize again for rejecting you that time you…"

"I told you there's nothing to discuss, or apologize for. I've forgotten it entirely."

"I don't want you to feel upset, or think it's come between us."

"Of course it hasn't."

"Good."

"Good," she said. She took a bite of quiche. "Delicious."

"Thank you."

They ate in silence for several minutes.

"And another thing," he said. "I think I haven't clearly explained the vision for TruthTeller."

She smiled at her plate, unsure whether he could see the shift in her expression. "You've explained it quite thoroughly. Many times."

"Then why did you go off and buy a house without discussing it with me?"

"Did you really just say that?"

"Yes, because you should have."

"It's my life and my decision. My money. There's nothing to discuss with you, or anyone else."

"Part of the vision…"

"I understand the vision, Sean. But I became part of this company because of your vision for the product. Not for your working environment utopia."

"The two are interconnected."

"In your mind."

"Not only that."

"Yes, only that."

"I can't have you leave."

"It's a done deal."

"It doesn't have to be. I don't think you realize how this will fracture everything. The balance is gone."

"Don't be dramatic."

"I need you to stay, at least until the product is launched."

She laughed. "And when is that? Never, if it means I'll leave?"

"You haven't given this a chance." He gestured toward the ceiling, sweeping his arm out past her shoulder to indicate the dining room and the rest of the house beyond.

She pushed her plate away. She picked up the half-eaten piece of toast and slid off the bar stool, grabbing her cup with her free hand.

"Where are you going?"

"To eat in peace. This is a perfect example of why I need to get out of here."

"Get out? You make it sound like a prison."

"Sometimes, that's what it feels like."

"Hyperbole isn't helpful."

"Is it hyperbole?" She smiled.

"Please wait. I'm not finished."

She took another bite of toast and put her cup on the end of the counter. "I don't want to talk about this. I need to move into my own place and it's not going to affect TruthTeller...at all."

"It affects me."

"Maybe it does, but that's not the issue."

"And that affects TruthTeller."

"That's your problem."

"Please sit down."

"Stop trying to pressure me. I don't like it, and your attitude will sour everything. Do you want to destroy the whole company over a silly argument about who sleeps where?"

He stood and took a step toward her. It seemed like an attempt at intimidation, but she didn't move. If he wanted to stand too close, that was his discomfort to deal with. She could take it. He would find out she had no intention of yielding her ground, physically or psychologically.

"Maybe the company is already destroyed." His voice was glum and sulky.

She picked up her cup and took a sip of espresso. It was cold.

"I've told you before, my feelings about Alex," he said.

"And what does that mean?"

"That she's a predator. I can't manage her without you living here. If you leave, I'm going to have to cut her loose."

She put her cup on the counter again, too hard. The sound of ceramic on granite was sharp and jarring. She balanced the piece of toast on top of the cup. "You can't do that."

"I absolutely can."

"Are you threatening me?" She laughed. "I think you are. That's not how you manage a company, that's not how you build solid working relationships. You thought I wanted out of here before…"

"You can fuss all you want," he said. "Actions have consequences. Cause and effect. You want to leave and unbalance things, but I need someone to manage the unruly person you hired."

"Unruly?" She laughed again.

"It's not a game. I'm serious. If you leave, Alex is gone." He picked up her toast and cup. He went to the sink and poured the espresso down the drain. He dropped the toast in the trash.

She didn't like that gesture at all. The espresso may have been cold and muddy and the toast no longer crisp — she didn't care about not consuming any more — but he'd done it to exert his control. She wanted to rush across the room and tackle him to the ground, pummel his chest. There were only a few moments in her life when she'd felt such an urge toward violence. He was a great guy — fun and smart, creative and knowledgeable. But right now she hated his guts. He was absolutely threatening her, and the problem was, she couldn't immediately think how she would escape. She was not giving up her house, but she couldn't do nothing and watch Alex lose her job, get deported.

For a moment, she imagined her life without Alex. That life looked dull. It felt as if there would be a shortage of oxygen.

40

Portland

Jake was taking *The Book of Sharks* back to the school library. For good. He'd had enough of it, read all the interesting stories, looked at the pictures multiple times. He was moving on to other things. Now, he was studying deep sea life — creatures that live down where human beings can't go without special equipment. He was into freakish species of the deep like the dragonfish, which looks even worse than it sounds, and the frilled shark that swallows its prey whole, and the Blobfish, which lives at depths of almost three quarters of a mile where the pressure is one hundred times greater. The fish isn't really a blob, it just turns into one as it suffers the effects of decompression coming up from the depths of the ocean.

My parents weren't aware of this shift in his interests. I'm not sure they would have liked the freakish aspects — his fascination with creatures disturbing to look at, his fascination with a touch of the morbid. Although, since those fish had been designed by the same creator they believed had formed each of them and their children, my parents couldn't very well reject them for being unpleasant and unworthy of our interest. But they didn't like us putting undue attention on the abnormal, whether it was at the bottom of the ocean or written about online or in the books we read or the television shows we watched. The Bible didn't count.

I wanted Jake to check the book out again, just for me.

"It's a pain. I'm not going to do that," he said.

"Why not?"

"You've read it more times than I have. You must have it memorized by now."

"I like the pictures too. And I like re-reading things."

"That's a waste of your brain. There are millions of books in the world. You shouldn't read the same one over and over."

"I don't see why not, if it's interesting. A lot of those millions of books are probably boring."

"You don't know if you haven't tried them."

"I said *probably*. Besides, I've read enough boring books to know that a bunch of ones I haven't read would also be boring."

"You only read kid books. You don't know what you're talking about."

"I want the shark book."

He grabbed the book off his nightstand and shoved it into his backpack. He put his hand on my shoulder and nudged me toward the bedroom door. I made myself trip on the stack of paperbacks on the floor.

"Watch out."

"Can I look at it now? You're not taking it back until tomorrow."

He sighed. He pulled it out of his backpack and handed it to me. "I want it back before dinner."

"You sound like Mom."

"Maybe there's a reason she sounds like that."

I took the book and went to my room. Instead of

opening it, I stared at the cover. I wanted the book. I wasn't allowed unsupervised time on the computer. I only went to the school library when the whole class went for library day, and those visits were short and restricted to books on our reading list. It was a big list, but still...

There had to be a way to keep this book.

I tried to think of how I could make it mine without him knowing for sure I'd taken it. Maybe there was a way to make him think he'd lost it. I opened the book slowly and turned to the diagram of a nurse shark. I studied the different pieces of its anatomy. The nurse shark has a spiral valve that helps make up for the short intestine compared to other animals, allowing the shark more time to absorb nutrients. I couldn't stop looking at that strange organ.

An hour later, I walked down the hall to Jake's room. He was seated at his desk, his back to the door. He was leaning over a math book, tapping his pencil eraser on the page as if the solution to the problem would emerge at the sound of repeated taps.

"Here's the book," I said.

"Just drop it on my bed."

I stepped into his room and placed the book on his bed. I stood there for a moment, still thinking about how I could make that book mine.

"What are you doing?" he said.

"Nothing."

"Then get lost."

I picked up the book. "I'll put it in your backpack for you."

"Fine. Thanks. It's right there." He turned partially, pointing his pencil at his pack on the floor, leaning against the side of his dresser.

I'd already seen it sitting there. I wasn't blind, but I didn't want him to tell me to forget it, so I said nothing. I went to his pack and unzipped the outer pocket. "Right here?"

"Sure."

I put the book inside and zipped it closed.

In my room, I set my alarm clock for three in the morning. I turned the volume down to the lowest setting. At bedtime, after my mother came in for prayers, I placed the clock under my pillow so I would hear it.

There was a rule in our house that all backpacks and jackets had to be lined up near the side entrance the night before. The purpose was to prevent last-minute morning scrambles. And that way, my father could take a peek to ensure homework was done well and there was no contraband buried beneath our schoolbooks.

I woke at three and crept downstairs.

I unzipped Jake's pack and removed the book. I zipped it partially closed, leaving a gap that would suggest it was possible for the book to have fallen out. I tossed his jacket on top, covering the partially unzipped outer pocket, and returned to my room. I re-set the alarm for six, turned up the volume, and placed the clock on my nightstand.

I slid the shark book into a Ziploc bag and taped the bag to the back of my large desk drawer. There was enough space between the drawer and the back of the enclosure that the drawer was still able to close without leaving a gap at the front.

The next morning, there was the usual chaos of dressing, fighting over bathroom time, breakfast, packing lunches, and getting into the car for the trip to the high school first, followed by the elementary school. There was always a lot of activity and confusion, despite the orderly set-up with backpacks and coats.

Of course Jake blamed me, once he realized the book was missing. Who else would have taken it?

But he couldn't be *sure*.

The zipper wasn't closed. The book *could* have fallen out. Someone else might have slipped it out, although that was unlikely.

What worked in my favor, was that he forgot to return the book to the library the day after I'd taken it. It was hard to argue that it was absolutely impossible for the book to have fallen out in the three days it took him to remember. It could be anywhere. It had rained between the morning after I took it and the day he remembered to return it to the library.

He knew I'd done it. But he couldn't be absolutely, one hundred percent *sure*.

41

Sydney

Suggesting that Carmen was getting busy on the TruthTeller Facebook page was one of the most profound understatements imaginable. The next time I opened the page, I had to get up and leave the office in order to think straight. I mixed a martini and took several icy cold sips. I considered taking the drink to my bedroom and having a cigarette along with it, but finally decided I'd prefer to keep the drink beside me at my desk, sipping slowly while I tried to clean up the mess Carmen had made.

Despite the ability Facebook offers to prevent people from posting their comments on your page, I'd left that feature on and unmoderated. It seemed important to have an open community. When you call yourself TruthTeller, you'd better make an effort at being truthful. If you want people to engage, you can't set security options that prevent them from engaging. Carmen had taken full advantage.

At the top of the page, she'd posted a selfie capturing a close-up of her left eye, eyebrow, and a section of her thick, dark hair brushing across her temple. Below the selfie was a string of comments that I had to count three times to get an accurate total — fifty-three.

Carmen Dunn: *Guess who?*

Carmen Dunn: *Recognize my eyes? Or I should say, my eye. You said you could drown in them. Remember?*

Carmen Dunn: *Like how my hair is long again? You said I looked exotic with long hair.*

Carmen Dunn: *I know you're there, Sean.*

Carmen Dunn: *Your heart and soul is all over the name, and the vision for this company. I'd recognize you anywhere, even without a profile pic.*

Carmen Dunn: *Very intriguing video. Whoever she is, that woman sure has gotten under your skin. I know what you're thinking in that video. I know exactly what you're thinking…because I KNOW you.*

Carmen Dunn: *I have so much to say. I wonder how many comments I'll end up leaving? I bet I could write a hundred things and I still wouldn't be finished.*

Carmen Dunn: *I'll never be finished. Some people find it easy to remove people from their lives. Me? Not so much. Once someone has my heart, she has it forever. So does he. I cherish human beings for the miraculous creatures they are. They shouldn't be treated lightly, tossed aside.*

Carmen Dunn: *I guess I gave away who it is, didn't I. So I didn't need my mysterious selfie after all.*

Carmen Dunn: *Or maybe I didn't give anything away. Maybe there are quite a few women who might say the same things to you.*

Carmen Dunn: *In fact, I know that's the truth. TruthTeller! Ha. My sister could write every one of these messages. You know that and I know that.*

Carmen Dunn: *Of course, you also know it's not her that's writing these things. How could she?*

Carmen Dunn: *I'm guessing you'll show up here. Eventually. I can't believe you've delegated something as important as your Facebook presence to an employee.*

Carmen Dunn: *You do know it's important for you to show your face, right?*

Carmen Dunn: *Are you being lazy or mysterious or something else? I can't decide. I'm thinking it's lazy.*

Carmen Dunn: *As soon as I wrote that, it occurred to me it might not be lazy or mysterious. It might be that you're a tiny bit afraid. When you leave such a mess behind you, as you slash and burn your way through other people's hearts, showing up on social media might be downright terrifying.*

Carmen Dunn: *Are you terrified, Sean?*

Carmen Dunn: *Are you worried about payback?*

Carmen Dunn: *But that's not really what I want. You know it's not what I want, although at this point, maybe I am wanting it more than I did at first.*

Carmen Dunn: *Are you reading these messages Sean?*

Carmen Dunn: *If you send your lackey to respond, I'm not going to be happy. Man up. I hate that phrase, but in this case, it's definitely appropriate. Own your company, own your social media, own what you've done. Give me the courtesy of a fucking response!*

Carmen Dunn: *I wonder where you got the idea for your app? Pretty clever.*

Carmen Dunn: *I wonder where you live and what you do all day.*

Carmen Dunn: *I wonder if there's a new woman in your life. I'm guessing, after all this time, there must be. Maybe the woman in the video, and you're already tired of her.*

Carmen Dunn: *How is life treating you, Sean? How is life? You used to say that a lot. Do you still?*

Carmen Dunn: *You've kept yourself very well hidden on line, but I guess that doesn't work when you want to launch a new company. Can't stay in the shadows.*

Carmen Dunn: *Of course, I'm still blocked. And I don't have* your address. *I don't have anything, Mr. Farmer. You are a hard man to track down. But then, suddenly, here you are.*

Carmen Dunn: *But I still don't see you. I don't see any comments from you. I don't know your thoughts about your vision for your company, only what you funnel through Alex-an-dra. It's like you need your own one-person PR company now, is that it?*

Carmen Dunn: *If you aren't reading this, I wonder if she'll show you the page.*

Carmen Dunn: *I wonder a lot of things.*

Carmen Dunn: *I'm not going away.*

The rest of the comments were similar, but became less interesting and somewhat repetitious. I stared at the flood of words, every single one of them *liked* and *wowed* and *heart-ed*, a few sad faces thrown in for variety, by the ever-present Jane and Lara, eager to see conflict at the expense of TruthTeller. I wondered what other Facebook pages those two stalked, encouraging trolls to speak their minds. I'd read a lot about trolls themselves, but had never witnessed this sort of troll fan club phenomena.

Their activity ensured that Carmen's trolling remained front and center in everyone's feed. Her mixture of humiliation and rage was stunning. I'd known she wanted something, and now I wished I was back in that wondering state. Had meeting her forced this into the open? But I didn't see that I'd had a choice. It all kind of evolved on its own.

As I ate an olive and watched the screen, I was notified that someone was typing a comment. I couldn't imagine she had any more to say.

The comment posted, failing to acknowledge the other fifty-three, as if they were irrelevant.

Anita Goyant: *Hi Sean. Cool page. So glad I found you on line!*

This was followed by a comment consisting of nothing but two pink hearts. Then…

Anita Goyant: *Loved your dinner party. Exquisite. Like you. LOL. Thanks for inviting me. I love that we're reconnecting.*

And then, as if it wasn't enough, another wordless comment with eight red hearts.

I took a long swallow of my drink, ate the second olive, and closed the Facebook page.

42

As Tess placed her foot on the bottom step of the staircase, she heard one of the office doors open. A moment later, Alex walked around the corner and into the foyer. She was carrying an empty martini glass, chewing something, presumably one of those over-sized olives she couldn't seem to get enough of.

"I was coming to see you," Tess said.

"I'm kind of busy."

Tess laughed. "Busy? Busy drinking your lunch?"

"I needed a treat."

"We should talk."

Alex stared at her. It was unusual for Alex's face to show a reaction to anything Tess said to her, but now, her eyes widened and she glanced over her shoulder at the hallway leading to the offices. "About what?"

"Not here," Tess said.

"Okay."

"Let's go to your room."

In the same involuntary spasm, Alex's chin lifted slightly and her gaze darted toward the top of the stairs, then quickly returned to Tess's face. "Too claustrophobic."

"Since when?"

"I'd rather go out."

"Out where? It's cold."

Alex turned and began walking toward the kitchen. "I

need to wash this glass."

Tess followed. "We can talk in the billiards room. That's private, more or less."

"Why so secretive?" Alex plucked out the plastic swizzle stick and dropped it into the recycling container. She turned on the water and ran the glass under the stream. She placed it in the bottom of the sink and picked up the sponge. She squirted soap into the glass and began wiping it.

"Why are you having a martini in the middle of the day?"

"I told you."

"I'm going to make tea. I need to calm down."

"I could mix two more martinis."

Tess shook her head. "I need my mind clear. Really clear."

"Sounds ominous."

Alex moved away from the sink and began drying the glass.

Tess filled the kettle with water. "Do you want any?"

"No thanks."

When the tea was finished steeping, she went into the billiards room. Alex followed, and Tess closed the door.

"I'll get right to it," Tess said. She pulled a coaster toward the edge of the side table and placed her mug on it. "Sean more or less threatened me. When I move out, he's going to fire you."

Alex walked to the table and picked up the red striped ball. She turned it around in her hand. She set it down and rolled it toward the cue ball, knocking the white ball against the opposite side. "I guess that was backwards. I should have rolled the cue ball."

"Is that a metaphor for something?"

Alex shrugged. She reached over and picked up the eight ball. She cupped her hand around it and appeared to squeeze, her fingers immobilized by the solid, glossy plastic. "It's probably just an excuse."

"What's an excuse?"

"He's not that thrilled with me. He hasn't been since the beginning."

"True. But he thinks he can force me to stay by threatening your position. So I suppose he's not technically threatening me."

Alex nodded.

Tess picked up her mug and sat on the loveseat. She crossed her legs, hoping that settling into the room and her seat and her tea would settle her thoughts. She took a small sip, testing the temperature. Still too hot. "I don't think I have to say this, but buying the house is a done deal. I'm moving out."

Alex opened her hand and studied the eight-ball.

"Nothing's changed, for me," Tess said.

"I know."

"But I feel badly about the impact on you. Even if it's just an excuse, it doesn't give you a lot of options."

"If he actually does it."

"You think he won't?"

"Who ever knows what that guy will do?" Alex laughed. She held the eight ball up, level with her eyes. "These are supposed to be magic, right? They give you answers."

"I wonder where that came from?" Tess said.

"No idea."

Alex laughed. "It's like the app. Looking outside yourself for answers. Never a good idea." She placed the ball on the table and gave it a shove. It rolled to the opposite end, hit the felt-covered lip and spun back toward the center.

"The app is looking inside of you, so that's not really true," Tess said.

"I suppose." Alex hoisted herself onto the edge of the pool table. She crossed her ankles and swung her legs slightly.

"I just wanted you to know," Tess said.

"I appreciate it."

"I feel terrible, but…"

"It's not your fault."

"I know, but I did bring things to a…a breaking point."

"Maybe."

"What are you going to do?" She took a sip of her tea.

"Nothing. I think there's a fifty-fifty chance he thought he could freak you out and that you would decide to stay and he won't really follow through."

"He knows I already bought the house. I can't undo it."

"In his world, with the kind of money he has, you can undo anything you want."

Tess nodded. Alex was right about that. Even outside of his world, it wasn't impossible to turn around and sell the house. But it irritated her that he thought she was that weak, that easily manipulated. That he cared so little for what she wanted.

"I think it might just be words, hoping you'll cave."

"Maybe. Shouldn't you at least think about options?"

"Are you thinking about options? With the provocateur?" Alex laughed.

"No, not that. But I have a decent amount of contacts in Sydney from CoastalCreative customers I worked with over the years."

"Are you legally obligated to TruthTeller?"

"No. I'll lose any profit potential, obviously."

Alex leaned back, planting her hands on the pool table to support herself.

"That damages the felt," Tess said.

"It's good to know what he's thinking, but I don't need to do anything right now." Alex sat up straight again.

"It's a risk, doing nothing."

"I'll survive."

"If he fires you, you'll have to leave Australia."

"I know."

"You don't seem very worried."

"I don't tend to worry about things."

Tess laughed. "Everyone worries, at least a little."

"Do they?"

"Worry is a healthy thing. It's legit concern for your future."

Alex wriggled off the pool table. "I have some savings."

"I bet you do."

Alex smiled. "Not as much as you, of course."

Tess felt blood rush to her neck and cheeks. She lifted the mug to her lips, hoping her skin wasn't flushed with color. She took a sip of tea. She hated that infusion of blood, even if it wasn't visible. She had every right to the assets she'd acquired over the years. She was older than Alex, had a solid, successful career that she'd worked hard at. Extremely hard. There was no need to blush, and yet obviously, at some deep level, there was a strong flicker of guilt or shame or something that caused her body to respond. And it shouldn't. She was angry that it was so deep inside she couldn't even identify it or determine where it originated.

She drank some tea, uncrossed her legs, and stood. "I guess I'm glad that you're not freaked out."

Alex's smile emerged slowly. "Have you ever seen me freak out?"

"No."

"But I appreciate that you told me."

"I wonder why he's so obsessed with having everyone live here? Things would be working a lot more smoothly in getting this product to market if we weren't consumed with our living situation half the time," Tess said. "It's funny. Paying for everything was supposed to take our minds off of all those life details. Instead, it's the opposite."

Alex nodded.

They walked beside each other to the door. Alex opened it and stepped to the side, allowing Tess to go through first.

Damien laughed. *Chardonnay time!*

"I can't wait to get him out of that cage," Tess said.

"Should we take him up on that?" Alex said.

"On the Chardonnay? It's only one-thirty."

"So? Might as well enjoy the place while we can."

Dangerous woman.

Tess took a sip of tea. "A glass of Chardonnay would be nice. And maybe sneak another guilty cigarette on your balcony."

"Not right now," Alex said. "I'd rather sit on the back patio. I'll turn on the fire."

While Alex poured wine, Tess stood several feet away, watching. Alex didn't care that she might be fired, didn't care that firing meant immediate exit from Australia, didn't seem to care it meant separation from her de facto boyfriend, or whatever that was with Gavin. She looked calm and happy, focused on nothing but pouring a cold glass of wine, anticipating the warmth of an afternoon fire on a chilly day.

On the other hand, Tess felt her tension growing more solid. She desperately wanted a cigarette, but Alex was strangely protective of her personal space. She sighed and accepted the glass Alex placed in her hand.

43

Gavin and I were lying half propped up in his bed, drinking hot chocolate, naked.

I'd spent the afternoon and evening doing everything I could think of to avoid Facebook. An entire bottle of wine with Tess, before she called an Uber to take her tipsy self off for a walk around her new property, peeking in the windows, unable to control her anticipation of the moment she would have the key in her hot little hand.

She seemed worried about my future, but not worried enough to suggest she might talk to some of her contacts about a position for me. Although I expected she would probably come through for me if Sean actually made good on his threat.

The future wasn't important yet. There were too many other things, not the least of which was my complete lack of a plan to fix the results of my unfortunate lust for taking John's prized possession. It felt as if the telescope had grown into a mammoth piece of glass and metal, swollen far beyond its actual size, weighing me down. Its heavy presence in the front of my thoughts was not the image I should be focused on when I was trying to conjure up images of weightlessness for my swimming lessons.

While we sipped chocolate, I'd told Gavin about Sean's threat. He agreed with me that it was unlikely Sean would actually follow through. He thought Sean was determined to have what he wanted, and came close to temper tantrums when he wasn't getting his way, but ultimately adapted when he didn't get what he wanted. Still, it wasn't completely outside the realm of possibility.

I was slowly picking information about Sean's past out of Gavin's brain while he lay in a chocolate and post-sex-induced fugue. He said he knew nothing about Terri except that she was dead. He also knew that the carved wood statue in Sean's bedroom reminded Sean of Terri in some way. That's why he kept it close, likely still feeling something for her, although Gavin had no idea what that might be. He knew nothing at all about Carmen.

He didn't know any more about Anita than what he'd already told me.

Before I asked more, I figured it was my turn to share a secret, an even exchange to keep him talking. I moved closer and held my mug with one hand. I dipped my finger into the chocolate and rubbed the liquid on his nipple. I licked it off. "Did you know Terri was pregnant when she died?" I said.

"Yes."

"With Sean's child?"

"Yes, did he tell you?"

"No. Terri's sister, the woman stalking him on Facebook, told me." I decided in that moment to keep the rest of my knowledge about Carmen a secret for now.

"You're kind of confusing me," he said.

"Why?"

"Talking about a dead woman and doing that thing with the chocolate. One or the other." He laughed, rather nervously, I thought.

He put his mug on the nightstand and slid lower in the

bed. "Why are we talking about Sean anyway?"

"Because I need to know what's going on with him. My future is in his hands."

"I thought it was in my hands." He put his hands on the sides of my head and turned my face toward him. He gave me a long, deep kiss, managing to avoid spilling my drink.

After a few minutes, I moved away and took a few sips of chocolate. He rested his head on my belly and I continued sipping the warm, subtly sweet liquid while I stroked his hair. Then, I probed deeper. "How did you meet him? I don't think you've ever said."

"I was a contractor at his first start-up."

"And you stayed in touch?"

"We get along. We both like tech, talking about tech."

I nodded, even though he couldn't see me. Perhaps he felt the small muscles inside my belly tighten as I moved my head. "And how did you get involved with TT?"

"He contacted me, asked if I was interested."

That told me nothing. Of course, Sean had contacted him. I wanted to laugh, but didn't want to derail my progress. "But how, specifically?"

"He knew I was a good coder, he only wanted one guy, not a team. I liked the idea of working on my own."

"And why did you decide not to have a stake? Or didn't he offer one?"

"I told you. I didn't want one."

"But why?"

"We already talked about this."

"I think there's more to the story." I circled my finger around his ear.

He sighed.

"Do you believe in the usefulness of the app?" I said.

"More or less. I think it's cool, the technology capabilities are cool. I don't see the need for it personally, but I can see why a lot of people might find it helpful. All those horoscope readers. There are tens of millions of them, so…a good market."

I wondered why I hadn't thought of taking an astrology-centric approach on Twitter. Or Facebook. It was a good idea. Although probably too far after the fact at this point. My days were coming to an end here, I could feel it. Either Carmen would blow up Facebook and Sean would fire me for that, or he would follow through on his threat to Tess. Or anything, really.

At the core, I think Sean was afraid of me. He liked being in charge. And not being able to *manage* me, or more truthfully — manipulate me — scared him. Once he found out the same was true of Tess, the poor man wouldn't know what to do.

"Did you ever meet his family?" I said.

"What makes you ask that?"

"Curious about his background."

Gavin heaved a deep, defeated sigh.

Several minutes passed.

"Did you?" I said.

"No."

"Why did you sigh?"

"It's a…he had a rough go of it."

"How?"

"His father bolted when he was a kid — eight years old or so. Well, I'm not sure his father wasn't really there to begin with. But when Sean was in primary school, he disappeared completely."

"That's rough."

"His siblings all had different fathers. His mom was a hippie type, a free spirit. Sort of let the kids raise themselves. Or rather, she expected Sean to be a bit of a father. He was fifteen before the other kids came along. She had Sean when she was fifteen herself."

"Wow."

"And then she has three other kids, three other guys, all within about three years."

I didn't know what to say. Obviously Sean had an overdeveloped sense of responsibility. "Is he close to them? Do they still think of him as a father?"

"They're dead."

I put my mug on the nightstand. "That's…" I couldn't find the right word. Sad, of course. Upsetting. Terrible. Tragic. Actually I could find the right word, because those sympathetic thoughts weren't the words that came to mind first. The word that came to mind was — weird. How weird and freakish and probably frightening to have all of your siblings die.

"That's terrible," I said. I picked up my mug again and drank the rest of the chocolate.

"It is."

"Was it a car accident?"

"No."

"Do you know how?"

"Yes."

"Why are you not saying."

"I probably shouldn't have said anything. But you kind of circled around to it…and now I'm not sure what to say. I don't think he likes…I know he doesn't like talking about it. I don't think he would want me talking about it."

"Then how do you know anything about it?"

"It came up once. A long time ago. When we were getting high."

"Well what happened?"

"I don't know if I should say."

"You can't do that now. After telling me all that. What's the big deal? It's not like I'll tell him I know."

He sat up. "Are you sure? I don't know if I can trust you."

I smiled. "I haven't told anyone about the dead finger under your bed."

"Not yet." He returned my smile, although a barely perceptible tremor shot through his lips.

"I won't tell him. I promise. And when I promise, you can trust me."

"I guess it doesn't matter." He moved onto his side, propping his head up with his hand. "They drowned. On Sean's watch."

"Oh. I can see…no wonder he was so upset about Karen drowning in his pool."

"Well anyone would be."

"Even more, though. How could they all drown at once? Were they small?"

"No. He was in his twenties, so they were, I don't know. Between ten and twelve, I guess?"

"Then how…"

He put his hand on my leg. "They were swimming at this lake, a remote place somewhere near their house. And there was a sunken boat they were messing around with. It was an old wooden fishing boat with a small cabin. They swam under water into the cabin. All three of them. The boat was leaning half on its side, snagged on some boulders. And all that water movement, the kids' bodies bumping the interior, caused it to tip over and sink deeper. They were trapped."

"That's awful."

"Yes."

We were quiet for a long time, twenty minutes or more. His hand rested on my leg, not moving the entire time. His eyes were closed. My thoughts drifted around what he'd said. I wondered if his thoughts were doing the same, around Sean's dead girlfriend and dead child and dead siblings. It was a lot for one man. I could see that.

Finally, he spoke. "He was there with them, at the lake. But he wasn't close by. He'd snuck off into the woods, trying to nail the girl he was with. Sorry. I shouldn't say it like that."

"No worries." I patted his shoulder.

"So. Guilt. Survivor's guilt. But worse, knowing they were his responsibility."

I couldn't imagine.

"Anyway. I think it's clear why his head is a little messed up sometimes. Two girls and a boy, all dead. Sometimes I feel like…" He rolled onto his back. "The whole thing with this house, wanting to take care of us by giving us all this, wanting us to live here. I feel like he's trying to recreate that family. I know it sounds fucked up, an over-analysis of the situation… But I can't help thinking about it, when we're having dinner together. Or whatever."

The idea was a bit of a stretch. But maybe not. People do strange things trying to escape the past, wishing for do-overs. Look at all the men who divorce their wives and start second families. This time, they aren't going to work eighteen hours a day. This time, they aren't going to travel all the time. They'll be there for the kids. Everyone wants a chance to start over. It's the theme of thousands of movies and books. We love second chances.

"Don't tell him any of this," Gavin said.

"I won't."

"Sometimes I think he's a little off, like I said. Tries too hard. So I try to keep my distance to some extent."

"Then why are you here at all? If you don't trust him enough to be a stake-holding founder of the company, why do you trust him enough to live here?" I laughed. "Or maybe you don't, since you've always kept your door locked."

"Exactly."

"Why don't you trust him?"

He looked at me, then turned and picked up his mug. He began drinking the cold chocolate, undeterred by the skin that had formed across the top.

44

It was late Saturday night. The house had been silent all evening. As far as I knew, Sean had been in his room. Tess had gone out to dinner after surveying her new house. She'd returned without providing any information about where she'd eaten and what job inquiries she was spreading around Sydney. Gavin was sleeping, satiated.

After the flood of self-revelation and complaints from Carmen, I'd closed the Facebook page on the office computer and hadn't returned. Now, I took my laptop, a new pack of cigarettes, and a martini onto my balcony. I had to see what was going on, even if I didn't have a single thought about how I might resolve it.

It was like being in the center of a frozen pond, hearing the sound of ice cracking all around, and not knowing where to step that won't plunge you into frigid water. And then, if you do fall through sheets of crumbling ice, if you drift even slightly with some unfrozen current beneath the ice, you end up with a thick hard layer above your head that prevents you from ever reaching oxygen again.

Not that I've been on a frozen pond. I don't even know how to ice skate.

I lit a cigarette and slowly smoked the entire thing without touching my drink. When I was finished, I opened my laptop and launched Facebook.

There were twenty-five new comments, most of them

nested under Carmen's stream of consciousness. None of them were from Sean, so that was the first good thing. I didn't think he would have seen it and not made his rage known throughout the house, but you never know. Maybe he would think it was clever and witty to fire me on line.

A few of the comments were from Carmen's cheerleading squad. The rest were from others who had followed other threads on our page. They smelled blood. They wanted to know the details of Carmen's relationship with Sean. They wanted to know why he wasn't showing his face, they wanted to know why he was shutting her out. They wanted to know why Carmen's sister couldn't post her own comments, speculating whether something had happened to her. They were far too curious. Like me. Fortunately none of them had descended into attacking the TruthTeller brand. Yet.

Anything I might post in response to Carmen was likely to release another stream of memories, accusations, and musings. As I re-read what she'd written I realized the best approach was a standard strategy for combatting trolls — ignore. Suck out their oxygen, and that oxygen consists of your emotional upset. Every word you type, every emotion you reveal, fuels them and feeds them and fills them with renewed energy for further attacks.

I would say nothing to Carmen.

However, I had to make an effort to get control of the page.

I put my martini on the small table beside me. I turned on the outdoor light and angled it so only part of the beam fell on the martini. I took several photographs of it, then edited the best photo to emphasize the contrast of shadow and light. I posted the image with a comment that it was the purest, most satisfying drink in the world.

Many, many people disagree with that sentiment. My opinion was sure to generate a bit of conflict that would divert energy from the flood of Carmen's emotional vomit.

Immediately there was a comment that scotch was the purest, most satisfying drink…from Carmen, of course. I was annoyed at myself for not having foreseen her instant response. I took a sip of my drink, followed quickly by another. I lit a cigarette and inhaled deeply, blowing out the smoke slowly, gently. Exhaling is the calming part of smoking, that release of smoke and breath and energy. The settling down of your body as it realizes the pleasure of releasing something toxic.

Two guys popped up to say martinis were good as long as they didn't veer off into *girl* martinis. Then they started an exchange about Appletinis and espresso martinis and every other combo of fruit and side beverages you can think of.

Carmen added a photograph of a shot of scotch.

A moment later, she posted a photograph of the interior of The Baxter Inn.

I closed my eyes, trying to remember whether there would have been a chance for her to surreptitiously take a photograph of me. I remembered her at the bar, ordering drinks. I remembered me at the table, studying the menu. I truly hoped she hadn't been thinking so far ahead that it would have occurred to her to take my picture.

I waited, smoking and sipping my drink and thinking about how off track I was in my effort to start social media buzz for the TruthTeller app.

I added another comment under the martini discussion.

Alex Teller: *Everyone should post a pic of their fav drink. Cheers!*

Within ten minutes, there were five photographs — beer, of course, were two of those. There were also pictures of a gin and tonic, a martini with a single olive on a glass stir stick, and a Cosmo.

I scrolled back to Anita's comments and hit reply to her statement that she was glad to be reconnecting with Sean.

Alex Teller: *Hi Anita, Sean delegated TruthTeller Facebook activity to me. He probably won't see this. But glad you commented. Thrilled you liked the party. Cheers!*

I added the martini emoji at the end.

Instead of Anita, Carmen popped up. She was everywhere.

Carmen Dunn: *Delegated is one word for it. Shirking is another. Coward.*

I sipped my drink and stared at her words. Part of me thought I should just give up. I wasn't going to win this battle. What she wanted was, in her words, the only thing that mattered in her life. What I wanted was control of the Facebook page and there was no way for me to win that unbalanced battle.

Jane and Lara both clicked thumbs up. Did these women ever sleep? Maybe they were friends of Carmen's, maybe she told them when she was going to be online and asked them to be ready and waiting to react. It was a somewhat paranoid thought, but then, as they say, sometimes paranoia isn't that at all — sometimes, there *is* a conspiracy, sometimes people *are* out to get you. My own activities come to mind. A number of men, and some women, would do well to be a bit paranoid around me.

Anita responded to my comment with the weeping emoji.

The page went silent for half an hour, during which time I smoked two more cigarettes and finished my martini.

And then, as soon as I let go of my expectation of more trouble, there it was — a photograph of me, sitting in the shadowy back corner of The Baxter Inn. The only good thing about it was that you couldn't truly see my face. Carmen had been too far away when she'd taken the shot, and it was too dark, producing a grainy image. Plus, I was leaning over the menu and my hair covered the side of my face.

I've spent my entire adult life trying to conceal my identity on line. How did I know that was her only photograph of me? It felt as if I'd let down my guard and allowed everyone to use me — Sean to get to Tess, Carmen to get to Sean, Anita to get to Sean. I wanted a vacation from all of them.

The photograph was a delicate threat. It didn't feel like she wanted to expose me to the others on the page. It felt like she wanted me to know she would show it to Sean. Of course, Sean was ignoring her, so I'm not sure how she thought that might happen. But the chill ran down my spine all the same.

I put out my cigarette and typed a private message to Carmen — *Can we meet at The Baxter Inn again? I might have an idea.*

I did not have an idea at all, but hopefully I'd come up with one by the time I descended those steps and saw her in the dark corner of the cellar, waiting for me. I closed the laptop, ate the last olive, left the martini glass, the cigarette pack, and my lighter on the table. I went inside and placed the laptop on my desk. I took off my clothes and slipped between the cool sheets. With a single exhale, I was asleep.

45

Walking down the stairs into The Baxter Inn felt like a retreat from the flow of humanity. The bar was so filled with shadows and so devoid of any natural light, it had the atmosphere of a bomb shelter. The last time, it had reminded me of a stately library, so perhaps my expectation of what might happen with Carmen had colored my perception.

Before I reached the cellar floor, I saw Carmen at the same table as before. Two glasses of scotch were already waiting, the warm gold color seeming to glow from all the way across the room, beckoning me.

I settled across from her and gave her a tiny smile. A tired smile, I imagined, I hoped.

She picked up her glass. "Cheers." She took a sip. "What's your idea?"

I curled my fingers around my glass but didn't drink. "Not so fast." I smiled. "I need to understand what's going on. You know how Sean is…" I waited. I stroked the rim of my glass. I dipped my finger into the scotch and licked it. The taste was warm and soothing, I had to admit that, but I still longed for the sharp, refreshing thrill of a martini.

Her features relaxed very slightly and she gave me a smile that was best described as a smirk. "In what way?"

"You know."

"Do I?"

"Reactive."

She nodded. I took a sip of my drink, letting the relief pour through me. It was a perfect description for him and I was glad to see I'd hit the right note. "I want to help you get in touch with him, but he's so stubborn. You know that. I already suggested he should contact you, but he flat-out refused."

"Of course he did."

"Do you know why?"

She shifted her position, leaning one silk-blouse clad forearm and elbow on the table. It looked uncomfortable, bone pressing into wood with nothing but a delicate piece of fabric between her skin and bone and solid wood. She leaned closer. "I know why, but I'm not going to talk about it."

"Knowing would really help."

"We're not friends. I'm talking to you for one reason. You live in his house and you have complete access to him. You need to get creative. You saw what I can do if you don't make something happen."

"I did. Very clever of you. How do you know Jane? And Lara?"

"Who are they?"

I peered into her eyes, trying to read whether there was something hidden there. It didn't seem so, but I couldn't be sure. "They respond to everything you post."

She shrugged. "Whatever."

That could mean she knew them and wasn't going to say, or that she wasn't even aware of their presence, so caught up with her own pain and whatever else was circling inside her head.

"So you're not going to tell me why you want to talk to him?" I said.

"I don't *want* to talk to him. I need to. It's imperative."

"But you won't say why?"

"It's irrelevant to you."

I nodded. "Fair enough."

She was holding fast to her determination, and I couldn't think of a way to unwind her resolve.

"Enough bullshit," she said. "What's your idea?"

I picked up my drink and took a sip. I reached into my bag and pulled out my phone. I unlocked the screen and tapped through to my email, hoping my brain would come up with something that might keep things moving forward. Without looking up, I said. "Do you mind getting us a bowl of pretzels?"

"We aren't going to be here that long."

"I'm hungry. And they were so good. Perfect with the…"

"Do you even *have* an idea?"

I looked at her. I gave her a self-deprecating smile.

"I do. But I'm really craving pretzels."

She sighed. She stood and walked to the bar while I scrolled mindlessly through my email.

Sean wouldn't listen to me, no matter what I said. He certainly wouldn't talk to her in person, not after refusing to send a text message or make a phone call. My asking again would make him less inclined.

Once he saw them, he would blame her river of comments on me, tell me it was my job to fix it, to make her go away, to clean up the mess. But it wasn't my job. If this were a normal job, there wouldn't be an angry woman stalking him. That doesn't happen in other social media jobs.

Yes, there are trolls, but not like this, not personalized trolls. She had a different reason for trolling and one that would keep burning even if I starved her of attention.

46

We were both starting on our third shot of scotch before Carmen finally let some useful information slip out. Treating her to the second drink, and then offering the third before she jumped up to take care of it herself, helped move things in the right direction.

For nearly an hour she'd danced around all of Sean's flaws, repeating them in an infinite loop alongside her grief for her sister.

From my perspective, the accident hadn't been his fault at all. But in her mind, it was one of those — *if this hadn't happened, then the other thing never would have taken place* scenarios. That kind of thinking is very appealing because it seems true on the surface. Yet no one will ever know what might have happened had a chain of events been interrupted and re-directed. It's like speculation about the possibility of time travel, it makes the brain ache and splinter into fragments, thinking about changing the past and wondering how those changes play out.

It's still wildly appealing for some reason I can't quite grasp. Maybe it makes people feel there's a purpose to events? Or that events are connected? I really don't know.

In Carmen's mind, if Sean hadn't dumped her so coldly, then he never would have wound up meeting her sister several years later. And if he hadn't broken up with Terri and if he hadn't gotten her pregnant, as if Terri had no part whatsoever in this getting pregnant, then Terri wouldn't have wanted to go hiking in Nepal to heal her soul. Carmen wouldn't have agreed to go along to support her sister's healing.

In that convoluted scenario of *what if*, Terri would still be alive. Carmen didn't seem to realize that her first part of the *what-if* train suggested she and Sean would still be together. But she couldn't know any of that. A desire to go hiking in Nepal doesn't come out of nowhere. More likely, that desire was already there, developed over several years. Terri still would have gone hiking and still would have fallen to her death.

Finally, with her eyes covered by a glaze of alcohol, she revealed a facet of her anger that wasn't tied to Sean dumping her sister. Sean, she said, was deeply messed up because he'd been neglectful and irresponsible all his life. As a result, his brother and sisters had suffered a tragic death.

I leaned back slightly, directing my gaze toward my seductive glass of scotch, and waited.

"You don't look surprised," she said. "Or shocked."

"I knew about the accident."

"Oh." She sipped her drink. "It was terrible. So horribly sad. Horrible." Her eyes filled with tears. She blinked them away, and the anger returned. "He did not handle it well. And it was his fault. Totally his fault."

"It's so sad. I can't imagine. When was this?"

"About seven...I shouldn't pretend...I know exactly when it was. Eight years ago this coming November. It happened on November third."

"You remember the date?"

She looked down at the table. Her voice shrank. "I was

there. I was the girl. Did you know about the girl?

Gavin's voice wafted through my mind — ...*trying to nail the girl he was with.*

"You?"

"He wanted to have sex. I didn't. He was my first." Her eyes grew hard and glassy. "I should say my only. But that's another...I'm not getting into that."

I nodded. I leaned forward, giving her a comforting, encouraging smile.

"He kept bugging me, grabbing at me, telling me it was *time*. It was the perfect place. A quiet forest, so spiritual because there were no human sounds, no human eyes. I kept telling him we should watch the kids. He said they were terrific swimmers. And they were. But that boat. I didn't think...I'd heard about it, but you couldn't see it from the surface. And I never imagined they would...We were making out, and then, I just let him. I don't even know why. He was older, and I guess I wanted to be sure we were together, or something like that. I honestly don't know anymore.

"That day, I felt that maybe he really loved me, I was sure of it. We did it, and then we fell asleep. When we came back to the shore of the lake, the kids were gone." Her pupils shrank to pinpricks despite the darkness of the bar. "We thought they'd walked home without us. But something didn't feel right. Still, we walked back to his mom's place and they weren't there. It was a few hours before we put together what happened. The police and divers came. Paramedics. It was awful. The worse thing I've ever experienced. Until Terri. All those kids, their sweet little faces, and just...the life wiped out of them. Lying beside each other on the beach after they pulled them out of the water." She looked down at the table, seeming to stare right through the thick wood.

When she finally started talking again, her voice was rough. "He fell apart. I never knew a man could cry like that. It was horrible. He was sobbing...wailing, actually. He was cursing himself, and everyone. Cursing life. Anyway..." She raised her head slightly and put both hands over her face.

For several minutes she was silent again. I left my drink on the table, unsure whether I wanted more. I was starting to feel a bit of a buzz. I wanted it to stay mellow, not turn into feeling ripped and unable to keep the upper hand with Carmen, if I even had the upper hand.

Talking through her fingers, she began again... "He disappeared. He never broke up with me. I just never heard from him again. Eventually I got myself together and I was doing okay. I went to school, I became a researcher for a newspaper in Queensland. I love my job. It took forever to feel like a whole person, but I do. I'm seeing a guy now." She lowered her hands and gave me a hesitant smile.

I returned it.

"We're taking it slow. I know it's lame that it took me so long...eight years to get over Sean. But it was a terrible thing. I felt guilty too, that if I'd held my ground..."

I didn't agree with her, didn't even move my head, just kept my eyes locked on hers.

"When Terri said she was with him, that she was in love with him. I couldn't believe it. I felt betrayed by her as much as by him. I'm not even really sure how they hooked up again after all that time. He'd only met her once or twice when he was with me. But then I wondered, did he have his eye on her the whole time? Who knows."

She closed her eyes for a moment. She sighed gently.

"And now he's eyeing your roommate." She gave a short burst of laughter. "He should be mourning my sister. But no, always after someone new." Her lids snapped open, she picked up her glass, and took a healthy slug. "I just hurt so much. Every day. Not because I want him back, that's long gone. But my sister. She was so beautiful and so kind. She gave everything to him and he wouldn't even take responsibility for his child. And now...she's gone. Evaporated into thin air. I'll never see that little baby's face. I'll never give my sister a hug or hear her laugh. So many things about her, she was such a beautiful person and she's been wiped off the earth as if she never existed." As she spoke, tears poured down her face.

I wasn't sure whether she knew the tears were there. She didn't wipe them away. Neither did she seem to have trouble seeing me through the film of salty liquid. She just kept sipping scotch and letting those tears wash across her cheeks.

"All I need is a chance to talk to him."

"Why, with all that, do you want to see him at all?"

"There's unfinished business. I've told you more than enough to show you why you should help me."

"Is it about the statue? You haven't explained..."

"I don't see why you're being so stubborn. Just arrange for me to meet him. Invite me over, or something. Tell me where he lives. Even that would be enough."

I thought about Sean's dinner parties. I took a sip of scotch. He would fire me for sure. He might even make a huge show of it, refusing to let her inside the house, then throwing me out.

I pictured him following me to my room while I packed, all of them seeing the telescope...

On the other hand, he wouldn't want to blow up in front of his guests, people he wanted to impress. He wouldn't want to upset Tess while he was trying so hard to lure her back into his vision…

"Our company is having these dinner parties, to get people familiar with the app."

She furrowed her brow.

"I know, it sounds a little pointless. But that's what we're doing. Why don't you come? There are only ten or twelve people at each one, but he won't act out when other people are watching." I smiled.

Relief, and whatever else, melted across her face. I gave her the address and the date and told her to dress up.

"You bet I will," she said.

I didn't finish my drink.

When I emerged onto the street level, the sun was going down and the sky was filled with clouds bathed in a warm, soft pink. I walked for several blocks, going nowhere, watching the shadows grow longer around me.

47

Gavin and I stood in the center of the salt water pool. It was a relatively warm morning without a breeze, which helped my willingness to be in the water. The beach was deserted despite the pleasant weather.

I hadn't mentioned it to Gavin, but this was the day. It had to be. Avoiding what I needed to do was making it worse. Alongside that was the precarious situation with my job. Before I knew it, I might be on a plane to San Francisco. I hadn't seen a kangaroo, or a Koala, but after going this far, I was not leaving Australia until I learned at least the basics of swimming. Until I could put my face in the water, knowing it would hold me in its arms without strangling me.

I was not leaving the water today until I floated on my face. I needed to make it work. I needed to learn how to do this, to take back my power, I guess you could say. Instead of letting every single body of water from a bathtub, to a bucket filled with floating apples, to the oceans covering two-thirds of the planet, threaten me.

"Should we do some more back floating?" Gavin said. He put his hand on the back of my head, running his fingers through my hair, pressing gently on the base of my skull until I felt the muscles in my neck become more pliable.

"Sure." I lowered myself and fell into the support of his arms. After a moment of staring up at the slowly lightening sky, he moved his arms away and I floated.

"Try kicking your feet. Gently. Just little flutters up and down."

I did. And I moved. I felt my body gliding slowly away from him.

"Good," he said. "Very good."

I kicked a bit more. Feeling my body move across the surface was kind of a trip. I felt like a duck, paddling its webbed feet, propelling itself around, turning this way and that, occasionally shoving its head in the water and coming up with bugs and tiny fish, wiggling and fluffing its tail, the feathers instantly dry. Of course, I wouldn't shove my head under the water, but I still felt like a duck.

Kicking also made me feel more stable, preventing my lower legs from drifting below the surface as if they meant to drag me down.

"That's great." Gavin said. "It's easy, isn't it."

"How do I stop?"

He laughed. "Just lower your legs and hips. Move your arms about like this." He demonstrated waving his arms in figure eights through the water. "And then you can find your footing."

I did and managed to stand up without getting my head into the water. "I guess it's time," I said.

"You're sure?"

I nodded.

He moved toward me and held out his arms for me to lay prone, my face toward the bottom of the pool. I moved closer to him and took three long, slow breaths. I closed my eyes and held my breath quietly inside, just to remind myself what it felt like. Then I let it slide quietly out of my nostrils. It seemed perfectly doable with oxygen right there, waiting to get sucked inside at a moment's notice, less than a moment, in the flick of an eyelid.

"Ready?"

He instructed me to reach my arms over my head to help balance out my weight, to help me think of relaxing my shoulders into the water.

"The tighter you make your muscles, the more likely you'll feel like you're sinking."

"I thought you said I couldn't sink."

"You can't, but if you're tense, it can feel as if you are."

I nodded.

"Ready?" He lifted me so I was prone on the surface, my head stretched up, the water lapping at my chin.

I stretched out my arms and put my mind to turning all my muscles into something soft and light — whipped butter came to mind. I took a slow, shallow breath, put my face in the water, and let my breath slowly escape. As my breath disappeared and water pushed against my skin, I counted, too fast, I could feel it was too fast, but the counting helped. I made it to forty-eight before I lifted my head, gasping for air.

Gavin moved me so that my feet could find the bottom. I stood and he wrapped his arms around my waist and put his lips close to my ear, almost touching it. "Not so terrible after all?"

I shook my head. I had a burning urge to try it again.

I launched myself onto the water, taking a breath as I did. This time I only made it to thirty-two, my counting less frenzied. I stood again and sucked in air. It was addictive. I think it wasn't the floating itself that was addictive, but the knowledge that I was in control. The success. Each time I floated and kept my face down, my desire swelled to something almost unmanageable.

After about twenty minutes of this, he asked whether I wanted to try kicking. I did. That wasn't as successful — maintaining a feeling of weightlessness and moving my legs in a somewhat rigid up and down motion fought against each other. I was only able to keep my face in for a few seconds at a time.

I floated two more times and we got out of the pool. We dried off and went to breakfast at a place that served Bloody Marys. I felt I'd earned one. Gavin didn't disagree.

While we ate eggs and corn fritters and sausages, I told him about Carmen.

He seemed disinterested in hearing the story from her perspective. Even though it was the same story he'd told me two days earlier, or maybe because of that.

The conversation, if you can call it that, faded quickly. I still wanted to know why he didn't trust Sean. The more he dodged the question, the more curious I'd become, but there was no way to make my interest appear artful and casual. I plunged in, no longer caring whether I was prying. "You never said why you don't trust Sean. Is there something I should be concerned about?"

"No."

"Then what is it? Why don't you trust him?"

"Because he broke it off with Terri right before he got all that cash. They had a thing going, for sure. They were a couple. He brought her to all the company picnics. They were *living* together. And then he decides it's over. Just like that.

"And it was over for him because he couldn't stand the thought of someone having that level of influence in his life. I get that the company was his. It was his idea. His work. It's not that I think she had a right to his good fortune, but it was still a shitty thing to do. He knew what he was going to get out of that sale. And he dumped her before she might make some kind of claim on his fortune. Before she could persuade him to marry her for the baby's sake. Who does that? Breaks up with his pregnant girlfriend?"

Probably a lot of people, but I didn't say that. Gavin was clearly upset about it.

"So, no, I don't trust the guy. I don't want to be in business with him beyond my salary. I don't want to be responsible for his crazy decisions or what happens to the product when it's for sale. I don't want to be chained to him."

"Then why are you here at all? Staying in the house? Working for him?"

"I told you when I first met you. It's who I am. I'm a developer. I love writing code. And having sole control of that development was appealing."

I didn't point out the irony.

"I get so lost inside my own head, it's like a state of altered consciousness…almost spiritual."

I laughed.

"It's not funny."

"Well, it sort of is."

"You just haven't found the work that you're meant to do. So you can't understand."

I have. I've definitely found that work. I don't get paid, obviously. But thinking of what I do shone a different light on his altered consciousness comment. Maybe he was right. A little bit. A tiny bit right.

I do feel lost in another place when I'm preparing to kill someone, working to make society better, mostly for women, but for men too.

But I would never call it spiritual. Not in a thousand years.

48

The Friday before Sean's third dinner party, I scheduled the works for myself — a complete overhaul of my body.

Before my pampering, I'd gone for a ten-mile run. It took over an hour, but felt good as all that sweat and tension bled out of me. My muscles stretched and burned to the breaking point, which made me think it would have been a good idea to take swimming lessons after running. My body would already be relaxed without any mental effort, the muscles drained of tension. The exertion of a run calmed my mind and that silent drifting would allow me to float. I wasn't sure why that hadn't occurred to me earlier.

The refresh of the rest of me would start with an hour-long deep-tissue massage, followed by a facial, followed by a haircut — blunt chop to the middle of my neck. It was also time for a color change. I'd decided on a dark blonde, streaked reddish brown.

While I was stretched out on the massage table, my face pressed into that cloth-covered head support, open in the center, it occurred to me the position was similar to floating. Through that porthole, I watched the boot-clad feet of the masseuse occasionally come into view and allowed my mind to wander to job possibilities.

It wasn't a topic I liked to spend time on, but with all the things facing me, I had to take at least a few minutes to consider my future.

I liked Australia and wasn't ready to leave, but unless Tess came up with an opportunity for me, it was unlikely I'd be able to find something on my own. An American with no contacts to speak of, and sketchy marketable skills, was not at the top of the desirability list for jobs that paid what I needed in order to continue my quest for a nest egg that would last the rest of my life.

If I was lucky, I could wind up my tenure with TruthTeller and still see part of the country. If I was lucky. So far, luck had followed me through my life. It might not seem lucky, being born to people who were blinded by their unwavering belief in a book filled with stories of brutality and threats of future torture, interspersed with some lovely inspiration and thought-provoking stories and instructions for getting along with fellow human beings.

But I had been lucky. I had a roof over my head and food in my belly. I had people who made sure I went to school and saw the doctor and dentist. I had siblings who made growing up entertaining and fun and challenging, in a good way.

I could argue that growing up with daily indoctrination opened my mind to my own thoughts. There's nothing like the invading thoughts of others, and the pressure to conform and to accept without questioning, to help shape your own mind into a separate entity.

My parents never grasped that I was different from most people. Or rather, they did, but they didn't like it and they didn't know what to do about it. So they did what they believed was right and battled me to the breaking point over every little thing. But more or less, we survived.

So yes, I'm a lucky woman.

I hoped that luck would play out into a nice vacation and an interesting job. I was fed up with social media. I think that's part of the reason I was taking such terrible risks with Sean's displeasure. It was boring half the time, but still a siren's call of fascinating communication that was anything but that. Social media is akin to the Emperor's New Clothes — every business and entrepreneur is touting their strengths and the benefits of their offerings on social media, thinking that because everyone else is using it, they will be left behind if they don't get involved.

No one wants their company ignored because they've failed to use the latest tools and gimmicks and gadgets to find success. Every single restaurant and store has those ubiquitous icons plastered on the glass and printed on the menus.

I wanted a job that had nothing to do with social media. I also wasn't keen on going back to the spreadsheets and PowerPoint slides that dominated my life at CoastalCreative.

But I had no idea what I could do.

I was trained for nothing.

As the masseuse's fingers drilled into the muscles between my shoulder blades, I wondered whether she liked her job. I wondered the same while my hair was being cut, falling across my shoulders and onto the floor in dark clumps.

Now, sitting in the pedicure chair, my feet bathing in a warm tub and my fingers soaking in soapy water, I stared at the open magazine splayed across my yoga pants.

The page was open to a picture of an actress's home in the hills of LA. It wasn't my taste. The decorating was stiff and overdone — too many vibrant paint colors, too much furniture, too many framed prints and drawings and photographs hanging on the walls, too many tables filled with objects meant just to take up space and look nice, but appearing claustrophobic to me. What did appeal to me was the location. There wasn't another house in sight, at least not visible in the photographs. Plenty of open space surrounded the house, filled with small gardens and clusters of trees, water features and secluded patios.

I could be very happy in that spot, with a different architect and decorator, of course.

"Lusting?"

I looked up. The woman seated in the chair beside me smiled. She had short hair, the color similar to my new color, without the streaks. She wore lots of makeup and a very expensive looking blouse, a rather risky choice when there's lots of bright enamel liquid within splatter distance, harsh chemicals, and oil for hand and foot massages. I prefer a washable top and pants when I'm in a nail salon.

"It's not entirely my taste," I said.

"A bit fussy. Impersonal."

I nodded, surprised she could see that much detail from where she sat.

"Are you here on holiday?" she said.

"No. I'm on a work visa."

"How are you liking Australia?"

I closed the magazine. "I love it."

"Where do you work?"

"I work for a technology start-up."

She didn't push it.

"How about you?"

"PR." She smiled.

I could see the PR personality in her face and the way she

smiled. There was something extremely polished and slick about her. Not necessarily in a phony way, but just hyper-aware of the impression she's making.

"Do you work for a big company?" I said.

"I have my own firm. We do custom PR for all kinds of businesses, several industries."

"How do you like it?"

She laughed. "You're very refreshing."

"Thank you."

"And I love it," she said.

"You don't feel like you're adding to all the phoniness out there in the world?"

"You're blunt." She smiled.

"I don't see the point in not asking questions, if I have a question that needs to be asked."

"I agree. Although I don't always act on that belief." She held out her hands and inspected her nails, running first one, then the other index finger over the tips of the nails on the opposite hand.

"So do you? ...feel like you're adding to the phony images?"

"Not at all. I see it this way." She leaned toward me. "Everything in the world has good points and bad points — every company, every product, every human being."

"That's true."

"My job is to highlight the good points and downplay the bad."

"That makes sense."

"So I don't see it as phony at all. It's all about putting your best foot forward, right?" She lifted her foot where bright blue polish was drying on her toenails. She wriggled her toes and rotated her foot as if she was showing off all angles.

"How did you get into PR?"

"I studied communications in college. Worked for a few companies, moving my way up, then wanted to put my own vision out there. I wanted more freedom."

"I suppose that's why everyone wants to start their own endeavor. Freedom," I said.

"Absolutely."

The manicurist indicated to the woman that her toenails were dry. The woman eased her way out of the chair, pulled her credit card out of her purse, and slipped her feet into flip flops. "Nice chatting with you, however briefly."

"Same here."

"I hope you get your dream house," she said.

"I will." Getting that dream house required more focus, a better job, meaning — more money. Still, those better jobs seemed to keep coming my way, so maybe I was more focused than I realized.

"Such confidence," she said.

"It's the only way to be."

"I agree."

When she left, I settled back and closed my eyes while cherry red enamel was painted on my fingernails and toenails by two women talking quietly to each other, which allowed my thoughts to drift.

I couldn't afford to spend a lot of time imagining a hilltop home or a career path that was suited to me and perfectly to my liking. For now, I needed to figure out a job, period. Soon.

49

Carmen was late.

The evening was scheduled to start at six, beginning with appetizers and champagne, of course. The so-called cocktail hour would last until seven.

I hadn't told Carmen how much time she had to slip in late while people were drifting about the house sipping champagne and her entrance would be less noticeable. She wasn't aware the dinner itself began at seven. I'd assumed she would show up within a few minutes of the time I'd provided.

Yet, she was late.

People were gathering in the dining room, champagne flutes abandoned beside snack plates, crumpled white napkins littering the patio and great room.

Sean had taken a more formal role this time. He wouldn't be seated at the head of the table. He'd given that spot to Tess, placing me at the foot again. He was wearing an apron and performing the services of waiter and sommelier. He believed it would make everyone more comfortable if he remained in the background. The previous parties had been too close to family style, he said. He wanted his guests to feel wined and dined, whatever that meant.

His black apron covered a white, long-sleeved shirt with the cuffs rolled up, and he wore black tuxedo slacks. His hair was slicked back and secured with a black elastic band.

Tess seemed fine with her prominent position.

There were no place cards this time, which had helped me disguise the identity of my guest. He'd told Tess and me where we were sitting, and assigned Gavin to the center of the table on my left to be sure he could communicate with the maximum number of people. The rest was left to chance.

Sean had wanted to complete the evening with a slide show presentation about TruthTeller, but we'd persuaded him that was completely contradictory to the mood he'd insisted he was trying to create. Gavin assured him he would maneuver the app and its features into conversation. Tess said the same. I didn't make a commitment and he didn't seem to notice.

My goal for the evening was to make sure no violence broke out when he saw Carmen.

He'd encouraged us repeatedly to invite other guests. I'd told him that morning I'd invited a woman who worked as a researcher for a newspaper. He thought the role sounded fascinating and didn't ask any questions. I agreed it sounded like an interesting job. I would have considered pursuing something similar if not for the fact that Carmen had mentioned the pay was almost insulting.

That was the trouble with technology jobs. I wasn't all that interested in technology overall, but jobs with those companies paid so much better than other jobs, it was hard not to go searching in that direction.

I lingered a few feet from my chair, wondering whether Carmen had decided to blow it off. At the same time, I couldn't imagine her doing that after all she'd done to get close to Sean. Maybe she just wanted his address, maybe she had something else in mind. I hoped she wasn't unstable in ways I hadn't noticed, that I hadn't put us at risk of something more sinister than a dinner party with an unwanted guest.

After all, I knew nothing about her but what she'd told me. None of those things might be true.

The doorbell rang while Sean was in the kitchen taking the pork tenderloin out of the oven. It smelled divine. Our wine glasses were filled with dark, rich Cabernet, and the small plates with tiny salads consisting of nothing but arugula, paper-thin slices of onion, sprinkled with a few pine nuts, and a light vinaigrette were settled in the center of the dinner plates at each place.

He'd told us to take our seats, and people were just now pulling out chairs and fidgeting to get themselves situated.

I stepped away from the table and walked to the front door. A thrill ran down my spine and continued along my legs as I anticipated what might happen. I doubted Carmen would bring up her issue, whatever it was, immediately or in front of all those people. I wondered if Sean would ask her to leave the minute he saw her.

If he did, she wouldn't comply, of course.

It could prove to be exciting, and hopefully in a good way. Drama without tragedy, or violence.

I opened the door.

Carmen looked completely different. One side of her head was shaved over her ear. Dark red streaks ran through her hair, coming out of the exposed scalp at her part line. It forced you to look twice, to be sure her head wasn't bleeding. She wore red lipstick, and her foundation made her skin almost colorless. The front light hit the side of her head and her shoulder, leaving the rest of her face in shadows, which sharpened her new look.

She'd taken my instructions to dress for a formal dinner and worn a black strapless dress that hit mid-calf. Her black high heels had a platform under the balls of her feet, allowing even longer heels. Because of my surprise at her hair, which I shouldn't have given a second thought to, given my frequent hair changes, I didn't say anything about dinner already starting or the nature of the party so far, or Sean's decision to be our server. I simply took in the dramatic effect. I opened the door wider. "Hi. We're just getting to the table. I have a place for you beside me."

She followed me across the foyer, pausing at Damien's cage. It's hard not to pause there, but I'd assumed she would smell the pork and the rest of the meal and realize we needed to get to the table.

"Hello there," she said.

Dangerous woman.

I wanted to laugh. Clearly Sean would agree.

Carmen did laugh. "You're a smart bird," she said.

Delicious mango, Damien chortled. He followed this with a laugh of his own. From the corner of my eye I could see the end of the table where my seat was. Oscar, the sports promoter, was seated to my left and I saw his head jerk toward the foyer in response to the bird's cackle. It seemed as if he hadn't noticed Damien in the several times he'd been in and out of the house. He looked alarmed.

"The dining room is this way," I said.

Carmen turned away from Damien and followed me.

I indicated the chair beside mine. Oscar jumped up, walked around behind me, and pulled out the chair for Carmen. He introduced himself. She sat down without giving him her name.

"Can I get you a glass of champagne?" he said.

She looked up at him and shook her head. He did a slight double-take and backed away.

As her head turned and I saw her face up close, no longer darkened by the shadows of the front porch, I noticed what had made Oscar move so suddenly. She wore contact lenses that turned the irises of her eyes blood red. It seemed a bit much, but the look was very compelling, hard to turn away from.

As I took my own seat, I thought about the theatrical change in her appearance. I hoped she wasn't going out of her way to enrage Sean by focusing all the dinner party attention on that self-confident hair style and those eyes.

I wanted him to take responsibility for whatever was causing this woman to sabotage our Facebook page, and my job, but I didn't want a full-on battle. I hoped I hadn't set one up.

50

Sean walked into the dining room carrying the platter with the pork tenderloin sliced into perfect ovals. As he passed through the doorway and looked at his guests, his feet stopped moving. His throat and lungs froze. The woman sitting beside Alex…no…she was dead. He struggled to take a breath, still standing just inside the entrance, unable to move any part of his body. It wasn't her. Of course not. She was dead. Mangled after a plunge of several hundred feet.

It wasn't her.

It was Carmen. She'd done things to her hair, her eyes and skin, maybe, or possibly just because she was a bit older, her face had taken on the shape and coloring of Terri's.

As he looked at them, neither one yet noticing he was standing there, he wasn't sure which woman he hated more — Carmen or Alexandra.

Alexandra, for inviting that woman into his home.

Carmen, for finding a way back into his life.

Alexandra, for working overtime to shatter his equilibrium.

Carmen, for thinking she could dictate his grief.

Alexandra, for not managing the situation with Carmen when it was nothing but a social media hiccup.

Carmen, for taking what belonged to him.

Alexandra, for defying him.

She hadn't defied a direct request, it was the spirit of

things. She did this to light him up, to blow apart everything he cared about in this house and with this venture. She wanted to destroy him, for the sheer pleasure of destruction.

Carmen, for just being there, for existing, for…of course it wasn't her fault his brother and sisters had drowned that day. It was his. All the blame was on him. But he loathed the sight of her.

He was relieved that he had enough self-discipline to stop the molten lava of emotion that roiled inside him, the frozen sensation replaced by hot, thick, deadly liquid. It moved fast despite its consistency, turning his organs and bones and muscle into fuel for the raging mass, set to consume everything in its path.

He stood in the entrance to the room, gripping the tray, his fingers beginning to ache, and then losing their sensation and then trembling, in danger of letting go. He tightened his grip. He turned and placed the tray on the long narrow table near the entrance. He rubbed his hands on his pants.

Demanding that Carmen leave the party was out of the question. It would spoil the evening. No one would interact naturally after that. He had no choice but to suck it up. He had to be the consummate host and get rid of her later, either as soon as he could set her straight in a private setting, or simply ushering her out the minute the others left.

His fury at Alexandra for fucking up his life in this way continued to burn.

He was pleased with his decision to serve the meal. At least that gave him repeated opportunities to leave the room, it kept his discomfort from infecting the others, and gave him space to think about how he was going to handle this.

Knowing that Carmen now knew where he lived was the

worst. How was he going to keep her away? He couldn't take out a restraining order. Getting the police involved was out of the question. He was in the right morally, but legally…

The meal went quickly. There was a lot of laughing and wine drinking. Everyone praised the food and his artful preparation. The few times he passed behind Gavin's chair, he heard Gavin explaining the functionality of the app. He hoped Gavin didn't get too geeky, rambling off on technical details that no one understood or cared about. So far, the things he was saying sounded appropriate for the audience.

He'd even heard Tess mention it once when he refilled her wine glass.

Alex, of course, was devoting all her attention to Carmen.

He couldn't believe this was happening. He returned to the kitchen, grabbed a beer out of the fridge, and took a long swallow. He had to think, but it was almost impossible.

While everyone was finishing the last of the wine in their glasses, he made espresso and plated the chocolate cake he'd purchased for dessert. It took longer than expected, trying to keep the white plates free of smeared frosting as he lifted each gooey wedge out of the box and placed it in the center of a plate.

He changed playlists on the sound system to soft rock.

When he returned to the dining room, Alex and Carmen were gone.

He took a deep breath and began passing around the plates of cake. Everyone moaned and made extensive phony sounds over the rich appearance and their undying love for anything chocolate. He poured coffee, cleared wine glasses, and when he finally had them settled in with chocolate-laden forks, he went into the living room. Alex and Carmen weren't there.

It made sense to check the billiards room, even the offices and the patio. But he had a bad feeling and didn't want to waste time there.

He jogged up the stairs and walked stealthily along the hallway, turning right at the end. The door to his bedroom was closed, but that meant nothing. Without slowing his forward movement, he pressed on the handle, pushed the door open, and charged into the room.

Carmen and Alex stood on either side of the wood carving. Each woman had a hand on one of the statue's hips. For a moment, he had the impression of three women carrying on a conversation, the statue as full of life as the other two, despite her rather flamboyant pose — her back arched and her arms lifted above her head, her face tilted toward the sky as if she were drinking in the entire universe.

"Get the fuck out of my room!"

Carmen and Alex turned their heads slightly, they said nothing, and they didn't move their hands off the figure's hips.

"I said…"

"We heard you," Carmen said. "But this belongs to me."

"It belongs to me," he said.

"It most definitely does not, and you know it."

Alex lowered her arm and took a step away from the statue. "It belongs to Carmen?"

"I'm not discussing it. Get out of my room."

"What are you going to do about it?" Carmen said. "You can't call the police. In fact, if you did, they'd be more interested in what I have to say." She laughed. "And now, I know where you live. You can't stop me from taking her back." She moved her hand and stroked the side of the figure's face.

"I have a dinner party I'm supposed to be hosting. I can't..."

"Then go host it," Carmen said.

Alex stood with her arms loosely folded across her ribs, gazing at him with that tiny smile, enjoying the tension between him and Carmen, doing nothing. Nothing but stirring the pot. Inviting Carmen here, bringing her to his room.

Had Carmen asked about the statue or had Alex volunteered information? It didn't matter. He pointed toward the door. "I want you to leave so I can get back to my guests. Now."

"I'm not leaving," Carmen said.

"Do I have to drag you out?"

"Really?" Carmen laughed. "That's your solution?"

He walked closer and grabbed her wrist, trying to wrench her hand away from the statue.

"Let go of me."

"Stop touching it."

"After all this time? Never seeing it, never a chance to touch it? I don't think so. You owe me. Big time."

He had to get them out of there. He had to get back downstairs. He glanced at the doorway. Maybe Tess could help...but she wouldn't. She seemed to think she owed him nothing personally. All she thought she owed were the tasks of her job while collecting her paycheck. Like a common worker, not an executive, a visionary. Maybe he'd over-estimated her. Of course he knew he hadn't, it was the unbearable frustration of watching everything fall apart, the feeling of exposure twisting his thoughts inside out.

He tightened his grip on Carmen, yanking her toward him. He lowered his head and hissed softly. "Don't think you're getting to me with what you did to your hair. It's sick. And your eyes are disgusting, by the way."

Carmen smiled, a rather saintly smile, meant to give the impression of someone above it all, someone looking down at him, seeing nothing but a twisted knot of ugly emotion.

From downstairs, the voices changed volume. People were moving away from the table. He heard the clatter of plates. They were clearing their own dishes! This was spoiling everything. "Get out."

"I'm taking her home." Carmen placed her hand on the statue's left breast. It remained there while she held his gaze.

Alex faded from his peripheral vision. No one was in the room but him and Carmen. And the statue. Their memories. Their failures and sins. Yes, sins. It wasn't too big of a word.

So many people had died and he would never have them back.

The statue was everything. He would not allow Carmen to take it.

51

In the end, Sean went back to his guests…our guests, in theory. I stayed with Carmen and the statue. She assured me the statue belonged to her, that Sean knew this, no matter what he said. She would arrange for a truck to pick it up during the coming week.

The moment she mentioned the truck, I thought of the albatross on my closet floor. She was offering a possible escape route. I had two or three days to figure out how I could get that telescope properly packaged, out of my room, down the stairs, and onto that truck.

Carmen was the last to leave, but Sean didn't speak to her again.

During our time in Sean's room, I learned that the statue had been the centerpiece of a memorial in her garden. It reminded her of the spirit of her sister. Although the figure wasn't obviously pregnant, the sense of freedom revealed her personality and the love in her heart, and the knowledge of her child.

A few weeks after the carving was installed, it disappeared in the middle of the night. She hadn't seen or heard it being removed from her garden. She had no proof, but she had a pretty strong idea it was him. She didn't elaborate on how she knew. She'd tried to contact him and that was when he blocked her.

She'd spent nearly a year trying to find it, and him. He

disappeared from the online world and no one seemed to know where he was living. There was a vague belief that he was in or around Sydney. She couldn't understand how he'd disappeared as surely as her sister, as if he'd never existed. Yes, Sydney was a good-sized city with over four million people, but you couldn't simply disappear. And yet, he had.

Given the story of his relationship with Carmen, and Terri, and the statue, it was surprising that Sean hadn't been even more unglued when I posted the photograph, opening the door to Carmen. He must have been furious when she popped up with her provocative comments. He'd held it together rather well, I thought.

But he was wealthy. Why go to the risk and trouble of stealing it? The struggle for ownership was rather childish and pointless. It was a memorial that was important to Carmen, why did he need to take it? Why didn't he commission his own statue?

On Sunday morning I went for a run to clear my head. Despite the rage Sean would direct at me for bringing Carmen closer instead of getting rid of her, I thought my position with TruthTeller was stable for a few more weeks. As long as Tess was in the house, as long as Sean was hoping to keep her there, he probably wouldn't fire me.

If Carmen's appearance was going to cause him to terminate my job, he was biding his time. And maybe he was. Maybe it would be something dramatic. I would come home from a run or a swim lesson to find all my belongings on the front lawn.

A locked door wouldn't keep him out of my room. If he didn't have a duplicate key, he could still easily crowbar his way in. And then, all my secrets would be exposed.

I ran faster, increasing my speed until I was in a full sprint. After a quarter of a mile I slowed and took an easy jog the rest of the way back to the house.

Anita was standing on the front patio. She wore jeans and boots that went up over her knees. She had on a drape-y white top and her hair was pulled up with a barrette, a few strands artfully escaping around her face. When she saw me, she started down the walkway toward the gate.

I grabbed part of the iron fence and pulled my foot up behind me, stretching my quadriceps. She stopped a few feet away from me.

"Why are you here?" I said.

"I need to see Sean."

"Why?"

"None of your business. Please tell him I'm here."

"I'm not his personal assistant. If he didn't answer the door, he's not interested in seeing anyone."

"I don't know if he heard the bell."

"He heard it."

I switched legs, stretching the opposite muscle. "If you want to get in touch with him, send a text or something."

"I know he wants to talk to me."

"How so?"

"I heard the other woman who works with him is leaving his company. I want to apply for her job."

I laughed and put my foot on the ground. I started around her. She grabbed the back of my shirt.

"Let go."

She took a step forward, clenching her fists as if she planned to punch me. "Don't laugh at me." Her eyes burned with fury and tears and a touch of pleading.

"The *other woman* is not leaving the company."

"I'm not talking to you about this. Tell him I'm here."

I jogged up the walkway and put my key in the lock. She hurried up behind me. Her breath was hot on the skin of my face.

"Are you lying to me?" Her voice was low, with a growling quality that I don't think I imagined.

"About?"

"You're fucking him. I can tell. I can smell it on you."

I laughed. I was no longer sure she was simply pushy and pathetic, angry and desperate. She teetered on the sharp edge of instability. At the parties, she'd been okay, if annoying — talking too much, socially clueless. When she arrived to clean up his kitchen, she was simply weird. Now...I wondered if Sean knew she was off balance. Surely he wouldn't have invited her if he thought she was unhinged, possibly dangerous. What the hell did she want? What made her think she could snag a marriage proposal from him?

I pulled my key out of the lock and turned to face her. "How do you know Sean?"

"I told you."

"Remind me."

She heaved a sigh and folded her arms. "I don't owe you any information. I'm here to talk to Sean and you're a roadblock. If you're not fucking him, you have no right to prevent me from talking to him. And even then..."

"This is my home too, and I'm not going to let you inside when I have no idea who you are."

"Just for the record, it's not *your* home." She took a deep breath. "I was his personal trainer."

"What else?"

"We had a strong spiritual connection. He always said that. He said it was as if I knew his body from the inside. Isn't that beautiful? That's why I know he wants to see me. That's why he invited me to his dinners. He wants to feel that intensity again."

I folded my arms.

"So tell him I'm here. I can wait inside." She took another step toward me.

"I can't do that."

"You said you would."

"No I didn't."

"You implied it."

"Did I?"

She moved even closer. Her warm breath was right in my face now, laced with the odor of coffee and possibly eggs, which until that moment, I hadn't realized you could smell on someone's breath.

"I need to see him. He said I was welcome any time."

I thought about Sean's face when he saw Carmen. I expected that no matter what he'd said to anyone last night, he'd forgotten it immediately.

"You're acting like this is your house and it's not. It belongs to him. He talked about it during our workouts, every single step when he was having it built. I know about the design of the swimming pool and waterfall, I know why he wanted the atrium, and I know the bathroom floors are heated."

I shrugged. "Good for you."

"He told me I was a huge asset to the party. I kept things real. He wouldn't have made it through the evening without me. And he said that other girl doesn't want to be in his company any more."

I had no doubt Sean might have said a lot of things. Some of them she might have heard, some she might be making up. But even the words he'd actually uttered came from some uncontrolled part of his mind because all his conscious thoughts were about Carmen and that statue.

It was also entirely possible that with Anita's propensity for hanging on for dear life, he'd said whatever was required to get her out the front door so he could be alone. So he could scurry up to his bedroom, lock the door, and pine over that statue.

"You're trying to keep him for yourself. He might have a physical thing with you, but he's connected to me physically *and* spiritually. That's unbreakable. You can't stop him from being attracted to me just because you live there. You can block me from seeing him all you want, but it won't change how he feels."

"If you know how that man feels about anything, that's quite remarkable."

She glared at me. She widened her eyes in that way she had, refusing to let her lids relax into a normal blink, hoping that by staring me down she might convince me to relent.

I put my hand on her shoulder and gave her a healthy shove. She stumbled back, tripped on the leg of a patio chair and half fell. She cried out as if I'd kicked her in the knee with steel-toed boots.

I put my key in the lock. I turned it quickly, opened the door, slipped inside the house, and closed it behind me. As the door was closing, she shouted again, a cry of visceral pain — physical *and* spiritual, I guess you could say — "I know you're lying. You have the look of a liar. I can see it. I can smell it. And you're not having him just because you live there."

I ran up the stairs, eager to get into the shower and wash the sweat and her desperation off my skin.

52

Portland

Jake didn't speak to me for two weeks after *The Book of Sharks* went missing and he had to pay the school library seventeen dollars out of the money he earned mowing the grass for several of our neighbors. At dinnertime he looked down at his plate, shoveling food into his mouth. He pretended not to hear me when I asked for the platter of chicken or a bowl of peas to be passed, forcing Tom to reach across at an angle, grabbing the requested item.

I continued asking for food and condiments that were in close proximity to Jake. He continued to ignore me. My parents seemed oblivious to this game. Tom was irritated, but preferred to pass the food and get on with eating rather than arguing with Jake.

Jake and I rarely passed each other in the hallway, but when we did, he made gestures at me — pointing two fingers at his eyes and then targeting them at me, to let me know he knew what I'd done.

He never accused me outright, and that puzzled me.

He knew I'd done it, I knew he knew, and yet, no words were exchanged.

I wasn't sure whether he was worried he'd get in trouble for picking on his little sister, or worse, get assigned extra prayer time and Bible memorization for making an accusation he couldn't prove. The other possibility was that he was actually protecting me. If he brought our parents into the situation, I would be in trouble for looking at a book I'd been told not to read. It was possible he knew my punishment would be worse than the seventeen dollars.

Most of the time, there was a strange protection among the Mallory kids. Even when we were fighting, most of the time we aligned ourselves with each other against our parents and other adults. It was better to wrestle it out and try to win by sheer force of will against a sibling rather than risk unwanted attention or punishment from the hand of god himself.

As the silence entered its third week, Jake woke one morning and said he had a bad headache. He couldn't go to school. Usually illness had to be proven with a thermometer or a raging cough or vomit. Headaches were unprovable, but maybe because Jake was a pretty straight-forward kid who mostly enjoyed school, the headache was believed and he was allowed to stay in bed.

A glass of water sat on his nightstand, the bottle of ibuprofen beside it. A warm washcloth was placed across his forehead, refreshed by my mother every half hour until she left to drive us to school and run her Tuesday errands.

Jake had the house to himself.

I hadn't believed the headache, proving, I suppose, that I had some of my father's blood in me — cynical about a claim I couldn't verify with my own eyes or ears. The difference between us was that my father set that cynicism aside for religious matters.

When I came home from school, I went immediately to my room. It was obvious Jake had been in there, but he'd covered his tracks well. Nothing was moved more than a few inches. One corner of the bedspread hung lower than the others, suggesting he'd shoved his arms between my mattress and box spring, feeling for the book. My pillow was disarranged and my bedroom slippers near my closet door had been moved ever-so-slightly.

I went to my desk. I pulled out the bottom drawer and felt the back where the shark book was inside it's plastic bag, taped to the wood. It was still securely in place. I closed the drawer and picked up my backpack, settling it on my desk chair. I went to my dresser and looked at my reflection in the mirror. I smiled. I studied my teeth, comparing the smooth edges to the teeth of sharks. I didn't have to look at the book to remember what they looked like.

The second floor was silent.

I took off my shoes and walked carefully along the side of the hall where nothing creaked until I was a few feet from Jake's room. I listened, but heard nothing. His door was closed but not latched. I thought I would be able to hear his breathing, or the occasional squeak of a bedspring as he turned. There was nothing.

Surely he wasn't dead. He'd been alone all day while my mother shopped for staples and cleaning supplies at the discount warehouse, went to the bank, and put in her volunteer hours at the church childcare center. At school, listening to classmates who were allowed unrestricted internet access, I'd heard stories of kids getting sudden headaches or other weird disruptions in their bodies, dying without warning.

I crossed the hall and pushed open his door.

He was lying on his side, staring at the doorway, waiting

for me all that time. "Where is it?" he said.

I stared back at him.

"You owe me seventeen bucks."

"You get to do whatever you want. I have to follow more rules. It's not fair."

He raised his right fist in the air. He released his thumb, pointing it toward me. "One, I cannot do *whatever I want.*" He released his index finger. "Two, I'm older than you."

I held up my middle finger. "Three, I'm a girl and I'll always have more rules."

He slammed his arm down on the covers. "Don't do that."

"What?"

"With your finger. Don't you know what that means?"

I lowered my hand. I'd seen kids do it, I knew it wasn't a friendly gesture, I knew it was absolutely forbidden, but I was ten. I didn't know precisely what it meant. "What does it mean?"

"Fuck off."

It seemed as if there was more to it than that, but it seemed as if he was done explaining.

"How are you going to pay me?" he said.

"I don't owe you anything."

"I told you not to lie to me. I know you have it."

I shrugged again. "Do you want some milk?"

He rolled onto his back. "You're impossible."

"Do you?"

"Sure. Whatever."

I went downstairs and filled two glasses with milk. My mother asked what I was up to and I explained I was taking a glass of milk to Jake. She smiled and offered me two oatmeal cookies for each of us. "It's good that you have a servant heart," she said.

I nodded.

I carried the milk and cookies upstairs on a small tray. I sat on Jake's floor and we drank our milk and ate cookies and didn't speak.

When we were finished, Jake rolled onto his side, turning his back toward me. "You can leave. Take the glass. And you need to figure out how to get me the seventeen dollars."

53

On Sunday afternoon Tess suggested we go for a run together. I'd already been running that morning, and I don't like running in the afternoon. Unless it's cold and cloudy, I start to feel as if my body is burning up from the inside.

"We should talk," she said.

The choices for a private conversation, away from the eyes and ears and curiosity of our CEO, were going out for a drink or going for a run. I agreed to the run. A few extra miles would help counter the dinner parties coming at us every other week, delivering excess butter and cream, chocolate and cheese.

We ran at a slow jog, focused on talking rather than pushing our bodies to work hard. She didn't waste any time getting to the point. "These dinner parties are too much."

"I kind of like them."

"Under normal circumstances, yes. But Sean's more intense than ever. I feel like he's watching me all the time. I can hardly think."

I wondered whether she'd seen the video. Probably not, or she would have mentioned it. I imagined she would be further creeped out by that image, and for a brief moment, I considered taking it down as soon as we finished our run. On the other hand, maybe she should see it. Maybe she needed a better understanding of what she was dealing with. Maybe we all did.

I let my mind wander back over my experience of Sean since we'd first met. He'd always been sure of his own ideas and determined to be in charge, excited about his vision, wanting us to absorb his enthusiasm and every facet of what he considered important. Had he changed? Was his behavior becoming stranger as we began to pull away? Was his grip becoming tighter as he realized not only was he losing that grip, he'd never really had it to begin with?

"Did something happen?" I said.

"No. I just wonder if working with him is seriously not healthy. It might be better for me to get out now. Maybe I shouldn't wait until I have a new position. Just resign. As soon as my house closes."

"You can afford that? To have a house, a condo, and no job?"

"I can manage for a few months. And I'll find something faster if I'm not juggling Sean and the work here."

We turned, headed toward the park. I looked forward to the shade. It was partly cloudy, but the sun was starting to slice through in sharp blades so that even at our slow pace, I felt its heat. I pulled up my tank top and tucked it under the edge of my sports bra.

Tess turned toward me and smirked. "That's attractive."

"I'm hot."

She slowed her pace even more and I did the same. I didn't want to walk. I'd agreed to the afternoon run partly for the exercise.

"I can't do anything without looking up and seeing him — watching me eat, standing in the doorway, always there when I turn around. I don't like it."

"What about your visa?"

She heaved a sigh. "Yeah. I guess I'm in denial."

"Do you have any possibilities?"

"I have two interviews the week after next."

"That's good."

I waited for her to offer some contact names for me. She said nothing.

"Working with him won't feel as intense once you move out of his house."

"That's true." She laughed sharply. "I had a dream he locked me in the cage with Damien."

"Maybe you're *letting* him get to you. Just do your job. Ignore how he behaves." I thought about the trolls. Ignoring bad behavior was the commonly cited rule for combatting bullying and trolls. But did it really work?

Girls, and to be fair, many boys, but especially girls, are raised to ignore the harassers and bullies, the unwanted comments and the uninvited suggestions that we smile or calm down.

Just ignore him, honey.

If you ignore him, he'll go away.

Don't pay any attention and he'll get tired of it.

Ignore even the more egregious forms of harassment — the subtle attacks and the aggressive encroachments on parts of our bodies, all the way to rape, which of course, we are not supposed to ignore. A woman is to fight like hell, or it's her fault.

Most of the time, it doesn't work.

It works only in that it doesn't turn the interaction ugly, or cause upset or conflict, or jeopardize your job or your friendships or your position in a group. But it doesn't work in that it makes the bully stop. You can ignore until your face turns red with all the reactions that you're gripping inside as if you're holding your breath while minutes tick past, and it prepares to explode out of your body without any consent from your conscious mind.

I didn't like that I was telling Tess to do something that we both knew doesn't work.

Ignoring implies the other person isn't doing anything wrong. At the same time, no one wants to be that chick who says, *Can't I just smoke my cigarette in peace without you turning it into some perverted fantasy?* Suddenly all the conversation at the party stops and the majority of the men and half the women wonder *who invited that bitch*, and suddenly the guy who thinks he's legit in making his suggestive comment hates your guts and everything becomes awkward and it's All. Your. Fault.

Fueled by her circular thoughts, she was running faster. I had to sprint to catch up with her.

When I did, she said, "I'm tired of ignoring things I don't like."

I ignored that. "So why did you say we need to talk?"

"I wanted you to know where my head was at. That you really need to take your own head out of the sand and figure out where you're going. In case it becomes unbearable. In case Sean makes good on his promise."

We ran past a large pond covered with lily pads, circled around it, and angled off in a direction I'd never taken. I waited for her to offer some sort of help. It was rather weak of me, expecting her to help me, relying on her as if she owed me. But we were friends, sort of. And she'd brought me into this job and she'd lured me to Australia and I thought she would feel she owed me a bridge to the future.

"I don't know anyone here, so my only option is to go back to the US," I said.

"I'd hate to see you leave."

"For now, I don't have a choice."

"Well, just so you know."

We ran for nearly half a mile without talking. I turned over ideas in my mind, trying to think about where I might land. Returning to San Francisco, trying to get back into CC seemed the easiest, and fastest option. I didn't want that, but something interesting might come out of it. The threat of exposure had been reduced to embers, especially without Tess. I was sure of that. My thoughts drifted, finally returning to Sean. "Did you meet Carmen last night?"

"The infamous TruthTeller troll? Yes, I met her, briefly."

"She told me some things about Sean. Things that explain...even more, maybe.

Tess stopped running.

I had to turn and jog back to where she stood.

"What things?"

I told her about Sean's sisters and brother, about his neglect of their safety and his relationship with Carmen. I didn't mention the statue. "Carmen thinks he's trying to take care of a family substitute — we're his sisters and Gavin is his brother. Trying to make up for his failure, trying to recreate what he lost."

"That's ridiculous."

"Gavin hinted at that idea too."

"No one does that," she said.

"Maybe not consciously. But wanting us all together, always under his watchful eye."

"He just likes to control people," she said.

"Exactly."

"Well, what does that explain?"

"That's why he's so freaked out about you leaving."

"It doesn't change my decision."

"I'm not saying it should influence your plans, I just thought you needed to know."

"What are you saying?"

Suddenly, I wasn't sure. It explained things to me, and maybe that was enough for me, having an explanation.

54

There wasn't a lot she needed to pack. Tess surveyed her room — clothes and jewelry, a few framed prints and some aboriginal artwork she'd bought to decorate her walls and shelves, making the place as if it belonged to her. The trunk of her car was full of flattened cardboard boxes she'd purchased at a packing supply store, along with tape, bubble wrap, and a permanent marker.

Her new home would be ready in two weeks, so packing was somewhat premature when there would only be seven or eight cartons, but she had to put her eagerness to escape into something tangible. There was no harm in starting now. Tomorrow she'd buy a transport cage for Damien and a new perch so she didn't need to take the one Sean had installed in the foyer cage.

She went outside and popped the trunk of the car. She lifted five flattened boxes and the roll of plastic wrap out of the trunk. She cut across the lawn to the front patio, putting her supplies on the ground to free her hand for a moment while she opened the door.

Before she touched the handle, the door swung wide. Sean stood there, legs spread, blocking her entrance. "I'm guessing you don't care so much about Alex after all? Willing to leave her hanging in a foreign country without a job or a valid work visa?"

Tess sighed. She picked up the flattened boxes and

plastic. "Excuse me."

"You really have no qualms about discarding someone you pitched to me as critical to the success of the company?"

"I'm not discarding anyone. And I'm not responsible for Alex."

"I was dead serious when I said I can't have her living here, can't have her as part of this company without your supervision."

"I have no doubt you were serious. Please move so I can get these things inside."

He backed out of the doorway, turned and sat on the bottom step of the spiral staircase, effectively blocking her progress again.

She carried her things inside and shoved her foot against the door to close it. "Please get out of my way."

"I've done everything for you."

"All I'm doing is moving into my own place. You act as if you own me."

"It's just such a betrayal. I agreed to hire Alex. I gave you a beautiful home and a nice office, and covered almost all your living expenses. I'm paying you a superb salary and you have a stake in my company. Why are you so greedy? And ungrateful? Worse, why don't you care about your friends?"

"Because none of those things are business transactions, except the salary and the profit share. We agreed on those, and they're comparable to what I'd be worth in any similar position."

"I let you have this damn cage so your bird could live in the foyer and terrify all my guests."

"If they're terrified by a cockatoo, there's something very wrong with them."

He waved his arm over his head as if to brush away the things she'd said. He put both hands on the sides of his head, exerting pressure that was obvious in the position of his arms and wrists. "You can't leave."

"I'm not going to keep having this same conversation. If you want to fire me, that's your call. If you want to fire Alex, that's your decision. But you can't make me stay in this house. Please get out of my way."

He remained seated, spreading his legs slightly to ensure it would be even more difficult for her to climb past him, dragging her boxes and plastic up the stairs.

"Please don't do this," he said.

"It's done."

He stood and came toward her. He tugged the roll of plastic out of her arms and dropped it on the floor. She clung to the flattened boxes as he put his hands on either side of her face and kissed her, touching her lips gently with his own, then with more force, then opening his mouth.

She wrenched away. "What is that supposed to be?"

"It's what you wanted."

"It is not what I wanted."

"But you came into my room and…"

"That's over. It was a mistake. We agreed to forget it." She picked up the plastic. "I'm not sure what's going on with you, but you better take a careful look at yourself if you don't want this whole venture to dissolve."

"It's already dissolving. Without you, without…I need this to work."

"It's not working."

"I need you here. I had a vision and I thought you shared it. We talked about it. I don't know what happened. Murder.

The detectives. Karen's suicide. It wasn't supposed to be like this."

"You can't shove your vision down other people's throats. You have to entice them."

"You're not trying."

"I did try. It's not for me."

"You didn't try hard enough."

"I said, it's not for me. You need to respect my decision."

They stood facing each other. Her arms ached from holding the stack of cardboard. She wasn't sure she had the strength to carry the unwieldy armload up the stairs at this point. "What do you want from me?"

"I want you here."

"Why is that so important?"

"People take each other for granted. It's so easy for relationships to become superficial, unless you're committed, unless you share all the pieces of your lives. Unless…"

She waited.

He stared at her. After a moment he seemed to be staring past her, looking not at the door or the hallway to the offices, but somewhere else entirely.

"Unless, what?" she said.

"People should be together. They should look out for each other. They shouldn't be going off to work, leaving their children with a stranger, or with someone who doesn't understand the weight of the responsibility."

He looked like he might cry. What was the matter with him? She had no idea what he was after. Caregivers understood their responsibilities. Why would he think otherwise? Unless Alex was right, and this was about his own failure of responsibility. She didn't really care. He needed to work out his issues with a therapist, not his colleagues.

"People should be connected and…"

"Well you can't make them."

"I tried to do something for the three of you and all you did was fight me. I wanted to do something good. I wanted to share what I have, to share our thoughts and our lives. I wanted a family."

"We're not your family."

"An adopted family. Lots of people choose their own families. And none of you are connected to your birth families. We could have this one."

"It's a business, not a family."

"Those are arbitrary lines. It can be both — a business becomes a family when everyone is emotionally invested. And a successful business needs emotional investment."

She let the boxes fall to the floor, her shoulder exhausted from trying to keep them secured under her left arm. They slid away from each other. She bent down and re-stacked them. She picked them up, readjusting her grip, and started up the stairs.

"You can't go," he said.

"I'm going." When she reached the landing, she forced herself to turn toward her room without looking down over the railing.

55

Once again, Gavin and I stood in salty water, our legs warm but our shoulders cold in the morning air. He was demonstrating the movements for the breast stroke. He thought it would be easier to learn that first before the traditional crawl. The breast stroke made it easier to remain relaxed and afloat, and the built-in rhythm made it easier to take in air more frequently.

Standing still, he bent forward and went through the coordinated motions of pulling his arms out to the sides that would thrust his body forward, lifting his head for air, tucking his arms and pushing them up over his head to glide even farther.

After a minute or so of this. He swam back and forth beside me, demonstrating the frog-like kicks. I marveled that a human and a frog could move their legs in such a similar fashion, and that there was a single creature who lived on land and in the water, a creature with legs, as if its sole purpose was to show human beings how to swim.

Of course there are other legged animals that swim — dogs, even horses. But their hips are so different from ours. Frogs look like tiny alien beings that could be re-imagined as half human and half fish.

I watched Gavin swim the width of the pool twice. It looked complicated, getting the legs to work at the right juncture with the arms. It wasn't complicated for the mechanics themselves, but very complicated when you considered you were without oxygen for half of each cycle.

He told me to keep my feet planted but lean forward to practice the upper body movements first.

Each bob up for air felt less panicky than the previous one, and after a while, I got the rhythm of it.

He'd brought along a small Styrofoam board and he demoed how to hold the board and practice the leg movements with the bobbing head. I followed his example easily, although I lifted my head about twice as many times as he had. There were only two tries during which I swallowed a bit of water and had to stop to cough it out.

The sensation of water in my mouth and throat was becoming less horrible. I realized it didn't have to gush in without stopping, that it really would not gush in unless I deliberately inhaled. And even then, it went down my throat, the passage to my lungs attempting to close of its own volition, which caused the choking and coughing. It was clear my body wanted to protect itself.

Our bodies do tend to take care of themselves. They grow skin over cuts and scrapes, making it appear as if the wound never even existed. The lungs grow new cells, so much so that if you get on it early enough, you can even wipe out most of the negative effects of smoking.

The body grows new hair and nails, constantly replenishing itself as if it won't stand for anything you might do to diminish it. The body will grow larger muscles if you help it along, and increase the amount of oxygen it can process, improving the functioning of the heart.

It does all these amazing things according to its own directive, independent of our minds. Of course our minds have to do the running and lifting parts, but the growth and expansion happens on its own.

Until it doesn't.

Suddenly, one day, the body decides it's finished and just craps out like a car that runs out of gas.

Thinking about this allowed me to go the entire length of the pool holding onto the Styrofoam board, kicking like a frog. It also made me think about putting more serious effort into stopping the smoking habit, helping my lungs along in their desire to heal themselves.

When he decided I had the frog kick well in hand, Gavin decreed it was time to put the pieces together. He told me to float for a few seconds and then start moving. He explained that if I couldn't get the coordination quite right, it would work to gently paddle my feet, just to keep my legs near the surface, and do that upper body stroke without the frog kick.

I launched myself into a floating position and pulled my arms out to the sides, lifting my head for air. He was right. I loved this part. It was like the entire stroke was designed for the sole purpose of breathing. As my arms came down along my sides, I kicked my legs like the happiest frog on the planet, gliding forward.

I was swimming.

I was so excited, I sucked in water. I coughed and started to sink. I found the bottom and stood.

It was the greatest feeling in the world. Almost as good as eating steak or having sex. Not quite as good, but pretty damn amazing.

Gavin clapped for me, which made me feel like a little kid, and seemed rather patronizing. At the same time, I didn't care. I knew how to swim. I closed my eyes and turned my face toward the sky. I imagined coming to the pool every morning, running for three or four miles along the streets surrounding Bondi Beach, then going for a quick swim.

After we finished our celebration, Gavin demonstrated how the breast stroke could be done quite easily without ever putting your face in the water. I splashed his face several times and accused him of tricking me, but I was laughing. And I knew that submerging my face was required in order to feel at home in the water.

I didn't quite feel at home, but neither did I feel we were enemies any longer.

56

That evening I was supposed to meet Carmen at The Baxter Inn. She definitely loved that place, and loved her scotch. There were hundreds of bars in Sydney. Every single one of them served scotch. She could have offered to meet at any one of them, asking whether I might enjoy something else to drink. Obviously I hadn't fallen in love with the stuff. I would call it a warm friendship, but that's all.

I told the Uber driver to drop me three blocks away so I could walk. I wanted to be a pedestrian in a big city, a new shape to myself that came from the constant knowledge that I was a person who knew how to swim. Did the streams of pedestrians moving around me all have that skill? Had all of them grown up in and around the water? Maybe I was nothing special, just catching up to the rest of the human race.

Even those thoughts couldn't puncture my elation. I was no longer handicapped, burdened by a secret that occasionally dictated my social life. Of course, I do have a much bigger, and more threatening secret to conceal, but in the normal pieces of my existence, my thoughts regarding water's desire to take my life were something I had to talk around. It was a topic of conversation I had to avoid. Not that people discuss swimming itself, but associated activities — cruises and water skiing, beach trips and pool parties and kayaking. Committing murder doesn't typically come up in conversation, so I don't always view it as a secret per se.

Now I was in control. I could walk along the Circular Quay, beside other locals and tourists from around the world, without giving excessive attention to the nearby water, to its depth, to the possibility of a wild altercation between drunken strangers inadvertently shoving me over the side. I could even consider a boat ride, although I supposed I had a bit more practicing to do before that could happen. Managing the breast stroke for twenty feet in water where I could stand up wasn't quite the same as a boat capsizing in thirty or forty feet of water, half a mile from shore.

Still. I felt that I walked differently. I felt people could see my success in the way I carried myself.

Carmen was sitting on a bench near the back corner of the bar. The table we'd sat at before was occupied. She held two glasses of scotch. She wore the same outfit she'd worn to Sean's party, which was an odd choice for a Tuesday night. She looked like she was going to a club. Maybe she was. And if that was the case, why hadn't we met at the club so I could have a damn martini?

I sat beside her. "Why so dressed up?"

She ignored my question and handed a glass to me. We toasted and took exploratory sips.

"I'd rather not deal with Sean, so I wanted to check when you could be there to meet me and the delivery truck I'm hiring. If you could give me some times when he won't be around, that would be even better."

"Does he know you're taking it?"

"I told him I was."

"Our bedroom doors lock. I should check to make sure he hasn't started locking his." I took another sip. Why hadn't we done this over a private chat on Facebook? It seemed like a lot of effort to meet in person simply to work out delivery logistics.

"If he doesn't allow you to get in there, tell him I *will* call the police."

"How would you prove it belongs to you, and that he's the one who stole it?"

"It's a custom piece. I have registration papers."

"Then why couldn't you get it back before this?"

"The police talked to him right after he took it, but there was no physical evidence he'd been anywhere near my house. He offered to let them search his place and it wasn't there. So..."

She shrugged and looked away from me.

"So why did we need to meet?"

"I need to be sure there are no misunderstandings. I need to be *sure* you know how important this is. It belongs to me and I've missed it terribly. He had no right..."

"I have a pretty good idea how important it is. But we could have arranged the delivery in a message or two..."

"It's his Facebook page. Any message I send you, he can see."

"We could have texted."

She took another sip of her drink and turned to look across the room. She sighed. "It's just really important that it's handled carefully. That he doesn't interfere. That nothing happens to it."

I thought about the telescope.

"Do you have a delivery company in mind? I could make the arrangements, when I know he won't be there. The less back and forth communication, the simpler it will be."

"I want a private driver. Not a truck with a whole bunch of other stuff on it."

"No other stuff at all?"

She shook her head.

"Reputable delivery companies are very careful. You can insure it."

"Insuring it's a waste of money. I want *my* statue, not a knock-off."

"Well it's still…"

"I don't need the money. It's not about the money. I want the statue."

"Why don't you let me arrange the truck."

She shrugged. "I guess that's okay." She sipped her drink. "But I still need to be there. I'll follow the truck in my car."

"That's a big commitment. Isn't the drive more than twenty-four hours?"

"You don't get it."

"I guess not."

"They have to understand it needs to be packaged like it's glass. Okay? I'll be there to supervise, but they need advance warning, so they bring the right materials."

"Absolutely."

"Maybe I should do it." She tilted her glass, watching thick gold liquid glide toward the edge. She straightened the glass and tilted it the other way. This time, the scotch ran almost to the rim.

"Really, it's easier this way. Less chance of tripping over Sean if I'm the one coordinating."

"You're right, I think. I'm just concerned."

"About what?"

"He doesn't want to let go of it," she said.

"He will. He can afford to commission his own, if it's that important to him."

She sipped her drink.

"I'll arrange it for Thursday night. Does that work? And I'll do it late. Have them come around eleven or so, if that's okay with you. I'll just have to figure out how to get him out of the house, which is why I should be managing everything."

"Do you think anyone would pick up that late?"

"People will do anything, if you make it worth their while."

She smirked. She pulled her hair over one shoulder and combed her fingers through the dark red strands.

"What made you do your hair like that for the dinner?"

"Don't you know?"

I shook my head.

"Terri did her hair like this, after he deep-sixed her."

"Oh."

"I wanted to look like her. I wanted him to think about what he did. I wanted him to remember."

"You wanted to haunt him a little?"

"Something like that."

"Did it work?"

"He didn't like it. I know that. Didn't you hear what he said? To be honest, I thought he might freak out a bit, but he didn't. He was just pissed. He's difficult to understand. So emotional with some things, and cold with others. I don't know." She swallowed the rest of her scotch. "I want him out of my life, and once I have the statue, I'll be free. I'll never have to see or speak to him or think of him again."

It struck me that Sean felt the same way…including wanting the statue.

57

I set the alarm for five-fifteen to make sure I had plenty of time for a run and a circuit with weights. My visits to the workout room had been erratic and I was annoyed with myself. A full set of weights and yoga supplies were fifty feet from my bedroom door. The room was quiet with a lush garden outside the floor-to-ceiling windows. I had the place to myself. What was my problem?

I love lifting weights. I'd been dedicated to lifting weights when I had to get in the car and drive to a gym. I'd been dedicated when I had to wrestle for a turn with the bench press and the squat cage, waiting for guys who extended their time so they could put on a bit of a show with their grunting, grimacing moves and swelling muscle mass. I was dedicated when I had to lug a duffel bag of clothes and makeup, and take a shower in a bathroom thick with steam, and once again, wrestle for a place — this time for counter space and electrical outlets.

Now, I had everything spread at my feet, and I managed to miss it more than I made it in there. It wasn't at the top of my mind, I suppose. It might have been the lethargy of the house. Maybe my lack of discipline was also the result of a terrific lover less than twenty steps from my bedroom door. Maybe it was wine and Grey Goose vodka that I didn't have to pay for, and food that seemed to magically appear in the fridge and cabinets.

I was a slug. Except for my running. And swimming. The lessons had also diverted me, but it still wasn't an excuse. It wasn't as if I was working ten-hour days, barely able to squeeze in a few swim lessons.

I dressed in ankle length navy blue leggings and a white tank top. I put on a white hoodie and my running shoes and yanked my hair into a stubby ponytail. I hurried down the stairs.

As my feet hit the foyer floor, Damien remarked, *Dangerous woman.* He immediately settled back to sleep, as if he'd been talking from the edge of a dream. I went out the front door and locked it behind me.

I set my playlist to Chopin, did some stretches, and turned right from Sean's front walkway, headed toward the park. I liked it more than running along the wide, curving streets with their stately homes. Those routes had been interesting when it was all new, but now, the differences in architecture compared to Oregon and California that struck me in the beginning had faded to familiar. It's too bad that so many things, most things, have a way of becoming commonplace. I suppose if I concentrated more, those magnificent homes would have still sparked my interest, but I liked the park. It was more secluded, and I didn't have to think about crossing streets.

I soaked up the jungle-like atmosphere with its overgrowth of trees and the curving paths and the moist feel of the air from all that lush plant life. I felt as if I was miles outside of the city.

I passed two other runners, but other than that, the place was deserted until the sun began to rise.

On my second loop around the perimeter, I heard the

faint thud of footsteps behind me, just barely discernible above the sound of piano keys. The feet pounded at a slightly more rapid pace than my own. I moved to the right to let the runner pass, remembered the opposite sides of the road thing, and moved left.

No one passed, and the sound faded to nothing.

I slowed, trying to soften the impact of my own feet. There was still no thud of another pair of feet. I stopped and turned. No one was there.

I was surrounded by enormous plants, shrubs taller than me with faded pink blossoms, holding on despite being well into winter. There wasn't another person in sight and there was no fork in the path at that point where another runner might have veered off.

After standing there for a moment, trying to figure out what I'd heard, I resumed my running. I completed the loop and turned back to the meandering pathways that curved and crisscrossed the park. I headed in the direction of the pond Tess and I had passed during our run.

The water wasn't even visible there were so many lily pads, tightly growing side-by-side, round leaves overlapping one another. It looked uncomfortable and suffocating. I was curious whether there were fish or frogs underneath, and if so, did the fish like swimming without ever receiving a glimpse of sunlight? I was sure the frogs could wiggle their way through the thick tangle of stems and flat, rubbery leaves to make their way up, but it still seemed like the plants should be thinned out occasionally.

I heard footsteps again, gaining on me. I stopped and turned. I saw a flash of white shoes, the rest of the figure dressed in black from head to toe, including a hood. The runner turned abruptly, stumbling across moss-covered ground rather than onto a connecting path, disappearing among the trees.

I pulled out my earbuds, wrapped the cord around my phone, and stuffed the whole thing back in the holder. I didn't like this interference, but I wasn't about to go home before I completed four miles. I pulled my phone out again and checked the app. I still had a mile left. I started again, turning at every intersecting path I reached, with no clear plan for where I was headed, only hoping to catch the person dogging me.

When I passed the pond a second time, I saw the figure up ahead, standing off to the side, watching. In a burst of speed I sprinted toward the grove of trees. The person turned and ducked behind some shrubs, but not fast enough. I recognized those deliberately widened eyes.

Anita.

I ran the circle of pathways that brought me back to the pond again, then headed toward the park exit, hoping she would show herself.

She didn't. I wasn't going to chase her through the park. She must have known I'd seen her and very likely recognized her. Of course, based on her earlier rather odd behavior, it was unlikely she cared much about that. Maybe she simply wanted to annoy me. She was very good at that.

I headed back to the house, running at a slow jog, my mindset shattered by the interruption.

About three blocks from Sean's house, I heard footsteps. I turned.

Anita ran toward me. "Wait!" She stopped, breathing hard. She put her hands on her thighs and bent her knees slightly. She looked at the ground, breathing even more loudly.

I waited for her performance to end.

She continued with the labored breathing and I began to think she wanted me to ask whether she was okay.

"Is there something you need to say? I need to get going."

"Trying to catch my breath." She straightened. "You might be able to run fast for a long time, but it's still not safe to run in the dark."

"Thanks for the alert." I turned and started running again.

She came up beside me. "It's not safe for a woman to be alone in such a secluded area when it's dark. Do you know that most rapes happen before dawn, not late at night as people assume?"

"I've heard that."

"Then you shouldn't run there. When it's not light."

"I can take care of myself."

"Not just rape. Other things can happen."

"I'm sure they can."

Now, she was perfectly in control of her breath, so I was sure the earlier panting had been some sort of act for my benefit, although I had no idea why. After all, she was a personal trainer. Why would she want to give the impression she was completely out of shape?

"So when is the next dinner party?" she said.

"I have no idea. Ask Sean."

"I haven't heard back from him."

I shrugged. We were at the house now. I stopped at the front gate. I stretched my calves and hamstrings while Anita chattered about how amazing the dinner parties were and what a charming host Sean was and how she was so excited that he wanted to reconnect with her, but now he seemed standoffish and maybe someone was badmouthing her. "You wouldn't do that, would you?"

"Nope." I unlatched the gate.

"You should invite me in. For a coffee or a smoothie."

"No I shouldn't."

"After we ran together? That's sort of rude."

"We didn't run together. I was running and you were following me."

She smiled. "Does he worry about you? Running in the dark?"

"Why would he worry about me?"

"Because men want to protect their ladies."

There was so much wrong with that, I wasn't sure where to start. I stepped inside the gate and moved to close it between us. There was no point in starting with any of it. She wasn't someone I could have a rational conversation with and it wasn't worth the effort to try to correct her ridiculous views, starting with her belief that Sean and I were together. "Please don't follow me again."

"I wasn't following you. I was just…"

"Don't do it again."

"I know he wanted to reconnect with me. He was very excited when he invited me to dinner. And you aren't going to interfere. He said he was single when he asked me, and now…you aren't going to insert yourself and I'm not going to allow you to talk shit about me and convince him to ignore my messages.

I lifted my hand in a slight wave and ran to the front

door. I unlocked it and went inside without looking back. I hoped he wouldn't invite her to the next party.

58

Tess had another message from Trystan. He was still in Sydney. He was working with a client for the entire month of August. He wondered if she'd like to meet for a drink.

The fact that he didn't suggest dinner made her think it meant nothing. It didn't sound like he was hitting on her, and even if he was, so what? She wasn't drawn to him. Maybe he was just extraordinarily friendly. More likely, he wanted to extend his network in Australia. It sounded as if his job, whatever that was, involved knowing a lot of people. Trying to form a connection to her made sense from that perspective. It was possible he was putting out a net for new clients.

She would stop by her house first. She wasn't sure why she had this compulsion to drive by nearly every day and check on it. You would think she'd never owned her own home before. But she just loved looking at it. She loved how unusual it was and she loved walking around the yard, imagining her future. She supposed she loved the fact that she owned property outside of the US. It made her feel very cosmopolitan.

Australia was a fantastic place. She could easily spend the rest of her life here. Despite the unpleasant experiences with Sean, she loved the country. Life was calmer. It seemed cleaner and less…desperate, maybe, than the places she'd lived in the US. Of course, there weren't as many people.

That was part of it, but she still felt there was something to the atmosphere that soothed her.

She pulled on her riding boots and adjusted her leggings, smoothing them around the top edge of each boot. She stood and slipped her arms into a jacket and looped a scarf around the back of her neck.

Before heading downstairs, she went to Alex's room and knocked on the door. No answer. She needed Alex to tell Sean she wouldn't be around for dinner. If the drink was pleasant, she planned on suggesting she and Trystan grab Tapas. Either way, she didn't want an exchange with Sean. It was too exhausting. Too complicated for a simple message that she was going out.

For a brief moment she considered just not showing up for dinner. It was Gavin's night to cook, and Gavin would let her absence run off his back like water. But respect was too engrained. Sean could try to control her life, try to force her to mold to his will, but she still felt the need to be polite. His behavior was on him, hers was her own responsibility.

She knocked again. She was sure Alex was home. She pressed the handle. Locked. Of course it was. Behind the locked door, nothing but silence.

Suddenly almost numb, as if she'd lost consciousness, she found herself reaching into her purse. She pulled out her makeup case and removed a metal hair clip. Alex was hiding something. She needed to know what it was. It was that simple.

She had no idea how to pick a lock. She wasn't even sure it was possible with a hair clip, but she felt compelled to give it a shot. The clip only went into the keyhole a quarter of an inch. It bent slightly. She pushed harder and wiggled it, but there was…

"Do you need to get into my room?"

She turned.

Alex stood about six feet away. She was barefoot, her fingertips tucked into the pockets of her jeans, a white sweater making her skin look warm and rosy. Her newly blonde hair was pulled back into a messy ponytail, too short for the sides to be properly restrained.

Tess yanked the clip out of the lock. "Sorry. I guess my curiosity got the best of me."

"I know how that is." Alex smiled.

Alex didn't seem angry or even all that disturbed. Her calm reaction made Tess feel more uncomfortable.

"I guess that's why I have to lock it," Alex said.

"Maybe so." Tess smiled. She dropped the clip into her purse. "Just wanted to let you know I'm going out. Will you let them know I won't be here for dinner."

"Sure. You couldn't just text them?"

"I'm not in the mood to deal with Sean."

"But you're in the mood to break into my room?"

"I wasn't…" She stopped talking, studying Alex's smile. It was lingering and almost sad, but also triumphant, if it were possible to have those two things embodied in a single expression.

"I like my privacy," Alex said. "I thought you did too. In fact, I thought that's why you were moving out."

"Not privacy. Freedom."

"I like freedom too," Alex said.

Tess moved away from the door. "Sorry."

"Nothing to apologize for. You didn't get in."

"Sorry for trying to invade your space. For going where I

don't belong. Where I'm not wanted."

"Wow. That's a lot. You didn't get there, so no worries."

Tess felt more disoriented. Trying was the same as doing, that was her belief. Although she supposed if you applied that to work — Alex *trying* to manage social media, but not succeeding, was that the same as doing? The two things didn't map to each other. So trying wasn't the same...but her intent... Her head ached. From time to time, Alex did this to her. "Well, I'll get going. Have a good evening," she said.

"Where are you going?"

She hadn't wanted to say, but now she felt obligated. Alex had been so nice, really, very nice about the attempt to break into her room. "Checking on my house and..."

"You sure check on it a lot. Is something wrong with it?"

"No." She felt herself blush, like a little girl, excited about getting a new pair of shiny shoes or a ballet costume. "I like seeing it."

"I can understand that."

Again, she felt unbalanced. No matter what response she expected, she received something else. So much of human interaction happened by rote, expected greetings and comments and reactions. With Alex, it was often something different. Maybe that was part of the appeal. Alex made Tess feel awake, alive, in a way that other people didn't always.

"And then what?" Alex moved closer, her expression eager.

Was this all a game? Alex knew Tess was on the defensive and was going to push, trying to make her squirm, after seeming to let her off the hook. "A drink with Trystan."

Alex nodded. "I'd love to get to know him better."

"I'll probably invite him to Sean's dinner party again. If I still work here, that is."

"Isn't that the truth," Alex said. "He keeps threatening, but nothing happens. It makes me almost wish he would pull the trigger and be done with it. He knows he can toy with us. It's not so easy for Americans to find jobs."

"Are you looking?" Tess said.

Alex shrugged. "I'm thinking about it."

"That's a start."

"A rather pathetic one."

Tess laughed. It wasn't funny, but she needed to dissolve the tension surrounding them.

Alex moved closer. "Please don't try to go into my room again. It makes me think you don't trust me."

"Ditto for the locked door," Tess said.

"And yet, it looks like I had a good reason."

It was a circular conversation. She was tired and now she really looked forward to that drink. And dinner. She would definitely suggest dinner. She needed an evening without mind games. "Have a good one." She walked around Alex and hurried down the hall. She descended the stairs without looking back. The truth was, she didn't trust Alex. But she still liked her. It was a very confusing feeling.

59

For nearly two months, Jake didn't say another word about *The Book of Sharks*.

Late at night, when everyone was asleep, I slipped the book out of its hiding place. Like kids all over the world, I took a flashlight beneath my covers and read. I couldn't stop reading about the power contained in a shark's body, and the sophistication of such seemingly simplistic creatures. I studied the pictures until they were imprinted on my brain.

I tried to figure out why everyone thought sharks were so terrible when it isn't their fault they're drawn to blood. It isn't their doing that they have all those murderous teeth. Every cell of their bodies is designed to move quickly and devour prey. Bodies made of cartilage rather than bone make them light in comparison to other ocean creatures. They have smaller toothlike scales that are different from regular fish scales. These denticles allow water to flow over the shark's body, minimizing drag. A shark's nose contains super-sensitive cells that can detect a single drop of blood in an Olympic-size swimming pool! They can smell blood from miles away. Their hearing allows them to pick up sounds from a long distance, identifying wounded prey.

Their teeth are attached to their jaws by soft tissue and they fall out all the time. This is part of what makes them so good at devouring prey — worn or broken teeth are constantly replaced by new, sharper teeth.

When I'd had my fill for the night, I put the book in the bag and re-sealed the tape holding it behind my drawer.

Jake didn't ask again for the money, and he no longer behaved as if there was anything wrong between us.

One night in late April, I put my hand under my pillow as I always did when I was getting ready to fall asleep. I felt a scrap of paper. I pulled it out and turned on the bedside light. It was a note from Jake.

Meet me in the greenbelt tomorrow at 4:45pm.

The greenbelt was the strip of wooded land between the backyards on our street and the backyards on the next street over. It was thick with trees — a forest in the middle of the suburbs. From the center of it, you could only see glimpses of the nearby homes.

Four-forty-five was a very specific time. I assumed he chose that time because it was my job to set the dinner table at five. I was still thinking about his demand for seventeen dollars, but the note didn't mention it.

Just before our meeting time, I pulled on rubber boots because it had been raining every day, which wasn't that unusual in Portland, and the reason all of us owned a pair of rubber rain boots. I put on a hooded jacket and slipped out the living room door onto the back porch. My mother was busy in the kitchen, assuming all her children were in their rooms, doing homework, not creeping around among the trees, squishing their feet in mud.

Returning wet, soil-caked boots to the mud room would be difficult, but I would worry about that later.

I crossed the first part of our backyard and walked

carefully down the slope of damp earth and wet grass toward the trees. I entered the wooded area and glanced in either direction. Even though it was spring and several hours until sunset, the thick dark clouds and towering trees made it feel like dusk.

I stood, not sure which way to turn. I decided to wait for him to find me. The fallen logs were too wet to sit on, so I waited, growing increasingly antsy from remaining still, and starting to think about my table-setting responsibilities. If I wasn't there at five, my mother would go up to my room. At least three or four minutes had passed so far.

"I'm over here." His voice seemed to come from inside one of the trees.

I took a few steps forward. He moved out from behind a massive redwood. He was clutching the sides of his jacket, holding something inside.

"Why did you lie to me?" he said.

"I didn't."

"You stole the book. It didn't just *fall* out of my backpack. That part of my backpack doesn't unzip far enough for anything to *fall* out."

"It could happen."

"I told you not to lie to me. I hate lying."

I said nothing.

"I don't like you making a dupe out of me. I'm not stupid, and I don't like you acting as if I am."

"I don't think you're stupid."

"I don't like you thinking you can outsmart me with a bald-faced lie, because you can't."

"I don't think that."

"Stop!" His voice was loud, angry. It reminded me of my

father's voice, and I wondered if all my brothers would sound like him when they became adults. "Maybe those big eyes and that stare work on mom, and even dad, sometimes. But it doesn't work on me. Why do you have to lie? Even when it doesn't matter?"

I stared at him.

"You're doing it again. I'm not going to rat you out. I really want to know."

His own eyes were opened rather wide. Did he know that? Was he imitating me or did he not realize he was doing it? Maybe it was a family trait, maybe we all did it. I tried to remember whether I'd seen my parents staring like that.

"Look. I know you took it, and you know you took it. Just be straight with me. That's all I'm asking. I don't want the seventeen bucks. I don't need the book back."

If I told him the truth, he would always know I'd lied. But it seemed as if he already did know, so maybe it wouldn't hurt anything. "I wanted to learn about sharks. I don't see why I can't. There's nothing in the Bible that says girls can't learn stuff about the world."

"You're right."

"I don't like having different rules for girls."

"The rules are different, I get that." He reached inside his jacket. He pulled out a rectangular object wrapped in a white plastic bag with red printing on it that I couldn't read. He handed it to me. He moved closer and stood over me, blocking the water dripping from the trees so I could open the bag without it getting wet.

I opened the bag and pulled out a thick book about sharks. I thumbed through it. There weren't as many photographs, and there were a lot more words, but I was a good reader. I read above my grade level. Probably because my parents restricted TV and expected us to read every evening. In fact, reading the Bible at home, and memorizing verses at Sunday School, probably helped as well. It's not as if the Bible is easy reading.

The book had more information about sharks than I could imagine anyone knowing.

"It's for you."

I looked at him. "Thanks."

"I don't like people lying to me."

"I don't either."

"Then why do you do it?"

"It makes things easier."

He laughed. He took the book and put it back inside the bag. "Hide it wherever you hid the other one. I couldn't find it, I doubt anyone else will."

We walked back to the house and I thought about how lucky I was. I also couldn't help thinking that I'd gotten what I wanted, and more. I would still lie when it was easier, but I would try not to lie to Jake.

60

Sydney

Tess and Trystan had arranged to meet at a bar in The Rocks. She took an Uber to avoid dealing with traffic and parking, or worrying about having one extra drink. Not that she planned to drink a lot. One drink. Some wine with dinner. That was all.

Trystan was already seated at the bar.

As she approached, he pulled his jacket off the stool beside him. He ordered a wheat beer and she ordered a Pinot Grigio. They sipped their drinks and talked about Sean's dinner party.

Trystan thought Sean was an interesting guy, trying a bit too hard, obviously, but very passionate about his app and about life in general. He was impressed that Sean cooked and served the meal and was, frankly, also impressed with his effort to buck the trend that insisted social media was a requirement for success, to try something different to get the word out about his product.

He said there was no telling how things could play out when you got people together and talking in real life, communicating with that other ninety percent that was said to come from tone and body language. It was entirely possible a dinner party offered greater probability for attention than the idea of capturing interest in the narcissistic pandemonium of the internet.

Thinking over Alex's difficulty in getting social media to work for them, Tess agreed. She didn't want to fly in the face of the latest thinking on global marketing techniques, but she knew first-hand it wasn't as easy as it was made out to be. Everyone talked about it as if they were pros, with proven methods to make it effective, but mostly the guidelines you read were platitudes, an echo chamber of suggestions that sounded good but were mostly filled with gaps — such as assuming you already had thousands hanging on your every Instagram shot.

She told Trystan about the struggles they'd had with social media, leaving out the Carmen issue.

"I looked at your Facebook page," he said.

She nodded, curious but not wanting to look as if she was.

He swallowed the last of his beer. "Do you want another? Or should we grab dinner?"

"There's a Tapas place three blocks from here," she said.

"Excellent."

He paid for the drinks and they walked to the Tapas restaurant, Facebook forgotten. As they walked, she decided she preferred it that way. She wasn't curious after all. He knew next to nothing about the TruthTeller app. She would feel she was betraying Alex if she and Trystan started critiquing her mistakes and failures. Alex was right — it was hard to get people to care about your bullshit.

When they were seated and finished ordering the first few plates, a bottle of wine open between them, he settled back on the cushioned bench. "Have you given any thought to potential candidates for the position I'm trying to fill?"

She picked up a coconut crusted prawn and dipped it into the orange-flavored sauce. She took a bite. "Not a lot. Some, I suppose." And she had. For no other reason than the precarious state of TruthTeller. Mentioning his request to Alex had come to mind several times. The trouble was, she couldn't see Alex in any kind of assistant role. Not at all.

"Any names you care to share with me?"

"Not really."

"That sounds evasive."

"I know."

She ate the rest of the prawn. "Things at TruthTeller are less than ideal right now."

"I'm sorry to hear that."

"In fact, please keep it to yourself, but I'm interviewing."

"Is that right." He ran his finger down the menu, pausing at a mac and cheese dish. "The app is very intriguing, and it's hardly had a chance. Are there issues with it?"

"No. It's coming together perfectly. And I'm excited about that aspect." She'd better be careful here, with Mr. Provocateur. She didn't want word getting out to trash the app. It was amazing how difficult it was to generate interest and how very easy for a few bad experiences or rumors to cause a product to crash and burn. "Gavin is a stellar programmer. It functions even better than we'd anticipated. It does have a lot of potential."

"You can stop selling me," he said.

She took a sip of wine. "There are personnel challenges."

"Aren't there always. The biggest problem for business worldwide. And governments, for that matter."

"And relationships. The human race." She laughed and he joined her.

"What sort of personnel issues? There are only four of you."

"Maybe that's the problem. It's too confined, too... I don't know. Sean is a very intense person, and that affects everything. Absolutely everything."

"I can understand that."

"I've decided it's not the right place for me, despite how much I believe in the product."

"And your protégé?"

Tess laughed. "Protégé? You better not let her hear you say that."

"Duly noted." He stabbed his fork into a thin slice of beef and put it in his mouth. After he'd finished chewing, he put down his fork. "Is she also interviewing?"

"I suppose. She's a little secretive about that."

He nodded. "Would she be a good fit for my position?"

Tess shrugged. She'd had too much wine. Her tongue was too loose, but she spoke anyway. That was the trouble with wine. You knew you should stop talking, but your tongue had a different idea. "I thought about it. But she's..."

"Not easily managed?"

"Why do you say that?"

"Her attitude. It's obvious. I know you know. I'm sure you saw it the minute you met her."

She tried to remember the first time she and Alex had met. She honestly couldn't remember any specifics of her reaction. "Maybe. I don't recall."

"Should I approach her? Or will you mention it?"

"You're interested in a PA who's difficult to manage?"

"I want someone who thinks for herself. She clearly has that attribute."

Tess smiled. "Clearly."

"It's not as easy to find as you might think."

She agreed, but still… She took several sips of wine and settled back to survey the room. It was long and narrow, the tables small, in keeping with the small plates, she supposed. Two walls were lined with a cushioned bench. They were seated at a table in the back corner where both of them could take advantage of the comfortable seating. The room was dark, making it difficult to see the food, but it was all delicious so the lack of visibility wasn't much of a disadvantage.

"What do you think?" he said.

She shrugged. "I don't know if she wants to try to stay in Australia." She took a sip of wine. "It's hard to say. You never know with her. She might think it sounds boring, might think it's too subservient a role, or she might eat it up."

He raised his hand to the waiter and ordered a dish of mac and cheese and a spicy broccoli plate. "Anything you want?"

Tess shook her head.

He lifted his wine glass toward her. "Here's to difficult employees."

"Why don't you come to the next dinner party? You can ask her yourself."

"I think I will. Thanks for the invite."

She told him she'd text him the date and they finished the meal talking about New York City, a place she loved as much as he apparently did. He lived there and she never had. Maybe, someday.

61

Finding a bonded driver with a small enclosed truck wasn't difficult. For an extra three hundred bucks, she was thrilled to drive straight through to Queensland. Yes, a she. It wasn't what I'd expected. And I was a little disturbed by my bias — both ways. I was startled to know there were female truck drivers, and I perceived a woman as more inclined to take care with what Carmen decreed was precious cargo.

Carmen loved that statue more than she seemed to love human beings. Although I'd also seen that tendency in Sean. He was maniacally territorial the first time he found me in his room admiring it. The statue was gorgeous, I agreed that it was difficult to stop looking at it, seductive and expertly crafted, containing a life-likeness that only a superb artist can extract from a piece of wood.

I still couldn't conceive of why Sean had stolen it right out of Carmen's yard. And he thought I was predatory?

I was also a little surprised she would leave something so valuable in a garden. She'd said it was surrounded by a wall, accessed through a locking gate. But to hear her describe it, there was no doubt it was a garden, still very much exposed. She'd had a small gazebo built that sheltered the statue from the weather. The statue looked like it had cost thousands, more likely, tens of thousands. The wood and craftsmanship were exquisite. It didn't seem like a piece of artwork that belonged in a garden.

The next part of my mission was slightly more difficult.

The stolen telescope lurking in my closet was going to be on that truck, but first, I had to find a recipient.

I'd considered offering it to Carmen. The odds of her mentioning it to anyone who knew me, to anyone who lived in New South Wales, for that matter, were extremely low. But they weren't non-existent. It was best to find a stranger.

After a bit of searching, I came across an organization that provided subsidized after school programs for kids. They occasionally had weekend hiking events, game days, and movie nights.

I bought a burner phone. I called *Kidz Learn for Fun*, asking whether they'd ever thought about stargazing as an evening activity. They were thrilled to accept the telescope. They were shocked by my generosity. I thought about the shark book and the wiping out of my seventeen-dollar debt all those years ago. *That* was generosity. This was an escape from trouble, ridding myself of an affliction. The passing on of something that didn't belong to me. I arranged for it to be dropped off at the house they'd converted into a quasi-school to fit their mission.

They gushed. They invited me to their first stargazing event so the kids could thank me properly. I said I preferred to be anonymous. I pointed out that the Bible clearly demands quiet gifts — *Don't sound a trumpet over your charitable giving. When you give, your right hand should not know what your left is doing.* In other words, keep your mouth shut and quit naming buildings after yourself because you laid down a pile of cash. Quit letting the recipients of your generosity photograph you and talk about how wonderful you are, throwing lavish parties and nailing up brass plaques.

I suppose the desire for appreciation is human. It makes both sides feel better, but still…

I purchased brown packaging paper, bubble wrap, plastic tape, and scissors. Trying to locate a pair of scissors in Sean's house would risk arousing his curiosity. The telescope was well-secured inside the rolled-up carpet. All I had to do was stuff bubble wrap in both ends of the tube formed by the rug and wrap it with multiple layers of paper so it wouldn't tear easily.

Once I was locked inside my room, I opened my laptop and put on a YouTube performance by Taylor Swift, as loud as I could bear — loud enough to drown out the noise of cutting and wrangling a large roll of paper, but not loud enough to bring someone knocking on the door asking me to decrease the volume of a performer they weren't fond of. But I thought a performer they weren't fond of would keep them away as well.

I put the telescope on the bed. I unrolled the rug and re-rolled it, making sure it was as snug as possible. I pulled the telescope toward me so that one end hung over the edge of the bed. I wrapped several lengths of tape around the carpet, then turned it and did the same at the other end. Several squares of bubble wrap stuffed into the openings made the packing solid. I taped those in place as well.

Rolling the paper out from one side of the room to the other was easy. I placed the telescope at one end and began pushing it forward, keeping the paper tucked around it. That was not quite as easy. It kept wanting to veer left, leaving the paper uneven. It probably didn't matter that it was perfectly wrapped, but I didn't want a sloppy mess that ended up looking like a badly concealed pipe bomb.

I wrote the name and address of the Kidz place on the side with permanent marker and carried the package back into the closet. Only one more day and I'd be rid of the thing. Then I could unlock my door and Tess would stop asking about it. I could invite Gavin into my room and he wouldn't make jokes about dead bodies under my bed.

62

Thursday morning I went for a run. Gavin had suggested a swim, but I insisted it was too cold. I agreed I needed to get back in the water to cement my victory, but I was still having too much fun reveling in the memory of that victory. The reveling was more fun than actually putting my face in the water. It wasn't that my aversion had returned, it was just nice to coast for a while.

We don't always have to be stepping up to the next level. We don't always have to be striving and pushing. Gliding is nice too. Not unlike the breast stroke itself, pull, kick, thrust, and glide. Every time I glanced out at the swimming pool, I thought about my victory. I imagined myself in that pool, swimming with the easy movement of a shark from one end to the other, unfazed by Sean's interference.

I headed to the park and followed my usual circuit. I'd learned to look forward to running past the lily-pad-encrusted pond. It was easy to pass by because it hardly looked like water at all. At the same time, it was more sinister than water — a garden of large damp leaves and flowers, standing upright and fresh-faced, hiding the fact that beneath was dark, murky water, waiting. And how easily those lily pads might trap someone underneath. So easy for your body weight to sink through them. They would close over the spot, and clawing your way out would not be nearly as easy.

As I ran, I half expected Anita to pop out from behind a

large, leafy tree or slip among the smooth trunks of a cluster of gracefully leaning palms. As I rounded each curve, I glanced to either side. When I passed through more densely planted areas, greenery reaching over the path more than it should, I looked behind me. I was alone.

After four miles, the sun still wasn't up, but the sky was growing light. I turned back toward Sean's. I pushed myself to a sprint and arrived at his street in less than five minutes. As I took a slow jog down the street, I began stretching my arms overhead, ready for a half hour in the weight room, followed by a hot shower.

I stopped at the gate and lifted the latch.

Anita was sitting in one of the lounge chairs on the front patio. She was stretched out as if it were midday and she was sunning her face. She wore a short black skirt, over-the-knee black leather boots and a black shiny, skin-tight sleeveless shirt with a mock turtleneck. Her ankles were crossed. Her hair was wild and tangled. Dark pink lipstick coated her lips.

"What are you doing here?" I said.

"Waiting for you."

"Why?"

"You know why."

I pressed my palm against one of the stucco columns and pulled up my left foot, stretching my quad. After a few minutes, I switched legs. "I don't like that you keep showing up unannounced."

"Too bad."

"What do you want?"

"You know what I want."

"This isn't the way to get it."

"It? Don't you mean him?"

"If he was interested, you'd be hearing from him."

"Not likely, not now."

I didn't want this conversation again.

"Of course I'll see him at the next dinner party. But…."

"He hasn't planned another dinner."

"Are you sure? He already invited me."

"Is that right?"

"Yes. So you can talk shit about me all you want. He's not listening. His true feelings will win out."

I sighed. "Whatever." I went to the door.

"What are you doing now?"

"None of your business."

She crossed her legs in the opposite direction. "Tell him I'm here."

"I've already explained what you need to do."

"So a girl can't surprise a guy?"

"Not here."

She sat up and leaned forward slightly. "I don't like you."

"I'm not surprised."

"Why do you have to be such a bitch?"

"I'm a little confused. One minute you think I'm seeing Sean, and the next minute you think I can help you get close to him. Which is it?"

"When I figure out what you're up to, I'll know which it is."

"Okay." I went to the front door.

"There's something not right about you. I think you want to hurt him. Like that red-eyed woman… inviting her to his dinner party. You could feel the hate coming out of her. I think she wants to hurt him too. He's a sensitive man and people don't get that. You for sure want to come between him and me. I don't know if you're sleeping with him or what. Maybe you're the type that has to beat the boys, emasculate them. Or maybe..."

I put my key in the lock.

"You think that you can get him by acting as if you're the mistress of this house. But it doesn't work like that."

"Thanks for sharing your thoughts." I turned the key.

She jumped off the lounge chair. "He came into the gym and he was so sweet. He was super affectionate. I hadn't seen him in ages, and he invited me to dinner. He said I would add a lot and it wouldn't be a success without me there."

He needed to fill an empty chair, was what I thought, but it was Sean's business to make that point clear. My guess was that he'd dumped her, as he seemed prone to do when some emotional wave hit him, and he needed to sweet talk her into attending the party. To fill a chair. I smiled.

"He kissed me."

That also meant nothing. What sort of kiss? On the cheek? A graze across her lips? Did they make out? I doubted it was the latter, but asking for clarification would give credibility to her story.

"Did you know that?" she said.

"How would I know that? And why do you think I care?"

"Because you think you're going to get him. The minute you opened the door that first night, you knew I was a threat." She grinned.

Did I imagine she was salivating?

"It happens to me all the time." She sighed. "All the fucking time. I'm always the femme fatale."

Clearly she thought that term meant something entirely different than it does. I smiled.

"Why are you laughing? It's the truth. All. The. Time."

She moved closer, exposing uneven layers of her lipstick. "Even though you live here, you haven't been able to get him. Not really. You haven't touched his soul. He's a good person. A spiritual person. He needs someone deep, someone who isn't all flash."

She eyed me up and down and I wondered how she thought a running outfit was flashy. I'm certainly flashy at times, but not when I'm sweating all over navy blue and white spandex, thick running shoes on my feet, my new haircut falling out of the elastic band.

"I know you started talking shit because he's changed. He's completely different from how he was the day he invited me."

"Nice talking to you." I opened the door and slipped into the house, closing it quickly behind me.

Damien shouted — *Delicious mango!*

"Not now." I walked to his cage. He looked horrified, his crown feathers standing straight up. He had plenty of food and water. He was probably lonely. People passing through the hallway threw him a phrase to repeat, but otherwise, he was too far from conversation to overhear anything but laughter and he never had someone sitting there, listening to him chatter. I opened one of the windows into his cage. I put my hand inside. He eyed it, but stayed on his perch. His feathers remained straight up. "Don't worry, you'll be moving to a much nicer place, soon."

He bobbed his head.

All the while, Anita pounded her fist on the door, likely the cause of those feathers standing up in fright. I decided I would start waking at four o'clock to go running. Unless

Anita planned to spend the entire night waiting for me, it was unlikely she would show up that long before sunrise.

63

On Thursday afternoon, Sean was in the office, making phone calls with one hand, setting up an E-vite for the next dinner party with the other.

I ran up the stairs two at a time and raced down the hall and around the corner to his room.

His door was locked.

Of course it wouldn't be that easy. Still, I could have killed him. I had no plan, short of arm-wrestling him into opening it so the driver could package and remove the statue.

Carmen was planning to arrive at nine p.m., which was overkill since the truck wasn't coming until eleven, but she wanted to be *absolutely one-hundred-percent sure* that nothing went wrong. She was not leaving without the statue. If she had to burn down the house around it, she would. That sounded both impressive and ridiculous. Obviously she wouldn't allow the statue to become collateral damage, but still I sort of believed she was half serious. I closed my eyes and thought of the glistening red irises she'd worn to the party.

I went to my room and out to my balcony for a smoke, trying to think how I would either get the key, get Sean to unlock the door, or…I didn't have any other ideas. Through each drag on my cigarette, I thought about possible ways to get the statue out of his room. I'd thought he would come to accept the inevitable. Now, it was clear he hadn't.

I lit a second cigarette and let out a long stream of

smoke. The breeze grabbed it and carried it away the moment it drifted past the overhang of my balcony.

Carmen said she could prove her ownership. Why was he hanging onto it as if she had no rights? He seemed confident in his position. Was she lying to me? All of those stories she'd fed me. Because I knew some of them were true, I'd believed everything she'd said. I dropped the half-finished cigarette into the water and carried the glass downstairs. I picked out the cigarette bumps and dumped them in the trash, washed and dried the glass, and took the trash bag outside so soggy tobacco didn't stink up the kitchen.

I made two cups of espresso and went to the doorway of Sean's office. "I made you a coffee."

He turned to the doorway and glowered at me. That lowered brow and sullen stare had become his constant expression since the night Carmen showed up at the party. He hadn't spoken to me beyond what was required over meals or the most minimal of exchanges about work. And those were extremely minimal. He seemed to be putting all his hope for product promotion into the nineteen-nineties marketing plan Tess had developed, and his nineteen-sixties dinner parties. Social media no longer had his interest, which was just as well.

Despite the glower, he didn't say no to the espresso. I entered the office and put the drink beside his keyboard. He looked at it and turned his attention back to the screen. "What do you want?"

"I need to talk to you about the statue." I settled on the couch and took a sip of my drink. I put the tiny cup and saucer on the table and settled back. I crossed my legs.

"I'm not interested in talking about it."

"I have some questions."

"It has nothing to do with you."

I took a sip of espresso. "Things aren't going well here. With TruthTeller."

"No shit."

"Tess is leaving, no matter how big of a tantrum you throw."

He sighed.

"Do you want to blow up the entire company?"

He pushed the espresso cup away from him. The ceramic scraped across the surface of the desk. Then the room was silent. He began clicking around on the computer but I couldn't see the screen from where I sat.

"Do you?" I said.

"I believe in this app," he said.

"We all do." It wasn't entirely true. I thought the app was clever. I thought it was unique. I thought it might be successful, but did I *believe* in it? I don't think so. I didn't think it would transform people's lives or anything like that. I didn't think it would become a must-have app on every phone in every country.

"But I wanted to do more than just develop an app," he said.

His voice was clear and laced with passion, not whining and self pity. It surprised me.

"Tens of thousands of guys are developing apps," he said.

"And girls."

He shifted in his chair and stared at me.

"Girls are developing apps as well."

"It was an expression."

I gave him a chastising smile. "An archaic expression."

"Okay, fine. *Girls* and guys," he said.

"You want too much from us," I said. "It feels like you want to own us."

"Excellence comes from high expectations, next-to-impossible expectations. Extreme performance."

"Maybe."

He turned back and clicked around some more.

"Do you want to blow it up?" I said.

"I don't know."

"Carmen is going to help you with that, if you don't let her take the statue."

He laughed.

"Did you take it from her yard?"

"Yes."

"So it does belong to her?"

"What does that even mean?"

It made no sense. He was making me tired. "She's hired a truck," I said. "They're picking it up tonight."

He shrugged.

"Your bedroom door is locked."

"Because I don't want people going in there. You. Her. It's my space. I've shared everything I have with you and you still needed to invade the one small corner I kept for myself."

"I need the key to your room, or the door left unlocked."

"If you can convince Tess to stay, I'll let you have the key."

"She's already gone. Mentally."

He pushed his chair away from the desk. He stood and went to the window. He turned and leaned against the windowsill. "So you have to take everything from me — a room in my house, my food and wine, my good will, my privacy, Tess, my vision, and now this."

"I didn't take Tess. And *this* isn't yours."

"She understood my vision, until you…"

I stood. "No one understands your vision. It's in your mind. It might help if you would find a vision that looks at the future instead of letting the past create this weird fantasy. Some kind of replacement family." I held out my hand. "Please give me the key."

"You don't understand. The statue is rightfully mine."

"You know it's not."

He reached into his pocket and dug out his keys. He slid one off the ring, crossed the room, and dropped it onto my outstretched palm. It hit bone and bounced to the floor. I bent and picked it up. I didn't understand why he thought the statue was rightfully his, when clearly it was not, but I had the key. It no longer mattered what sort of fantasy he'd built around that artfully formed block of wood.

Everything went smoothly after that.

Sean left the house without me having to orchestrate it after all. He looked lost.

Still, Carmen planted herself in his room, convinced that at the last minute, he would show up and prevent her from getting access. The truck arrived a few minutes before eleven and the driver spent twenty minutes packing the statue in foam and wood supports and plastic wrap.

While Carmen supervised the process, I went to my room and got the telescope. I hadn't seen Tess or Gavin all evening, so I felt relatively safe taking my package downstairs and out to the driveway. I stashed it at the front of the truck's storage compartment, covering it with blankets meant for wrapping furniture. The driver knew to look out for it. She had the information regarding its destination, and she knew not to mention it to Carmen under any circumstances. Another two hundred dollars had quelled her curiosity.

As the truck pulled away from the curb, followed by Carmen's Prius, I stood on the patio in the darkness. After the exertion of helping to maneuver the statue down the staircase, the night air was refreshing against my overheated body.

I stood for a long while, looking at the stars, thinking about how beautiful they were without the aid of a telescope.

64

The dinner party had the same format as the previous one — Sean in a white shirt, black slacks, and apron, serving his guests. The meal was beef that he'd pounded within an inch of its life, brushed with mustard and formed into rolls containing sautéed onion and marjoram, topped by a veal broth and port wine gravy. There were whipped potatoes, Brussels sprouts browned in butter, olive oil, and garlic and sprinkled with fresh Parmesan cheese, all of it preceded by a crab and arugula salad with avocado-lime dressing.

Once again, the three TruthTeller employees were arranged for maximum contact with Sean's guests. Anita was there, of course, seated at Tess's left. Inviting her was a mistake on Sean's part, but he didn't seem to realize that.

Trystan was at my left. I spent most of the evening talking to him, neglecting to keep an eye on Anita. Not that it was my job to track her movements. I let her presence blur and fade to the back of my mind.

I stabbed my fork into the first piece of crab meat, raised it to my mouth, and as it touched my lips, he said, "Did Tess mention I have a position you might like to interview for?"

She hadn't. I shook my head.

He explained that he wanted a personal assistant.

I ate some arugula. The sharp tang of it, along with the word *assistant*, left a bitter taste on my tongue. Working as someone's assistant was not the sort of job that would move me forward. It sounded like a giant step backwards. No wonder Tess hadn't mentioned it.

"You look disinterested," he said.

"Do I?"

"Well you certainly don't look intrigued."

"I don't have any information."

"You're turned off by the title. And really, I need to come up with a different title. The role is so much more than that. This isn't one of those deals where you pick up my dry cleaning and schedule dinner meetings."

"Good to know," I said. "If I decide to interview."

"Picking up dry cleaning isn't a good career move," he said.

I laughed. "Dry cleaners deliver. Why does anyone need to pick up anything?"

He laughed with me. From the hallway, Damien joined us.

"That bird is something else," he said.

"He seems almost human."

"A lot of them do. It's hard to keep in mind they're simply mimicking."

I ate more crab and took a sip of wine. Conversation buzzed around me. Rising above the hum, I heard Gavin talking about the app and its connection to people interested in their horoscopes. I smiled.

"I have a suite with four offices on East Fifty-third," Trystan said. "There's a team of two, and the assistant would…"

"If you're planning on coming up with a better title, and I think you should, then you need to figure that out before you define the job. After all, if you're a provocateur, shouldn't this other position have a much more provocative title? Assistant is to provocateur what a can of spam is to filet mignon."

He laughed. This time, Damien and I both let him carry on by himself.

"I'll give that some thought. Are you interested? In an interview?"

"I still don't know what I would be interviewing for."

"You just said…"

I picked up the wine bottle a few inches from his plate and topped off his glass. I topped off my own. "I did. I was just pointing out the flaw in your approach to hiring."

"Fair enough. This person would manage the staff in terms of what projects they're working on, give input into where they should focus, and balance the workflow. Most important, she or he would participate in brainstorming sessions where we dig into the backgrounds and habits of the clients we're working with, trying to think outside the box in solving their problems, coming up with strategies for upping their game."

"Do or do not. There is no try," I said.

He laughed.

"I'm surprised you have a team, even if it's a small one. Something about your title makes you sound like a lone wolf."

"I am, for the most part. But I need researchers who study the latest in psychology and group dynamics, personal growth, goal setting, those sorts of things. They need to do the paperwork applying those concepts to our clients."

Our salad plates had been removed and we were now eating our way through beef so tender, it could be cut with the side of my fork. Sean really was a terrific chef. I would

miss the amazing food I'd eaten in his house. But then —
New York City restaurants. I imagined those would keep me
satisfied for quite some time. Probably longer than a job with
the provocateur would keep me content.

"This person I'm looking for would join me in client
meetings. She would pick up on signals I might miss, and add
another, informed perspective to our brainstorming because
of her presence in those meetings. He or she needs to have a
strong personality. The people I work with are at the top of
their game. They're aggressive and they know what they want
out of life. They cut to the chase. No time for niceties."

That certainly sounded like me. I wondered what Tess
had told him.

"Our clients need to hear the truth, brutal truth. Despite
their self-awareness and ability to get what they want, the self-
discipline that leads to that, they have blind spots. Often
significant blind spots. Everyone does, and blind spots cause
us to lie to ourselves. Our clients need to hear the truth
without any concern for being polite or avoiding insults."

I could do that. But I also have a fluid relationship with
the truth. The truth is perfect when it's on my side, but I
don't see truth telling as the golden virtue everyone seems to
think it is. And I also think there's a lot more lying going on
than we ever want to admit, and not just lying to ourselves.

It looked as though my procrastination was going to be
rewarded by pure luck, or whatever you want to call it.

I took a forkful of whipped potatoes and looked toward
the other end of the table. Tess was leaning to her left. Anita
leaned in toward her, talking furiously into Tess's ear.

Tess wasn't even bothering to nod or murmur in
response. She sat like a stone carving, her eyes wide, while

Anita talked and talked.

It occurred to me that Anita might be talking shit about me. Usually people who accuse others of that are very adept at it themselves. Would Tess listen to that? I didn't think she would, under normal circumstances. In this case, maybe she felt she needed to keep the mood of the dinner subdued and it was best to listen without comment.

I turned my attention back to Trystan. "It sounds interesting."

"Should we set up an interview?"

"Sure."

He suggested drinks. "What do you like to drink?"

"Martinis…vodka martinis."

"If you can let go of the vodka for an hour or two, there's a place that serves gins from all over the world. They make one of the best martinis I've ever had."

I thought of The Chimera Bar in San Francisco where Jen started her climb out of working as a call girl and into bartending. They had also claimed the best martinis, not an assertion you can necessarily prove. But, he'd said *one* of the best, which nudged me to give him a bit more trust. "I'll give it a try."

"Good. It's called The Barbershop."

He took out a card and wrote down the date and time. I ate the last few bites of potato, holding the card in my left hand. When I was finished I excused myself and took the card up to my room.

Opening the door, knowing I had nothing to hide, that I could leave the door wide open, was a pleasant sensation. I looked around my room. Despite the luxurious house, I was living in a relatively small space that didn't have much to say for itself beyond the private balcony. Living in New York, if the salary was good enough to get me a decent place of my own, seemed much more appealing all of a sudden.

Maybe I was bored. Tired of Sean and social media, cooped up in a palatial house, not meeting many Australians or seeing anything of the country. It was beyond disappointing. Maybe a vacation to Australia, with the purpose of getting to actually experience the place, instead of spending my time trying to get attention on social media, would be better. Tess could show me around.

I put the card on my desk and placed an empty bud vase over the edge as if I needed to secure its position. I went out onto the balcony and smoked a cigarette, enjoying each exhale, listening to the night sounds, and thinking about how much I loved the atmosphere but couldn't wait to escape.

I left my room and turned the corner toward Sean's room. His door was also unlocked. I opened it and stepped inside. Anita was sprawled on the bed, sipping a glass of champagne. Her head was propped on her hand, her elbow bent. "Get lost," she said.

I stepped out and closed the door. I could see myself going for a run in Central Park.

65

When everyone was gone, including Anita, who had come drifting down the stairs after the others had finished their angel food cake drizzled with a sweet lemon sauce, and the cheese and fruit platter, served with espresso and after-dinner drinks, I suggested Sean should have a beer and watch TV, or crash. I would clean up the kitchen. He was startled, but didn't argue.

The silent house surrounded me as I lost myself in the beauty of scraping plates and lining them up in the dishwasher. I scrubbed knives and pots. I ran a small, soft sponge inside of wine glasses and champagne flutes, polishing them dry.

My mind grew calm and slowed its frantic circling around questions about the interview and a possible move to New York City. The description of the work had been specific enough to convince me to interview, but unstructured enough that I wondered whether it would be perfect, or more aggravating than my current job.

Before I got into bed, I sat on the balcony and smoked half a cigarette. I thought about nothing.

The next morning, I went for a run at four. I ran the circuit at the park, and then went farther, ending up running nearly eight miles. It was exactly what I'd needed. I felt loose and energized. I was ready to take on anything...

...Except what I found.

The minute I stepped into the foyer, I knew something was off.

Damien was muttering with a slightly frantic undertone. I walked toward him. A flash of movement in the living room caught my eye. I turned and saw Anita collapsed in one of the armchairs. She held an espresso cup and saucer a few inches above her crossed legs. She wore jeans and boots and a baggy gray top that was falling off one shoulder.

I walked into the living room. "How did you get in here?"

She smiled. "Scared you?"

"No."

"Liar."

"I'm not scared."

"You should be. The bird sure is." She laughed. "He's smarter than you."

My skin grew cold, the sweat like a thin sheet of ice across my back. "How did you get in?"

"Does that matter?"

I pulled out my phone. "I'm calling the police."

"Do you really think Sean will back you up on that?"

I held my phone in front of me. "What do you want?"

"You have a lot of questions."

"Very simple questions."

"I'll answer the first one. That other girl, Tess, was moving some boxes into her car. She left the front door wide open."

"When was this?"

"Last night."

"You've been here all night?"

"Not really all night. I came in at one and it's not even

six, so…really, I've been here all morning."

"And now you can leave."

"Why should I?"

"Because you don't belong here."

"I do. You're the one who doesn't belong here. That other girl made it quite clear."

"What do you mean?" I hated that I was talking to her. The feeling of knowing she had power over me was loathsome. But she was right. It was unlikely Sean would look kindly on me calling the police. In fact, he would be furious if the police knocked on the door, for any reason. And he obviously wasn't bothered by her since he kept inviting her to his parties.

Tess was another matter.

Anita gave me a slow, curving smile that turned into a grin somewhat like The Joker's. The bright lipstick was her usual Pepto-Bismol pink instead of lurid red, but the effect was similar. "You're dying to know what she said."

I tried to think back on the evening. When I'd looked, Anita was doing all the talking. But I'd been caught up in imagining my future in New York. I hadn't kept my eye on them the entire meal, far from it.

"You want to know what she said but you don't want to ask me because you don't like that I'm running the show here. I told her all about me and Sean. She agreed we seem to be soul mates."

I wanted to laugh. I swallowed the desire, turned, and started to walk out of the room. She was going to win if I continued talking to her. It was highly likely that Tess hadn't said anything at all, and Anita thought she could unearth some sort of insecurity in me that would have me begging to know how my friend had betrayed me.

The way things were progressing, I would be gone soon. If Anita wanted to sneak into the house, if she wanted to roll out a sleeping bag on the living room floor, if Sean was ambivalent about having her around, it had nothing to do with me. Still, all my self-preservation senses continued to hum, and I wasn't sure why.

She raised her voice. "I could do your job. Both of your jobs."

I kept walking.

She called after me. "Since you're too proud to ask, I'll tell you. Chatting on social media. What a joke. I do that all the time. So that's taken care of. And fucking Sean, I could do that better than you."

I knew with absolute certainty Tess would not have suggested or implied that I had anything going with Sean. But possibly, Anita might have gotten that impression through simple observation. There had always been electricity between Sean and me. And even our battle for control sparked an energy that could be interpreted as something else. Lust and loathing can be closely related. Like love and hate.

I don't know when Anita left or whether anyone else in the house spoke to her.

I spent an hour in the weight room and then shocked myself by going to the laundry room and changing into my bathing suit that had been hanging there since my last lesson. I went outside and eased my way into the bathwater comfort of the pool. I swam from one end to the other. Twice.

66

One thing that was appealing about the idea of living in New York City was the subway system. And the proximity of everything. So, two things. Manhattan is only thirteen miles from one end to the other and a little over two miles wide. I looked it up. I can run ten miles with only moderate effort. Walking for thirteen wouldn't even break a sweat.

Taking Uber everywhere was tiresome. Ordering a ride is easy, getting to your destination is painless, and payment takes no thought. Safety is at least superior to walking through a crime-prone area or getting behind the wheel yourself when you've had a martini or two. It's a useful and simple system.

But using Uber feels like there's this other person required in order to accomplish the most insignificant tasks of your life. You often have to talk, or at the least, exchange greetings. There's the unknown of a stranger's car and the frustration when a route is taken that you don't consider optimal. There's something about the whole dynamic that intrudes on your thoughts, on your effort to make the most of travel time by reading email or surfing the web, or even just surfing through your own thoughts.

I love walking and would rather do it than ride.

I imagined the subway would become familiar. Familiar faces and routes and the interiors of the trains. Even taking a cab, when it's late or you're dressed up, seems easier, slightly more anonymous. I can't say why.

I took an Uber to The Barbershop bar. I marveled over its clever shout-out to speakeasies as I entered through the subtle door at the back of the full-service barbershop and walked down the stairs to the slightly-below-street-level bar.

Trystan was seated on a sagging green couch in the corner near the alley entrance. He stood and walked toward me. We shook hands and went to the bar.

After the bartender's explanation of the various gin offerings that I might like, based on other kinds of alcohol that I preferred, he mixed me a martini. I'd chosen his first recommendation — a gin made in Tasmania, which felt like the right thing to do in Sydney. Part of their recipe for distinctive martinis included a selection of tinctures, which added zest to the drink. I chose lemon and he added a beautiful twist of lemon peel to complement it. Trystan ordered the same.

We sat at a small corner table.

An interview over a drink was an unusual choice, but I took it as a good omen that it foreshadowed an unusual job.

Trystan told me about himself, his education — NYU — his working life, and then his decision when he turned thirty-two that he needed to do something wildly different. He couldn't see himself sitting in a cubicle or a tiny office every day, emerging an old man at the end of a so-called career. He couldn't tolerate a lifetime of doing what others told him to do, thinking what others told him to think, acquiescing to authority.

In the end, he feared he would question why he'd even spent time on the earth. He had to live an interesting life, he had to answer only to himself, and he had to feel like every day was a worthwhile adventure.

The idea of a daily *adventure* was a little fanciful for me, but the rest of what he said convinced me I was headed to New York City. I hoped my excitement didn't show on my face, didn't glitter in my eyes, didn't slip out in the speed with which I spoke or the intensity of my breathing.

He asked about my life. That was a bit of a challenge. I had to give the impression I was providing a complete picture and at the same time, hide an awful lot of things, because he wasn't only interested in my work life.

"I want to get a sense of who you are," he said. "I want to understand your world-view and how you make decisions."

He liked that I hadn't finished college. It wasn't a reaction I was used to. Most people see that as a red flag demonstrating a lack of commitment. He liked that I'd only studied what interested me. He thought it *said something* that trudging toward a degree was unimportant to me. Not many resisted the herd mentality that a degree was required for a successful career. It showed intelligence and a sense of power and self-knowledge and self-confidence.

I thought his reaction showed a tendency to flatter, but I couldn't be sure. He seemed genuine.

I sipped my martini, surprised that I not only enjoyed the gin, I didn't miss the olives, refreshed by that slender twist of lemon.

He asked questions about my time at CoastalCreative, about the people I worked with, about my aspirations there, about my performance reviews, of which there had only been one, and about my relationship with Tess. He asked what I liked and what I hated about my jobs, actually using that word — *hated*. He inquired about my skills with spreadsheets and PowerPoint and my interactions with customers. He seemed rather curious about Steve for some reason I couldn't figure out. I wasn't sure what I'd said to make Steve stand out from the others I'd mentioned.

I talked about my social media job. "I'm bored with it. I hope that's not any part of this position."

He laughed. "I don't even have a Facebook account. At the end of the day, we still live in a physical world with other human beings. That's what defines life." He sipped his martini, holding my gaze.

Talking about my TruthTeller job segued into a discussion of Australia. I told him about learning to swim, leaving out the history of why that milestone had never been achieved when I was a child. He didn't push for more information. I wouldn't have given it. I'm not even sure why I mentioned it at all. I suppose he was easy to talk to. That would be something to watch out for...talking too much.

We ordered another round of martinis, this time with gin from New Zealand. He told me what he loved and hated about New York City — its design as a city made for walking, theater, restaurants, and a wide variety of interesting people were in the love category. He hated the garbage and the homeless issues.

As the last of the gin and vermouth was drained from both our glasses, he offered me a job. He said he'd known when he first spoke to me, for no more than three minutes, that I'd be a good fit.

It might seem risky to make such a decision based on no information, but our dinosaur brains are gathering information with every intake of breath. We know when someone is a threat and we know when we're attracted, we know so many things that we don't even realize we know.

Deep inside, the animal part of us is deciding what it thinks of every single human interaction. Trystan, like me, acknowledged that fact, even if he didn't say it in quite that way. Working with him seemed promising.

It was rash, but he was definitely a man who knew his own mind and followed his instincts. How could he not be, when people paid him to help fine-tune their own instincts?

He said he'd come up with a job title — Client Satisfaction Manager. It wasn't nearly as sexy as Provocateur, but the salary was better than what I was making at TruthTeller, significantly better, so what did a title matter? I wondered whether Tess had played a part in the salary, or it was simply what he thought I was worth.

I preferred to think the latter.

67

At four-ten the next morning, I was headed down Sean's
street toward the park. Rachmaninoff was pounding into my
brain. Lists of things to do circled around the notes, which I
hate when I'm running. I had to figure out when I was leaving
Australia, book my flight, get my things ready for shipping. I
had to tell Gavin. And Sean. And Tess. I absolutely had to see
a kangaroo.

I expected Tess had a pretty good idea I was headed back
to America, but I still needed to talk to her.

There were other things I needed to get started on — the
search for an apartment, starting with a study of the layout of
New York. I needed to traipse through some online forums
to figure out what neighborhoods were the best fit for me. I
had to figure out what I was going to do with the Facebook
page — leave it a mess for Sean to discover on his own, or
delete all of Carmen's comments and the video of Sean and
Tess. And the statue photograph, for that matter. Deleting it
all was winning my mental battle, so far.

As I entered the park, I passed a man running, his leash-
less dog trotting beside him. The dog slowed, then turned
and followed me for a few yards, checking me out with a
thorough sniffing. The man whistled for the dog, who
ignored him. After another twenty feet or so, the man chased
after us. He grabbed the dog's collar and apologized. He
clipped a leash to the collar. They left the park and I was

alone, just as I liked it.

I ran the circumference and then turned toward the interior.

As I rounded the curve toward the pond, I saw someone waiting in the semi-protective cover of a fifteen-foot shrub. I knew it was Anita. I'd hoped that running this early would have gotten her out of my hair, but I should have realized when she sat up all night in our living room — the clock meant nothing to her.

Perhaps she never slept at all. That wildness in her eyes might be the burning of a brain that never allowed the restoration and sorting out of life that comes from spending time in the realm of dreams.

She stepped out in front of me and held up her left hand like a self-appointed traffic cop. I stepped to the side, prepared to run around her, but she moved quickly to block me.

In her right hand was a knife. A rather small knife, slightly larger than a steak knife, which wasn't that big of a surprise given her over-confidence in other areas. Still, a six-inch blade can kill you if it's inserted in the right spot. And working as a personal trainer probably gave her more knowledge of anatomy than most.

She grabbed the cord to my earbuds and yanked them out. "The only thing between me and everything that should be mine, is you." She grabbed the edge of my shirt and swung the knife toward me. I jumped out of the way and stumbled to the opposite side of the path. She lunged at me, the knife pointing straight at the unprotected space below my ribcage. I jumped back and to the side again. My heel landed in soft grass and damp earth, sinking slightly, then skidding, pulling me closer to the pond.

Even with my eyes fixed on that blade, I felt the strange sensation I've experienced so many times before — the water behind me reaching out its arms, trying to pull me into its center. But this time, it didn't have the strength it had all those other times. We were equal opponents. Almost.

Anita rushed at me again, her blade flashing, despite the lack of direct light. There's something about the metal of a knife blade that makes itself known even in near-total darkness. The sky was an inky gray. The sun would be up soon, but it was dark enough and early enough that the chance of someone passing by was slim.

I grabbed her wrist and she twisted, dragging the blade across my upper arm. The fabric of my shirt tore slightly and I could feel the blade scrape at my skin, but not enough to draw blood. I tightened my grip and twisted hard. She was still trying to get closer to me, working to get her footing. I kicked her knee. She cried out and collapsed slightly. I grabbed the other wrist.

We wrestled like that for a moment, me holding both wrists, trying to keep my face outside the arc of the knife, Anita pushing against my arms, trying to knock me off balance and find some leverage to turn the knife on me.

As we struggled in our weird, silent dance, I felt myself sliding a bit where the ground sloped down toward the pond. Before it happened, I knew we were going into the water. The thick covering of lily pads wouldn't keep us from sinking.

She pushed against me. She was strong and more muscular than she looked. "Stop fighting me. You can't win. You won't win." Her voice was rough, filled with the effort of her breathing and rage.

I tightened my grip on her wrists, squeezing with every ounce of strength I could find.

She cried out, then cut off her cry, letting the pain contort her face instead, not wanting me to think I'd forced her to whimper.

And then, without warning, we were in the water.

I wasn't sure how it happened. It could have been the sloped ground, the water pulling us toward it, the sheer force of both our bodies pushing against each other. Possibly all three.

The lily pads held us for a moment, like an inadequate hammock, and then we sank. The pond wasn't deep. My feet found the bottom. Still holding her wrists, I pushed myself to a standing position, my head and shoulders shoving through the thick leaves. The sky felt darker somehow, as if the earth had changed its mind and reversed direction, turning us away from the sun.

When I pulled her hands above the lily pads, the knife was still there.

She'd also found her footing and our struggle continued the same as it had on dry ground, but with much more difficulty, our feet sliding around the mucky bottom, water weighting our clothes and hair.

I tried to think how I was going to change our fight from an equally balanced wrestling match.

"I'm stronger than you," she hissed. Her teeth were clenched, her voice tight and filled with determination.

She was wrong. She might be a trainer, but she wasn't a runner, and I could hear her breathing hard from the exertion. I also doubted she had the same upper body strength. I could tell by looking, that first night she'd appeared at the door, her narrow shoulders covered by nothing but spaghetti straps. Not many women can bench-press as much as I can. Not because they can't, but because they don't work at it as diligently and passionately as I do.

I kept my grip tight, but stopped moving, digging my feet into the thin layer of muck to find something firmer below. She thought I was tiring and she twisted her hand, trying to draw the knife closer to my face.

I waited half a second, then moved my leg as quickly as was possible with the water and my wet leggings and the stems of the lily pads. I shoved the bottom of my foot into her already injured kneecap and knocked her off balance. I twisted her arm out to the side. She screamed but didn't loosen her grip on the knife.

I continued forcing her arm out to the side. I heard cartilage crack. And then her arm lost its strength, and now the knife was driving itself into her side, sliding between her ribs. It's not quite right to say it was driving itself, because I was pushing, but it did seem to take on a life of its own, finding the spot where it could complete its passage into her flesh. I really can't bear the sight of blood coming out of someone's body, but the dark water overpowered the worst of it.

She started to collapse and her breathing became strained. Her legs buckled and I lowered her into the water. When her head disappeared beneath the surface, she began kicking and thrashing, which had the effect of tangling her arms and legs in the densely growing stems of the lily pads. Her struggle didn't last long, and I really didn't have to hold her down, the lily pad stems took care of that.

It was a strange sensation, because I could feel her body

in my hands, pushing against my legs, but I couldn't see her with the covering of vegetation.

When she stopped moving, I reached down, keeping my head out of the water, and felt around for the knife. I pulled it out of her side.

I climbed out of the water. I shoved the knife inside the sleeve of my shirt, and ran as fast as I could back to Sean's. Inside the laundry room, I turned the knife around, studying the handle. I saw that it wasn't one of Sean's after all. I stripped off my clothes and wound them around the knife. I dried myself with a beach towel and wrapped it around my torso. I ran upstairs carrying the bundle, once again, forced to lock my door behind me.

After scrubbing and rinsing my body twice and shampooing my hair, I dressed in clean workout clothes. I buried my damaged phone inside my pillow for the time being. I added the purchase of another burner phone to my growing list of details to take care of.

I blew my hair dry, shoved my wet clothes with the sharp, bloody nougat center into a small backpack, grabbed some trash bags from the kitchen, and went out for a run.

This time, I went in the opposite direction, looping around less familiar streets and ending up at the tiny cluster of stores that included the neighborhood pie shop. The sun was just coming up. I put my wet clothes in a trash bag, tied it several times, and dropped it into the dumpster. I wrapped the knife in another trash bag, put that package inside a third bag, and continued running. I was getting tired, nearing three miles, not counting the earlier run that was cut short, and my wrestling workout. Finally, I passed the perfect spot. Behind a gas station, a garbage truck was extending its automated claw to empty a dumpster. I darted up to the side of the dumpster, lifted the lid a few inches, and dropped the bag inside. I was already past the fuel pumps when the claw engaged with the dumpster and began to raise it into the air.

All the things on my to do list that had cluttered my mind at the start of my run came back to me. I wasn't sure how long Anita's body would stay tangled in the stems of the lily pads.

68

Tess's eyes teared up as she stood in the doorway, ready to leave Sean's house for the last time. Sean had leased a suite of three offices downtown, a concession that had helped her decide to continue working with TruthTeller until the app was launched. She wanted to be *deliberate* about her next move, she said. I, on the other hand, was excited to make another leap into the unknown. Deliberation is overrated.

A few of her tears might have been stirred up by saying good-bye to working with me, I wasn't sure. She hugged me, holding on for several seconds, and I returned the hug warmly.

Damien was in his travel cage near her feet, muttering with a definite tone of anticipation. *Delicious mango. Good-bye. Delicious mango.* He seemed bothered that he had nothing in his cage but generic seed and kibble mix. He moved around, sidling back and forth on the perch. He bobbed his head at no one in particular. He pecked at the seed, and I could have sworn I saw him spit out the kibble, but I might have imagined it.

The enormous cage he'd occupied for such a short time looked more sinister than ever, empty and without purpose. The cage door stood open, as if the structure were waiting for, possibly welcoming, its next occupant. Of course, there wouldn't be one. I expected Sean would break down the pieces and leave it for recycling pick-up.

He hadn't come out of his room all morning, sulking like a two-year-old, refusing to say good-bye.

Tess was reeling out memories as she picked up Damien's cage and moved closer to the front patio, recalling how thrilled we'd been at the start of our Australian adventure, re-telling the events of the day I arrived in Sydney. She recalled our game of badminton and how we'd marveled over the size and beauty of the house. We'd had some great times, but it was hard, she said, not to think about all the death surrounding the place. It was impossible not to feel excited to escape the oppressive atmosphere of spending all your time with the same four people.

She didn't say a word about whether she'd nudged Trystan in my direction or whether she'd proposed a salary range to him or whether she'd done anything to find potential interview opportunities for me in Australia. Maybe she needed a break from me. Or maybe, she was so unsure about her own future, I was the furthest thing from her mind.

She took a few more steps away from the house. "When are you telling Sean?"

"After I let Gavin know."

She nodded.

"I think Gavin sort of knows."

"So when is all that happening?"

I shrugged. "Soon."

She smiled in that motherly way she occasionally had. "Can you define *soon*? The minute the door closes behind me? Tonight? Tomorrow? Three weeks from now?"

"I honestly don't know."

"Milking it as long as you can?"

"Actually, trying to get a virtual sense of New York, and

get started looking for an apartment. There are a lot of things to work out."

"Not that many."

Damien muttered that it was *Chardonnay time*.

"I think he's ready to go," I said.

"The reason I'm asking about your timeline, is I have an idea."

"What's that?"

"We've been in this house twenty-four-seven. Except for those few trips downtown. You should see a bit of Australia before you leave," she said.

I needed to get out of Australia. I needed to be far away from any upcoming inquiries about a woman's body floating among the lily pads in the nearby park. Once her body rose to the surface, once they identified her, and once they talked to her co-workers, there was a good chance the police would end up at Sean's front door. "Maybe. I did want to see a kangaroo. It's ridiculous that I've been here all this time and haven't seen one. I thought they were wild."

"Not in Sydney. Anyway, I was thinking you could stay with me for a while, get out of this place as fast as possible but still have time to make arrangements for New York."

I felt a tightness that had worked its way up my spine over the past few days slowly unwind.

"We could do a few touristy things in Sydney — there's a speed boat trip to Fort Denison that's amazing. We could fly down and check out Melbourne. All the time I've spent there was inside office buildings and hotels. It's a beautiful place and I want to see more of it."

Either way, I'd be in Australia for at least another week. Staying with her would put a little extra space between the inevitable investigation of Anita's death and me. Plus…a vacation. "That would be fantastic."

"So wrap it up here…fast." She smiled.

I'd never seen her look so giddy, and I appreciated that she'd nudged me out of the nest.

69

Sean continued to lurk in his bedroom long into the afternoon. I wondered if he would stay there until the house had disgorged all of its occupants. As far as I could tell, at four o'clock, he hadn't eaten anything or even ventured out for a cup of espresso or a beer. Presumably he was staying hydrated with tap water from his bathroom sink.

Gavin reminded me that although the air was on the cusp of a wintry chill, the swimming pool remained at its usual close-to-bathwater temperature. He gave me a knowing look — my final lesson. Or maybe just a bit of fun.

"I need to tell you something first," I said.

We stood in the living room, looking out at the pool. Sun splashed across the water, belying the cold air. We'd come into the room for a warm-up of hot chocolate and stayed on the couch for nearly an hour, not talking much, until he came up with the swimming idea.

I didn't really need another lesson. I hadn't told him about the two lengths of the pool I'd already swum by myself. And obviously he knew nothing about my wrestling match with Anita and her knife and the thick stems and resilient leaves of the water lilies. His lessons had already put down deeper roots than he realized.

"I have a pretty good idea what you want to tell me," he said.

"What's that?"

"I overheard you at the party — setting up your interview with Trystan."

I smiled. "And here I thought you were absorbed with telling everyone about the life-changing benefits of TruthTeller."

"You're never off my radar." He gave me a small, affectionate smile. "But I've always known you, from the minute we first said hello. And I've always known what this was, between us."

We didn't say any more. He washed the mugs and we went upstairs to change into our swimsuits.

He dove into the pool at the deep end while I walked down the steps into the shallow end, pausing for a moment on each concrete step, despite the frigid air brushing across my skin, urging me to slip below the warm water. I preferred the chill over a sudden plunge.

Finally I was in. I swam two lengths without stopping. Gavin gushed with praise. He showed me the mechanics of the crawl. I tried a few strokes, but decided it required a lot more work, on a warmer day.

With the lesson complete, such as it was, we stayed in the shallow end, our knees bent to keep our shoulders below the surface. It was a pleasant feeling — sharp, cold air on my face and warm liquid stroking the rest of my body. There was no sensation that it was plotting to pull me under the surface.

Clouds moved in front of the sun, stirring up a shivering breeze. We climbed out, dried off, and took a long, soapy shower in my bathroom. He didn't ask why he was welcome in my room again. Maybe he thought it was because this was our last time. We stayed in bed until we were starving. We ordered pizza and ate the entire thing while watching rugby on the great room TV. I drank beer with my pizza, just to be friendly.

"So, I'm going to be out of here tomorrow," I said.

"A clean break?"

"Not just that. Tess and I are going to hang out and be tourists before I go home."

He looked at me. "*Home.*"

There was nothing else to be said.

The word had emerged without a conscious choice on my part. I guess America was still my home. I wondered what Tess would say in a similar situation.

70

It was with her usual style, including her flamboyant disregard for anyone else, that Sean found out Alex was leaving. Professionalism wasn't high on her list of priorities.

After a day spent in his room, trying to rest, trying to sort out the future, he came downstairs to find her in the middle of the foyer surrounded by shipping boxes. "Leaving?"

She smiled. "I think it's for the best."

He shrugged.

"You were going to fire me anyway."

"Was I?"

"It was an empty threat?" She smiled, her lips tight, her teeth hidden, but that didn't mean they weren't there, sharp as ever.

He shoved his hands in his pockets. He felt strangely torn about her leaving. The house, and his life, had been full of energy when they were all here, and a large part of that was due to Alex. He hated to admit it, but he had to be truthful with himself if he was going to do a re-set on his life. He was simultaneously afraid of her, disliked her, and admired her. Most of all, he was frustrated with his inability to figure her out. Maybe he was too quick to categorize, too eager to label her and put her in a box that he could manage rather than to truly understand who she was. Selfish. Irresponsible. Narcissistic. Predatory.

"Tess is gone. You said if she didn't stay in the house…"

"That's not why you're leaving and you know it," he said.

Alex cocked her head, reminding him of the bird, the cage behind her desolate without the murmuring, laughing cockatoo.

"Then why am I?" she said.

"I think you're the type who's always leaving." There he was, categorizing again. He regretted saying it, as he regretted saying so many things he'd said to her, but he wasn't going to admit it now.

"And what type are you? The type who's always dumping women who become inconvenient?"

"No."

"It's a bit of a pattern," she said.

"You don't understand the circumstances."

"I think I do."

He decided to stop there. He wasn't going to defend himself, especially to her. And the things he'd done weren't completely defensible. Dropping Carmen — that was defensible. Not the most admirable move, but after what happened to Callie and 'Licia and Dave...He blamed himself. Entirely. It was entirely and completely him, not Carmen. He'd carry that forever, but he still couldn't look at her. He couldn't see her and remember her scared and excited eyes when they'd made love. The image of her face, as her eyes finally closed with satisfaction, was burned into his mind alongside the faces of his sisters and brother, their eyes closed forever, mouths twisted in confusion, unsure what had happened to their lives.

Anita. Well that was a mindless hook-up in the midst of unbearable pain. And Terri...ending their relationship had been a mistake. A terrible mistake that would echo throughout the rest of his life. He shivered.

"Are you feeling okay?" Alex said.

"I'm fine."

"Have you eaten anything while you were locked in up there?" She nodded at the curving staircase.

He shook his head.

"You probably should."

He didn't acknowledge her comment.

"I deleted all of Carmen's posts and the photograph of the statue from the Facebook page. I deleted my photo. But the page is still there, if you want to use it. There are still quite a few fans of TruthTeller."

He stared at her. That's what she thought was important?

"I guess you don't care about social media," she said.

"Not really."

"So what are you going to do?"

"Not sure." The day sequestered in his room had yielded no new thoughts. He had no idea what might happen next. It was a rather pleasant feeling on one level. Another part of him felt his purpose had dissolved.

"I guess without the wooden muse, there isn't much inspiration in your room."

"Don't say that. If you hadn't…it should be mine."

"You're very territorial about something that doesn't belong to you."

"You don't understand." He sighed. He sat down heavily on the bottom step. He propped his elbows on his knees and put his face in his hands.

The foyer was silent. Without the bird, there was a vacant feeling to it. His thoughts pressed against his skull. He didn't know why he wanted to tell her and he was pretty sure he would be adding that to his list of regrets, but the words started coming of their own volition.

"Carmen had the statue commissioned. It was gorgeous. And it looked like Terri, even though the artist never met her. Terri, before she did that thing with her hair. It really did." He sighed. "Then, Carmen found another specialty artist to work with the sculptor."

He swallowed. "The other artist was a woman who took cremated remains and worked them into the grain of the wood. She would carve out small slivers and pockets and press in the ashes. The whole thing was finished with a resin to keep them in place. So Terri...and our child...are in there forever." He sighed. He pressed his face into his hands with more force. "It should be mine. I know they're sisters. I get that. And I broke up with Terri. But the baby...Carmen had no right to do that. The ashes should have been shared."

He stopped talking. He didn't regret telling Alex after all. For some strange reason, it was a relief. A relief to make her understand why it was so invasive when she entered his room, sat in his chair, gazed at his statue, treating it as if it were a simple work of art that anyone could enjoy. Every time he's seen her in his room, it felt as if she'd stolen something from him.

The silence between them deepened.

She didn't speak, didn't offer condolences or words of understanding or pithy comments about letting go. For once, he appreciated her pointed silence.

71

During my final week and a half with Tess, I saw more of Australia than I had in the entire three and a half months I'd lived there. We spent five days in Melbourne, mostly eating and drinking and shopping. We visited an animal preserve where I fed wallabies and got to see an entire field full of kangaroos, including a Joey in its mother's pocket.

Back in Sydney, we visited the aquarium where I saw a platypus. We ate dinner at the Opera House and went to a comedy show inside that magnificent building. She took me to Cafe Sydney. We walked across the Harbor bridge. We took a late-night tour of the Rocks, led by a man who told stories of murder from the days when Sydney was occupied primarily by convicts. Woven through his history were stories of untimely death and murder, and the associated legends of haunted rooms and houses and strange events. After getting our chills, we went to The Barbershop and drank gin martinis.

We had lots of great conversations. We recalled our time with TruthTeller. We talked about swimming lessons and sex and careers. We talked about Gavin and Sean. We talked about everything imaginable, but I didn't tell her about the woman and her child embedded in the statue.

I love the feeling of an airplane accelerating down the runway, then lifting gracefully into the clouds. I don't think I'll ever get tired of that sensation of incredible speed, of rising into the sky, of going somewhere different.

I looked out the window as Sydney shrank to a model city. Below me were three dead bodies I was leaving behind, and as I leafed through the brochure from our haunted tour, I hoped their ghosts kept their silence.

Some people say silence, in certain circumstances, is a lie of omission. To me, lying is a matter of survival, for obvious reasons. In other cases, lying simply gets me what I want. And as I told Jake, lying is often just easier. The line between truth and lies is difficult to find. The things we say shift and change shape even as we're speaking. As Pontius Pilate asked, *What is truth?*

I put the brochure in the pocket behind the seat ahead of me. The memory of Sean's tattoo drifted across my thoughts. People choose tattoos because they have meaning, deeper symbolism, for the bearer. The shark symbolized something to Sean. It reflected a part of how he saw himself. I had to believe that meant he knew very well he was also a predator.

Sean Farmer might have been a candidate for murder. Don't think it didn't cross my mind. But really, why? Yes, he discarded women the moment they became inconvenient, uninteresting, or reminded him of tragedy. I didn't like that about him, but now that he'd been discarded himself, I had a feeling his behavior would become less predatory.

Now that the statue and all it embodied had been ripped out of his life, it was possible he would put his ghosts to rest.

A Note to Readers

Thanks for reading. I hope you liked reading about Alexandra as much as I enjoy writing her stories.

I'm passionate about fiction that explores the shadows of suburban life and the dark corners of the human mind. To me, the human psyche is, as they say in Star Trek — the final frontier — a place we'll never fully understand. I'm fascinated by characters who are damaged, neurotic, and obsessed.

I love to stay in touch with readers. Visit me at my website: CathrynGrant.com

To find out when the next Alexandra Mallory novel is available you can sign up for my new book mailing list here: CathrynGrant.com/contact.

As a thank you for signing up, you'll receive a free Alexandra short story — *Death Valley*.

www.ingramcontent.com/pod-product-compliance
Lightning Source LLC
Chambersburg PA
CBHW031314280626
47169CB00019B/1532